The Chase

CLIVE CUSSLER

PENGUIN BOOKS

PENGUIN BOOKS

Published by the Penguin Group
Penguin Books Ltd, 80 Strand, London WC2R 0RL, England
Penguin Group (USA) Inc., 375 Hudson Street, New York, New York 10014, USA
Penguin Group (Canada), 90 Eglinton Avenue East, Suite 700, Toronto, Ontario, Canada M4P 2Y3
(a division of Pearson Penguin Canada Inc.)
Penguin Ireland, 25 St Stephen's Green, Dublin 2, Ireland (a division of Penguin Books Ltd)
Penguin Group (Australia), 250 Camberwell Road, Camberwell, Victoria 3124, Australia
(a division of Pearson Australia Group Pty Ltd)
Penguin Books India Pvt Ltd, 11 Community Centre, Panchsheel Park, New Delhi – 110 017, India
Penguin Group (NZ), 67 Apollo Drive, Rosedale, Auckland 0632, New Zealand
(a division of Pearson New Zealand Ltd)
Penguin Books (South Africa) (Pty) Ltd, 24 Sturdee Avenue, Rosebank,
Johannesburg 2196, South Africa
Penguin Books Ltd, Registered Offices: 80 Strand, London WC2R 0RL, England

www.penguin.com

First published in the United States of America by G. P. Putnam's Sons,
part of the Penguin Group (USA) Inc, in 2007
First published in Great Britain by Michael Joseph 2007
Published in Penguin Books 2008
Reissued in this edition 2011

003

Set in Monotype Garamond
Typeset by Palimpsest Book Production Limited,
Falkirk, Stirlingshire
Printed in England by Clays Ltd, St. Ives plc

ISBN: 978-0-241-95642-7

www.greenpenguin.co.uk

To Teri, Dirk, and Dana
No father was blessed with more-loving children

GHOST FROM THE PAST

4-6-2 Pacific Locomotive

April 15, 1950
Flathead Lake, Montana

It rose from the depths like an evil monster in a Mesozoic sea. A coat of green slime covered the cab and boiler while gray-brown silt from the lake bottom slid and fell off the eighty-one-inch drive wheels and splashed into the cold waters of the lake. Ascending slowly above the surface, the old steam locomotive hung for a moment from the cables of a huge crane mounted on a wooden barge. Still visible under the dripping muck, beneath the open side window of its cab, was the number 3025.

Built by the Baldwin Locomotive Works of Philadelphia, Pennsylvania, 3025 rolled out of the factory on April 10th of 1904. The "Pacific" class was a common large-sized, high-drive-wheeled steam engine that could pull ten steel passenger cars long distances at speeds up to ninety miles an hour. She was known as a 4–6–2 because of her four-wheeled truck in the front, just behind the cowcatcher, the six massive drive wheels below the boiler, and the two small wheels mounted beneath the cab.

The crew on the barge watched in awe as the crane operator orchestrated his levers and gently lowered old 3025 onto the main deck, its weight settling the barge three inches deeper in the water. She sat there almost a minute before the six men overcame their wonderment and detached the cables.

"She's in remarkably good shape for sitting underwater for almost fifty years," murmured the salvage superintendent of the battered old barge that was nearly as ancient as the locomotive. Since the nineteen twenties, it had been used for dredging operations on the lake and surrounding tributaries.

Bob Kaufman was a big, friendly man, ready with a laugh at the slightest hint of something jovial. With a face ruddy from long hours spent in the sun, he had been working on the barge for twenty-seven years. Now seventy-five, he could have retired long ago, but as long as the dredging company kept him on he was going to keep working. Sitting at home and working jigsaw puzzles was not his idea of the good life. He studied the man standing beside him, who was, as close as he could figure, slightly older.

"What do you think?" Kaufman asked.

The man turned, tall and still lean in his late seventies, hair full and silver. His face was as weathered as buckskin. He stared at the locomotive thoughtfully through eyes yet to rely on glasses. They gleamed blue with a tinge of lavender. A large silver mustache covered his upper lip as if it had been planted there many years ago. It matched his eyebrows, which had become bushy with age. He lifted an expensive Panama hat off his head and dabbed at his forehead with a handkerchief.

He walked over to the salvaged locomotive, now sitting solidly on the deck, and focused his attention on the cab. Water and muck poured down its ladders and spilled across the deck of the barge.

"Despite the grime," he said finally, "she's still aesthetically pleasing to the eye. Only a question of time before a railroad museum comes up with the funds to restore her for display."

"Lucky a local fisherman lost his outboard engine and dragged the bottom to find it or the locomotive might have been down there another half century."

"Yes, it was a stroke of luck," the tall, silver-haired man said slowly.

Kaufman stepped over and ran a hand over one of the big drive wheels. A sentimental expression crossed his face. "My daddy was an engineer with the Union Pacific," he said quietly. "He always said the Pacific-type locomotive was the finest he ever drove. He used to let me sit in the cab when he brought a train into the yard. The Pacific class was used mostly to haul passenger cars because it was so fast."

A team of divers, wearing suits of canvas sandwiched between layers of rubber, stood on a platform as it was raised from beneath the surface of the cold water. They wore the Mark V brass hard hat, large weight belts around their chests, and diving boots with canvas tops, brass toes, and lead soles that weighed thirty-six pounds. Altogether, the divers wore one hundred fifty pounds of equipment. They tugged at their umbilical cords, leading to the surface-supplied diving air pump, as the platform was raised and swung down to the deck. They were no sooner aboard than another team climbed down ladders and stood on the platform as it descended into the waters of the lake, still icy from the long Montana winter.

The tall man watched silently, looking out of place among the barge's crew in their grease-stained work clothes and overalls. He wore neatly pressed brown slacks with an expensive cashmere knit sweater under a cashmere jacket. His shoes were highly polished and had amazingly kept their shine on the oil-soaked deck, amid the rusting cables.

He eyed the heavy layers of silt on the steps leading to the cab and turned to Kaufman. "Let's get a ladder over here so we can climb into the cab."

Kaufman gave an order to a nearby barge crewman and a ladder soon appeared and was propped against the lip of the cab's floor behind the engineer's seat. The superintendent went up first, followed by the elderly observer. Water dripped in sheets from the roof while dissolved coal merged with the silt flowing through the open door of the firebox onto the metal floor.

At first, it looked like the cab was empty. The maze of valves, pipes, and levers mounted over the boiler was coated with layers of ooze and the tentacles of green weed growing from it. The muck on the floor of the cab was ankle-deep, but the tall, quiet observer did not seem to notice it coming over the tops of his shoes. He knelt down and studied three humps that rose from the ooze like small hills.

"The engineer and fireman," he announced.

"You sure?"

He nodded. "I'm sure. The engineer was Leigh Hunt. He had a wife and two children, both grown now to middle age. The fireman was Robert Carr. He was going to be married after the run."

"Who was the third man?"

"Name was Abner Weed. A tough customer. He forced Hunt and Carr to operate the engine with a gun in their backs."

"They don't look pretty," Kaufman muttered, repelled by what he saw. "I'm surprised they didn't turn into skeletons."

"There would be nothing left of them if they died in salt water, but the cold, fresh water of Flathead Lake preserved them. What you see is the adipose tissue in which fat is stored. It breaks down over time when immersed, giving the body a waxy, soapy look called saponification."

"We'll have to call the sheriff and get a coroner out here."

"Will that delay the operation?" asked the stranger.

Kaufman shook his head. "No, it shouldn't slow things down any. As soon as the team of relief divers attach the lift cables, we'll bring up the coal tender."

"It's important that I see what's in the attached car."

"You will." Kaufman looked at the man, trying in vain to read his thoughts. "Better we tackle the tender first to simplify matters. If we concentrate on the car before it has been uncoupled from the tender, it might prove disastrous. It may not be as heavy as the locomotive, but unless we're very careful it might break into pieces. It's a far trickier operation. Besides, the front end of the baggage car is half buried under the tender."

"It's not a baggage car. It's a boxcar, or freight car."

"How could you know that?"

The observer ignored the question. "Raise the coal tender first. You're in charge."

Kaufman stared down at the ugly lumps that had once been humans. "How did they get here? How could a train come to be lost in the middle of the lake all these years?"

The tall man gazed out over the calm blue lake. "Forty-four years ago, there was a ferry that carried railcars loaded with lumber back and forth across the lake."

"It sure is strange," said Kaufman slowly. "Newspapers and the Southern Pacific officials reported that the train was stolen. As I recall, the date was April 21, 1906."

The old man smiled. "A cover-up by the company. The train wasn't stolen. A railroad dispatcher was bribed to charter the engine."

"Must have been something valuable in the freight car to kill for," said Kaufman. "Like a shipment of gold."

The old man nodded. "Rumors circulated that the train was carrying gold. If the truth be known, it was not gold but hard cash."

"Forty-four years," Kaufman said slowly. "A long time for a train to go missing. Maybe the money is still inside the car."

"Perhaps," said the tall man, looking toward the horizon at a vision only he could see. "Just perhaps we'll find the answers when we get inside."

THE BUTCHER BANDIT

Cromwell with his Harley and Boxcar

I

January 10, 1906
Bisbee, Arizona

Anyone seeing an old derelict sot slowly swaying down Moon Avenue in Bisbee that afternoon would have mistaken him for what he was not, a man who had grown old before his time working the mines that ran through the mineral-rich mountains under the town. His shirt was grubby and he smelled unwashed. One suspender held up torn and ragged pants that were stuffed into scuffed and worn boots that should been thrown in the trash gully behind the town long ago.

Snarled and greasy hair straggled to his shoulders and merged with an uncut beard that hung halfway down his protruding stomach. He looked through eyes so dark brown they were nearly black. There was no expression in them; they seemed cold and almost evil. A pair of work gloves covered the hands that had never held a shovel or a pick.

Under one arm, he carried an old gunnysack that appeared empty. Almost whimsically, the dirty burlap had DOUGLAS FEED & GRAIN COMPANY, OMAHA, NEBRASKA stenciled on it.

The old man took a minute and parked on a bench

at the corner of Moon Avenue and Tombstone Canyon Road. Behind him was a saloon, mostly empty because it was the middle of the day and its usual patrons were hard at work in the mines. The people walking and shopping in the little mining town paid him no more than a quick, disgusted glance. Whenever they passed, he pulled a whiskey bottle from a pant pocket and drank heavily before recapping it and putting it back. No one could have known it was not whiskey but tea.

It was warm for June; he guessed the temperature to be in the high nineties. He sat back and looked up and down the streets as a trolley car passed, pulled by an aging horse. Electric-motored trolleys had yet to come to Bisbee. Most of the vehicles on the streets were still horse-drawn wagons and buggies. The town had only a handful of automobiles and delivery trucks, and none was in evidence.

He knew enough about the town to know that it was founded in 1880 and named after Judge DeWitt Bisbee, one of the moneymen behind the Copper Queen Mine. A good-sized community, its population of twenty thousand made it the largest city between San Francisco and St. Louis. Despite the many miners' families that lived in modest little wooden buildings, the main economy was based around saloons and a small army of shady ladies.

The man's head nodded to his chest; he looked like a drunk who had dozed off. But it was an act. He was conscious of every movement around him. Occasionally, he glanced across the street at the Bisbee

National Bank. He watched with interest, through half-closed eyes, as a truck with chain drive and solid-tired wheels rattled up to the bank. There was only one guard, who got out of the truck and carried a large bag of newly printed bills inside. A few minutes later, he was helped by the bank's teller to lug a heavy chest through the door and onto the truck.

The man knew that it was a shipment of gold, a piece of the three million ounces that had been produced at the local mines. But gold was not what piqued his interest. It was too heavy and too risky for one man to dispose of. It was the cash that brought him to Bisbee, not the prized yellow metal.

He watched as the truck moved away and two men, whom he had identified as security guards at the giant Phelps Dodge Mining Company, walked out of the bank. They had delivered the cash to pay the mining company payroll the following day. He smiled to himself, knowing the assets of the Bisbee National Bank had risen to a new level.

He had watched the people who came and went from the bank for nearly two weeks until he could identify them by sight. He had also noted the time when they came and went. Satisfied now there was no one in the bank except one teller and the owner/manager, he looked at his watch and nodded to himself.

Leisurely, the old derelict rose, stretched, and ambled across the brick street and trolley tracks to the bank, carrying the large, empty gunnysack over one shoulder. Just as he was about to enter, a woman unexpectedly walked past. She gave him a look of loathing, stepped around him, and went inside. She was not in his plan, but he decided to deal with the matter rather than wait. He checked the street and followed her into the bank.

He closed the door. The teller was in the vault and the woman waited until he reappeared. The derelict removed a model 1902 Colt .38 caliber automatic from his boot, struck the woman on the nape of the neck with the barrel, watching with detachment as she slowly folded to the wooden floor. It happened so suddenly and silently that the owner of the bank did not see or hear anything from his office.

Then the drunken miner suddenly turned bank robber leaped sprightfully over the counter, entered the owner's office, and put the gun barrel to his head. "Resist and you'll be shot dead," he said in a low but forbidding tone. "Now, call the teller into your office."

The bald, fat, shocked bank owner looked at him with brown eyes widened with fright. Without argument, he called out, "Roy, come in here."

"Be right there, Mr. Castle," Roy called out from inside the vault.

"Tell him to leave the vault open," said the bank robber quietly, with a sharp edge to his voice.

"Roy, don't close the vault door," Castle complied as ordered, his eyes crossing as they focused on the gun pressing against his forehead.

Roy stepped from the vault, a ledger under one arm. He couldn't see the unconscious woman lying under the counter. Suspecting nothing, he entered Castle's office and abruptly stiffened when he saw the robber holding a gun to his boss's head. The robber pulled the gun barrel away from Castle's head and motioned with the muzzle toward the vault.

"Both of you," he said calmly, "into the vault."

There was no thought of resistance. Castle rose from his desk and led the way into the vault while the robber stepped quickly to the window to check the street for anyone heading for the bank. Except for a few women shopping and a passing beer wagon, the street was quiet.

The interior of the vault was well lit, with an Edison brass lamp hanging from the steel ceiling. Except for the chest containing the gold, stacks of bills, mostly the payroll for the mining companies, covered the shelves. The robber threw the gunnysack at the teller.

"Okay, Roy, fill it with all the greenbacks you have."

Roy did as he was told. With trembling hands, he began sweeping the piles of bills of various denominations into the sack. By the time he was finished, the sack was stretched to the limit of its burlap fibers and seemed to be the size of a well-filled laundry bag.

"Now, lay down on the floor," ordered the robber.

Castle and Roy, believing the robber was now

about to make his getaway, stretched out flat on the floor, with their hands stretched over their heads. The robber pulled a heavy woolen scarf from one of his pockets and wrapped it around the muzzle of his automatic. Then he systematically shot both men in the head. It sounded more like two loud thumps than the sharp crack of gunfire. Without another second's hesitation, he heaved the sack over one shoulder and walked from the vault without looking back.

Unfortunately, he wasn't finished. The woman under the counter moaned and tried to rise to her elbows. With utter indifference, he leaned down, lowered the gun, and shot her in the head like he had the bank owner and teller. There was no remorse, not the slightest hint of emotion. He didn't care whether any of them left families behind. He had murdered three defenseless people in cold blood with as little interest as he might have shown stepping on a column of ants.

He paused to search for one of the shell casings he thought he'd heard fall to the floor from inside the scarf wrapped around the gun but could not find it. He gave up and walked casually from the bank, noting with satisfaction that no one had heard the muted gunshots.

With the gunnysack bulging with cash slung over his shoulder, the man walked through the alley running behind the bank. Stepping into a small alcove under a stairway where he would not be seen, he took off the grimy clothes, removed the gray wig and beard, and threw everything in a small valise. Now revealed in an expensively tailored suit, he perched a bowler hat at a jaunty angle on his head and its neatly brushed carpet of red hair. He slipped on a necktie and knotted it before also tossing the scuffed boots in the valise. He was a short man, and the soles and heels of the boot had been raised nearly two inches. Next, he pulled on a pair of English-made leather shoes, with lifts in the heel to make him appear taller, before turning his attention to a large leather suitcase he had hidden under a canvas tarp along with a Harley-Davidson motorcycle. Glancing up and down the alley every few seconds, he transferred the huge pile of cash from the gunnysack to the suitcase, which he strapped on a rack over the rear wheel of the motorcycle. The valise containing his disguise he tied on a front rack.

At that moment, the man heard shouting coming down the alley from Tombstone Canyon Road. Someone had discovered the bodies in the Bisbee National Bank. Unconcerned, he pushed the motorcycle forward and started the three-horsepower, twenty-five-cubic-inch one-cylinder engine. He threw one leg over the seat and rode deserted back alleys to the railroad yard. He moved unseen along a siding where a freight train had stopped to take on water.

His timing was perfect.

Another five minutes and the freight train would have moved back onto the main line and headed toward Tucson. Without being noticed by the engineer and the brakeman, as they pulled a big pipe down from the wooden tank into the tender for water to make steam, the man took a key from his vest pocket and opened the padlock to the door to a boxcar that was marked with a painted sign that read O'BRIAN FURNITURE COMPANY, DENVER. He slid the door open on its rollers. The presence of the boxcar in this time and place was no coincidence. Acting as a fictitious representative of the equally fictitious O'Brian Furniture Company, he had paid cash for it to be included in the freight train passing through Bisbee, en route from El Paso, Texas, to Tucson, Arizona.

He took a wide plank, attached by brackets to the side of the boxcar, and used it as a ramp to ride the Harley-Davidson aboard. Then he quickly closed the rolling door and reached through a small hinged opening to replace the lock as the whistle on the engine tooted and the train began moving forward from the siding onto the main track.

From the outside, the boxcar looked like any other that had been in use for several years. The paint was faded, and the wooden sides were dented and chipped. But its appearance was deceptive. Even the lock on the door was fake, making it look like the car was buttoned up tight. It was the inside that was the most deceptive, however. Instead of an empty interior or one packed with furniture, it was luxurious, ornately constructed, and furnished as ostentatiously as any private railcar belonging to the president of a railroad. Mahogany paneling spread over the walls and ceiling. The floor was covered by a thick carpet. The décor and furniture were extravagantly magnificent. There was an opulent sitting room, a palatial bedroom, and an efficient kitchen with the latest innovations for preparing gourmet meals.

There were no servants, porters, or cooks.

The man worked alone, without accomplices who might reveal his true name and occupation. No one knew of his clandestine operations as a bank robber and mass murderer. Even the railroad car had been built and decorated in Canada before being secretly transported across the border into the United States.

The robber relaxed in a plush leather settee, uncorked a bottle of 1884 Château La Houringue Bordeaux, chilled in buckets, and poured himself a glass.

He knew the town sheriff would quickly form a posse. But they would be looking for an old mangy miner who murdered while in a drunken fit. The posse would fan out, searching the town, almost certain he was too poor to own a horse. None of the townspeople had ever seen him come and go on horseback or driving a buggy.

Immensely pleased with himself, he sipped the wine from a crystal glass and studied the leather suitcase. Was this his fifteenth, or was it his sixteenth, successful robbery? he mused. The thirty-eight men and women and two children he had killed never entered his mind. He estimated the take of the mining payroll at $325,000 to $330,000. Most robbers wouldn't have come close to guessing the amount inside the case.

But it was easy for him, since he was a banker himself.

The sheriff, his deputies, and the posse would never find the murdering robber. It was as if he had disappeared into thin air. No one ever thought to connect him with the dapper man riding through town on a motorcycle.

The hideous crime would become one of Bisbee's most enduring mysteries.

2

September 15, 1906
The Mississippi River Below
Hannibal, Missouri

Soon after the twentieth century was born, steamboating on the Mississippi began to fade. Few passenger steamboats still reigned in style. The *Saint Peter* was one of the last grand passenger boats to have survived the onslaught of the railroads. Two hundred fifty feet long and seventy-five feet wide, she was a splendid example of palatial elegance, with side-curving stairways, plush passenger cabins, and a magnificent main dining room with the finest food to be found anywhere. Ostentatious salons were provided for the ladies while the men smoked their cigars and played cards in handsome rooms adorned with mirrors and paintings.

Card games on steamboats plying the river were notorious for their cardsharp gamblers. Many passengers left steamboats poorer than when they boarded. At one table in the gambling room of the *Saint Peter*, in a quiet corner away from the main action, two men were enjoying a game of five-card stud.

At first glance, the scene looked like any other in the room, but a closer look revealed that no chips sat on the green felt table.

Joseph Van Dorn calmly studied his hand before laying down two cards. "A good thing we're not in this for the money," he said, smiling, "or I would owe you eight thousand dollars."

Colonel Henry Danzler, director of the United States government's Criminal Investigation Department, smiled in return. "If you cheated like I do, we'd be even."

Van Dorn was a congenial man in his early forties. His cheeks and chin were buried under a magnificent red burnsides beard that matched what remained of the hair that circled his bald dome. His face was dominated by a Roman nose, and his brown eyes looked sad and melancholy, but his look and manner were deceiving.

Irish-born, he bore a name known and respected throughout the country for tenacity in tracking down murderers, robbers, and other desperados. The criminal underworld of the time knew he would chase them to the ends of the earth. Founder and chief of the renowned Van Dorn Detective Agency, he and his agents had prevented political assassinations, hunted down many of the West's most feared outlaws, and helped organize the country's first secret service agency.

"You'd still deal yourself more aces than me," he said affably.

Danzler was an enormous man, tall and mammoth in girth, weighing slightly over three hundred pounds, yet he could move as effortlessly as a tiger. His salt-and-pepper hair was immaculately trimmed and brushed, shining under the light that streamed in through the boat's big windows. His blue-green eyes had a soft glow to them, yet they seemed to analyze and record everything going on about him.

A veteran and hero of the Spanish American War, he had charged up San Juan Hill with Captain John Pershing and his black "Buffalo Soldiers" of the Tenth Cavalry and had served with distinction in the Philippines against the Moros. When the governments Criminal Investigation Department was authorized by Congress, President Roosevelt asked him to become its first director.

Danzlet opened the lid of a large pocket watch and stared at the hands. "Your man is five minutes late."

"Isaac Bell is my best agent. He always gets his man – and occasionally a woman, too. If he's late, there's a good reason."

"You say he's the one who apprehended the assassin Ramos Kelly before he could shoot President Roosevelt?"

Van Dorn nodded. "And he rounded up the Barton gang in Missouri. He shot and killed three of them before the other two surrendered to him."

Danzler stared at the famous detective. "And you think he's the man to stop our mass murderer and bank robber?"

"If anyone can stop the killer, Isaac can."

"What is his family background?"

"Very wealthy," answered Van Dorn. "His father

and grandfather were bankers. You've heard of the American States Bank of Boston?"

Danzler nodded. "Indeed. I have an account there myself."

"Isaac is very affluent. His grandfather left him five million dollars in his will, thinking Isaac would take his place as head of the bank one day. It never happened. Isaac preferred detective work to banking. I'm lucky to have him."

Danzler caught a shadow on his arm. He looked up and found himself looking into soft blue eyes with a slight violet cast, eyes that had looked over horizons to see what was beyond. The effect was almost mesmerizing, as though they were searching deep into Danzler's inner thoughts.

Danzler could size up a man as precisely as he could a horse. The intruder was tall and lean, stood well over six feet, and weighed no more than one hundred seventy-five pounds. A large flaxen mustache that covered his entire upper lip conformed with the thick mass of neatly barbered blond hair. His hands and fingers were long and nimble and hung loosely, almost casually, at his sides. There was a no-nonsense look about him. The colonel judged that this was a man who dealt with substance and did not endure fools or insignificant and phony candor. He had a determined set to the chin and lips that were spread in a friendly smile. Danzler guessed his age at about thirty.

He was dressed immaculately in a white linen suit without a wrinkle. A heavy gold chain dipped from a left vest pocket that was attached to a large gold watch inside the right pocket. A low-crowned hat with a wide brim sat squarely on his head. Danzler might have pegged him as a dandy, but the look of elegance was betrayed by a pair of worn leather boots that had seen many hours in stirrups. Bell carried a thin valise and set it down beside the table.

"Colonel Danzler," said Van Dorn, "this is the man I told you about, Isaac Bell."

Danzler offered his hand but did not rise from his chair. "Joe here tells me that you always get your man."

Bell grinned slightly. "I'm afraid Mr. Van Dorn has exaggerated. I was ten minutes too late when Butch Cassidy and Harry Longabaugh sailed for Argentina three years ago from New York. Their boat pulled away from the dock before I could apprehend them."

"How many agents or law enforcement officers were with you?"

Bell shrugged. "I intended to handle the matter on my own."

"Wasn't Longabaugh the Sundance Kid?" asked Danzler.

Bell nodded. "He got the nickname when he tried to steal a horse in Sundance, Wyoming. He was caught and spent eighteen months in jail."

"Surely you didn't expect to subdue them without a fight."

"I think it is safe to say that they would have

resisted," said Bell, without explaining how he would have single-handedly captured the former members of the infamous Wild Bunch.

Van Dorn sat back in his chair, made no comment, and gave the colonel a smug look.

"Why don't you sit down, Mr. Bell, and join our little game?"

Bell looked at the empty table quizzically and then at Danzler. "You appear to have no chips."

"Just a friendly little game," said Van Dorn, shuffling the deck of cards and dealing out three hands. "So far, I owe the colonel eight thousand dollars."

Bell sat down, the quizzical look altered to one of understanding. The game was a pretense. His chief and the colonel were sitting in the corner away from the other gamblers and playing as if they were in a serious game. He laid his hat in his lap, picked up his cards, and acted as if he were deep in thought.

"Are you familiar with the swarm of bank robberies and murders that have occurred around the western states in the past two years?" Danzler inquired.

"Only in conversation," replied Bell. "Mr. Van Dorn has kept me busy on other cases."

"What do you actually know about the crimes?"

"Only that the robber murders anyone in the bank during the act, escapes like a spirit, and leaves no evidence behind that might incriminate him."

"Anything else?" Danzler probed.

"Whoever he is," answered Bell, "he is very, very good. There have been no leads and no breaks in the investigation." He paused and stared at Van Dorn. "Is that why I've been called here?"

Van Dorn nodded. "I want you to take over the case as chief investigator."

Bell threw down a card, picked up the card that Danzler dealt, and slipped it in the fan, which he held in his left hand.

"Are you a lefty, Mr. Bell?" asked Danzler out of curiosity.

"No. Actually, I'm right-handed."

Van Dorn laughed softly. "Isaac can draw the derringer he hides in his hat, cock it, and pull the trigger faster than you can blink."

Danzler's respect for Bell grew during the conversation. He drew back his coat and revealed a 1903 Colt .38 caliber hammerless automatic. "I'll take Joe's word for it, but it would be interesting to put it to the test—" Danzler had not finished the sentence when he found himself staring into the twin muzzles of a derringer.

"Age has slowed you, Henry," said Van Dorn. "Either that or your mind wandered."

"I have to admit, he is very fast," Danzler said, visibly impressed.

"What office will I work out of?" Bell asked Van Dorn as he slipped the derringer back in his hat. where it fit in a small pocket inside the crown.

"The crimes have occurred from Placerville, California, in the west, to Terlingua. Texas, to the east," replied Van Dorn. "And from Bisbee, Arizona, in the south, to Bozeman, Montana, in the north. I think it best if you operated in the center."

"That would be Denver."

Van Dorn nodded. "As you know, we have an office there with six experienced agents."

"I've worked with two of them three years ago," said Bell. "Curtis and Irvine are good men."

"Yes, I forgot," Van Dorn said, now recalling. "I might add, Colonel, that Isaac was responsible for the apprehension of Jack Ketchum, who was later hung for two murders committed during a train robbery." He paused and reached under the table and produced an identical valise to the one Bell had carried into the gambling salon. Bell then passed his empty valise to Van Dorn. "Inside, you will find the reports on all the crimes. Every lead so far has led up a blind alley."

"When do I start?"

"At the next landing, which is Clarksville, you will depart and take the first train to Independence. From there, you will be given a ticket on the Union Pacific express to Denver. You can digest and study what little clues and evidence we've gathered. Once you arrive, you'll take up the hunt for the murdering scum." A look of anger and frustration clouded Van Dorn's brown eyes. "Sorry, I didn't give you a chance to pack when you left Chicago, but I wanted you to start as soon as possible."

"Not to worry, sir," Bell said with a faint smile. "Fortunately, I packed two suitcases for the duration."

Van Dorn's eyebrows raised. "You knew?"

"Let's say I made an educated guess."

"Keep us informed on your manhunt," said Danzler. "If you need any help from the government, I'll do all in my power to assist you."

"Thank you, sir." Bell acknowledged. "I'll be in contact as soon as I get a firm grip on the situation."

Van Dorn said, "I'll be working in our Chicago office. Since transcontinental telephone service has yet to run from St. Louis across the prairie to Denver and beyond to California, you'll have to telegraph me on your progress."

"If any," Danzler muttered sarcastically. "You're up against the best criminal brain this country has ever known."

"I promise I won't rest until I capture the man responsible for these hideous crimes."

"I wish you good luck," Van Dorn said sincerely.

"Not to change the subject," Danzler spoke with satisfaction as he laid his card hand on the green felt, "I have three queens."

Van Dorn shrugged and threw his cards on the table. "Beats me."

"And you, Mr. Bell?" said Danzler with a crafty grin.

Isaac Bell slowly laid his cards on the table one by one. "A straight flush," he said matter-of-factly. Then, without another word, he rose and walked briskly from the salon.

3

Late in the morning, a man drove an old wagon, hitched to a pair of mules, past the cemetery outside the town of Rhyolite, Nevada. The graves had simple wooden fences around them, with the names of the deceased carved on markers made of wood. Many were children who had died of typhoid or cholera, aggravated by the hard family life of a mining town.

The July heat in the Mojave Desert was unbearable under the direct rays of the sun. The driver of the wagon sat beneath a tattered umbrella attached to the seat. Black hair fell past his neck but just short of the shoulders. His head was protected by a stained Mexican sombrero. His unseen eyes peered through the stained-blue glass of spectacles, and a handkerchief wrapped the lower half of his face, to keep out the dust raised by the mules' hooves. The manner in which he was hunched over made it difficult, if not impossible, to determine his build.

As he rode by, he stared with interest at a house a miner had built using thousands of cast-off saloon beer bottles embedded in adobe mud. The bottoms of the bottles faced outward with the mouths facing in, the green glass casting the interior in an eerie sort of light.

He came to the railroad tracks and drove the mules along the road next to them. The tops of the rails gleamed like narrow twin mirrors in the blinding sun. These were the tracks of the Las Vegas & Tonopah Railroad, which would through the middle of the residential district of the town.

The wagon rolled slowly past more than eighty railcars on a siding. They had been unloaded of their incoming freight. The empty cars were now being filled with outgoing ore for the mills. The driver took a brief glance at a boxcar being coupled to a thirty-car train. The lettering on the side said O'BRIAN FURNITURE COMPANY, DENVER. He glanced at the dial of his cheap pocket watch – he carried nothing that might help identify him – and noted that the train was not scheduled to leave for Las Vegas for another forty-four minutes.

A quarter of a mile later, he came to the Rhyolite train station. The substantial building was a mixture of Gothic and early Spanish styles. The ornate depot had been built of stone, cut and hauled from Las Vegas. A passenger train that had steamed in from San Francisco sat alongside the station platform. The passengers had disembarked, and the seats cleaned by porters, and the train was now filling with people heading back toward the coast.

The driver reached the center of town, where the streets were bustling with activity. He turned to stare at a large mercantile establishment, the HD & LD PORTER store. Beneath the sign was a slogan painted on a board that hung above the front entrance. It read *We handle all things but Whiskey.*

The 1904 gold rush had resulted in a substantial small city of solidly constructed buildings built to last a long time. By 1906, Rhyolite was a thriving community of over six thousand people. It had quickly graduated from a busy tent town to an important city meant to stand far into the distant future.

The main buildings were constructed of stone and concrete, making the small metropolis of Rhyolite the major city of southern Nevada. A four-story bank came into sight, a fine-looking structure that gave it a look of substance and wealth. Half a block away, a three-story stone office building was going up.

There was a post office, an opera house, a twenty-bed hospital, comfortable hotels, two churches, three banks, and a large school. Up-to-date, Rhyolite boasted an efficient telephone system and its own electrical-generating plant. It also had a booming red-light district and forty saloons and eight dance halls.

The man driving the wagon was not interested in anything the town had to offer except some of the assets of the John S. Cook Bank. He knew that the safe inside could hold over a million dollars in silver coins. But it was far easier to carry cash from the payrolls of the mines, and he had yet to take a single silver, or gold, piece. He figured that with eighty-five companies engaged in mining the surrounding hills, the payroll take should be quite considerable.

As usual, he had planned well, living in a boardinghouse for miners while entering the Cook Bank on numerous occasions to make small deposits in an account he had opened under a false name. A brief friendship was struck up with the bank's manager, who was led into thinking the town newcomer was a mining engineer. The man's appearance had been altered with a wig of black hair, a mustache, and a Vandyke beard. He also walked with a limp, which he said was the result of a mining accident. It proved to be a flawless disguise with which to study the banking habits of the citizens and the times when the bank was doing little business.

As he drove the wagon and mules into town toward the Cook Bank, however, his image had been changed from that of a mining engineer to that of a small-time freight hauler to the mines. He looked like any one of the town's haulers, struggling to make a living in the broiling heat of the desert during summer. He reined in the mules at the rear of a stable. When he was certain no one was observing him, he lifted a dummy dressed exactly the same as himself and tied it to the seat of the wagon. Then he led the mules back toward Broadway, the main street running through town. Just before reaching the concrete walkway in front of the bank's entrance, he slapped the mules on their rumps and sent them off, pulling the wagon down the street through the main part of town, his dummy likeness sitting upright on the seat and holding the reins.

He checked for customers approaching the bank. None of the people milling around the town seemed headed in that direction. He looked up at the four-story building, glancing at the gold paint on the windows of the upper floor advertising a dentist and a doctor. Another sign, with a hand pointing downward, indicated that the town post office was in the basement.

He strolled into the bank and looked around the lobby. It was empty except for a man making a withdrawal. The customer took his money from the teller, turned, and walked from the bank without glancing at the stranger.

There goes a lucky man, the robber thought.

If the customer had bothered to notice him, he would have been shot dead. The robber never left anyone behind to identify the least detail about him. Then there was always the possibility, although slim, that someone might see through his disguise.

He had learned from conversations in the neighboring saloons that the bank was run by a manager for a company of men who were owners of the region's most productive mines, especially the Montgomery-Shoshone Mine whose original claim had grossed nearly two million dollars.

So far, so good, thought the robber as he leaped over the counter, landing on his feet next to the startled teller. He pulled the automatic from his boot and pressed the muzzle against the teller's head.

"Do not move, and do not think of stepping on

the alarm button under the counter or I'll splatter your brains on the wall."

The teller could not believe what was happening. "Is this *really* a holdup?" he stammered.

"It is that," replied the robber. "Now, walk into the manager's office very slowly and act as if nothing is happening."

The frightened teller moved toward an office with a closed door whose etched glass made it difficult to see in or out. He knocked.

"Yes, come on in," came a voice from the other side.

The teller Fred pushed open the door and was roughly shoved inside, losing his balance and falling across the manager's desk. The sign on the desk, HERBERT WILKINS, was knocked to the floor. Wilkins swiftly took in the situation and reached for a revolver under his desk. He was five seconds too late. The robber had learned about the weapon from the manager himself, while talking at a nearby saloon.

"Do not touch that gun," snapped the robber, as if he were psychic.

Wilkins was not a man who frightened easily. He stared at the robber, taking in every inch of his appearance. "You'll never get away with it," he said contemptuously.

The robber spoke in a cold, steady voice. "I have before and I will do so again." He motioned toward the imposing safe that stood nearly eight feet high. "Open it!"

Wilkins looked the robber square in the eye. "No, I don't think I will."

The robber wasted no time. He wrapped the muzzle of his automatic in a heavy towel and shot the teller between the eyes. Then he turned to Wilkins. "I may leave here without a dime, but you won't live to see it."

Wilkins stood, horrified, staring down at the spreading pool of blood around Fred's head. He looked at the smoldering towel where the bullet had passed through, well knowing it was unlikely that anyone in the building had heard the gunshot. As if in a trance, he walked to the safe and began turning the combination lock to the required numbers. After half a minute, he pulled down on the latch and the massive steel door swung open.

"Take it and be damned!" he hissed.

The robber merely smiled and shot Wilkins in the temple. The bank manager had barely struck the floor when the robber strode quickly to the front door, slammed it shut, hung a CLOSED sign in the window, and pulled down the shades. Then he methodically cleaned out the safe of all bills, transferring them into a laundry bag he carried tied around his waist under his shirt. When the sack was filled until it bulged in every seam, he stuffed the remaining bills in his pant pockets and boots. The safe cleaned of all money, the robber stared briefly at the gold and silver coins inside and took just one gold souvenir.

There was a heavy iron rear door to the bank that

opened onto a narrow street. The robber unlocked the door's inside latch, cracked the door open, and scanned the street. It was lined on the opposite side with residential houses.

A group of young boys were playing baseball a block from the bank. Not good. This was entirely unexpected by the robber. In his many hours of observing the streets around the Cook Bank, this was the first time he had found children playing in the street behind the bank. He was on a time schedule and had to reach the railyard and his secret boxcar in twelve minutes. Shouldering the bag so his face was shielded on the right side, he walked around the ball game in progress and continued up the street, where he ducked into an alley.

For the most part, the boys ignored him. Only one stared at the poorly dressed man toting a big sack over his right shoulder. What struck the boy as odd was that the man wore a Mexican sombrero, a style that was seldom seen around Rhyolite. Most men in town wore fedoras, derbies, or miner's caps. There was also something else about the raggedy man . . . Then another boy yelled, and the boy turned back to the game, barely in time to catch a pop fly.

The robber tied the sack around his shoulders so that it hung on his back. The bicycle he'd parked earlier behind a dentist's office was sitting there behind a barrel that had been placed to catch runoff water from the building's drainpipe. He mounted the seat and began pedaling along Armagosa Street, past the red-light district, until he came to the railyard.

A brakeman was walking along the track toward the caboose at the end of the train. The robber couldn't believe his bad luck. Despite his meticulous planning, fate had dealt him a bad hand. Unlike with his other robberies and murders, this time he had been noticed by a stupid young boy. And now this brakeman. Never had he encountered so many eyes that might have observed him during his escape. There was nothing he could do but see it through.

Luckily, the brakeman did not look in the robber's direction. He was going from car to car checking the grease in the axle boxes of the trucks and wheels the boxcars rode on. If the brass sleeve that rotated inside the box did not receive enough lubricant, the friction would heat the end of the axle to a dangerous level. The weight of the car could break the axle off and cause a disastrous crash.

As the robber cycled past, the brakeman did not bother to look up. He instead went about his business, trying to complete his inspection before the train departed for Tonopah and then on to Sacramento.

Already, the engineer was looking at his gauges to make sure he had enough steam to move the heavy train. The robber hoped the brakeman would not turn back and witness him entering his private boxcar. Quickly, he unlocked and slid open the door. He threw the bicycle inside and then climbed a small ladder up to the door, dragging the heavy money sack over the threshold.

Once inside the boxcar, the robber peered down

the length of the train. The brakeman was climbing aboard the caboose, which housed the train crew. There was no sign he'd witnessed the robber enter the boxcar.

Secure inside his palatial car, the robber relaxed and read a copy of the Rhyolite *Herald.* He could not help but wonder what the paper would print the following day about the bank robbery and the killing of its manager and teller. Again, as he had so many times earlier, he felt no remorse. The deaths never entered his mind again.

Later, besides the mystery of how the robber/killer had escaped without a trace, the other puzzle was the wagon found outside of town on the road toward Bullfrog. The wagon was empty and appeared to have been driven by a dummy. The posse that chased it down was mystified.

Sheriff Josh Miller did put two and two together, but his speculation went nowhere. Nothing made sense. The desperado left no clues.

The robbery and murders in Rhyolite became another enigma that went unsolved.

4

The summer sunlight heightened the contrast of colors in the mile-high altitude of Colorado. The sky was free of clouds, a vivid blue that spread over the city of Denver like a quilt. The temperature was a comfortable eighty-one degrees.

Isaac Bell closed the door to his stateroom and left the train by stepping off the observation platform at the rear of the Pullman car. He paused to look up at the clock tower of the Gothic-style Union Station. Built of stone hauled down from the Rocky Mountains, the imposing three-story structure stretched a quarter of a mile.

The arrowhead-tipped hands of the huge clock read 11:40. Bell lifted his large gold watch from the vest pocket of his tailored linen suit and glanced at the hands that pointed to Roman numerals. His time was 11:43. He smiled at himself with satisfaction, knowing for certain that the big clock-tower clock was three minutes slow.

He walked down the redbrick platform to the baggage car, identified his trunks, and hailed a porter. "My name is Bell. Could you please see that my trunks are sent to the Brown Palace Hotel?"

The porter smiled broadly at the gold coin Bell laid in his hand and rubbed it almost reverently. "Yes, sir, I'll deliver them myself."

"I'm also expecting a large wooden crate on a later train. Can I count on you to make sure it is delivered to the Union Pacific freight warehouse?"

"Yes, sir, I'll take care of it." Still rubbing the gold piece, the porter grinned broadly.

"I'd be grateful."

"May I take that for you?" said the porter, nodding at the valise in Bell's hand.

"I'll keep it with me, thank you."

"Can I hail you a taxi?"

"That won't be necessary. I'll take the tram."

Bell strolled through the high-ceilinged grand lobby of the depot, with its majestic hanging chandeliers, past the rows of high-backed oak waiting benches and out the main entrance, flanked by twin Grecian columns. He crossed Wyncoop Street onto 17th Street and passed under the newly erected Mizpah Arch, a gatelike structure with a pair of American flags flying on top that was built to welcome, and bid farewell to, train travelers. *Mizpah*, Bell knew, meant watch-tower in ancient Hebrew.

Two ladies wearing light summer dresses, gloves, and ornate hats decorated with flowers drove by in an electric battery-powered car. Bell doffed his hat, and with nods and smiles they acknowledged the attention of the attractive man as they motored up 17th Street toward the state capitol building.

Horse-drawn wagons and carriages still outnumbered the few automobiles that chugged up and down the streets of the city. A Denver Tramway Company trolley car clanged around the corner off Wazee Street and approached the end of the block, where it stopped to let off and take on passengers. The horse-drawn railways were a thing of the past and electric trolleys ruled the streets, reaching every neighborhood in Denver.

Bell climbed the steps and gave ten cents to the motorman. The bell was clanged and the big red trolley clattered up 17th Street. Three-and four-story brick buildings filled the next fourteen blocks. The sidewalks were crowded with people on a typical business day. The men wore black or gray suits and ties, while the women strolled in the long dresses whose skirts rose just above the ankles. Most of the women wore flamboyant hats and carried parasols.

He observed with interest a store that was selling Cadillac motorcars. The awnings were rolled out, shadowing the windows and revealing the vehicles inside. He glanced at the street signs so he could recall the location. An enthusiast of motorcars, he owned a Locomobile race car that had been driven by Joe Tracy in the 1905 Vanderbilt Cup road race on Long Island, in New York, placing third. Bell had converted it to street driving by adding fenders and headlamps.

He also owned a bright red motorcycle. The newest racing model, its V-Twin engine put out three and a half horsepower. It had an innovative twist grip throttle, weighed only one hundred twenty pounds, and could whip over the roads at nearly sixty miles an hour.

When the trolley rattled to a stop at California and 17th Streets, Bell stepped down the stair to the pavement and sauntered over to the sidewalk. It had been three years since he had set foot in Denver. Tall buildings stood on almost every corner, and the construction never stopped. He walked a block to the Colorado Building, a brown stone structure that rose eight stories on 16th and California Streets.

The windows were high and shielded by awnings that matched the brown exterior of the walls. The overhang above the top floor stretched nearly ten feet over the sidewalk far below. Hedgecock & Jones and the Braman Clothing Company occupied the street level. Above them were several different businesses, including the Fireman's Fund Insurance Company and the Van Dorn Detective Agency.

Bell turned into the lobby and moved through a group of office workers who were streaming out of the building on their lunch break. The floor, walls, and ceiling were beautifully constructed of green Italian marble the color of jade. He entered an Otis elevator behind two pretty young ladies and moved to the rear of the car as the operator closed the steel scissor-gate door. As was the custom, Bell played the gentleman and removed his wide-brimmed hat.

The elevator operator pivoted the handle on the curved throttle housing, sending the elevator toward the upper floors at a leisurely pace. The women exited at the fifth floor, chatting gaily. They both turned and gave Bell a bashful glance before disappearing down the hallway.

The operator stopped the elevator and opened the door. "Eighth floor, and a good afternoon to you, sir," he said cheerily.

"Same to you," replied Bell.

He exited into a hallway painted a muted Mexican red above with walnut wainscot halfway up the wall below. He turned right and came to a door with etched lettering on the upper glass that advertised THE VAN DORN DETECTIVE AGENCY. Beneath was the agency's slogan: *We never give up, never.*

The antechamber was painted white, with two padded wooden chairs and a desk, behind which a young woman sat primly in a swivel chair. Van Dorn was not a man to waste money on ostentatious décor. The only embellishment was a photo of the head man hanging on the wall behind the secretary.

She looked up and smiled sweetly, admiring the well-dressed man standing opposite her. She was a pretty woman, with soft brown eyes and wide shoulders. "May I help you, sir?"

"Yes. I'd like to see Arthur Curtis and Glenn Irvine."

"Are they expecting you?"

"Please tell them Isaac Bell is here."

She sucked in her breath. "Oh, Mr. Bell, I should have known. Mr. Curtis and Mr. Irvine did not expect you until tomorrow."

"I managed to catch an earlier train out of Independence, Missouri." Bell looked at the sign on her desk. "You're Miss Agnes Murphy?"

She held up her left hand, displaying a wedding band. "Mrs. Murphy."

Bell smiled his beguiling smile. "I hope you don't mind if I simply call you Agnes, since I'll be working here for a time."

"Not at all."

She rose from her desk, and he could see she wore a pleated blue cotton skirt with her white fluffy blouse. Her hair was piled atop her head in the fashion of the Gibson girl, which was so popular then. Her petticoats rustled as she went through the door to the inner offices.

Always curious, Bell moved around the desk and looked down at the letter Mrs. Murphy had been typing on a Remington typewriter. It was addressed to Van Dorn, and spelled out the superintendent of the western states' displeasure at having Bell come in and take over the unsolved case. Bell had never met Nicholas Alexander, who headed the Denver office, but he was determined to be courteous and polite to the man despite any antagonism.

Bell moved away from Mrs. Murphy's desk and stood looking out the window over the rooftops of the city when Alexander walked into the anteroom. He looked more like the bookkeeper of a funeral parlor than the chief investigator who had unraveled many crimes and brought the offenders to full justice. He was a short man, his head barely coming up even with Bell's shoulders. He wore a coat that was too large and his trousers were baggy. The high collar of his shirt showed wear and sweat stains. His head was devoid of hair except around the temples and at the rear; the eyebrows were trimmed as neatly as his hair. A pair of pince-nez glasses were clipped to the bridge of his nose in front of almost-sad-looking gray-green eyes.

Alexander held out his hand as his lips spread into a smile that was completely lacking in humor. "Mr. Bell, I'm honored to meet Van Dorn's finest agent."

Bell didn't buy the compliment since there was no hint of warmth about it. "The honor is mine in meeting you," Bell replied, nearly biting his tongue. It was obvious Alexander simply thought of Bell as an interloper into his private territory.

"Please come on back. Before I show you to your new office, we'll have a talk."

Alexander abruptly turned and strode stiffly through the door into the inner offices. Mrs. Murphy stood aside and smiled sweetly as they passed.

Alexander's office was positioned in the only corner with a panoramic view of the mountains; the other offices were small and windowless. Bell observed that they were also doorless, offering almost no privacy. Alexander's domain was embellished with cowhide sofas and chairs. His aspen desk was expansive and completely barren of paperwork. Though Alexander's suit was a poor fit and bore wrinkles, he was fastidious about his working habits.

He seated himself in a high-backed chair behind his desk and motioned Bell to sit in an uncushioned wooden chair on the opposite side. The only thing missing for intimidation, Bell thought, was a platform under Alexander's work space so he could look down on his employees and visitors like a minor god on Mount Olympus.

"No, thank you," Bell said quietly. "After sitting on a train for two days, I'd prefer a softer seat." He lowered his long frame onto one of the sofas.

"As you wish," said Alexander, not pleased with Bell's superior demeanor.

"You were not here when I worked on a case three years ago."

"No, I came six months later when I was promoted from our Seattle office."

"Mr. Van Dorn spoke very highly of you," Bell lied. Van Dorn had not mentioned him.

Alexander folded his hands and leaned across the empty wasteland of his desk. "I trust he briefed you on the murderer and his operations."

"Not in conversation." Bell paused to hold up the valise. "But he gave me several reports that I examined while riding on the train. I can see why the felon responsible for the robberies and murders is so difficult to pin down. He plans his criminal ventures with extreme care and his techniques appear to be flawless."

"All reasons why he eludes capture."

"After absorbing the material, I do believe his fetish

for detail will be his undoing," said Bell thoughtfully.

Alexander looked at him suspiciously. "What, may I ask, brought you to that conclusion?"

"His jobs are too perfect, too well timed. One small miscalculation could prove his last."

"I hope we can have a close relationship," Alexander said with veiled animosity.

"I agree," said Bell. "Mr. Van Dorn said I could have Art Curtis and Glenn Irvine on my team, if it is all right with you."

"Not a problem. I wouldn't go against Mr. Van Dorn's wishes. Besides, they told me they worked with you a few years ago."

"Yes, I found them to be dedicated agents." Bell came to his feet. "May I see my office?"

"Of course."

Alexander came from behind his desk and stepped into the hallway.

Bell saw that all the offices were quite small and quite plain. The furniture was sparse and there were no pictures on the walls. Only one other agent was present in the office, a stranger to Bell whom Alexander did not bother to introduce.

Before Alexander could point out a closet office, Bell asked innocently, "Do you have a conference room?"

Alexander nodded. "Yes, on the opposite side of the hallway from the offices." He stopped, opened a door, and stood aside as Bell walked in.

The conference room stretched nearly thirty feet and flowed fifteen feet to the side. A long pine table, stained dark and with a polished surface, sat beneath two massive, circular chandeliers. Eighteen leather captain's chairs were spaced evenly around it. The room was paneled in pine that matched the table, the floor carpeted with deep red pile. High windows rose on one wall, allowing the early-afternoon sunlight to illuminate every corner of the room.

"Very nice," said Bell, impressed. "Very nice."

"Yes," said Alexander with pride showing in his bloodhound eyes. "I use it frequently for meetings with politicians and influential people in the city. It gives the Van Dorn Detective Agency significant respect and an image of importance."

"It will do nicely," Bell said matter-of-factly. "I'll work in here."

Alexander looked directly at Bell, a fiery look in his eyes that suddenly glowed with anger. "That's not possible. I won't permit it."

"Where is the nearest telegraph office?"

Alexander seemed taken back. "Two blocks south on Sixteenth Street and Champa. Why?"

"I'll send a message to Mr. Van Dorn requesting the use of your conference room as an operations center. Considering the importance of the case, I'm sure he will give it his blessing."

Alexander knew when he was licked. "I wish you well, Mr. Bell," he conceded. "I will cooperate with you any way I can." He then turned and left Bell to return to his suite in the corner. He paused in the doorway. "Oh, by the way, I've reserved a room for you at the Albany Hotel."

Bell smiled. "That won't be necessary. I've booked a suite at the Brown Palace."

Alexander appeared confused. "I can't believe Mr. Van Dorn would allow that on your expense account."

"He didn't. I'm paying for it out of my own funds."

Not aware of Bell's prosperous situation, the superintendent of the western states looked completely bewildered. Unable to comprehend, but not wanting to ask questions, he returned to his office in a daze and closed the door, utterly defeated.

Bell smiled again and began spreading out the papers he'd carried in the valise on the conference table. Then he stepped into the anteroom and approached Agnes Murphy. "Agnes, could you let me know when Curtis and Irvine show up?"

"I don't expect them back until tomorrow morning. They went up to Boulder on a bank fraud case."

"All right, then. And would you call the building maintenance superintendent and have him come up? I have some alterations to make in the conference room."

She looked at him questioningly. "Did you say the conference room? Mr. Alexander seldom allows the help to step inside. He keeps it mostly to entertain the town bigwigs."

"While I'm here, it will be my office."

Agnes looked at Bell with newly found respect. "Will you be staying at the Albany Hotel? That's where most all visiting agents stay."

"No, the Brown Palace."

"Mr. Alexander consented to the extra expenditure?" she asked warily.

"He had no say in the matter."

Agnes Murphy stared after him as if she had just seen the Messiah.

Isaac Bell returned to his office and rearranged the chairs to the conference table so he could have a large work space at one end. After a few minutes, the building superintendent arrived. Bell explained the alterations he wished to make in the room. The end wall was to have a layer of soft material so a map of the western states and towns the killer had hit could be pinned to it. Another layer was to be installed on the inside wall for information, photos, and drawings. The superintendent, after Bell had offered him a twenty-dollar gold piece, promised to have the installation accomplished by noon the next day.

Bell spent the rest of the afternoon organizing and planning his hunt for the bank killer.

At precisely five o'clock, Alexander stuck his head in the door on his way home. "Are you settling in all right?" he asked icily.

Bell did not bother to look up. "Yes, thank you." He finally looked into Alexander's angry eyes. "By the way, I'm making some changes in the room. I hope you don't mind. I promise to put it back exactly the way it was when the case is closed."

"Please see that you do." Alexander swung his head in a gesture of dismissal and left the office.

Bell was not happy that things were not going well between Alexander and him. He had not planned to get in a game of quarrelsome loggerheads with the head of the agency's office, but if he hadn't gone on the attack he knew that Alexander would have walked all over him.

5

Built in 1892 by Henry C. Brown on the spot where he used to pasture his cow before he struck it rich, the hotel was fittingly named the Brown Palace, for the "Queen City of the Plains," as Denver was called. Constructed of red granite and sandstone, the building was in the shape of a ship's bow. The men who made their fortunes in gold and silver stayed there with their wives, who took afternoon tea, and their daughters, who danced away the nights at opulent balls. Presidents McKinley and Roosevelt had stayed there, as well as a few emperors and kings and other members of foreign royalty, not to mention the celebrities of the time, particularly famous stage actors and actresses. The Brown Palace was also embraced by locals and visitors alike because it was the anchor to the busy financial and cultural district of the city.

It was nearly dark when Bell walked through the 17th Street entrance of the Brown Palace Hotel. He checked in at the desk and looked around the magnificent lobby, which was situated in an atrium that reached up to the ninth floor. The pillars and wainscoting, freighted in by railroad from Mexico and carved from golden onyx, reflected the pastel light that filtered down from the massive stained-glass ceiling.

Over seven hundred wrought-iron panels graced the balcony railings, ringing the lobby from the upper floors.

What was not generally known was that the owner of the Navarre Hotel and restaurant across the street had had an underground rail system dug from the Brown Palace to his own establishment in order to accommodate gentlemen wishing to enjoy the ladies of an upstairs brothel without being seen entering or leaving.

Bell was given his key and entered the elevator, telling the operator which floor his suite was on. A woman stepped in behind him. She stopped at the mirrored wall, turned, and faced the door. She was dressed in a long blue silk gown with a large bow in the back. Her fire opal red hair was fine and silken, pulled back in a bun with curls streaming from it. There were two large feathers rising from the hair. She had an engaging charm about her. She stood tall and erect and nubile, Bell guessed probably between twenty-five and twenty-seven, perhaps younger, judging by her swan neck and face as smooth as alabaster. Her eyes were a golden brown. She was, in Bell's mind, unusually attractive – not quite beautiful, maybe, but very lovely by any standard. He also noticed she wore no wedding ring.

The woman was dressed as if she meant to attend a party in one of the hotel's ballrooms, Bell reasoned. He was right as usual. The elevator stopped on the second floor, which held the ballrooms and dance floors. He stood aside, hat in hand, and made a slight bow as she exited onto the landing.

She threw him a smile with surprising warmth and nodded, and said, in a mellow yet husky tone, "Thank you, Mr. Bell."

At first, it slipped by Bell. Then it hit him like a hammer on a thumb. He was stunned that she knew him, and positive he'd never seen her before. Bell gripped the arm of the elevator operator. "Hold the door open a moment."

By now, she had mingled in with a crowd that was funneling through the arched doorway of the hotel's grand ballroom. The women wore ravishing gowns in extravagant colors – crimson, peacock blue, emerald green – with ribbons, sprigs, and feathers in their hair. The men were dressed in their finest evening clothes. A banner over the doorway read BENEFIT FOR ST. JOHN'S ORPHANS.

Bell stepped back, nodding at the elevator operator. "Thank you. Please take me up."

Bell unlocked the door to his suite and found a study, living room, ornate bath, and bedroom with a canopied bed, all furnished in Victorian elegance. His trunks had been opened and his clothes packed in the dresser and hung in the closet by a maid, a service provided to those who reserved suites. The trunks were not in sight. They had been moved from the room and stored in the basement storage area. Bell lost no time in taking a quick bath and shaving.

He opened his watch and read the time. Thirty

minutes had elapsed since he stepped from the elevator. Another fifteen minutes were taken to tie his black tie and insert the shirt studs and cuff links, usually a job that took four hands. It was one of the few times he wished he had a wife to help. Black socks and shoes came next. He did not wear a cummerbund but a black vest instead, with a gold chain running from the left pocket through a buttonhole to the big gold watch in the right pocket. Last, he slipped on a single-breasted black jacket with satin lapels.

One final view of his reflection in a full seven-foot mirror and he was ready for the evening, whatever it would bring.

The charity ball was in full swing when he walked inside the grand ballroom and stood unobtrusively behind a tall potted palm. The ballroom was spacious and majestic. The parquet dance floor was laid in an intricate sunburst design and colorful murals adorned the ceiling. He spied the mysterious woman, seated with her back to him, with three couples at table six. She appeared to be alone, without an escort. He sidled up to the hotel director in charge of the evening's event.

"Pardon me," said Bell with a friendly smile, "but could you tell me the name of the lady in the blue dress at table six?"

The director straightened with a haughty look. "I'm sorry, sir, but we frown on giving information on our guests. Besides, I can't know everybody who comes to the ball."

Bell passed him a ten-dollar gold certificate. "Will this jog your memory?"

Without a word, the director held up a thin leather book and ran his eyes over the entries. "The single lady at the table is Miss Rose Manteca, a very wealthy lady from Los Angeles whose family owns a vast ranch. That's all I can tell you."

Bell patted the director on the shoulder. "I'm grateful."

The director grinned. "Good luck."

An orchestra was playing a medley of ragtime and modern dance tunes. Couples were dancing to a song called "Won't You Come Over to My House."

Bell walked up behind Rose Manteca and whispered in her ear. "Would you please consent to dance with me, Miss Manteca?"

She turned from the table and looked up. Golden brown eyes looked into a pair of mesmeric violet eyes. She was smooth, Bell thought, but his sudden appearance in evening dress completely stunned her. She lowered her eyes and recovered quickly, but not before her face blushed red.

"Forgive me, Mr. Bell. I did not expect you so soon."

"So soon?" he asked. What an odd thing to say, he thought.

She excused herself to the people at the table and stood up. Gently, he took her by the arm and led her to the dance floor. He slipped his arm around her narrow waist, took her hand, and stepped off smartly with the music.

"You're a very good dancer," she said after he swept her around the floor.

"Comes from all those years my mother forced me to take lessons so I could impress the debutantes in our city."

"You also dress very well for a detective."

"I grew up in a city where the affluent men lived in tuxedos."

"That would be Boston, would it not?"

For once, in his years of investigation, Bell was at a loss, but he recovered and came back. "And you're from Los Angeles."

She was good, he thought. She didn't bat an eye.

"You're very knowledgeable," she said, unable to fathom his eyes.

"Not half as knowledgeable as you. What is your interest? How do you know so much about me? Better yet, I should ask why?"

"I was under the impression you like to solve mysteries." She tried consciously to look past him over his tall shoulder, but she was drawn into those incredible eyes. This was a sensation, a stirring she had not counted on.

The photographs she had been shown did not do him justice face-to-face. He was far more attractive than she had imagined. He also came off as highly intelligent. This she'd expected, though, and could understand why he was so famous for his intuition.

It was as though he was stalking her as she was stalking him.

The music ended and they stood together on the dance floor waiting for the orchestra to begin the next musical arrangement. He stepped back and ran his eyes from her shoes to the top of her beautifully styled hair. "You are a very lovely lady. What prompted your interest in me?"

"You're an attractive man. I wanted to know you better."

"You knew my name and where I came from before you met me in the elevator. Our meeting was obviously premeditated."

Before she could reply, the orchestra began playing "In the Shade of the Old Apple Tree," and Bell led her around the floor in a foxtrot. He held her against him and gripped her hand tightly in his. Her waist was small, made even smaller by a corset. The top of her head came up even with his chin. He was tempted to press his lips against hers but thought better of it. This was neither the time nor the place. Nor were his thoughts on romance. She was spying on him. That was a given. His mind was trying to formulate a motive. What interest could a total stranger have in him? The only possibilities he could conjure up were that she'd been hired by one of the many criminals he had put behind bars, shot, or seen hanged. A relative or friend out for revenge? She didn't fit the image of someone who associated with the scum he had apprehended over the last ten years.

The music ended, and she released his hand and

stood back. "You'll have to excuse me, Mr. Bell, but I must return to my friends."

"Can we meet again?" he asked with a warm smile.

She slightly shook her head. "I don't think so."

He ignored her negative reply. "Have dinner with me tomorrow night."

"Sorry, I'm busy," she answered, with a haughtiness in her voice. "And even in your fancy tuxedo you couldn't bluff your way into the Western Bankers' Ball at the Denver Country Club like you did tonight at the benefit for St. John's Orphans." Then she threw out her chin, swept up her long skirt, and walked back to her table.

Once seated, she stole a glance back at Bell, but he was nowhere to be seen among the crowd. He had completely disappeared.

6

The following morning, Bell was the first one in the office, using a skeleton key that could open ninety doors out of a hundred. He was sorting through bank robbery reports at the end of the long table when Arthur Curtis and Glenn Irvine entered the conference room. Bell rose to greet them and shook hands. "Art, Glenn, good to see you both again."

Curtis stood short and rotund, with a rounded stomach neatly encased in a vest whose buttons were stretched to their limit. He had thinning sandy hair, wide megaphone ears, blue eyes, and a smile that showed a maze of teeth that lit up the room. "We haven't seen you since we tracked down Big Foot Cussler after he robbed that bank in Golden."

Irvine placed his hat on a coat stand, revealing a thick head of uncombed brown hair. "As I remember," he said, standing as tall and as scrawny as a scarecrow, "you led us directly to the cave where he was hiding out."

"A simple matter of deduction," Bell said with a tight smile. "I asked a pair of young boys if they knew of a place where they liked to hide out from their folks for a few days. The cave was the only location within twenty miles, close enough to town so Cussler could sneak in for supplies."

Curtis stood in front of the large map of the western United States and thoughtfully studied the little flags signifying the killer's spree. There were sixteen of them. "Got any intuition on the Butcher Bandit?"

Bell looked at him. "Butcher Bandit? Is that what they're calling him?"

"A reporter from the Bishee *Bugle* came up with it. Other newspapers have picked it up and spread the term across the territory."

"It won't help our cause," said Bell. "With that name on everyone's lips, the law-abiding citizens will come down hard on the Van Dorn Detective Agency for not apprehending him."

"That's already started," Curtis said, laying the *Rocky Mountain News* on the table in front of Bell. He stared down at it.

The lead column was on the robbery and murders in Rhyolite. Half the column was devoted to the question "Why haven't law enforcement agencies made any progress in the case and captured the Butcher Bandit?"

"The heat is on," Bell said simply.

"The heat is on *us*," Irvine added.

"So what have we got?" asked Bell, pointing to a stack of files two feet high on the bank crimes piled on the desk in front of him. "I've studied the reports while coming west on the train. It appears that all we have is that we're not dealing with the typical cowboy turned bank robber."

"He works alone," said Curtis, "and he's devilish clever and evil. But what is most frustrating is that he never leaves a trail for a posse to follow."

Irvine nodded his head in agreement. "It's as though he disappears into the hell he came from before he leaves town."

"No tracks are ever found leading into the surrounding countryside?" asked Bell.

Curtis shook his head. "The best trackers in the business have come up dry every time."

"Any evidence he might have holed up in town until the excitement died down?"

"None that's ever turned up," replied Curtis. "After the robberies, he was never seen again."

"A ghost," murmured Irvine. "We're dealing with a ghost."

Bell smiled. "No, he's human, but a damned smart human." He paused and fanned out the files on the conference table. He selected one and opened it, the report on the robbery in Rhyolite, Nevada. "Our man has a very rigid modus operandi that he sticks with on every bank job. We believe he hangs around for a few days studying the town and its people before robbing the bank."

"He's either a gambler or a risk taker," said Curtis.

"Wrong on both counts," Bell corrected him. "Our man is bold and he's shrewd. We can assume he does his dirty work using disguises, since the people of all the towns he's struck never agree on the appearance of suspicious-looking strangers."

Irvine began pacing the conference room, occasionally examining a flag pinned on the map. "Citizens of the towns recall seeing a drunken bum, a uniformed soldier, a well-to-do merchant, and a small-time freight hauler. But none could tie them to the murders."

Curtis looked at the carpeted floor and shrugged. "How odd there are no witnesses who can give a credible identification."

"Nothing odd about it," said Irvine. "He murders them all. The dead can't speak."

Bell seemed to ignore the conversation as if he was lost in thought. Then his eyes focused on the map and he said slowly, "The big question in my mind is why he always kills everyone in the bank during the theft. Even women and children. What does he gain by the slaughter? It can't be that he simply doesn't want to leave witnesses to the robberies, not when he's already been seen around town in disguise . . . unless . . ." He paused. "There is a new definition created by psychologists for murderers who kill as easily as they brush their teeth. They call them sociopaths. Our man can kill without remorse. He has no emotions, does not know how to laugh or love, and has a heart that is as cold as an iceberg. To him, shooting down a small child holds the same sensitivity as shooting a pigeon."

"Hard to believe there are people that cruel and ruthless," muttered Irvine in revulsion.

"Many of the bandits and gunfighters of the past were sociopaths," said Bell. "They shot other men as easily as if they sneezed. John Wesley Hardin, the famous Texas badman, once shot and killed a man for snoring."

Curtis looked steadily at Bell. "Do you really think he murders everyone in a bank because he enjoys it?"

"I do," Bell said quietly. "The bandit gets a weird satisfaction from committing his blood crimes. Another peculiar factor. He makes his escape before the people of the town, including the town sheriff, realized what happened."

"So where does that leave us?" asked Irvine. "What avenues do we search?"

Bell looked at him. "Another of his routine habits is to ignore any gold and take only currency. Glenn, your job is to check out the banks that were robbed and study their records of the serial numbers on the stolen bills. Start in Bozeman, Montana."

"Banks in mining towns aren't in the habit of recording the identifying number of every bill that passes through their hands."

"You might get lucky and find a bank that recorded the numbers of the currency sent from large city banks to make the miners' payroll. If you do, we can trace them. The robber had to either spend the money or exchange the currency through bank deposits and withdrawals. A trail he can't cover up."

"He could have exchanged through foreign financial institutions."

"Maybe, but he would have to spend it overseas. The risk would be too great for him to bring it back into the U.S. I'm betting he kept his loot in the country."

Then Bell turned to Curtis. "Art, you check out all stagecoach and train schedules for any that departed the towns on the same day the robberies took place. If our man couldn't be tracked by a posse, he might easily have taken a train or stage for his getaway. You can begin in Placerville, California."

"Consider it done," said Curtis firmly.

"Are you going to remain here and act as a command post?" asked Irvine.

Bell shook his head and grinned. "No, I'm going out in the field, beginning with Rhyolite, and retrace the robberies. No matter how good the murderer is or how well he planned his crimes, there has to be a stone he left unturned. There must be evidence that's been overlooked. I'm going to question the mining town citizens who might have seen something, however insignificant, and failed to report it to the local sheriff or marshal."

"You'll give us your schedule so we can get in touch by telegraph if we come onto something?" said Curtis.

"I'll have it for you tomorrow," replied Bell. "I'm also going to travel through the mining towns that have large payrolls our man has yet to rob. Maybe, just maybe I can second-guess our butcher, set up a trap, and entice him to strike another bank on our turf." Then he pulled open a drawer and passed out two envelopes. "Here's enough cash to cover your travel expenses."

Both Curtis and Irvine looked surprised. "Before now, we always had to travel third class, use our own money, and turn in bills and receipts," said Curtis. "Alexander always demanded we stay in sleazy hotels and eat cheap meals."

"This case is too important to cut corners. Trust me, Mr. Van Dorn will okay any monies. I request, but only if we show results. The bandit may have everyone believing he's invincible and can't be caught, but he's not faultless. He has flaws just like the rest of us. He will be trapped by a small insignificant mistake he neglected. And that, gentlemen, is our job, to find that insignificant mistake."

"We'll do our best," Irvine assured him.

Curtis nodded in agreement. "Speaking for both of us, permit me to say that it is a real privilege to be working with you again."

"The privilege is mine," said Bell sincerely. He felt lucky to work with such intelligent and experienced operatives who knew the people and country of the West.

The sun was falling over the Rockies to the west when Bell left the conference room. Always cautious, he closed and locked the door. As he passed through the outer office, he ran into Nicholas Alexander, who looked like he'd just stepped out of an expensive tailor's shop. The usual shabby suit was gone and replaced by an elegant tuxedo. It was a new image of respectability that he didn't quite pull off. The inner polish simply was not there.

"You look quite the bon vivant, Mr. Alexander," Bell said graciously.

"Yes, I'm taking the wife to a fancy soiree at the Denver Country Club later this evening. I have many influential friends here in Denver, you know."

"So I've heard."

"A pity you can't come, but it's only for members of the club in good standing."

"I understand perfectly," Bell said, masking his sarcasm.

As soon as they parted, Bell went down the street to the telegraph office and sent a telegram to Van Dorn.

> Have set up a schedule of investigations by myself, Curtis, and Irvine. Please be informed that we have a spy in our midst. A woman, a stranger who approached me at the hotel, identified me by name, knew my past, and seemed to know why I was in Denver. Her name is Rose Manteca and she supposedly comes from a wealthy family of ranchers in Los Angeles. Please ask our Los Angeles office to investigate. Will keep you advised of our progress on this end.
>
> Bell

After he sent the telegram to his superior, Bell walked down the busy sidewalk to the Brown Palace Hotel. After a few words with the concierge, who provided him with a map of the city, he was escorted down to the storeroom and the boiler room beneath the lobby, where he was greeted by the hotel maintenance man. An affable fellow in stained coveralls, he led Bell to a wooden crate that had been dismantled. Under a single, bright lightbulb that hung from the ceiling, the maintenance man pointed at a motorcycle that sat on a stand beside the crate and gleamed a dazzling red.

"There she is, Mr. Bell," he said with satisfaction. "All ready to go, I personally polished her up for you."

"I'm grateful, Mr. . . ."

"Bomberger. John Bomberger."

"I'll take care of your services when I leave the hotel," Bell promised him.

"Glad to be of help."

Bell went up to his room and found hanging in the closet the tuxedo that had been cleaned by the hotel during the day. After a quick bath, he dressed and removed a long linen coat from the closet and slipped it on, the bottom hem dropping to the tops of his highly shined shoes. Next, he slipped on a pair of leggings to save his tux trousers from the oily liquid that often came out of the engine. Finally, he donned a cap with goggles.

Bell took a back stairway down to the storeroom. The red cycle, with its white rubber tires, stood as if it was a steed waiting to carry him into battle. He kicked the stand up to the rear fender, took hold of it by the handlebars, and pushed all one hundred twenty pounds of it up a ramp used by wagons to remove the hotel bedding for cleaning and to allow merchants to bring in food for the restaurant and room service kitchens.

Bell exited the ramp and found himself on Broadway, the street that ran past the state capitol building with its golden dome. He mounted the hard, narrow saddle that perched over the camelback fuel tank above the rear wheel. Because it was built for racing, the seat was level with the handlebars and he had to lean almost horizontal to ride the machine.

He pulled the goggles over his eyes, then reached down and twisted open the valve that allowed fuel to fall by gravity from the tank to the carburetor. Then he placed his feet in the bicycle-style pedals and pumped down the street, allowing the electrical current from the three dry-cell batteries to flow to the coil, producing a high-voltage spark that ignited the fuel in the cylinders. He'd only gone about ten feet when the V-Twin engine popped into life, the exhaust rattling in a high-pitched snarl.

Bell curled his right hand around the grip throttle and twisted it less than half its rotation, and the racing bike lurched forward by its single-speed chain drive and he soon found himself cruising down Broadway around the horse-drawn carriages and occasional automobiles at thirty miles an hour.

Because it was built for racing, the bike had no headlight, but a half-moon lit the sky, and the street was lined with electric lights, providing enough illumination for him to see a pile of horse dung in time to dodge around it.

After about two miles, he stopped under a streetlamp and consulted his map. Satisfied he was traveling in the right direction, he continued until he reached Speer Avenue, before turning west. Another two miles and the Denver Country Club came into view.

The big, high-peaked building was ablaze with lights that streamed from the numerous huge square windows that encircled the building. The drive in front of the main entrance was packed with parked carriages and automobiles whose drivers and chauffeurs stood in groups, conversing and smoking. Two men in white tie and tails could be seen checking the invitations of the people who entered.

Bell was certain he would cause too much attention by riding up to the entrance on his motorcycle. And, without an invitation, there was little chance of bluffing his way inside even though he was dressed for the occasion. Under the partial light from the half-moon, he turned the handlebars and rode through the night onto the golf course. Careful to stay off the greens and out of the sand traps, he made a wide circular detour and approached the caddy shack that sat behind the main building near the first tee. The interior was dark and the shack was deserted.

He shut off the ignition and coasted into a clump

of bushes beside it. He raised the motorcycle onto its kickstand and removed the long linen coat, draping it over the handlebars. Then he took off the leggings, cap, and goggles. Smoothing back his blond hair, Bell stepped into the light and began strolling up the path leading from the caddy shack to the stately clubhouse. The whole area was illuminated by lustrous electric lights through the windows and tall lamps beside a narrow road that ran from the street to the rear of the country club. Several trucks stood below a wide stairway rising to the rear entrance. Caterers in blue, military-tailored uniforms carried trays of dishes and utensils from the trucks into the kitchen.

Up the stairs, Bell went between two of the caterers, moving into the kitchen as though he owned it. None of the waiters rushing in and out of the dining-room doors carrying trays of food, or the chefs, paid him the slightest attention. For all they knew, the tall man in the tuxedo was one of the reigning managers of the country club. If he had a problem gaining entry into the dining room, it was thankfully eliminated. He simply pushed open one of the kitchen's swinging doors, and stepped into the crowd of refined members of the club, walking between the tables, his eyes searching for Rose Manteca.

After only two minutes scanning the tables, he spotted her on the dance floor.

Bell stiffened.

Rose was dancing with Nicholas Alexander.

He thought fleetingly of enjoying the expressions

on their faces when he walked up and asked to cut in. But discretion was a wiser choice than ego. He had seen more than he had bargained for. Now he knew the spy's identity. But Bell was certain that Alexander was not a paid agent for the Butcher Bandit and his female snoop. He was merely a fool and a dupe for a pretty face. He was pleased that they had not noticed him.

Bell placed a napkin over his arm and took hold of a coffeepot as though he was waiting on a table. He could hold up the pot in front of his face, should either Rose or Alexander look in his direction. The music stopped, and he watched as they walked back to a table. They were seated together, with Alexander between Rose and an older, heavily jowled woman Bell took to be the agent's wife. If it proved nothing else, it proved that they hadn't met casually for a dance. Seated together meant that their table was reserved in advance. They were no strangers.

Bell stared openly at Rose. She wore a red silk dress that nearly matched her flaming hair. This night it was a combination of a bun in the back and curls along the sides and front. Her breasts were pressed against silk fringe that edged the bodice of her dress and swelled into twin, white mounds. She was a beautiful woman from toes to hair.

Her lips were parted in a delightful laugh and her golden brown eyes twinkled in mirth. Her hand fell on Alexander's arm, indicating to Bell that she liked to be physical. A sense of excitement surrounded her that was contagious to those at the table. She was a charmer, gorgeous and ravishing, but her aura did not penetrate Bell. He felt no fire, no passion of arousal toward her. In his analytical mind, she was the enemy, not an object of desire. He saw through the transparent veneer of her loveliness to the cunning and guile beneath.

He decided he had seen enough. Quickly, he ducked behind a waiter who was heading back to the kitchen and walked beside him until they passed through the swinging doors.

As Bell put on the gear he'd left hanging on the motorcycle, he considered himself lucky. He had stumbled on a situation he had not fully expected but one he could profit from. As he rode back to the Brown Palace, he knew the only information that he'd feed to Alexander would be false and misleading. He might even conjure up a bit of trickery to beguile Rose Manteca.

That part of his plan intrigued him. Already, he felt as if he had a head start in tracking a cagey lioness.

7

Shortly after Bell returned to the office the next morning, a runner from the telegraph office brought him a telegram from Van Dorn.

> My chief agent in Los Angeles reports that he can find no trace of a Rose Manteca. There is no family by that name owning a ranch within two hundred miles of the city. It looks to me as if the lady has pulled the wool over your eyes. Was she pretty?
>
> Van Dorn

Bell smiled to himself. He stuffed the telegram in his pocket, walked to Alexander's office, and knocked on the door.

"Come in," Alexander said softly, as if talking to somebody in the same room.

Barely hearing the words, Bell stepped inside.

"You're here to report, I assume," said Denver's head agent without prelude.

Bell nodded. "I wanted to bring you up to date on our activities."

"I'm listening," Alexander said without looking up from the papers on his desk or offering Bell a chair.

"I've sent Curtis and Irvine out into the field to question the law enforcement officers and any witness to the robberies and killings," Bell lied.

"It's not likely they will dig up anything the local law officials haven't already provided us."

"I intend to leave myself on the next train to Los Angeles."

Alexander looked up, a suspicious expression in his eyes. "Los Angeles? Why would you go there?"

"I'm not," Bell answered. "I'm getting off in Las Vegas and taking the spur line to Rhyolite, where I plan to talk to witnesses, if any, on my own."

"A wise plan." Alexander almost looked relieved. "I thought for a moment that you were going to Los Angeles because of Miss Manteca."

Bell feigned surprise. "You know her?"

"She sat at my table with my wife and me at the country club party and dance. We've met on other occasions. She said you two had met at the Orphans Ball, and she seemed very interested in your work and background. She was especially fascinated by the bank robber/murderer."

I'll bet she was interested in my work, Bell thought. But he said, "I didn't know I made an impression on her. She did a pretty good job of brushing me off."

"My wife thought Miss Manteca was smitten with you."

"Hardly. All I learned about her was that she came from a wealthy family in Los Angeles."

"That's true," Alexander replied out of ignorance. "Her father owns a huge spread outside the city."

It was obvious to Bell that Alexander had neither investigated Rose nor bothered to be suspicious of her questions about him and the Butcher Bandit case.

"When do you expect to return?" asked Alexander.

"I should wind up the Rhyolite investigation and be back within five days."

"And Curtis and Irvine?"

"Ten days to two weeks."

Alexander refocused his attention on the papers atop his desk. "Good luck," he said briefly, dismissing Bell.

Returning to the conference room, Bell relaxed in a swivel chair and propped his feet on the long table. He sipped coffee from a cup Mrs. Murphy had brought earlier. Then he leaned back and stared at the ceiling, as if seeing something on the floor above.

So his suspicions about Rose Manteca were right on the money. She was not only a fraud but perhaps somehow connected to the Butcher Bandit, and sent to learn what she could of the Van Dorn Detective Agency's investigation. Bell's quarry could never be overestimated. He was no ordinary bandit. Hiring the services of a lovely spy was the work of a man who carefully thought out his operation. Rose, or whatever her true identity was, was good. She had no problem burrowing into the confidence of the Denver office director. The groundwork had been carefully laid. It was clearly the work of a professional. Employing a counterfeit meant the bandit had first-rate resources and a network of tentacles that could delve into government and the business community.

When Bell returned to the Brown Palace, he went to the desk and asked for Rose Manteca's room number. The clerk looked very official when he said, "I'm sorry, sir. We can't give out our guests' room numbers." Then a smug look came across his face. "But I can tell you that Miss Manteca checked out at noon."

"Did she say where she was going?"

"No, but her luggage was taken to the Union Station and placed on the one o'clock train for Phoenix and Los Angeles."

This was not what Bell had expected. He cursed himself for letting her slip through his fingers.

Who really was Rose Manteca? Why would she take the train for Los Angeles when there was no record of her living there?

Then another thought began to tug on Bell's mind. Where would his nemesis strike next? He couldn't even begin to guess and he found it frustrating. He had always felt as if he was in control of his earlier cases. This one was different, too different.

8

The blond-haired man with a thick, yellow-brown, pomaded handlebar mustache had a prosperous appearance about him. After walking through the train depot, he settled into the backseat of the Model N Ford taxicab and enjoyed a beautiful, cloudless day as he viewed the sights of Salt Lake City nestled beneath the Wasatch Mountains. He was dressed in the neat, dandified fashion of the day, but with a sophisticated business look. He wore a silk top hat, a black, three-button cutaway frock coat with vest and high rounded collar, and an elegant tie. His hands were encased in pearl gray kid gloves, and matching spats covered his midstep to just above the ankle over his shoes.

He leaned slightly forward as he stared from window to window, his hands gripping the handle of a sterling silver cane adorned with an eagle's head with a large beak on the end. Though it was innocent-looking, this cane was a gun with a long barrel and a trigger that folded out when a button was pressed. It held a .44 caliber bullet whose shell could be ejected and a new cartridge inserted in the barrel from a small clip in the eagle's tail.

The cab passed the church of the Latter-Day Saints

– the Temple, Tabernacle, and Assembly Hall. Built between 1853 and 1893, the six-foot-thick gray granite walls were topped by six spires, the highest bearing a copper statue of the angel Moroni.

After leaving Temple Square, the cab turned down 300 South Street and came to a stop in front of the Peery Hotel. Designed with European architecture only a short time earlier during the mining boom, it was Salt Lake City's premier hostelry. As the doorman retrieved the luggage from the rear of the cab, the man ordered the driver to wait. Then he entered through the cut-glass double doors into the stately lobby.

The desk clerk smiled and nodded. Then he glanced at a large clock standing in the lobby and said, "Mr. Eliah Ruskin, I presume."

"You presume right," answered the man.

"Two-fifteen. You're right on time, sir."

"For once, my train was punctual."

"If you will please sign the register."

"I have to leave for an appointment. Will you see my luggage is taken to my room and my clothing placed in the closet and drawers?"

"Yes, Mr. Ruskin. I will personally see to it." The clerk leaned over the registry desk and nodded at a large leather suitcase set securely between Ruskin's legs. "Would you like me to send your bag up to your room?"

"No, thank you. I'll be taking it with me."

Ruskin turned and walked out to the curb, cane

in one hand, the other clutching the handle of the suitcase, the weight of its contents tilting his right shoulder downward. He pushed it through the cab's door and reentered the backseat.

The desk clerk thought it odd that Ruskin hadn't left the bag in the cab. He wondered why Ruskin would lug such a heavy case into the lobby and then carry it outside again. He speculated that something of value must be inside. His thought soon faded when another guest showed up to register.

Eight minutes later, Ruskin stepped from the cab, paid the driver, and entered the Salt Lake Bank & Trust lobby. He walked to the security guard who was seated in a chair near the door.

"I have an appointment with Mr. Cardoza."

The guard rose to his feet and motioned toward a frosted-glass door. "You'll find Mr. Cardoza in there."

There had been no reason for Ruskin to ask the guard where to go. He could just as easily have seen the bank manager's office door. The guard did not notice that Ruskin had observed him closely, how he moved, his age, and how he placed the holster, containing a new .45 caliber Model 1905 Colt Browning automatic pistol, at his hip. The brief study also revealed the guard was not particularly alert and watchful. Day after day of seeing customers come and go without the slightest disturbance had made him listless and indifferent. He didn't appear to find anything unusual about Ruskin's big case.

The bank had two tellers behind the counter in their cages. The only other employees except for the guard were Cardoza and his secretary. Ruskin studied the big steel door to the vault that was open to the lobby to impress the customers and suggest that their savings were in solid, protective hands.

He approached the secretary. "Hello, my name is Eliah Ruskin. I have a two-thirty appointment with Mr. Cardoza."

An older woman in her fifties with graying hair smiled and stood up without speaking. She walked to a door with ALBERT CARDOZA, MANAGER painted on the upper part of the frosted-glass pane, knocked, and leaned in. "A Mr. Eliah Ruskin to see you."

Cardoza quickly came to his feet and rushed around his desk. He shoved out a hand and shook Ruskin's palm and fingers vigorously. "A pleasure, sir. I've looked forward to your arrival. It's not every day we greet a representative from a New York bank that is making such a substantial deposit."

Ruskin lifted the suitcase onto Cardoza's desk, unlocked the catches, and opened the lid. "Here you are, half a million dollars in cash to be deposited, until such time we decide to withdraw it."

Cardoza reverently stared at the neatly packed and bundled fifty-dollar gold certificate bills as though they were his passport to a banker's promised land. Then he looked up in growing surprise. "I don't understand. Why not carry a cashier's check instead of five hundred thousand dollars in currency?"

"The directors of the Hudson River Bank of New York prefer to deal in cash. As you know from our correspondence, we are going to open branch banks throughout the West in towns that we think have potential for growth. We feel it is expedient to have currency on hand when we open our doors."

Cardoza looked at Ruskin somberly. "I hope your directors do not intend to open a competing bank in Salt Lake City."

Ruskin grinned and shook his head. "Phoenix, Arizona, and Reno, Nevada, are the first of the Hudson River branch banks to open in the West."

Cardoza looked relieved. "Phoenix and Reno are certainly booming."

"Ever have a bank robbery in Salt Lake?" Ruskin asked casually while looking at the vault.

Cardoza looked at him quizzically. "Not in this city. The citizens would not allow it. Salt Lake is one of the most crime-free cities in the country. The Latter-Day Saints are upstanding and religious people. Trust me, Mr. Ruskin, no bandit would dare to attempt a robbery of this bank. Your money will be absolutely and one hundred percent safe once it's locked up in our vault."

"I've read of some fellow called the Butcher Bandit who robs and murders throughout the western states."

"Not to worry, he only strikes in small mining towns and robs payrolls. He wouldn't be stupid enough to try robbing a bank in a city the size of

Salt Lake. He wouldn't get past the city limits before the police shot him down."

Ruskin nodded toward the vault. "Very impressive repository."

"The very finest vault west of the Mississippi, built especially for us in Philadelphia," Ruskin said proudly. "An entire regiment armed with cannons couldn't break inside."

"I see it is open during business hours?"

"And why not. Our customers enjoy seeing how well their deposits are protected. And as I've mentioned, no bank has ever been robbed in Salt Lake City."

"What is your slowest time of day?"

Cardoza looked puzzled. "Slowest time of day?"

"When you have the least customer transactions?"

"Between one-thirty and two o'clock is our slowest time. Most of our customers have gone back to their offices after their lunch hour.

And, because we close at three, a number of customers come in for late transactions. Why do you ask?"

"Just curious as to how the traffic compares with our bank in New York, which seems to be about the same." He patted the suitcase. "I'll leave the money in the case and pick it up tomorrow."

"We'll close shortly, but I'll have my head clerk count it first thing in the morning."

Cardoza pulled open a drawer of his desk, retrieved

a leather book, and wrote out a deposit slip for the half-million dollars. He handed it to Ruskin, who inserted it into a large wallet he carried in the breast pocket of his coat.

"May I ask a favor?" Ruskin inquired.

"Certainly. Anything you wish."

"I would like to be on hand when your clerk does the count."

"That's very gracious of you, but I'm sure your bank has accounted for every dollar."

"I'm grateful for your trust, but I would like to be present just to be on the safe side."

Cardoza shrugged. "As you wish."

"There is one other request."

"You have but to name it."

"I have other business to conduct in the morning and cannot return until one-thirty tomorrow. And, since your business is slowest then, it should be a good time for the count."

Cardoza nodded in agreement. "You're quite right." He stood and extended his hand. "Until tomorrow afternoon. I look forward to seeing you."

Ruskin held up his cane as a good-bye gesture, dismissed Cardoza, and left the office. He walked past the security guard, who didn't give him a glance, and swung his cane like a baton as he stepped onto the sidewalk.

He smiled to himself, knowing that he had no intention of returning to the bank merely to count the contents of the suitcase.

9

The next afternoon, Ruskin walked to the bank, making sure he was seen on the street by the passing crowd and stopping in shops to browse, making small talk with the merchants. He carried his gun cane more as a prop than for protection.

Reaching the Salt Lake Bank & Trust at one-thirty, he entered and ignored the guard as he turned the key in the front entrance door, locking it. Then he turned the sign around in the window so that it read CLOSED from the street and pulled down the window shades, as the guard sat there in his bored stupor, not realizing that the bank was about to be robbed. Neither Albert Cardoza's secretary and the tellers nor the female depositor standing at the counter took notice of the intruder's unusual behavior.

The guard finally came alert and realized that Ruskin was not acting like a normal bank customer and might be up to no good. He came to his feet, his hand dropping to the holster holding his .38 Smith & Wesson revolver, and asked blankly, "Just what do you think you're doing?" Then his eyes widened in alarm as he found himself staring into the muzzle of Ruskin's .38 Colt.

"Make no resistance, and walk slowly behind the counter!" Ruskin ordered as he wrapped his gun in a battered, old heavy woolen scarf with burn holes in it. He quickly moved behind the counter before the clerks in their cages became alert and could make a grab for the shotguns at their feet. Never expecting their bank to be robbed, they hesitated in confusion.

"Don't even think about going for your guns!" Ruskin snapped. "Lay flat on the floor or you'll get a bullet in your brain." He motioned his cane at the frightened woman at the counter. "Come around the counter and lay down on the floor with the tellers and you won't get hurt," he said in a cold tone. Then he motioned the gun at Cardoza's secretary. "You, too! Down on the floor!"

When all were lying on the highly polished mahogany floor face-down, he rapped on Cardoza's door. Unable to distinguish voices outside his office, the bank's manager was not aware of the macabre event unfolding within his bank. He waited out of habit for his secretary to enter, but she did not appear. Finally, irritated at being interrupted, he stepped from his desk and opened the door. It took him a full ten seconds to comprehend what was happening. He stared at Ruskin and the gun in his hand.

"What is the meaning of this?" he demanded. Then he saw the people lying on the floor and looked back at Ruskin in utter confusion. "I don't understand. What is going on?"

"The first bank robbery of Salt Lake City," said Ruskin, as if amused.

Cardoza did not move. He was frozen in shock. "You're a director of a respectable New York bank. Why are you doing this? It makes no sense. What do you hope to gain by it?"

"I have my motives," Ruskin answered, his voice cold and toneless. "I want you to make out a bank draft for four hundred seventy-five thousand dollars."

Cardoza stared at him as if he was crazy. "A bank draft to whom?"

"Eliah Ruskin, who else?" answered Ruskin. "And be quick about it."

Mired in confusion, Cardoza pulled open a drawer, retrieved a book containing bank drafts, and hurriedly scribbled out one for the amount Ruskin demanded. When finished, he passed it across the desk to Ruskin, who slipped it into his breast pocket.

"Now, down on the floor with the others."

As if in the throes of a nightmare, Cardoza slowly lowered himself onto the floor next to his trembling secretary.

"Now, then, none of you move, or even twitch, until I tell you to."

Without saying more, Ruskin walked inside the vault and began stuffing the bank's currency into leather money sacks he'd seen earlier stacked on a shelf inside the huge five-ton door. He filled two of them, estimating the take at roughly two hundred thirty thousand dollars in larger denominations, none under ten dollars. He had planned well. From inside banking information, he knew that the Salt Lake Bank & Trust had received a large shipment of currency issued from the Continental & Commercial National Bank of Chicago for their reserves. The suitcase with his own money he left on another shelf of the vault.

Laying aside the sacks, he closed the vault door. It swung shut as easily as a door on a cupboard. Then he turned the bog wheel that activated the inside latches and set the timer for nine o'clock the next morning.

Unhurriedly, as if he was strolling through a park, he stepped behind the counter and ruthlessly shot the people lying on the floor in the back of the head. The muffled shots came so quickly, none had time to know what was happening and cry out. Then he raised the bank's window shades, so people passing on the sidewalk could see that the vault was shut and would assume the bank was closed. The bodies were conveniently out of sight behind the counter.

Ruskin waited until the sidewalk was clear of foot traffic and vehicles before he nonchalantly exited the bank, locked the door, and strolled leisurely from the building, swinging his cane. By four o'clock, he had returned to the Peery Hotel, had a bath, and come down to the restaurant, where he enjoyed a large smoked-salmon plate with dill cream and caviar accompanied by a bottle of French Clos de la Roche

Burgundy 1899. Then he read in the lobby for an hour before going to bed and slept like a rock.

Late in the morning, Ruskin took a taxi to the Salt Lake Bank & Trust. A crowd of people were clustered around the front door as an ambulance pulled away from the bank. Police in uniforms were in abundance. He pushed his way through the crowd, saw a man who was dressed like a detective, and addressed him.

"What happened here?" he asked courteously.

"The bank has been robbed and five people murdered."

"Robbed, murdered, you say? This is disastrous. I deposited half a million dollars in cash here yesterday from my bank in New York."

The detective looked at him in surprise. "Half a million dollars, you say? In cash?"

"Yes, I have my receipt right here." Ruskin flashed the receipt in the detective's face. The detective studied it for a few moments and then said, "You are Eliah Ruskin?"

"Yes, I'm Ruskin. I represent the Hudson River Bank of New York."

"A half million dollars in cash!" the detective gasped. "No wonder the bank was robbed. You better come inside, Mr. Ruskin, and meet with Mr. Ramsdell, one of the bank's directors. I'm Captain John Casale, with the Salt Lake Police Department."

The bodies had been removed, but large areas of the mahogany floor were layered in dried blood. Captain

Casale led the way to a man – a huge, fat man with a large protruding stomach behind a vest and massive watch chain. The man was sitting at Cardoza's desk, examining the bank's deposits. His brown eyes appeared dazed beneath the bald head. He looked up and stared at Ruskin, annoyed at the intrusion.

"This is Mr. Eliah Ruskin," announced Casale. "He says he deposited half a million dollars with Mr. Cardoza yesterday."

"Sorry to meet you under such tragic circumstances. I am Ezra Ramsdell, the bank's managing director." Ramsdell rose and shook Ruskin's hand. "A terrible, terrible business," he muttered. "Five people dead. Nothing like this has ever happened in Salt Lake City before."

"Were you aware of the money Mr. Cardoza was holding for my bank?" asked Ruskin flatly.

Ramsdell nodded. "Yes, he called me on the telephone and reported that you had come in and placed your bank's currency in the vault."

"Since Mr. Cardoza, God rest his soul, wrote me out a receipt, my directors will assume your bank will make good on the loss."

"Tell your directors not to worry."

"How much cash did the robber take?" Ruskin asked.

"Two hundred forty-five thousand dollars."

"Plus my half million," he said, as if agitated.

Ramsdell looked at him queerly. "For some inexplicable reason, the robber didn't take your money."

Ruskin simulated a stunned expression. "What are you telling me?"

"The bills in a large, brown leather suitcase," said Captain Casale. "Are those yours?"

"The gold certificates? Yes, they are from the bank I represent in New York."

Ramsdell and Casale exchanged odd looks. Then Ramsdell said, "The case you and Mr. Cardoza placed in the vault still contains your currency."

"I don't understand."

"It hasn't been touched. I opened and checked it myself. Your gold certificates are safe and sound."

Ruskin made a show of acting perplexed. "It doesn't make sense. Why take your money and leave mine?"

Casale scratched one ear. "My guess is, he was in a hurry and simply ignored the suitcase, not realizing it was filled with a king's fortune in cash."

"That's a relief," said Ruskin, taking off his silk top hat and wiping imaginary sweat from his brow. "Assuming the robber won't return, I'll leave it in your vault until such time as we require it to open our new branch banks in Phoenix and Reno."

"We are most grateful. Especially now that our currency on hand has been wiped out."

Ruskin looked around at the spread of dried blood on the floor. "I should leave you to your investigation." He nodded at Casale. "I trust you will catch the killer so he can be hung."

"I swear we'll track him down," Casale said

confidently. "Every road out of Salt Lake and all the train depots are covered by a network of police officers. He can't travel beyond the city limits without being caught."

"Good luck to you," said Ruskin. "I pray you will apprehend the fiend." He turned to Ramsdell. "I will be at the Peery Hotel until tomorrow afternoon, should you require my services. At four o'clock, I will board a train, to oversee the establishment of our new bank in Phoenix."

"You are most generous, sir," said Ramsdell. "I will be in touch as soon as we resume operations."

"Not at all." Ruskin turned to leave. "Good luck to you, Captain," Ruskin said to Casale as he made for the front entrance of the bank.

Casale stared out the window as Ruskin walked across the street toward a taxi. "Most strange," he said slowly. "If I know my train schedules, the next train for Phoenix doesn't leave for another three days."

Ramsdell shrugged. "He was probably misinformed."

"Still, there is something about him that bothers me."

"What is that?"

"He didn't look overjoyed that his bank's money was not taken by the robber. It was almost as if he knew it was safe before he walked in the door."

"Does it matter?" asked Ramsdell. "Mr. Ruskin should be glad his half a million dollars was overlooked by the robber."

The detective looked thoughtful. "How do you know it's a half a million dollars? Did you count it?"

"Mr. Cardoza must have counted it."

"Are you certain?"

Ramsdell began walking from the office toward the vault. "Now is as good a time as any to make a quick tally."

He opened the case and started to lay the first layer of stacked bills on a nearby shelf. The top layer consisted of twenty thousand dollars in gold certificate bills. Underneath, the rest of the case was filled with neatly cut and banded newspaper.

"Good God!" Ramsdell gasped. Then, as if struck by a revelation, he rushed back to the bank manager's office and opened a book that lay on the surface of the desk. The book contained bank drafts – but the final draft was missing and unrecorded. His face went ashen. "The murdering scum must have forced Cardoza to write a bank draft for the half million. Whatever bank he deposits it in will assume we authorized it and demand payment from Salt Lake Bank and Trust. Under federal law, we are bound to honor it. If not, the lawsuits, the prosecution from United States Treasury agents – we'd be forced to close."

"Ruskin was not only a fraud," Casale said firmly, "he was the one who robbed your bank and murdered your employees and customer."

"I can't believe it," muttered Ramsdell incredulously. Then he demanded, "You've got to stop him. Catch him before he checks out of his hotel."

"I'll send a squad to the Peery," said Casale. "But this guy is no buffoon. He probably went on the run as soon as he walked out the door."

"You can't let him get away with this foul deed."

"If he's the notorious Butcher Bandit, he's a shrewd devil who vanishes like a ghost."

Ezra Ramsdell's eyes took on an astute glint. "He has to deposit the draft at a bank somewhere. I'll telegraph the managers of every bank in the nation to be on the lookout for him and contact the police before they honor a draft made out to Eliah Ruskin for half a million dollars. He won't get away with it."

"I'm not so sure," John Casale said softly under his breath. "I'm not so sure at all."

10

The Butcher Bandit was a country mile ahead of him, Bell thought as the train he was riding slowed and stopped at the station in Rhyolite. He had received a lengthy telegram from Van Dorn telling of the Salt Lake massacre, as it had become known. A bank in a major city like Salt Lake was the last place he or anyone else expected the Butcher to strike. That was his next stop after Rhyolite.

He stepped from the train with a leather bag that held the bare essentials he carried while traveling. The heat of the desert struck him like a blast furnace, but because of the absence of humidity in the desert it did not soak his shirt with sweat.

After getting directions from the stationmaster, he walked to the sheriff's office and jail. Sheriff Marvin Huey was a medium-sized man with a head of tousled gray hair. He looked up from a stack of wanted posters and stared at Bell with soft olive brown eyes as the Van Dorn agent entered the office.

"Sheriff Huey, I'm Isaac Bell from the Van Dorn Detective Agency."

Huey did not rise from his desk nor offer his hand; instead, he spit a wad of chewing tobacco juice into a cuspidor. "Yes, Mr. Bell, I was told you'd be on the ten o'clock train. How do you like our warm weather?"

Bell took a chair across from Huey without it being offered and sat down. "I prefer the high-altitude cool air of Denver."

The sheriff grinned slightly at seeing Bell's discomfort. "If you lived here long enough, you might get to like it."

"I wired you concerning my investigation," Bell said without preamble. "I want to obtain any information I can that would be helpful in tracking down the Butcher Bandit."

"I hope you have better luck than I did. After the murders, all we found was a dilapidated, abandoned freight wagon and team of horses that he had driven into town."

"Did anyone get a good look at him?"

Huey shook his head. "No one gave him the slightest notice. Three people gave different descriptions. None matched. All I know is, my posse found no tracks from wagon, horse, or automobile leading out of town."

"What about the railroad?"

Huey shook his head. "No train left town for eight hours. I posted men at the depot who searched the passenger cars before it left, but they found no one that looked suspicious."

"How about freight trains?"

"My deputies ran a search of the only freight train that left town that day. Neither they nor the train engineer, fireman, or brakemen saw anyone hiding on or around the boxcars."

"What is your theory on the bandit?" asked Bell. "How do you think he made a clean getaway?"

Huey paused to shoot another wad of tobacco saliva into the brass cuspidor. "I gave up. It pains me to say so, but I have no idea how he managed to elude me and my deputies. Frankly, I'm put out by it. In thirty years as a lawman, I've never lost my man."

"You can take consolation in knowing you're not the only sheriff or marshal who lost him after he robbed their town banks."

"It still isn't anything I can be proud of," muttered Huey.

"With your permission, I would like to question the three witnesses."

"You'll be wasting your time."

"May I have their names?" Bell persisted. "I have to do my job."

Huey shrugged and wrote out three names on the back of a wanted poster, and where they could be found, handing it to Bell. "I know all these people. They're good, honest citizens who believe what they saw even if it don't match up."

"Thank you, Sheriff, but it is my job to investigate every lead, no matter how insignificant."

"Let me know if I can be of further help," said Huey, warming up.

"If need be," said Bell, "I will."

* * *

Bell spent most of the next morning locating and questioning the people on the list given him by Sheriff Huey. Bell was considered an expert at drawing on witnesses' descriptions, but this time around he drew a blank. None of the people, two men and one woman, gave correlating accounts. Sheriff Huey was right. He accepted defeat and headed back to his hotel and prepared to leave for the next town on his schedule that had suffered a similar tragedy: Bozeman, Montana.

He was sitting in the hotel restaurant, eating an early dinner of lamb stew, when the sheriff walked in and sat down at his table.

"Can I order you anything?" Bell asked graciously.

"No thanks. I came looking for you because I thought of Jackie Ruggles."

"And who might that be?"

"He's a young boy of about ten. His father works in the mine and his mother takes in laundry. He said he saw a funny-looking man the day of the robbery, but I dismissed his description. He's not the brightest kid in town. I figured he wanted to impress the other boys by claiming he'd seen the bandit."

"I'd like to question him."

"Go up Third Street to Menlo. Then turn right. He lives in the second house on the left, a ramshackle affair that looks like it may fall down any minute, like most of the houses in that area of town."

"I'm obliged."

"You won't get any more out of Jackie than you did from the others, probably less."

"I have to look on the bright side," said Bell. "As I said, we have to check out every lead, no matter how trivial. The Van Dorn Detective Agency wants the killer as much as you."

"You might stop by the general store and pick up some gumdrops," Sheriff Huey said. "Jackie has a sweet tooth for gumdrops."

"Thanks for the tip."

Bell found the Ruggles house just as Huey described. The entire wooden structure was leaning to one side. Another two inches, Bell thought, and it would crash into the street. He started up the rickety stairs just as a young boy dashed out of the front door and ran toward the street.

"Are you Jackie Ruggles?" Bell asked, grabbing the boy by the arm before he dashed off.

The boy wasn't the least bit intimidated. "Who wants to know?" he demanded.

"My name is Bell. I'm with the Van Dorn Detective Agency. I'd like to ask you about what you saw the day of the bank robbery."

"Van Dorn," Jackie said in awe. "Gosh, you guys are famous. A detective from Van Dorn wants to talk to me?"

"That's right," said Bell, swooping in for the kill. "Would you like some gumdrops?" He held out a small sack that he had just purchased at the general store.

"Gee, thanks, mister." Jackie Ruggles wasted no time in snatching the sack and savoring a green gumdrop. He was dressed in a cotton shirt, pants that were cut off above the knee, and worn-leather shoes that Bell guessed were handed down by an older brother. The clothes were quite clean, as befitting a mother who was a laundress. He was thin as a broomstick, with boyish facial features that were covered with freckles, and topped by a thicket of uncombed curly light brown hair.

"I was told by Sheriff Huey that you saw the bank robber."

The boy answered while chewing on the gumdrop. "Sure did. The only trouble is, nobody believes me."

"I do," Bell assured him. "Tell me what you saw."

Jackie was about to reach in the sack for another gumdrop, but Bell stopped him. "You can have them after you've told me what you know."

The boy looked peeved but shrugged. "I was playing baseball in the street with my friends when this old guy—"

"How old?"

Jackie studied Bell. "About your age."

Bell never considered thirty as old, but to a young boy of ten he must have appeared ancient. "Go on."

"He was dressed like most of the miners who live here, but he wore a big hat like the Mexicans."

"A sombrero."

"I think that's what it's called."

"And he was toting a heavy sack over his shoulder. It looked like it was plumb full of something."

"What else did you notice?"

"One of his hands was missing the little finger."

Bell stiffened. This was the first clue to identifying the killer. "Are you sure he was missing a little finger?"

"As sure as I'm standing here," answered Jackie.

"Which hand?" Bell asked, containing his mounting excitement.

"The left."

"You've no doubt it was the left hand?"

Jackie merely nodded while staring longingly at the gumdrop sack. "He looked at me like he was really mad when he saw I was looking back."

"Then what happened?"

"I had to catch a fly ball. When I turned around, he was gone."

Bell patted Jackie on the head, almost losing his hand in a sea of unruly red hair. He smiled. "Go ahead and eat your gumdrops, but, if I were you, I'd chew slowly so they last longer."

After he checked out of the Rhyolite Hotel and before he boarded the train, Bell paid the telegraph operator at the depot to send a wire to Van Dorn describing the Butcher Bandit as missing the little finger on his left hand. He knew that Van Dorn would quickly send out the news to his army of agents to watch out for and report any man with that disfigurement.

Instead of traveling back to Denver, he decided on the spur of the moment to go to Bisbee. Maybe – just maybe – he might get lucky again and find another clue to the bandit's identity. He leaned back in his seat, as the torrid heat of the desert grilled the interior of the Pullman car. Bell hardly noticed it.

The first solid clue, provided by a scrawny young boy, wasn't exactly a breakthrough, but it was a start, thought Bell. He felt pleased with himself for the discovery and began to daydream of the day he confronted the bandit and identified him by the missing finger.

THE CHASE QUICKENS

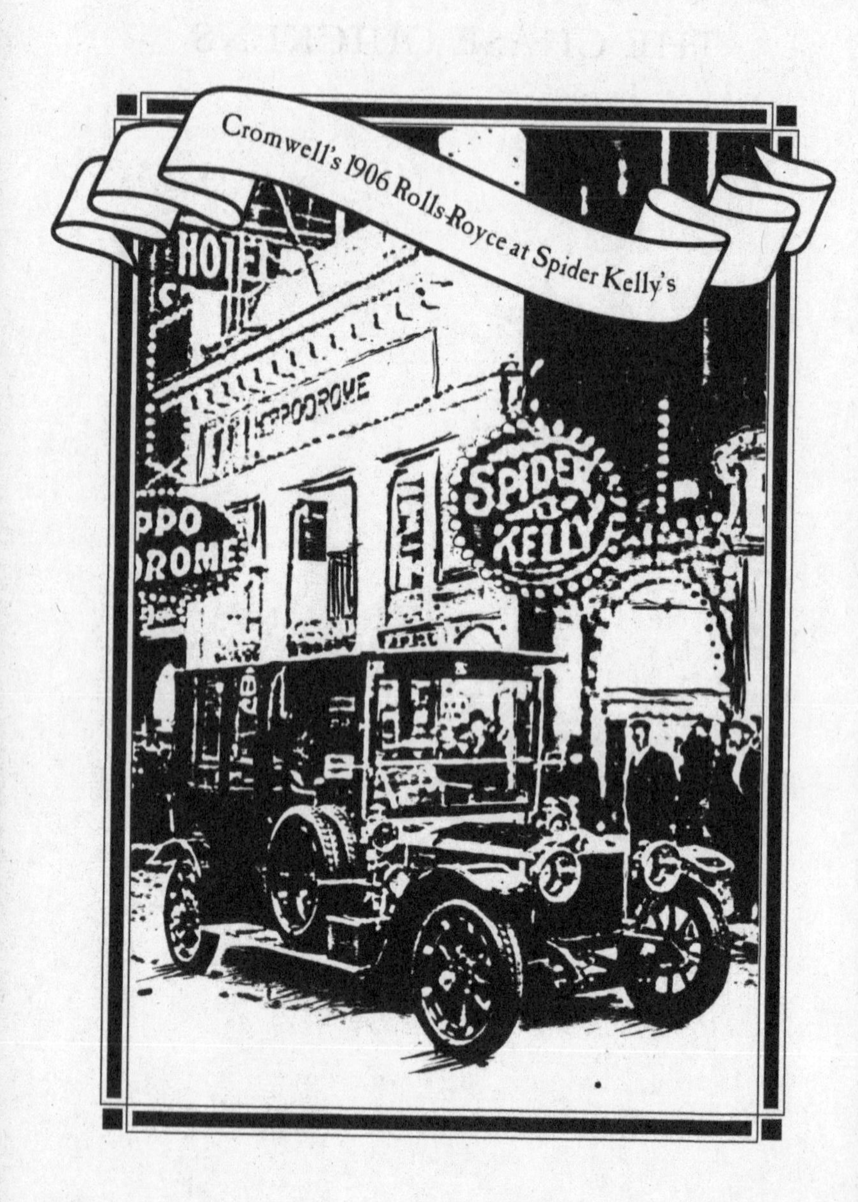
Cromwell's 1906 Rolls-Royce at Spider Kelly's
SPIDER
KELLY

11

March 4, 1906
San Francisco, California

The man whose last alias had been Ruskin stood in front of an ornate brass sink and stared into a large oval mirror as he shaved with a straight razor. When finished, he rinsed off his face and patted on an expensive French cologne. He then reached out and clutched the sink as his railroad boxcar came to an abrupt stop.

He stepped up to a latched window, disguised from the outside as if it were a section of the wooden wall of the car, cautiously cracked it, and peered outside. A steam switch engine had pushed ten freight cars uncoupled from the train, including the O'Brian Furniture car, through the Southern Pacific Railroad's huge terminal building, called the Oakland Mole. It consisted of a massive pier built on pilings, masonry, and rock laid in the San Francisco Bay itself, on the west side of the city of Oakland. The slip where the ferryboats entered and tied up was at the west end of the main building, between twin towers. The towers were manned by teams of men who directed the loading and unloading of the huge fleet of ferries that moved to and from San Francisco across the bay.

Because the Oakland Mole was at the end of the transcontinental railway, it was filled twenty-four hours a day with a mixed crowd of people, coming from the east and heading across the continent in the opposite direction. Passenger trains commingled with freight trains that carried goods and merchandise. It was a busy place in 1906, since business was booming in the sister cities of the bay. San Francisco was a thriving commercial center while much of the actual goods were manufactured in Oakland.

Ruskin checked a schedule and saw that his cleverly disguised mode of secret travel was on board the *San Gabriel*, a Southern Pacific Railroad ferry built to haul freight trains as well as passengers. She was a classic ferry, double-ended, her stern and bow surmounted with a pilothouse on each end. She was propelled with side paddle wheels powered by two walking-beam steam engines, each with its own smokestack. Ferries carrying trains had parallel tracks on the main deck for the freight cars, while the cabin deck housed the passengers. The *San Gabriel* was two hundred ninety-eight feet long, seventy-eight feet wide, and could carry five hundred passengers and twenty railroad cars.

The *San Gabriel* was to arrive at the Townsend and Third Streets Southern Pacific terminus, where the passengers would disembark. Then it would move on to Pier 32 at Townsend and King Streets, where its cargo of railroad cars would be taken to the city railyard between Third and Seventh Streets. There, the

O'Brian Furniture Company car would be switched to the siding of a warehouse the bandit owned in the city's industrial section.

Ruskin had ridden on the *San Gabriel* many times on his trips across the bay and looked forward to returning home after his venture in Salt Lake City. A great whoop echoed around the Mole from the boat's steam whistle as it announced her departure. She began to tremble when the tall walking-beam engines turned the big twenty-seven-foot paddle wheels that churned the water. Soon the boat was riding the glass-smooth bay toward San Francisco, no more than twenty minutes away.

Ruskin quickly finished dressing in an exactingly tailored conservative black business suit. A small yellow rose went in the buttonhole. He sat a derby hat on his head at a rakish angle and pulled a pair of suede gloves over his hands. He picked up his cane.

Then he bent down and gripped the handle to the trapdoor in the floor of the freight car and swung it open. He dropped a large, heavy suitcase through the opening. Then he slowly lowered himself to the deck between the rails, careful not to soil his clothes. Hunched down under the car, he made certain none of the crew were within view as he moved away and straightened up.

Ruskin was headed up a stairway to the cabin deck where the passengers rode when, halfway up, he met a crewman coming down. The crewman stopped and nodded at him, a serious expression on his face.

"Are you aware, sir, that passengers are not allowed on the main deck?"

"Yes, I'm aware." The bandit smiled. "I realized my mistake, and, as you see, I was turning around to return to the cabin deck."

"Sorry to have troubled you, sir."

"Not at all. It's your duty."

The bandit proceeded up the stairs and stepped into the ornate, highly decorated cabin deck where the passengers crossed the bay in style. He went into the restaurant and ordered a cup of tea at the stand-up bar, then walked outside onto the open forward deck and sipped as he watched the buildings of San Francisco grow larger across the bay.

The City by the Bay was already becoming a fascinating, romantic, cosmopolitan city. It had risen in stature since 1900, establishing itself as the financial and merchandising hub of the West. It was built on the foresight of entrepreneurs much like the meticulously dressed man standing on the deck with the huge suitcase. He, like they, saw an opportunity and moved quickly to seize it.

Not one for niceties, Ruskin finished his tea and then threw the cup overboard, not returning it to the restaurant. He idly watched a thick flight of sandpipers fly past the boat, followed by a trio of brown pelicans gliding inches above the water in search of small fish. Then, mingling with the throng, he moved down the forward stairway to the main deck, where the passengers disembarked the ferry onto the pier in front of the big, ornate, Spanish-style Southern Pacific terminus.

He walked briskly through the interior cavern of the terminus, lugging the big suitcase, and through the doors on the Townsend Street side. For the next few minutes, he stood on the sidewalk and waited. He smiled as a white Mercedes Simplex runabout rolled up the street and came to a tire-skidding halt at the curb in front of him. Under the hood was a massive four-cylinder, sixty-horsepower engine that could move the car as fast as eighty miles an hour. It was a marvelous contrivance of steel, brass, wood, leather, and rubber. Driving it was sheer adventure.

If the car produced a striking picture, so did the woman behind the steering wheel. She was svelte and wasp-waisted. Her red hair was adorned with a large red bow that matched her fiery hair. Her bonnet was tied under her chin to keep it from blowing away, and she wore a tan linen dress that came halfway up her calves so she could dance her feet deftly over the five floor pedals. She took one hand from the big steering wheel and waved.

"Hello, brother. You're an hour and a half late."

"Greetings, sister." He paused to grin. "I could only go as fast as the engineer drove the train."

She offered him her cheek and he dutifully kissed it. She inhaled the smell of him. He always used the French cologne she had given him. It smelled like a sea of flowers after a light evening rain. If he hadn't been her sibling, she might have had a love affair with him.

"I assume your trip was successful."

"Yes," he said, strapping the suitcase on the running board. "And we haven't a minute to lose." He climbed into the brown leather passenger's seat. "I must record the bank draft I obtained at the Salt Lake Bank and Trust before their agents show up to stop the transfer."

She pushed a laced-up brown leather shoe against the clutch and shifted expertly, as the car leaped down the street like a lion chasing a zebra. "It took two days for you to get here. Don't you think you're cutting it close? They would have contacted law enforcement officials and hired private agents, prodding them to check all the banks in the country for a stolen bank draft worth a fortune."

"And that takes time, not less than forty-eight hours," he added, clutching the side of the seat with a hand since there were no doors on the runabout for support as she made a sharp left turn up Market Street. He barely grabbed his derby with his other hand before it almost flew off into the street.

She drove fast, seemingly recklessly, but nimbly, smoothly whipping around slower traffic at a speed that turned heads and startled passersby. She hurtled past a big beer truck, pulled by a team of Percheron horses, that blocked most of the street, slipping between the stacked barrels on the street and the sidewalk filled with pedestrians with only inches to spare.

He bravely whistled a marching tune called "Garry Owen" and tipped his hat at the pretty girls coming out of the clothing stores. The big Market Street electric trolley car loomed ahead, and she crossed into oncoming traffic to pass it, sending more than one horse rearing up on its hind legs, to the anger and fist waving of their drivers.

Another two blocks through the canyon of brick-and-stone buildings, she came to a quick stop, skidding the rear tires when she hit the brakes, in front of the Cromwell Bank on the southeast corner of Market and Sutter Streets. "Here you are, brother. I trust you enjoyed the ride."

"You're going to kill yourself someday."

"Blame yourself," she said, laughing. "You gave me the car."

"Trade you my Harley-Davidson for it."

"Not a chance." She gave a cheery wave and said, "Come home early and don't be late. We've a date on the Barbary Coast with the Gruenheims to go slumming and take in one of the scandalous dance revues."

"I can't wait," he said sarcastically. He stepped down to the sidewalk before turning and unstrapping the suitcase. She saw that he strained as he lifted and knew it was crammed with stolen currency from the Salt Lake bank.

At the press of the accelerator pedal, the chain-driven Mercedes Simplex charged across the intersection and roared up the street, the thunder of the exhaust coming within a few decibels of breaking the storefront windows.

The bandit turned and looked with pride at the big, elaborately ornamented Cromwell Bank Building with its tall, fluted Ionic column and large stained-glass windows. A doorman in a gray uniform opened one of the big glass doors for him. He was a tall man with gray hair, and a military bearing that came from thirty years in the United States Cavalry.

"Good morning, Mr. Cromwell. Glad to see you back from your holiday."

"Glad to be back, George. How's the weather been in my absence?"

"Just like it is today, sir, sunny and mild." George looked down at the large suitcase. "May I carry that for you, sir?"

"No, thank you. I can manage. I need the exercise."

A small brass sign listed the bank's assets at twenty-two million dollars. It would soon be twenty-three, thought Cromwell. Only the fifty-year-old Wells Fargo Bank had higher assets, capital, and liquidity. George swung open the door, and Cromwell the bandit strode across the marble floor of the bank's lobby, past the beautifully carved desks of the managers and the tellers' windows and the counters without bars, totally open to the customers. The open tellers' area was a strange innovation by a man who trusted no one and robbed out-of-state banks to build his own financial empire.

The fact was, Jacob Cromwell no longer needed the additional income he stole for his bank. But he was intoxicated by the challenge. He felt he was invincible. He could match wits with any police investigators, not to mention the agents from the Van Dorn Detective Agency, until he died of old age. He knew from his spies that no one was remotely close to identifying him.

Cromwell entered an elevator and rode up to the third floor. He stepped out onto the Italian-tiled floor of the main office on the gallery above the bank's lobby. He walked into the grandeur of his suite of offices, the deep, ivory brown carpet muffling his footsteps. The walls were paneled in teak, with carvings depicting scenes of the nineteenth-century West, while the columns that supported the roof were sculpted in the manner of totem poles. The vast ceiling above had been painted with murals of the early days of San Francisco.

He employed three secretaries to handle his main business, along with much of his personal affairs. They were all beautiful women, tall, graceful, intelligent, and came from fine San Francisco families. He paid them more than they could make working for his competitors. The only requirement was that they all wear the same style and color dress, which the bank paid for. Every day was a different color. Today, they were wearing brown dresses that complemented the carpet.

They saw him enter and immediately came to their

feet and surrounded him, chatting gaily and welcoming him back from what they had been told was a holiday that took him fishing in Oregon. Although he had to use great restraint and willpower, Cromwell never carried on a love affair with any of the three women. He had strong principles about playing on his own turf.

After the niceties were over and the ladies returned to their desks, Cromwell asked his senior secretary, who had been with him for nine years, to come into his office.

He sat down at his massive teak desk and parked the suitcase underneath. He smiled at Marion Morgan. "How are you, Miss Morgan? Any new gentlemen friends lately?"

She blushed. "No, Mr. Cromwell. I spend my nights staying home and reading."

Marion was twenty-one when she finished college and came to work for Cromwell as a teller, and she had risen to manager. She had just turned thirty and had never married, which made many consider her an old maid. But the truth was, she could have had any one of the well-heeled men in town. She was an unusually ravishing and nubile lady who could pick and choose her suitors but had yet to select one for a husband. She was particular about men, and the Prince Charming of her dreams had not appeared. Her straw-blond hair was wrapped on her head, as was the fashion of the day, and her lovely facial features enhanced a long swan neck. Her corseted figure looked like the classic hourglass. She gazed across the desk at Cromwell through coral–sea green eyes, and a delicately shaped hand held a pencil poised above a notepad.

"I expect agents representing a bank in Salt Lake City to arrive at any moment to check our records."

"Are they going to examine our books?" she asked as if mildly alarmed.

He shook his head. "Nothing like that. I've heard rumors among my fellow bankers that a bank in Salt Lake City was robbed and that monies stolen might have been deposited in another bank."

"Do you wish me to take care of the matter?"

"No. Please, simply entertain them until I'm prepared to deal with it."

If Marion had any inquiries as to the uncertainty about Cromwell's request, she showed no curiosity. "Yes, of course, I'll see that they are comfortable until you wish to see them."

"That will be all," said Cromwell. "Thank you."

As soon as Marion left his office and shut the door, Cromwell reached into his breast pocket and brought out the bank draft from the Salt Lake Bank & Trust. Then he stood and went over to the large stand-up safe that held the bank's ledgers and records. He quickly, and expertly, doctored the books so that it appeared that the draft had already been received and the full amount paid to Eliah Ruskin. Cromwell also made entries that indicated the money had been deducted from his bank's liquid capital.

Cromwell did not have long to wait after finishing doctoring the records. The expected agents walked into his outer office twenty minutes later. Marion had stalled them, saying Mr. Cromwell was extremely busy. When a small buzzer beneath her desk sounded, she showed them into his office.

He was holding a telephone and nodded a greeting while motioning them to take chairs. "Yes, Mr. Abernathy, I will personally see that your account is closed and the funds transferred to the Bank of Baton Rouge in Louisiana. Not at all. Glad to be of service. Have a good trip. Good-bye."

Cromwell put down the phone with a dead line and no caller on the other end. He stood, came around the desk, and offered his hand. "Hello, I'm Jacob Cromwell, president of the bank."

"These gentlemen are from Salt Lake City," said Marion. "They wish to see you about a draft drawn against their bank." Then she swirled her skirt, a bare inch above the ankles, left the office, and closed the door.

"How can I help you?" Cromwell asked courteously.

One man was tall and gangly, the other short and stocky and sweating. The tall one spoke first. "I'm William Bigalow, and my associate here is Joseph Farnum. We are inquiring if any financial institution in San Francisco might have received a bank draft for four hundred and seventy-five thousand dollars drawn on the Salt Lake Bank and Trust."

Cromwell raised his eyebrows in mock apprehension. "What seems to be the problem?"

"The draft was made under duress by the bank manager before a bandit shot him dead and made off with it, including the bank's money in its vault. We're trying to trace its whereabouts."

"Oh, my," said Cromwell, throwing up his hands in a sign of distress. "That draft came into our hands yesterday afternoon."

The two agents tensed. "You have the draft?" Farnum queried expectantly.

"Yes, it is in a safe in our bookkeeping department." Cromwell's tone became grave. "Unfortunately, we honored it."

"You honored it!" Bigalow gasped.

Cromwell shrugged. "Why, yes."

"With a check, no doubt," said Farnum, in hope there was still time to stop the bandit from cashing it at another bank.

"No, the gentleman whose name was on the draft asked for cash and we complied."

Bigalow and Farnum looked at Cromwell in shock. "You paid almost half a million dollars in cash to someone who walked into your bank off the street?" Bigalow frowned severely.

"I checked the draft myself when my manager brought it to me for approval. It appeared perfectly legitimate."

Bigalow did not look happy. It would be his burden to contact the directors of the Salt Lake Bank and tell them their four hundred and seventy-five thousand dollars had vanished.

"What was the name on the draft?"

"A Mr. Eliah Ruskin," answered Cromwell. "He produced a file of papers that showed Mr. Ruskin was the founder of an insurance company that was going to pay off claims brought on by a fire that destroyed a city block in a town . . ." Cromwell paused. "I believe he said its name was Bellingham, in Washington State."

"Can you describe Ruskin?" asked Farnum.

"Very well dressed," offered Cromwell. "Tall, with blond hair and a large blond mustache. I didn't catch the color of his eyes. But I seem to recall that he carried an unusual cane, with a silver eagle's head."

"That's Ruskin, all right," muttered Farnum.

"He didn't waste any time," Bigalow said to his partner. "He must have caught an express train to get here in a little over a day."

Farnum stared at Cromwell skeptically. "Didn't you think that was an astronomical amount to pay a perfect stranger from out of state?"

"True, but, as I said, I personally checked the draft to make sure it wasn't a forgery. I asked him why he didn't draw on it from a Seattle bank, but he said his company was opening an office in San Francisco. I assure you that it was a bona fide draft. I could find no reason to be suspicious. We paid, although it took almost every dollar of currency we carried in the vault."

"The bank we represent won't be happy about this," Barnum pointed out.

"I'm not worried," Cromwell replied significantly. "The Cromwell Bank has done nothing illegitimate or illegal. We have adhered to the rules and regulations of banking. As to the Salt Lake Bank and Trust failing to meet their obligations, I'm not concerned. Besides their insurance company paying for the theft of the currency, I happen to know their assets are more than ample to cover a half-million-dollar loss."

Barnum addressed Bigalow without turning in his direction. "We had better get to the nearest telegraph office and notify the Salt Lake Bank and Trust directors. They won't he pleased."

"Yes," Bigalow nodded heavily. "They may not take this lying down."

"They have no choice but to honor the draft. It is safe to say the banking commission will agree in Cromwell Bank's favor, should the directors of the Salt Lake Bank wish to enter a protest."

The two agents came to their feet.

"We'll need a statement from you, Mr. Cromwell," announced Farnum, "stating the circumstances of the payment."

"I shall have my attorneys draw it up first thing in the morning."

"Thank you for your consideration."

"Not at all," said Cromwell, remaining seated. "I'll do all in my power to cooperate."

As soon as the agents left, Cromwell called in Miss

Morgan. "Please see that I am not disturbed for the next two hours."

"I'll see to it," she said efficiently.

Seconds after the door closed, Cromwell walked over and quietly locked it. Then he lifted the heavy suitcase under the desk onto the teak surface and opened it. The currency was piled loosely inside, some in stacks wrapped with paper bands.

Methodically, Cromwell began to count and stack the bills, wrapping the loose ones with bands as he inked in the amount. When he finished, he had his desktop filled with neatly piled bundles of cash, marked and counted. The tally came to two hundred forty-one thousand dollars. Then he carefully put the money back in the suitcase, slid the suitcase back under the desk, and opened several ledgers, entering deposits in bogus accounts, which he had set up previously to conceal money stolen over the years. Money that he used to build up the assets needed to open his own bank. Satisfied that he was covered by all the entries, he buzzed Miss Morgan and informed her that he was ready to deal with the day-to-day business of running a successful house of finance.

The banking hours were from ten o'clock in the morning until three in the afternoon. When closing time rolled around, Cromwell waited until the employees had all left for home and the bank was locked up. Now, alone in the bank's vast interior, he carried the suitcase down the elevator to the main floor and into the bank vault, which was still open according to his instructions. He placed the currency, one stack at a time, in the proper bins that were used by the tellers for customer transactions. The receipts he had made up would be turned over to his chief accountant in the morning, who would record the juggled deposits without knowing the serial numbers.

Jacob Cromwell felt pleased with himself. Swindling as well as robbing the bank in Salt Lake City had been his most bold undertaking to date. And he was not about to repeat it. The evil act would throw off his pursuers, who would think he was becoming more daring, and be led into thinking he might try robbing a major city's bank again. But he knew when not to press his luck. Such a robbery was extremely complicated. When he went out on a crime spree again, it would be in a small town yet to be selected.

After closing the vault and throwing the locks and timer, he went down to the basement and slipped out to the street through a hidden door that only he knew existed. Whistling "Yankee Doodle," he hailed a cab and rode to California Street, where he took the cable car up the steep, twenty-four-percent grade of the three-hundred-seventy-five-foot-high slope to his house on Nob Hill, the "hill which is covered with palaces," as Robert Louis Stevenson described it.

Cromwell's mansion amid mansions sat on a small picturesque lane called Cushman Street. The other monuments to wealth had been built by the bonanza-mining types and the big-four barons of the Central Pacific, later the Southern Pacific Railroad: Huntington,

Stanford, Hopkins, and Crocker. To the eye of a creative artist or designer, the mansions looked like monstrosities of architecture gone mad with ostentation.

Unlike the others that were built of wood, Cromwell and his sister Margaret's house was constructed of quarried stone and reflected more of a sedate, almost library-like exterior. There were some who thought it bore a striking resemblance to the White House in Washington.

He found his sister impatiently waiting. At her urging, he quickly readied himself for a night on the Barbary Coast. Yes indeed, he thought, as he dressed in his evening clothes, it had been a productive week. One more success to add to his growing sense of invincibility.

12

Irvine could not come up with currency serial numbers in Bozeman. Not only had the bank failed to record them; it had gone out of business due to the robbery. By the time their assets made up for the loss, the bank had collapsed, and the founder sold what few assets that were left, including the building, to a rich silver miner.

Irvine pushed on to the next robbed bank on his list and took the Northern Pacific Railroad to the mining town of Elkhorn, Montana, located at an elevation of 6,444 feet above sea level. A booming mining town with twenty-five hundred residents, Elkhorn had produced some ten million dollars in gold and silver from 1872 until 1906. The Butcher Bandit had robbed its bank three years earlier, leaving four dead bodies behind.

Just before the train pulled into the town station, Irvine studied, for the tenth time since leaving Bozeman, the report on the robbery in Elkhorn. It was the same modus operandi the bandit used on all his other robberies. Disguised as a miner, he entered the bank soon after the currency shipment had arrived to pay the three thousand men working the quartz lodes.

As usual, there were no witnesses to the actual crime. All four victims – the bank manager, a teller, and a husband and wife making a withdrawal – had been shot in the head at close range. Again, the shots went unheard, and the bandit escaped into the atmosphere without leaving a clue.

Irvine checked into the Grand Hotel before walking down the street to the Marvin Schmidt Bank, its new name taken from the miner who bought it. The architecture of the bank building was typical of the current style in most mining towns. Local stone laid with a Gothic theme. He walked though a corner door, facing the intersection of Old Creek and Pinon Streets. The manager sat behind a low partition not far from a massive steel safe painted with a huge elk standing on a rock outcropping.

"Mr. Sigler?" inquired Irvine.

A young man with black hair, brushed back and oiled, looked up at the greeting. His eyes were a shade of dark green, and his features indicated Indian blood in his ancestry. He wore comfortable cotton pants, a shirt with soft collar, and no tie. He lifted a pair of spectacles from the desk and set them on the bridge of his nose.

"I'm Sigler. How can I help you?"

"I'm Glenn Irvine with the Van Dorn Detective Agency, here for an investigation into the robbery a few years ago."

Sigler quickly frowned with an attitude of annoyance. "Don't you think it's a little late for Van Dorn to arrive on the scene? The robbery and murders took place back in 1903."

"We were not engaged to make an investigation at that time," Irvine retorted.

"So why are you here at this late date?"

"To record the serial numbers of the bills taken by the robbery, if they were listed in a register."

"Who is paying for your services?" Sigler insisted.

Irvine could imagine Sigler's distrust and incomprehension. He might have felt the same if he was in the bank manager's shoes. "The United States government. They want the robberies and murders to stop."

"Strikes me that the bastard can't be caught," Sigler said coldly.

"If he walks on two legs," said Irvine confidently, "the Van Dorn Agency will catch him."

"I'll believe it when I see it," Sigler said indifferently.

"May I see your register of serial numbers? If we have those from the stolen bills, we will make every effort to trace them."

"What makes you think they were recorded?"

Irvine shrugged. "Nothing. But it never hurts to ask."

Sigler fished around in his desk and retrieved a set of keys. "We keep all the old bank records in a storehouse behind the building."

He motioned for Irvine to follow him as he led

the way through a back door toward a small stone building sitting in the middle of the bank's property. The door protested with a loud squeak as it opened on unoiled hinges. Inside, shelves held rows of ledgers and account books. A small table and chair sat at the back of the storeroom.

"Sit down, Mr. Irvine, and I'll see what I can find."

Irvine was not optimistic. Finding a bank that kept a record of serial numbers of its currency seemed highly improbable. It was a long shot, but every avenue had to be followed. He watched as Sigler went through several clothbound ledgers. At last, he opened one and nodded.

"Here you are," Sigler said triumphantly. "The serial numbers our bookkeeper recorded of all the currency in the vault two days before the robbery. Some of the bills, of course, were distributed to customers. But most were taken by the bandit."

Irvine was stunned as he opened the book and stared at the columns of neatly inked numbers within the lines of the pages. There were several different kinds of large banknotes. Gold certificates, silver certificates, notes issued by individual banks were recorded in the ledger. United States Treasury serial numbers were printed vertically and horizontally on the sides; the local bank that issued them added their own number at the bottom. Most came from the Continental & Commercial National Bank of Chicago and the Crocker First National Bank of

San Francisco. He looked up at Sigler, now fired with elation.

"You don't know what this means," Irvine said, gratified beyond his greatest expectations. "Now we can pass out numbers on the stolen bills to every bank in the country where the bandit might have deposited them. Handbills with the numbers can also be distributed to merchants throughout the West, urging them to be on the lookout for the bills."

"Good luck," said Sigler pessimistically. "It's hardly possible that you can trace them back three years. Any one of them could have changed hands a hundred times by now."

"You're probably right, but hopefully the bandit is still spending them."

"Slim chance of that," Sigler said with a tight grin. "I'll bet a month's wage he spent it all a long time ago."

Sigler *was* probably right, Irvine thought. But Irvine was not discouraged. Bell had said that it would be an insignificant mistake that would trip the bandit up. Now it was only a question of getting the information out to banks and merchants and hope there would be a response that led to the whereabouts of the mysterious killer.

13

Curtis sat at a table in the Western Archives Division of the Union Pacific Railroad's office in Omaha, Nebraska, surrounded by high shelves filled with ledgers and account books of reports on train operations. During the nine days since he launched his search, he had scoured the records of four different railroads and the Wells Fargo stage lines trying to find a link for how the Butcher Bandit escaped capture after committing his robberies and hideous murders.

It was an exercise in futility. Nothing fell into place. He had begun with the stagecoach possibilities. Most of the stage lines were gone by 1906. Wells Fargo still held the monopoly, with lines extending several thousand miles over overland express routes in remote areas that were not serviced by railroads. But the schedules did not fall into the proper times.

There were sixteen hundred different company railroads across the nation in 1906, with two hundred twenty thousand miles of track among them. Fifty of the largest had a thousand miles of track each. Curtis had narrowed the number of companies down to five. They were the railroads with scheduled runs through the towns hit by the bandit.

"Would you like a cup of coffee?"

Curtis looked up from a train schedule record into the face of a little man standing no more than five feet two inches. His name was Nicolas Culhane, and his biscuit brown–streaked graying hair was brushed forward over his head to cover the receding baldness. The ferret brown eyes shifted with amazing frequency, and he wore a thinly clipped mustache whose pointed ends extended a good inch on either side of his lips. He walked with a slight stoop and wore spectacles with lenses that magnified his eyes. Curtis was amused at the helpful little man with the springy step. He was the perfect stereotype of a keeper of musty records in an archive.

"No, thank you." Curtis paused to glance at his pocket watch. "I never drink coffee in the afternoon."

"Having any luck?" asked Culhane.

Curtis shook his head wearily. "None of the passenger trains ran close to the time the bandit robbed the banks."

"I pray you catch the murdering scum," Culhane said, his voice suddenly turned angry.

"You sound like you hate him."

"I have a personal grudge."

"Personal?"

Culhane nodded. "My closest cousin and her little boy were killed by the Butcher at the bank in McDowell, New Mexico."

"I'm sorry," Curtis said solemnly.

"You must catch and hang him!" Culhane struck a fist on the table, causing the schedule book lying open to tremble and flip its pages. "He has got away with his crimes far too long."

"I assure you, the Van Dorn Agency is working night and day to bring him to justice."

"Have you found anything at all that might trace him?" Culhane asked anxiously.

Curtis raised his hands in a helpless gesture. "All we've discovered is that he is missing the little finger on his left hand. Besides that, we have nothing."

"Did you check out the stagecoach lines?"

"I spent a day in the Wells Fargo records department. It was a dead end. None of their schedules put them in town within four hours of the robberies. More than enough time for the bandit to evade capture."

"And the passenger trains?"

"The sheriff and marshals telegraphed surrounding towns to stop all trains and examine the passengers for anyone who looked suspicious. They even searched all luggage in hopes that one of the bags might contain the stolen currency, but they turned up no evidence, nor could they make an identification. The bandit was too smart. The disguises he used to rob and murder were too original and too well executed. The law officers had little or nothing to go on."

"Did time schedules work out?"

"Only two," Curtis replied tiredly. "The departure times on the others didn't coincide with the events."

Culhane rubbed his thinning hair thoughtfully. "You've eliminated stagecoaches and passenger trains. What about freight?"

"Freight trains?"

"Did you check out the departure times on those?"

Curtis nodded. "There, we have a different story. The trains I've been able to find in the right place at the right time left the robbed towns within the required times."

"Then you have your answer," Culhane said.

Curtis didn't reply immediately. He was tired, on the verge of sheer exhaustion, and depressed that he was no further along and had made no discoveries. Inwardly, he cursed the Butcher Bandit. It didn't seem humanly possible the man could be so obscure, so will-o'-the-wisp, so able to defy all attempts at detection. He could almost see the man laughing at the inept efforts of his pursuers.

At last, he said, "You underestimate the law enforcement officials. They searched the boxcars of all the freight trains that passed through the towns during the specified time limits."

"What about the boxcars that were switched onto local sidings to be hauled later to other destinations by incoming trains? He could have dodged the posses by hiding in a freight car."

Curtis shook his head. "The posses searched all empty cars and found no sign of the bandit."

"Did they check out the ones that were loaded?" Culhane questioned.

"How could they? The cars were locked tight. There's no way the bandit could have entered them."

Culhane grinned like a fox on a hot scent. "I guess nobody told you that the train brakemen all carry keys that will open the locks on the loading doors in case of fire."

"I was not aware of that angle," said Curtis.

The steel-rimmed spectacles slid down Culhane's nose. "It's certainly something to think about."

"Yes, it is," Curtis mused, his mind beginning to turn. "We're looking at a process of elimination. The posses claimed there were no tracks leading out of town to follow, which means our man didn't ride a horse. There is almost no chance he could have taken a stagecoach, and it appears unlikely he bought a ticket and traveled out of town as a passenger on a train. He also failed to be spotted in an empty boxcar."

"Which leaves loaded boxcars as the only means of transportation that was not examined," Culhane persisted.

"You may be onto something," said Curtis thoughtfully.

A peculiar expression crossed Curtis's face as he began to envision a new scenario. "That leaves a whole new avenue to follow. Now I have to go through freight car records to study the cars that made up those specific trains, who owned them, their manifest, and their ultimate destination."

"Not an easy chore," said Culhane. "You'll have to check out hundreds of freight cars from a dozen trains."

"Like a piece of a puzzle. Find the boxcar that

was parked on a nearby siding in all of the robbed towns on the days of the robberies."

"I'll be happy to help you with the Union Pacific freight records."

"Thank you, Mr. Culhane. Two of the freight trains in question were hauled by Union Pacific."

"Just tell me which towns they were at and I'll dig out the records that give the car's serial numbers, their ownership, and the agent who arranged and paid for their transportation."

"You've been a great help to me and I'm grateful," Curtis said sincerely.

"I'm the one who is grateful, Mr. Curtis. I never thought I would be instrumental in bringing the Butcher Bandit, the killer of my cousin and her child, to justice."

Four hours later, with Culhane's able assistance, Curtis had the information that gave him a solid direction to investigate. Now all he had to do was research the archives of the Southern Pacific, the Atchison, Topeka & Santa Fe, and the Denver & Rio Grande railroads to confirm Culhane's theory.

By nightfall, he was on a train to Los Angeles and the Atchison, Topeka & Santa Fe archives. Too inspired to sleep, he stared at his reflection in the window since it was too dark to see the landscape roll by outside. He was optimistic that the end of the trail seemed to be over the next hill and around the next bend.

14

The early evening came with a light rain that dampened the dirt street through town as Bell stepped off the train. In the fading light, he could see that Bisbee, Arizona, was a vertical town, with sharply rising hills occupied by many houses that could be reached only by steep stairways. On his way to the Copper Queen Hotel, he walked through the narrow, twisting streets, a maze flanked by new, substantial brick buildings.

It was a Saturday, and Bell found a deputy holding down the sheriff's office and jail. The deputy said the sheriff was taking a few days off, to make repairs to his house that had been damaged in a flood that had swept down the hills, and would not return to work until Thursday. When Bell asked him for directions to the sheriff's house, the deputy refused to give them, claiming that the sheriff was not to be disturbed unless it was an emergency.

Bell checked into the Copper Queen, ate a light dinner in the hotel dining room, and then went out on the town. He skipped having a drink in the Copper Queen Saloon and walked up to the infamous Brewery Gulch, lined with fifty saloons, known throughout the territory as the wildest, bawdiest, and best drinking street in the West.

He checked out four of the saloons, stepping into each and studying the action, before going on to the next one. Finally, he settled into a large, wooden-walled hall with a stage and a small band playing a ragtime tune while four dancing girls hoofed it around the stage. Moving through the crowded tables to the bar, he waited until a busy bartender asked, "What'll it be, friend, whiskey or beer?"

"What's your best whiskey?"

"Jack Daniel's from Tennessee," said the bartender without hesitation. "It won the Gold Medal at the St. Louis Fair as the best whiskey in the world."

Bell smiled. "I've enjoyed it, on occasion. Let me have a double shot glass."

While the bartender poured, Bell turned around, leaned his elbows behind him on the bar, and gazed around the busy saloon. Like most watering holes in the West, a large section of the room was given over to gambling. Bell's eyes went from table to table, looking for the right mix of poker players. He found what he had hoped to find, a table with men dressed in fancier clothes than the large number of miners. They appeared to be businessmen, merchants, or mining officials. Best of all, there were four of them, one short of a fifth player.

Bell paid for his whiskey and walked over to the table. "May I join you gentlemen?" he asked.

A heavyset man with a red face nodded and motioned toward an empty chair. "You're quite welcome to sit in," he said.

A man directly across the table shuffled the cards, looked across at Bell as he sat down, and began dealing. "I'm Frank Calloway. The others are Pat O'Leery, Clay Crum, and Lewis Latour."

"Isaac Bell."

"You new in town, Mr. Bell?" asked O'Leery, a big, brawny Irishman.

"Yes, I arrived on the six-thirty train from Phoenix."

"Business or pleasure?" O'Leery probed.

"Business. I'm an agent with the Van Dorn Detective Agency."

They all looked up from their cards and stared at Bell with inquisitive interest.

"Let me guess," said Crum, folding his hands over a rotund belly. "You're looking into the bank robbery and murders that took place four months ago."

Bell nodded as he fanned his hand and examined his cards. "You are correct, sir."

Latour spoke in a French accent as he lit a cigar. "A little late, aren't you? The trail is cold."

"No colder than it was five minutes after the crime," Bell countered. "I'll take two cards."

Calloway dealt as the players called out the number of cards they hoped would give them a winning hand. "A mystery, that one," he said. "No trace of the bandit was ever found."

"Uncanny," O'Leery said as he inspected his hand, his expression revealing he had nothing worth betting on. "I fold." His eyes briefly met Bell's. "Uncanny that he could escape into thin air."

"The sheriff found no sign of his trail," muttered Crum. "The posse returned to town looking as if their wives had run off with a band of traveling salesmen." He paused. "I'll bet two dollars."

"I'll raise you three dollars," offered Calloway.

Latour threw his hand toward the dealer. "I'm out."

"And you, Mr. Bell," inquired Calloway, "are you still in?"

Bell was amused that the stakes were not high, but not penny-ante either. "I'll call."

"Two queens," announced Crum.

"Two tens," said Calloway. "You beat me." He turned. "Mr. Bell?"

"Two eights," Bell said, passing his cards facedown to Calloway. Bell had not lost. He held three jacks, but he thought that losing would bring him closer to the other men's confidence. "Was there any clue to how the robber escaped?"

"Nothing I ever heard of," replied O'Leery. "Last time I talked to the sheriff, he was baffled."

"That would be Sheriff Hunter?" Bell inquired, recalling what he read in the agency report.

"Joe Hunter died from a bad heart two months after the murders," answered Latour. "The new sheriff is Stan Murphy, who was Hunter's chief deputy. He knows what went on as well as anybody."

"As nice as they come, if he likes you," Crum

said. "But get on his bad side and he'll chew you to bits."

"I'd like to talk with him, but I doubt if he'll be in his office on the Sabbath," said Bell, not mentioning the discouraging comments of Murphy's deputy. "Where might I find him?"

"We had a bad flood through town two weeks ago," replied Calloway. "His house was badly damaged. I suspect you'll find him up to his neck in repairs."

"Can you give me directions to his house?"

O'Leery waved a hand toward the north. "Just go up to the end of Howland Street and take the stairs. The house is painted green and has a small grove of orange trees alongside."

The talk moved to politics and whether Teddy Roosevelt could run for a third term in 1908 and, if not, whom he would pick as his successor. Bell lost three hands for every hand he won, easily putting the other men at ease as they realized the stranger was no gambling cardsharp. He swung the conversation back to the bank murders.

"Seems strange that no one saw the robber leaving the bank or riding out of town," said Bell idly as he played his cards.

"Nobody came forward," said O'Leery.

"And none saw the bandit enter or leave the bank," Latour added.

"There was an old drunken miner that hung around across the street from the bank," answered Calloway, "but he disappeared soon afterward."

"Sheriff Hunter did not consider him a suspect?"

Latour had no luck. He folded for the fifth time since Bell sat down at the table. "An old miner who was all played out and looked like he wasn't long for this world? He was the last one the townspeople thought had anything to do with the crime."

"More than once, I saw him sprawled on a sidewalk, drunk out of his mind," said O'Leery. "He couldn't have robbed a bank and murdered three people any more than I could become governor. I still think it was an inside job pulled off by someone we all know."

"It might have been a stranger," Bell said.

Calloway shrugged negatively. "Bisbee has twenty thousand inhabitants. Who's to recognize a stranger?"

"What about that fellow on a motorcycle?" Crum asked no one in particular.

"There was a motorcycle in town?" asked Bell, his interest aroused.

"Jack Carson said he saw a dandy riding one." Crum threw down a winning hand with a flush.

Latour took a long puff on his cigar. "Jack said the rider was well dressed, when he saw him pass through an alley. He couldn't figure out how someone riding one of those contraptions could wear clothes so clean and unsoiled."

"Did your friend get a look at the rider's face?"

"All Jack could tell was that the rider was clean-shaven," Calloway responded.

"What about hair color?"

"According to Jack, the fellow wore a bowler. Jack wasn't sure, as he didn't get a good look because the motorcycle went by too fast, but he thought the hair might have been red. At least, that's what he thought, from a glimpse of the sideburns."

For the second time that week, Bell found excitement coursing through his veins. A resident of Eagle City, Utah, another mining town where the Butcher Bandit left four residents dead, mentioned that he had seen a stranger riding a motorcycle on the day of the killing.

"Where can I find this Jack Carson?"

"Not in Bisbee," replied Crum. "The last I heard, he went back to his home in Kentucky."

Bell made a mental note to ask Van Dorn to try and find Carson.

O'Leery made another sour face at seeing his hand. "Whoever rode that motorcycle must have hung around town for a few days after the robbery."

"Why do you say that?" Bell probed.

"Because the sheriff and his posse would have spotted the motorcycle's tire tracks if the killer had ridden out of town immediately after the robbery."

"You'd think he would have been spotted if he stayed in town until the posse gave up the hunt."

"You would think so," said Calloway, "but he was never seen again."

"Was Carson a reliable witness?" Bell laid five dollars on the table. "I raise."

"Jack was a former mayor of Bisbee, an attorney highly regarded as an honorable man," Latour explained. "If he said he saw a man on a motorcycle, he saw a man on a motorcycle. I have no reason to doubt his word."

"You going to see Sheriff Murphy tomorrow?" Crum inquired, finally winning a hand.

Bell nodded. "First thing in the morning. But, after talking with you gentlemen, I fear there is little of importance he can tell me."

After nursing his drink during two hours of play, Bell was even, almost. He was only four dollars in the hole, and none of the other players minded when he bid them good night and walked back to his hotel.

The road that wound up to the street toward the sheriff's house was long, and muddy after a rainstorm that struck Bisbee in the middle of the night. Coming to a dead end, Bell mounted the steep stairway that seemed to go on forever. Despite being in excellent physical shape, he was panting when he reached the top.

Bell was in a happy mood. He had yet to learn what Irvine and Curtis turned up, if anything. But he was dead certain the man seen on the motorcycle was the Butcher Bandit after he removed his disguise as the old intoxicated miner. A missing finger and a hint of red hair was hardly a triumph. Even the hair color glimpsed by Jack Carson was a long shot. It was the motorcycle that intrigued Bell, not because the bandit owned one but because it fit that a shrewd and calculating mind would use the latest technology in transportation.

The primary question was, how did the bandit ride it out of town without being seen again?

Sheriff Murphy's house was only a few steps from the top of the stairway. It was small, and looked more like a shed than a house. The flood had pushed it off its foundation, and Bell saw that Murphy was busily engaged in propping it up in its new location, ten feet from where it had sat before. True to O'Leery's description, it was painted green, but the flood had devastated the orange grove.

Murphy was furiously wielding a hammer and didn't hear Bell approach. A great torrent of dark brown hair flowed around his neck and shoulders. Most of the lawmen in the West were not fat but lean and angular. Murphy had the body of a blacksmith rather than a sheriff. The muscles in his arms looked like tree trunks, and he had the neck of an ox.

"Sheriff Murphy!" Bell shouted over the pounding of the hammer against nails.

Murphy stopped with his hammer in midair and turned. He stared at Bell as he might stare at a coyote. "Yes, I'm Murphy. But, as you can see, I'm busy."

"You can keep working," said Bell. "I'm with the Van Dorn Detective Agency and would like to ask you a few questions about the bank robbery and murders a few months ago."

The name Van Dorn was respected among law

enforcement circles, and Murphy laid down the hammer and pointed inside the little house. "Come inside. The place is a bit of a mess, but I have coffee on the stove."

"After that climb up the hill, a cup of water would be nice."

"Sorry, the well got befouled by the flood and isn't fit to drink, but I carried a gallon up from a horse trough in town."

"Coffee it is," said Bell with a measure of trepidation.

Murphy led Bell into the house and offered him a chair at the kitchen table. There was no sign of the presence of a woman, so Bell assumed that Murphy was a bachelor. The sheriff poured two coffees in tin cups from an enamel pot that sat on the wood-burning stove.

"I don't know how I can help you, Mr. Bell. I sent a copy of my findings to your agency in Chicago."

"You neglected to mention Jack Carson's sighting."

Murphy laughed. "The guy on a motorcycle? I don't believe what Jack said he saw. The description didn't fit anyone I knew in town."

"The bandit could have changed his disguise," Bell suggested.

"There was no time for him to completely alter his appearance, retrieve his motorcycle, and ride off into the blue."

"The rider and his machine were never seen again?"

Murphy shrugged. "Strikes me odd that nobody else saw him except Jack. A man on the only motorcycle in town is bound to be noticed. And how could he ride out of town without leaving a trail?"

"I admit it sounds a bit far-fetched," said Bell, not wanting to discard the sighting.

"Jack Carson was an upstanding citizen not noted for being a hard drinker or a teller of tall tales. But I believe he was hallucinating."

"Was there any other evidence discovered that wasn't in your report?"

"There was something found after I sent the report to Chicago. Murphy rose from the kitchen table and pulled open a drawer of a rolltop desk. He passed Bell a brass shell casing. "This was found two weeks later, by a young boy playing on the floor of the bank while his father made a deposit. It was under a carpet. The bandit must have missed it."

Bell studied the cartridge. "Thirty-eight caliber. If it was ejected, it must have come from an automatic weapon, probably a Colt."

"That was my guess, too."

"May I keep it?" asked Bell.

"Sure. But I doubt you'll learn anything from it, except knowing it came from the bandit's gun. And even that is not cold, hard evidence."

"If not the bandit, then where did it come from?"

Murphy held up his hands in a helpless gesture. "I can't begin to guess."

Bell carefully held the cartridge in the palm of his hand. "Hopefully, we can obtain the bandit's fingerprints."

Murphy grinned. "You'll find mine as well as the young boy's and two of my deputies'."

"Still," said Bell optimistically, "our experts may be able to pull a print. We won't need a sample of the boy who found it. His print would be small. But I would like sample prints of you and your deputies. You can send them to my Chicago office."

"I've never taken a fingerprint," said Murphy. "I'm not at all sure how it's done."

"The science has been around for centuries, but only in the past few years is it catching on with law enforcement. The impressions on an object – in this case, the cartridge – are created by the ridges on the skin. When the object is handled, the perspiration and oils are transferred to it, leaving an impression of the fingertip-ridge pattern. To record the prints, a fine powder like ground-up graphite from a pencil is dusted on the surface. Then a piece of tape is used to lift the print for study."

Murphy sipped at his coffee. "I'll give it a try."

Bell thanked the sheriff and walked down the stairway. Three hours later, he was on a train back to Denver.

15

Cromwell's chauffeur drove the 1906 Rolls-Royce Brougham, made by the London coach maker Barker, with its six-cylinder, thirty-horsepower engine, from the garage to the front of the palatial Nob Hill mansion Cromwell had designed himself and constructed from white marble blocks cut and hauled by railroad from a quarry in Colorado. The front end had the appearance of a Greek temple, with high fluted columns, while the rest of the house was more simply designed, with arched windows, and a cornice that crowned the walls.

While the chauffeur, Abner Weed, a stony-faced Irishman whom Cromwell hired more for his experience as a wrestler than his expertise behind the wheel of an automobile, stood patiently by the Rolls out front, Cromwell waited for his sister in his study, sprawled comfortably on a leather sofa, listening to Strauss waltzes on an Edison cylinder phonograph. He was conservatively dressed in a dark wool suit. After listening to "Voices of Spring," he changed cylinders and played *Tales from the Vienna Wood*. The cylinders played two minutes of music each.

Cromwell glanced up from the machine as his sister

came into the room wearing a doeskin dress that fell around her nicely curved calves.

"A bit risqué, aren't we?" he said, eyeing her exposed flesh.

She spun around, swirling the skirt and showing off her legs up to midthigh. "Since we're going slumming on the Barbary Coast, I thought I'd dress like a soiled dove."

"Just be sure you don't act like one."

He rose from the sofa, turned off the phonograph, and held up her coat so she could slip into it. Even with his shoe lifts, he stood the same height as his sister. Then he followed her through the large, intricately carved front doors to the drive and the waiting Rolls-Royce. Abner, attired in his liveried uniform with shiny black boots, stood at attention, holding open the rear door. The Rolls was a town car, with an enclosed passenger compartment, the chauffeur in the open air with nothing but the windshield to protect him. As soon as Cromwell's sister was settled, he instructed the driver where to go. Abner shifted gears and the big car rolled silently over the granite stones laid in the street.

"This is the first opportunity we've had to talk since I came home," said Cromwell, secure in the knowledge that the driver could not hear their conversation through the divider window separating the front and rear seats.

"I know that your trip to Salt Lake City was successful. And our bank is another seven hundred thousand dollars richer."

"You haven't told me how you made out in Denver."

"Your spies in the Van Dorn Agency were quite accurate in their assessment of the investigation. The Denver office has taken on the job of lead investigator in the hunt for the Butcher Bandit."

"I hate being called that. I would have preferred something with more swank."

"Like what, pray tell?" she asked, laughing.

"The Stylish Spirit."

She rolled her eyes. "I doubt that newspaper editors would be enthused with that one."

"What else did you find out?"

"The head of the Denver office, Nicholas Alexander, is an idiot. After I flashed a few of my charms, he couldn't stop speaking about the hunt. He was angry he wasn't put in charge of the investigation and had no reservations about revealing pertinent information concerning the methods they were going to use to catch the notorious bandit. Van Dorn himself named his top agent, Isaac Bell, to the case. A handsome and dashing devil, and very wealthy, I might add."

"You saw him?"

"I met him, and, what's more. I danced with him." She pulled a small photograph from her purse. "I was waiting to give you this. Not the greatest likeness, but the photographer I hired was not very proficient at shooting photographs without setting them up in advance."

Cromwell switched on the dome light of the car and examined the photo. The photo showed a tall man, with blond hair and mustache. "Should I be concerned about him?"

Her eyes took on an evasive expression. "I can't say. He seemed more intelligent and sophisticated than our spies led me to believe. I had them check his background. He rarely if ever fails to find and apprehend his man. His record is quite admirable. Van Dorn thinks very highly of him."

"If, as you say, he is affluent, why is he wasting his time as a simple detective?"

Margaret shrugged. "I have no idea. Maybe, like you, he craves a challenge, too?" She hesitated as she adjusted an imaginary loose curl with her fingers.

"Where did he get his money?"

"Did I forget to mention that he comes from a family of bankers in Boston?"

Cromwell stiffened. "I know of the Bells. They own the American States Bank of Boston, one of the largest financial institutions in the country."

"He's a paradox," she said slowly, recalling her few minutes with him in the Brown Palace Hotel. "But he can also be very dangerous. He'll come after us like a fox chasing a rabbit."

"A detective who knows the inner workings of banking procedures is not good," Cromwell said, his tone low and icy. "We must be especially wary."

"I agree."

"You're certain he had no clue to your true identity?"

"I covered my tracks well. As far as he and Alexander

know, my name is Rose Manteca, from Los Angeles, where my father owns a large ranch."

"If Bell is as smart as you suggest, he'll check that out and prove Rose doesn't exist."

"So what?" she said impishly. "He'll never know my name is Margaret Cromwell, sister of a respected banker who lives in a mansion on Nob Bill in San Francisco."

"What other information did you pry out of Alexander?"

"Only that Bell's investigation is not going well. They have no clues that lead in your direction. Alexander was angry that Bell hadn't taken him into his confidence. He said that Bell was close-mouthed concerning his actions with a pair of agents known as Curtis and Irvine. All I could find out is, they're all out beating the bushes in search of a lead."

"That's good to hear." Cromwell smiled thinly. "They'll never consider that a banker is behind the robberies."

She gazed at him. "You could quit, you know. We no longer need the money. And no matter how careful, no matter how sharp-witted you are, it's only a question of time before you're caught and hung."

"You want me to give up the excitement and the challenge of achieving what no one else would dare and play the role of a stodgy banker for the rest of my days?"

"No, I do not," she said with a wicked sparkle in her eye. "I love the excitement, too." Then her voice softened and became distant. "It's just that I know it cannot go on forever."

"The time will come when we know when to stop," he said without emphasis.

Neither brother nor sister possessed even a tinge of repentance or remorse for all the men, women, and children Cromwell had murdered. Nor could they have cared less for all the savings of small businesses, miners, and farmers they had wiped out when the robbed banks, unable to refund their depositors, had to close their doors.

"Who are you taking tonight?" she asked, changing the subject.

"Marion Morgan."

"That prude," she scoffed. "It's a mystery to me why you keep her on the payroll."

"She happens to be very efficient," he retorted, not seeking an argument.

"Why haven't you ever taken her to bed?" she said with a soft laugh.

"You know I never play with my employees. It's a principle that has saved me much grief. I'm only taking her out tonight as a bonus for her work. Nothing more." His sister's dress was pulled to her knees and he reached over and squeezed one of them. "Who is the lucky man this evening?"

"Eugene Butler."

"That fop?" he taunted. "He's as worthless as they come."

"He's filthy rich—"

"His *father* is filthy rich," Cromwell corrected her. "If Sam Butler hadn't made a lucky strike when he stumbled onto the Midas gold vein, he'd have died broke."

"Eugene will be richer than you when his father dies."

"He's a wastrel and a sot. He'll spend his fortune so fast your head will swim."

"I can handle him," said his sister. "He's madly in love with me and will do anything I tell him."

"You can do better, much better," grunted Cromwell. He picked up a speaking tube and spoke to the driver. "Abner, turn left at the next street and stop at the Butler residence."

Abner held up a hand to indicate he understood. He stopped the Rolls in front of a huge mansion constructed of wood in the Victorian style of the day. Then he stepped from the car and rang the bell at the iron-gated front door. A maid answered, and he handed her Cromwell's calling card. The maid took it and closed the door. A few minutes later, the door reopened and a tall, handsome man with sharply defined facial features came out and walked toward the car. He could have passed for a matinee idol onstage. Like Cromwell, he wore a woolen suit that was dark navy rather than black, a starched collar, and a tie with a white-diamond pattern. He paused in the portico and sniffed the air, which was tinged with a light fog that rolled in from the bay.

Abner opened the Rolls's rear door, pulled down a

jump seat, and stood back. Butler got in and sat down. He turned to Cromwell's sister. "Maggie, you look positively stunning, good enough to eat." He left it there, seeing the fearsome, hostile look in Cromwell's eyes. He greeted Cromwell without offering his hand. "Jacob, good to see you."

"You look fit," said Cromwell as if he cared.

"In the pink. I walk five miles a day."

Cromwell ignored him, picked up the speaking tube, and instructed Abner where to pick up Marion Morgan. He turned to his sister. "What saloon on the Barbary Coast do you wish for us to mingle with the foul-smelling rabble?"

"I heard that Spider Kelly's was quite scrubby."

"The worst dive in the world," Cromwell said knowledgeably. "But they have good bands and a large dance floor."

"Do you think it's safe?" asked Margaret.

Cromwell laughed. "Red Kelly hires a small army of husky bouncers to protect affluent clientele like us from harm or embarrassment."

"Spider Kelly's it is," said Butler. "I even took my mumsy and dad there one evening. They truly enjoyed watching the mix of unsavory people who frequent the place. We sat in the slummers' balcony to watch the lowlife cavort."

The Rolls stopped in front of an apartment building on Russian Hill just off Hyde Street on Lombard, a fashionable but affordable district of the city. This area of Russian Hill contained the homes and meeting places where intellectuals, artists, architects, writers, and journalists engaged in lofty arguments and discussions – but mostly socialized and partied.

Marion did not stand on protocol. She was waiting out front, on the top step of her building. As the Rolls eased to the curb, she descended and then stopped as Abner opened the door for her. She was dressed in a short jacket over a blue blouse with a matching skirt that had a simple elegance about it. Her blond hair was drawn back and twisted into a long braid with a bow at the back of her long neck.

Cromwell stepped out and gallantly helped her into the backseat. The chauffeur pulled down the other jump seat in which Cromwell, in a courtly manner, seated himself. "Miss Marion Morgan, may I present Mr. Eugene Butler. And you've met my sister Margaret," he said, using her proper name.

"Miss Cromwell, a pleasure to see you again." Marion's tone was gracious but not exactly filled with warmth. "Likewise, Eugene," Marion acknowledged sweetly with familiarity.

"You know each other?" asked Margaret in surprise.

"Eugene . . . Mr. Butler . . . took me to dinner some time ago."

"Two years," Butler said good-naturedly. "I failed to impress her. She spurned all my later invitations."

"And advances," Marion added, smiling.

"Ready for a hot night on the Barbary Coast?" asked Cromwell.

"It will be a new experience for me," said Marion. "I've never had the courage to go there."

"Remember the old song," said Margaret:

> *"The miners came in 'forty-nine.*
> *the whores in 'fifty-one.*
> *And when they got together,*
> *they produced the native son."*

Marion blushed and looked demurely at the carpet on the floor as the men laughed.

A few minutes later, Abner turned onto Pacific Street and drove through the heart of the Barbary Coast, named after the lair of the Barbary pirates of Morocco and Tunisia. Here was the home of gamblers, prostitutes, burglars, con men, drunks, derelicts, cutthroats, and murderers. It was all there, debauchery and degradation, poverty and wealth, misery and death.

The infamous coast boasted more than three hundred saloons, wall-to-wall, within six city blocks, fifty of them on Pacific Street alone. It existed because of crooked politicians who were bribed by the saloon, gambling house, and brothel owners. The reputable citizens of the city complained publicly about the den of iniquity but averted their eyes because they were secretly proud of the distinction that their fair city of San Francisco more than equaled Paris, which bore the enviable reputation as the wickedest city in the Western Hemisphere, as a carnival of vice and corruption.

And yet the Barbary Coast was glitzy and glamorous, with loads of ballyhoo and skulduggery, a veritable paradise for people of honest means to go slumming. The unsavory who ran the dens of sin – in most cases, men – relished seeing the swells from Nob Hill enter their establishments because they had no scruples charging them exorbitant prices for admission and liquor, usually thirty dollars for a bottle of champagne rather than the going rate of six to eight. Mixed drinks in most saloons were twenty-five cents and beer a dime.

Abner slipped the Rolls through the revelers wandering the street and pulled to a stop in front of a three-story building that served as a hotel upstairs – in reality, a brothel, called a cow yard, which housed fifty women in rooms, called cribs. The main floor was for gambling and drinking, while the downstairs basement had a stage for bawdy shows and a large wooden floor for dancing. They stepped from the car, with the men in the lead to shield the ladies, who stared with fascination at a flashy uniformed barker on the sidewalk.

"Step right into Spider Kelly's, the finest drinking and dancing establishment on the coast. All are welcome, all will have the night of their lives. See the wildest show and the most beautiful girls to be found anywhere. See them kick their heels over their heads; see them sway in a manner that will shock and amaze you."

"I like this place already," said Margaret gaily.

Marion stared and clutched Cromwell's arm tightly and looked up at a sign largely ignored by the clientele that read NO VULGARITY ALLOWED IN THIS ESTABLISHMENT.

They entered a large, U-shaped entrance lobby decorated with framed panels of nude women dancing amid Roman ruins. A manager decked out in an ill-fitting tuxedo greeted them and escorted them inside. "Do you wish to go downstairs for the show?" he asked. "The next one starts in ten minutes."

"We would like a safe table away from the riffraff," said Cromwell in a demanding tone. "After we've enjoyed a bottle of your finest champagne, we'll go downstairs for dancing and the show."

The manager bowed. "Yes, sir. Right this way."

He escorted Cromwell's party through the crowded saloon up to a table on the slummers' balcony Butler had mentioned overlooking the main floor of the saloon. Soon a waitress wearing a thin blouse cut low across her breasts and a skirt that came well above her knees, showing an ample display of legs in black silk stockings held up by capricious garters, brought a magnum of Veuve Clicquot Ponsardin champagne, vintage 1892. As she eased the bottle into an ordinary bucket filled with ice, she brushed against the men and gave each an earthy smile. Margaret returned the smile, letting the waitress know that Margaret knew that besides serving customers in the saloon she also worked in the cribs upstairs. Surprised at seeing a Nob

Hill swell dressed in a revealing outfit, the waitress gave Margaret a lewd look.

"You know, dearie, a redhead like you is in high demand. You could name your own price."

Marion was stunned. Cromwell fought to keep from laughing, while Butler became outright indignant. "This is a lady!" he snapped. "You will apologize!"

The waitress ignored him. "If she's Jewish, she can make the top of the scale." Then she turned, gave a wiggle to her buttocks, and walked down the stairway.

"What does being Jewish have to do with it?" Marion asked naively.

"There is a myth going around," explained Cromwell, "that Jewish redheads are the most passionate of all women."

Margaret was enjoying herself as she gazed around the main floor of the saloon. She felt a giddy elation at seeing the sailors and dockworkers, the young and honest working girls who unknowingly were easily led astray, and the hardened criminals milling around the floor, which was littered with a small army of men too drunk to stand. Unknown to the others, including her brother, Margaret had visited the dives of the Barbary Coast on several occasions. And she was well aware that her brother Jacob often frequented the expensive and most exclusive parlor houses, where the royalty of the shady women plied their trade.

Marion found it disgusting and fascinating at the same time. She had heard the coast was the pit of bitterness and despair for the poor of San Francisco, but she had no idea how far humans could sink. She was not used to drinking and the champagne mellowed her after a while, and she began to see the depravity in a less-sickening light. She tried to imagine herself as one of those loose women, taking men to the cribs upstairs for as little as fifty cents. Horrified at herself, she quickly pushed the thought from her mind and rose unsteadily to her feet after Cromwell held up the empty bottle and announced that it was time for them to go downstairs.

The manager appeared and found a table that was occupied on the dance floor not far from the stage. Two couples dressed in soiled working clothes protested at having to give up their table, but the manager threatened them with bodily harm if they didn't move.

"What luck," said Margaret. "The show is just starting."

Cromwell ordered another magnum of champagne as they watched a well-endowed woman step onto the small stage and begin a Dance of the Seven Veils. It wasn't long before the veils dropped away and she was left with a scanty costume that left little to the imagination. Her abdominal muscles rippled as she gyrated and made several lusty contortions. When she was finished, the men in the audience threw coins on the stage.

"Well, that was certainly arousing," Margaret said sarcastically.

A small band began playing and couples moved onto the dance floor, stepping lively to a dance called the Texas Tommy. Butler and Margaret swirled around the floor with gay abandon as if they were one. Marion felt a self-conscious sense of embarrassment at being held close to her boss. In all the years she had worked for him, this was the first time he had ever asked her out. He was an excellent dancer, and she followed his lead gracefully.

The band changed tempo at different times so the dancers could move to the steps of the Turkey Trot and the Bunny Hug. Soon the dancers began to sweat in the confined, airless quarters of the basement. The champagne began to make Marion's head reel and she asked Cromwell if she could sit down for a few minutes.

"Would you mind if I left you for a little while?" Cromwell asked courteously. "I'd like to go upstairs and play a few hands of faro."

Marion was vastly relieved. She was on the verge of exhaustion, and her new shoes were causing discomfort to her feet. "Yes, please do, Mr. Cromwell. I could stand a breather."

Cromwell climbed the wooden stairway and walked slowly through the bustling gambling section until he came to a table where there were no players except the dealer. Two burly men stood behind the dealer and discouraged any customer from sitting at the table.

The dealer looked like he was born from a bull. His head sat like a chiseled rock on top of a neck that was as thick as a tree stump. His black hair was dyed, plastered down with pomade, and parted in the middle. His nose was flattened across his cheeks from being broken numerous times. His limpid eyes looked oddly out of place on a face that had seen more than its share of fists. He had the torso of a beer keg, round and abundant, but hard, without fat. Spider Red Kelly had been a fighter and had once fought James J. Corbett, knocking down the former heavyweight champion twice but getting knocked out himself in the twenty-first round. He looked up at Cromwell's approach.

"Good evening, Mr. Cromwell, I've been expecting you."

Cromwell opened the cover to his watch and glimpsed the hands on the dial. "Forgive me for being eight minutes late, Mr. Kelly. I was unavoidably detained."

Red Kelly smiled, showing a mouth full of gold teeth. "Yes, I would have also been detained if I was in the company of such a lovely lady." He nodded at the table. "Would you care to try your luck?"

Cromwell took out his wallet and counted out ten fifty-dollar National Bank notes printed by his bank under contract with the federal government. Kelly casually placed the bills in a small stack on the side of the table and pushed a stack of copper tokens advertising the saloon across the table. A typical faro layout of a suit of thirteen cards was painted on the table's green felt cover. The suit was in spades from ace to king, with the ace on the dealer's left.

Cromwell placed a token on the jack and one between the five and six in a bet called splitting. Kelly discarded the top card from the dealer box, displaying the next card, called the losing card. It was a ten. If Cromwell had bet on it, he would have lost, since the house wins any wagers placed on the displayed card. Then Kelly pulled the losing card out of the box, revealing the winning card. It was a five, Cromwell won the full bet, not half.

"Beginner's luck," he said as Kelly pushed the winning tokens across the table.

"What is your pleasure, Mr. Cromwell?"

"Nothing, thank you."

"You asked to see me," said Kelly. "What can I do to return the favors you've given me over the years, the generous loans and the help in keeping the police out of my place?"

"I need someone eliminated." Cromwell spoke as if he was ordering a beer.

"Here in the city?" asked Kelly as he dealt another hand.

"No. Denver."

"A man, I hope," said Kelly without looking up from the dealer box. "Place your bet."

Cromwell nodded and moved a token between the queen and jack. "Actually, he's an agent with the Van Dorn Detective Agency."

Kelly paused before pulling a card from the box. "Taking out a Van Dorn agent could have serious repercussions."

"Not if it's done right."

"What's his name?"

"Isaac Bell." Cromwell passed across the picture his sister had given him. "Here's his photo."

Kelly stared at it briefly. "Why do you want him removed?"

"I have my reasons."

Kelly pulled the losing card and revealed the winning card as the queen. Cromwell had won again.

Kelly gazed across the table at Cromwell. "From what I've heard, everyone who's killed a Van Dorn agent has been tracked down and hung."

"They were criminals who stupidly allowed themselves to be run down by detectives from the agency. If done in an efficient manner, Van Dorn will never know who killed Bell or why. Make it look like a random killing or even an accident. Leaving no trace would make it impossible for Van Dorn's agents to retaliate."

Kelly sank slowly back in his chair. "I have to tell you, Cromwell, I don't like it." There was no "Mr. Cromwell."

Cromwell smiled a grim smile. "Would you like it if I paid you twenty thousand dollars for the job?"

Kelly sat up and looked at Cromwell as if he was not sure if he believed him. "Twenty thousand dollars, you say?"

"I want it done by a professional, not some two-bit killer off the street."

"Where do you wish the deed to take place?"

There was never doubt that Kelly would do the job. The saloon owner was knee-deep in any number of criminal activities. Coming under Cromwell's spell for financial gain was a foregone conclusion.

"In Denver. Bell works out of the Van Dorn office in Denver."

"The farther away from San Francisco, the better," Kelly said quietly. "You got yourself a deal, Mr. Cromwell."

The "Mr." was back, and the transaction agreed upon. Cromwell rose from his chair and nodded toward the tokens on the table. "For the dealer," he said, grinning. "I'll have ten thousand in cash delivered to you by noon tomorrow. You'll get the rest when Bell is deceased."

Kelly remained seated. "I understand."

He pushed his way downstairs and through the dancers, who had stopped dancing. He saw they were watching his sister perform an undulating and provocative hootchy-kootchy dance on the stage, to the delight of everyone present. She had loosened her corset and let her nicely coiffed hair down. Her hips swiveled and pulsed sensually to the music of the band. At the table, Butler was sprawled in a drunken haze while Marion stared in awe at Margaret's gyrations.

Cromwell motioned for one of the managers, who also acted as bouncers.

"Sir?"

"Please carry the gentleman to my car."

The bouncer nodded, and with one practiced motion lifted the thoroughly intoxicated Butler to a standing position and threw him over his shoulder. Then the bouncer proceeded up the stairs, carrying Butler's bulk as lightly as if he were a bag of oats.

Cromwell leaned over Marion. "Can you walk to the car?"

She glanced up at him as if angry. "Of course I can walk."

"Then it's time to leave." He took her by the arm and eased her from the chair. Marion, unassisted but wobbly, went up the stairs. Then Cromwell turned his attention to his sister. He was not amused by her scandalous behavior. He grabbed her by the arm hard enough to cause a bruise and hauled her off the stage and out of the saloon to the waiting car at the curb. Butler was passed out in the front seat with Abner while Marion sat glassy-eyed in the back.

Cromwell roughly shoved Margaret into the backseat and followed her, pushing her into one corner. He sat in the middle between the two women as Abner got behind the wheel, started the car, and drove up the street that was ablaze with multicolored lights.

Slowly, Cromwell slid his arm around Marion's shoulders. She looked at him with a vague, unresponsive expression. The champagne had given her a sense of lethargy, but she was not drunk. Her mind was still clear and sharp. His hand squeezed one shoulder and there was a small pause in her breathing. She could feel his body pressing against hers in the narrow confines of the seat.

There was a time when Marion had found her boss appealing and felt a deep attraction to him. But in the years she had worked for him, he had made no effort to bridge the gap between them. Now, suddenly, after all this time, he was showing an interest in her. Strangely, there was no emotion or arousal surging within her. She felt as if she were repelled by him and she couldn't understand why.

Marion was relieved there were no further moves on his part. The one arm remained snaked around her waist and his hand rested lightly on her shoulder until Abner stopped the Rolls in front of her apartment house. Cromwell stepped to the sidewalk and helped her from the car.

"Good night, Marion," he said, holding her hand. "I trust you had an interesting evening."

It was as if she saw now something deep within him that she had never seen before and she felt repulsed by his touch. "It will be an evening I'll long remember," she said honestly. "I hope Mr. Butler and your sister recover."

"They'll be hungover tomorrow, and justly so," he said with a tight smile. "I'll see you Monday morning. There is a pile of correspondence I have to dictate. I want to have a clean desk when I leave on a business trip on Friday."

"You're leaving again so soon?"

"A bankers' conference in Denver. I must attend."

"Until Monday morning, then," she said with vast relief as he released her hand.

Marion climbed the steps to the door but turned and gazed at the Rolls-Royce as it pulled away into the street. Her mind acted without command. Things between her employer and herself would never be the same. There was a coldness about him that she was not aware of before and she cringed as she remembered his touch. All of a sudden, the lingering smell of the dance hall's smoke and sweat on her clothes sickened her.

She rushed upstairs to her room, turned on the faucets of her bathtub, frantically removed her clothes, and slipped into the soapy water to remove all memory of the decadent evening.

"What was your little meeting with Red Kelly all about?" asked Margaret after they let off Marion at her apartment.

"I hired him for a little job."

She stared at his face as it was reflected by the light of the passing streetlamps. "What kind of a job?"

"He's going to take care of Isaac Bell," he said matter-of-factly.

"You can't murder a Van Dorn agent!" Margaret gasped. "Every peace officer in the country would come after you."

Cromwell laughed. "Not to worry, dear sister. I

instructed Kelly to administer only enough damage to keep Bell in the hospital for a few months. That's all. Call it a warning."

Cromwell had blatantly lied to his sister. He would act surprised when Bell's murder was announced and claim the agent's death had been a mistake, that Kelly had gotten carried away. Inciting his sister's anger, he decided, was a small price to pay for eradicating the man who had become his worst enemy.

16

"Give it another coat," Cromwell ordered the two men painting his boxcar. The color had been the earth brown that most freight cars had been painted since the early days of the railroad. But Tuscan red was the newer color used by Southern Pacific to standardize their vast fleet of freight cargo haulers. Cromwell wanted a second coat because the O'BRIAN FURNITURE COMPANY, DENVER still bled through the freshly dried first coat.

Margaret, dressed in a woolen dress and short jacket to keep her warm against the cool breeze blowing in from the ocean through the Golden Gate, held a parasol against a light early-morning mist that fell in the city. They stood watching the painters on the loading dock of an empty warehouse her brother had leased under a pseudonym.

"Can you trust them?" she asked.

"The painters?" He stared at the four men busy brushing paint on the boxcar. "To them, it's just another job, another boxcar that needs to be tidied up. As long as they're well paid, they don't ask questions."

"About time you changed the name," she said. "Some sheriff or a Van Dorn detective is bound to discover that an O'Brian Furniture freight car was present in five of the towns that were robbed."

"The same thought crossed my mind," he said.

"What are you going to call it this time?"

"Nothing," answered Cromwell. "It will look just like another freight car belonging to the Southern Pacific Railroad."

"You could buy and decorate a new one. Why keep this old relic?"

"Because it looks like an old relic," he said with a slight laugh. "Built in 1890. The railroad is still using this model. I prefer it to look tired and worn from many years and thousands of miles of hauling freight. And because its outward appearance is so ordinary, no one would suspect its true purpose. Even your Mr. Hotshot Bell could never begin to guess its real purpose."

"Don't underestimate Bell. He's smart enough to get wise to your traveling hotel suite."

He gave her a sour look. "Not that smart. And even if he smells a rat, it's too late. The O'Brian Furniture car no longer exists."

Cromwell was proud of his aged boxcar. It was thirty-four feet long, with a capacity of forty thousand pounds. Empty, it weighed twelve thousand. Once the second coat was dry, the car would be finished off with the proper signage on its wooden sides, which would include a serial number under the letters SP, for Southern Pacific. The capacity and unloaded weight also would be lettered on one side, while the SP insignia sunrise – a white circle with SOUTHERN arched across the top, PACIFIC arched across the bottom, and LINES across the middle – would be painted on the opposite side. When finished, the boxcar would look like any one of thousands of cars belonging to the Southern Pacific.

Even the serial number, 16173, was correct. Cromwell had arranged for the number to be lifted from a car in the middle of a railyard, scrapped, and then transferred to his rolling suite.

Nothing was ever left to chance. Every move was carefully thought out, then rehearsed and rehearsed again and again. All possible contingencies were considered and dealt with. Nothing escaped Cromwell's attention, down to the last detail. No bandit in the history of the United States, including Jesse James and Butch Cassidy put together, came close to matching him in the number of successful robberies he pulled off and the amount of loot he collected. Or the number of people killed.

At the mention of Bell's name, Margaret's mind traveled back to when they danced together at the Brown Palace Hotel. She cursed herself for wanting to reach out and touch him. The mere thought of it sent a shiver down her spine. She had known many men, a great number of them intimately. But none had affected her as much as when she was in Bell's arms. It was a wave of yearning she could neither understand nor control. She began to wonder if she would ever see him again, knowing deep inside it would be extremely dangerous. If they ever did meet, he surely would learn her true identity and find a path to her brother Jacob.

"Let's leave," she said, angry at herself for allowing her emotions to lose control.

Cromwell saw the faraway look in her eyes but chose to ignore it. "As you wish. I'll return tomorrow to oversee the finished results."

They turned and walked through a door into the warehouse. Cromwell paused to lock the door and set a bar in place so no one could enter. Their footsteps echoed throughout the deserted interior of the building. The only furnishings were in one corner, two desks, and a counter that looked like the tellers' windows at a bank.

"A pity you can't lease this space out and put it to good use," said Margaret, fussing with her hat that had tilted to one side of her head when the pin slipped out.

"I must have a place to park the boxcar," Cromwell replied. "So long as it sits unnoticed on a siding, next to the loading dock of an empty warehouse whose owner cannot be traced, so much the better."

She gave her brother a suspicious glance and said, "You have that look on again."

"What look?"

"The one that means you're planning another robbery."

"I can't fool my own sister," he said with a grin.

"I suppose it's a waste of time trying to talk you into retiring from the robbery business."

He took her hand and patted it. "A man can't bear to give up a pursuit in which he excels."

She sighed in defeat. "All right, where this time?"

"I haven't decided yet. The first step is to make discreet inquiries in banking circles about payrolls. Then I have to select towns that have railroads and sidings for freight trains. The getaway is the most important part of the operation. Next is a study of the streets and location of the bank. Finally, I have to carefully plan the actual robbery itself, the timing and my disguises."

Margaret stopped beside the desks and counter. "And this is where you rehearse."

He nodded. "After our agents obtain a layout of the interior of the bank and I arrange the furnishings accordingly."

"You have it down to a fine science."

"I try," he said loftily.

"Your method of operation is becoming too polished, too sophisticated," she cautioned him.

He took her by the arm and gently squeezed. "I wouldn't have it any other way."

17

Bell came to the office directly from the train and found Irvine and Curtis already in the conference room waiting for him. He could tell the news was good because there were no frowns or grim looks on their faces. The jovial mood was enhanced by Irvine smoking a cigar and Curtis pulling a silver cigarette case from his coat pocket.

"You two seem to be in good spirits," said Bell, setting down his suitcase.

"We found some leads," Curtis said, lighting a cigarette. "Nothing earth-shattering, but a few small pieces to fit in the puzzle."

"How about you, Isaac, did you turn up anything?" asked Irvine.

Before Bell could answer, Agnes Murphy entered the conference room carrying a tray with three cups and a coffeepot. "Sorry to interrupt," she said sweetly, "but I thought you gentlemen might like some coffee."

Bell took the tray from her and set it on the long table. "That's very kind of you, Agnes."

She turned and started for the door. "I'll be right back." In less than a minute, she returned with a sugar bowl and cream pitcher. "I didn't forget. I just couldn't carry it all."

"You're a lifesaver," said Curtis with a broad smile, as he lightly kissed her on the cheek.

Bell and Irvine exchanged glances, smiling. They both knew that Curtis and Agnes were just pals and always teasing each other. Agnes gathered her skirts as she turned, left the conference room, and closed the door.

"Besides the coffee," said Bell, "it was thoughtful of her to close the door."

Curtis blew a smoke ring toward the ceiling. "She knows the score. Agnes has no more respect for Alexander than we do."

"You were about to say . . ." Irvine prompted Bell.

"I discovered that, besides a missing finger, he probably has red hair. And rides a motorcycle, which he's used on more than one robbery." Bell reached into his pocket and lifted out a small silk sack, opened it, and spilled the cartridge out on the table. "We now know the Butcher Bandit uses a thirty-eight-caliber Colt automatic. This shell casing was found under a carpet. The killer somehow missed it since he hasn't left any shells at his other bank hits. Sheriff Murphy of Bishee was a smart man and had the country coroner remove the bullets from the murder victims. They all came from a thirty-eight Colt."

"We can check sales of all thirty-eight Colt automatics," said Curtis.

"There couldn't be more than ten thousand of them," Irvine replied sarcastically. "It would take ten agents years to check out every gun dealer, salesman, and hardware store owner who sells thirty-eight Colt automatics."

"Art is right," Bell said as he stared at the brass cartridge. "It would be a tremendous long shot."

Curtis grinned like a fox. "Not if we have a lead to where the bandit hides out. Then we can check out dealers in the area."

"Good thinking," Bell agreed, not knowing what Curtis was about to reveal. "In the meantime, I'll send it off to Chicago and see if our agency experts can pull any fingerprints." He relaxed in a chair and tilted it back on two legs, propping a foot against the table. "Now, let me hear what you two have unearthed."

Irvine opened a bound ledger and placed the book on the table in front of Bell and Curtis. "I hit pay dirt in Elkhorn, Nevada. They had recorded the serial numbers of the fifty-dollar bills in their vault the day before the robbery."

"I can understand why," said Bell. "Fifties are counterfeited more than any other bill. As their bookkeeper itemized the bills, he must have studied each one and made sure they weren't bogus."

Irvine tapped the entries in the book with his finger as he looked at Bell. "You can request the Chicago office to put out bulletins to banks around the West to be on the lookout for them. Fifties will be easier to trace than fives, tens, or twenties."

"And a lot easier than ones," Curtis added.

"I'll see to it," Bell assured Irvine.

"I made a few inquiries on my own and actually came up with two banks in San Francisco where three of the bills showed up."

"Good work," said Bell. He then focused on Curtis. "Now, how about you, Arthur? Any luck on your end?"

"Did you find any passenger trains the killer might have escaped on?" Irvine queried.

"No. But freight trains are a different story."

"Weren't they searched by the posses?"

Curtis shook his head. "Not the ones that were loaded and locked."

"So where did you go from there?" inquired Bell.

Curtis broke out into a smile that spread and beamed. "It took many hours of digging in musty old railroad company records, but I did manage to make an interesting discovery. I found three cars that were on the sidings of towns that were robbed. Boxcar serial number 15758 was present in Virginia City and Bisbee during the robberies. In Virginia City, its cargo manifest was listed as fifty bales of barbed wire to be transported to a ranch in Southern California. Boxcar 15758 was empty when it sat on a siding waiting to be switched to another train in Bisbee."

"Empty," Irvine repeated, stirring restlessly in his chair.

"Yes, empty. It had hauled a load of pottery from Las Cruces, New Mexico, to Tucson, before being sent empty back to El Paso."

"So we can scratch that one," muttered Bell. "What about the others?"

Curtis referred to his notes. "Number 18122 was present at Elkhorn, Nevada, and Grand Junction, Colorado, when their banks were robbed. It was on the siding at Grand Junction waiting to be switched to a train to take it to Los Angeles. Its cargo was sixty cases of wine. At Elkhorn, it carried a load of mattresses, from a factory in Sacramento, California."

"So much for 18122," said Irvine. "It's not likely the bandit escaped to different locations."

Curtis fairly beamed. "I saved the best for last." Rising and walking to a blackboard, he wrote O'BRIAN FURNITURE COMPANY, DENVER on the black surface. Then he turned with a pleased expression on his face. "Now we come to a boxcar that was present at five robberies."

Both Bell and Irvine sat up suddenly in their chairs as Curtis caught their fixed attention. The agent had taken the bull by the horns and delved into an area no one had thought to go.

Bell, surprised at Curtis's unexpected revelation, said, "The car was in five towns on the day their banks were robbed?"

"I've made a list of towns, times, and its final destination."

Irvine nearly spilled his coffee as he set it back on the tray. "Don't you mean destinations, plural?"

"No. Destination, singular." Curtis laughed softly.

"In every instance, the furniture car from Denver went to San Francisco. I could find no record of it ever having been hauled to Denver or anywhere else. I can only assume it was a façade the bandit used to escape the posses."

Bell stared at the writing on the blackboard. "I'll bet a month's pay that a check of furniture stores in Denver will prove O'Brian Furniture does not exist."

"I think that goes without saying," Irvine summed up.

Bell turned to Curtis. "When was the last Southern Pacific Railroad account of the car?"

"It was put on a siding in the San Francisco railyards two weeks ago. At my last inquiry, it was still there."

"Then we've got to find and search it."

"And stake it out," said Irvine.

"That, too," replied Bell. "But we must be very careful not to alert the bandit that we're closing in on him."

Curtis lit another cigarette. "I'll leave on the first train in the morning for San Francisco."

"Irvine and I will join you." Bell then turned his attention to Irvine. "You mentioned that three bills turned up in San Francisco."

Irvine nodded. "That's right. One at the Cromwell National Bank of San Francisco and two at the Crocker National Bank."

Bell smiled for the first time. "It would seem, gentlemen, all roads lead to San Francisco."

"It's beginning to look that way," Curtis agreed, his enthusiasm growing.

The two agents stared expectantly at Bell as he studied the map with the flags marking the terrible crimes committed by the Butcher Bandit. The evidence was almost infinitesimal and could easily lead to dead ends. Yet there was satisfaction in what the three Van Dorn agents had gleaned. Meager as it was, they had little else to go on. But it was enough for a plan to form in Bell's mind.

"It might be like betting on a plow horse at the racetrack, but I think we may have an opportunity to trap the bandit."

"You have a plan?" asked Irvine.

"Suppose we plant stories in the local San Francisco newspapers revealing that a million-dollar payroll is being shipped by special train to a bank in a town populated by several thousand miners. The large amount would be because the mine owners have declared a special bonus for the workers to avert a threatened strike called by the miners' union over the demand for substantially increased wages."

Curtis pondered Bell's proposition and said, "The bandit could easily check out the story and find it's false."

"Not if we have one of us sitting in the telegraph office when the inquiry comes in and give the appropriate reply."

"We might even get lucky and discover who sent the telegram," said Irvine.

Bell nodded. "There is that, too."

Irvine gazed into his coffee cup as if he was a fortune-teller reading tea leaves. "It's a thousand-to-one shot. We all know that."

"No doubt about it," Bell said, "it's worth a try. And, if the scheme fails, we might still stumble onto another lead to the bandit."

"Got a mining town in mind?" Curtis asked.

"Telluride, Colorado," answered Bell. "Because the town is situated in a box canyon. Telluride is also the area where its miners struck the mine owners in 1901 and 1903, so another strike is quite plausible."

"If the O'Brian Furniture freight car shows up," said Curtis, "we'll know our man took the bait."

"Once the train pulls it onto the Telluride siding, the only way out is the way it came." Irvine sighed and smiled contentedly. "The bandit will be trapped and have no means of escape."

The atmosphere in the conference room crackled with expectation and hope. What had almost seemed like a lost cause was coming together. Three pairs of eyes trained on the giant wall map, traveled west toward the Pacific Ocean, and focused on the port city of San Francisco.

In the elevator that took him down to the street for his walk to the Brown Palace, Bell felt jubilant. Win, lose, or draw, the end of the game was in sight. Granted, it was still hazy and indistinct, but the cards were finally falling in Bell's favor. His thoughts turned to Rose and he found himself wondering for the hundredth time what connection she had with the Butcher Bandit.

What woman could be close to a man who murdered women and children? He began to believe that she might be as rotten as the bandit, if not more so.

Bell stepped from the Brown Palace elevator and walked to his suite. He pulled the key from his pant pocket and inserted it in the door lock. Before he could turn the key, the door slipped open a crack. The latch had not been fully engaged when the door had been closed.

Bell paused and tensed. His first thought was that the maid had forgotten to close the door and spring the bolt. It was a logical assumption, but an inner wisdom made him suspicious. The perception of something being not quite right had saved him on more than one occasion.

Bell had made many enemies during his years as a detective with Van Dorn. Several of the men he had captured and seen tried and sentenced to prison had vowed they would come after him. Three had tried and two had died.

If someone was waiting for him inside his room, it wouldn't be with a gun, he reasoned. Gunshots would echo throughout the hotel and bring a dozen staff running. For a criminal to escape from the ninth floor, he either would have to wait for an elevator or run down the stairs, neither a good choice for a successful escape.

Bell was aware that he was probably overexaggerating the threat, which could very well be nonexistent. But he hadn't survived this long without a suspicious mind. If someone was waiting inside his suite, he thought, they would do their dirty work with a knife.

He removed his hat and dropped it. Before it hit the carpet, his derringer was in his hand, an over-and-under, two-barrel, .41 caliber small handgun that packed a surprisingly heavy punch at close range.

Bell waggled the key in the door as if he was turning the lock. He pushed the door open and hesitated, staring around the foyer of the suite and the living room beyond before he entered. The smell of cigarette smoke greeted his nostrils, confirming Bell's suspicions. He only rarely smoked a cigar and then only with brandy after a gourmet dinner. With the derringer in hand, he stepped into the suite. Death, like a third man, was waiting inside.

A man was sitting on a settee reading a newspaper. At Bell's approach, he laid the paper aside and revealed a face as ugly as sin. The black hair was greasy and slicked flat. His face looked like it had been stomped on by a mule, and he had the body of a state fair prizewining boar. His eyes were strangely soft and friendly, a guise that fooled many of his victims. Bell was not fooled: he could see the man had the strength to spring like a tiger.

"How did you get in?" Bell asked simply.

The stranger held up a key. "Skeleton key," he said

in a voice that came like a rock crusher. "I never leave home without one."

"What is your name?"

"It won't matter if you know my name. You'll never get a chance to use it. But since you've asked, it's Red Kelly."

Bell's photographic memory shifted into gear and the recollection of a report he'd once read came back. "Yes, the infamous Red Kelly, boxer, Barbary Coast saloonkeeper, and murderer. You fought a good battle against world champion James J. Corbett. I once studied a report on you in the event you ever wandered beyond the California border. This is a mistake on your part. You have protection from crooked politicians that keeps you from getting extradited for crimes in other states, but that won't help you in Colorado. You're subject to arrest here."

"And who is going to arrest me?" said Kelly showing an expanse of gold teeth. "You?"

Bell stood loosely, waiting, and expecting a move from Kelly. "You wouldn't be the first."

"I know all about you, pretty boy," said Kelly contemptuously. "You'll bleed just like the other poor slobs I've put in the grave."

"How many detectives and police?"

Kelly grinned nastily. "Three that I can remember. After a while, the numbers began to fade."

"Your days of murder are over, Kelly," Bell said calmly.

"That'll be the day, pretty boy. If you think you can bully me with that popgun in your hand, you're wasting your breath."

"You don't think I could kill you with it?" Bell said.

"You'd never get the chance," Kelly retorted coldly.

There it was. Bell caught it instantly. The sudden shift in the eyes. He swung into a crouch and, in the blink of an eye, aimed and fired a shot into the forehead of the man who was creeping up behind him from where he'd been, hidden by a curtain. The report reverberated out the open door and throughout the atrium of the hotel.

Kelly glanced at the body of his henchman with all the interest of a horse that had stepped on a prairie dog. Then he smiled at Bell. "Your reputation is well founded. You must have eyes in the back of your head."

"You came to kill me," said Bell evenly. "Why?"

"It's a job, nothing more."

"Who paid you?"

"Not necessary for you to know." Kelly laid aside the paper and slowly got to his feet.

"Don't try for the gun in the belt behind your back," Bell said, the derringer as steady as a branch on an oak tree.

Kelly flashed his gold teeth again. "I don't need a gun."

He sprang forward, his powerful legs propelling

across the room as if he had been shot from a cannon.

What saved Bell in those two seconds was the span between them, a good eight feet. Any less distance and Kelly would have been all over him like an avalanche. As it was, Kelly struck him like a battering ram, a glancing blow that knocked Bell sideways over a chair and onto the grass green carpet. But not before he pulled the trigger of the derringer and sent a bullet into Kelly's right shoulder.

The brute was stopped in his tracks but did not fall. He was too powerful, too muscular, to fold with a bullet that did not penetrate his heart or brain. He contemplated the spreading of crimson on his shirt with the detached look of a surgeon. Then he grinned fiendishly. "Your little popgun only holds two bullets, pretty boy. Now it's empty."

"I wish you would stop calling me pretty boy," said Bell, leaping to his feet.

Now it was Kelly's turn to reach behind his back and retrieve his Colt revolver. He was just bringing it level to pull the trigger when Bell hurled his derringer like a baseball pitcher receiving the signal from the catcher to throw a fastball. At four feet away, he couldn't miss. The little gun, solid as a piece of quartz, thudded off Kelly's face just above the nose and between the eyes.

Blood gushed from the gash and quickly covered the lower half of Kelly's face. The blow staggered him more than the slug in his shoulder. There was no gasp of pain, no bloodcurdling cry. He made no sound other than a great sigh. The gun was still in his hand, but he did not lift it to aim. He couldn't. Bell put his head down and charged the strong man like a porpoise into a great white shark, accelerating with every step, thrusting his head into Kelly's stomach with all his strength. The ex-boxer merely grunted and brushed Bell away, throwing him halfway across the room with a strength nothing less than phenomenal.

Bell crashed into a wall with a crunch that forced the breath from his lungs. If the impact had been any harder, he'd have been in traction for two months. But his bone-jarring charge had not been in vain. During the collision of his one hundred eighty-five pounds against Kelly's two-fifty, he had snatched the revolver from the hand of the killer.

There was no command to cease another assault, no "Stop or I'll shoot." Bell had been through the mill and knew you don't waste words on a killer dead set on sending you to a marble slab at the county coroner's. He had no illusions about beating Kelly in a man-to-man fight. The murderer was stronger and more ruthless. Bell barely got off two shots before Kelly recovered enough to reach out and grasp Bell around the neck with the ferocity of a gorilla, his massive hands choking the life out of the detective. He fell against Bell, pressing him into the carpet, his massive weight crushing Bell's torso and pinning his arms so he couldn't fire the Colt again. Kelly squeezed calmly and purposely, as though the bullets he had taken were a mere annoyance.

Bell couldn't move, and there was no reaching up in an attempt to pull off the fingers digging into his neck. Kelly's strength went way beyond Bell's. Bell didn't doubt that he wasn't the first man Kelly had strangled. Unless he did something very rapidly, he wouldn't be the last. Blackness was edging his line of vision, and getting darker by the moment.

What stunned Bell more than the realization that he was only seconds away from death was what happened to the two bullets he had pumped into Kelly. He was certain he had struck the Goliath in the body. Bell looked up into two eyes that were as dark as evil and the blood that had turned the lower face into a horrific mask of crimson. What was keeping him alive, why wasn't his strength ebbing? The man wasn't human.

Then, perceptibly, Bell felt the pressure begin to ease slightly. Rather than try to pry the hands from around his neck, Bell reached up and embedded his thumbs in Kelly's expressionless eyes, knowing it would be the final move before darkness closed over him. In a violent, corkscrew motion, Bell twisted his body out from under Kelly.

The big boxer groaned and covered his eyes with his hands. Unseeing, he crawled toward Bell, who kicked out viciously, catching Kelly in the stomach. Only then did he see the two bullet holes seeping blood through Kelly's shirt below the rib cage. What kept him going? Bell wondered. He should have died before now. But, instead, Kelly reached out and grabbed Bell by the leg.

Bell felt himself being pulled across the carpet, now stained and soaked with Kelly's blood. He lashed out with his free foot. It bounced off Kelly, who acted as if he never felt it. The grip on Bell's calf tightened. Fingernails dug through his pants into his flesh. He was pulled closer to Kelly, seeing an agonized face, the eyes glaring with hatred.

It was time to end this ghastly fight. Bell's right hand still held the Colt. With deadly calm, he raised the barrel until the muzzle was only inches from Kelly's face, deliberately pulled the trigger, and sent a .44 caliber bullet into Kelly's right eye.

There was no terrible scream or horrible gurgling sound. Kelly exhaled an audible gasp from his throat and rolled over on the carpet like some great beast in its death throes crumpling to the earth.

Bell sat up on the floor and massaged his throat, panting from the exertion. He turned his head and stared at the doorway as men came rushing into the suite. They stopped in stunned shock at the sight of the sea of blood and the great hump of a man whose face was unrecognizable because of the bloody, congealing mask. The face looked particularly grotesque due to the gold teeth showing through the open lips that slowly became coated red.

Kelly had died hard, and for what? Money? A debt? A vendetta? Not the latter. Bell had never launched an investigation against the Barbary Coast giant. Someone must have paid him to kill and paid him extremely well.

Bell wondered if he would ever know the answer.

The next morning, Bell stepped out of the big porcelain bathtub, toweled off the water that dripped down his body, and gazed in the mirror. His throat didn't look pretty. It was swollen, with purple bruises so obvious that he could see the shape of Red Kelly's fingers where they had dug into his flesh. He put on a clean white shirt and was pleased to see that the high, starched collar, though it chafed his tender skin, covered the bruises.

They weren't the only purplish green marks on his aching body. He had several from falling over the chair, and from being thrown across the room and into the wall by Kelly's brute strength. They were tender to the touch and would not fade anytime soon.

After dressing in his trademark linen suit, Bell left the hotel and stopped off at the Western Union office and sent a telegram to Joseph Van Dorn that told of the attempt on his life. When he came slowly through the door of the office, Agnes Murphy openly stared at him. She stood up with a look of motherly concern in her eyes. "Oh, Mr. Bell. I heard about your unfortunate incident. I do hope you're all right."

"A few bruises, Agnes, nothing more."

Curtis and Irvine heard his voice and came from the conference room, followed by Alexander from his office. Both agents vigorously shook his hand – a bit too vigorously, Bell thought, wincing at the discomfort that traveled over his aching body. Alexander merely stood back, as if he was a spectator in an audience.

"Glad to see you alive and kicking," said Curtis. "We heard it was quite a fight."

"It was as close as I ever came to buying the farm," said Bell.

"After talking to you over the phone," said Curtis, "I wired your identification of Red Kelly to our San Francisco office. They're going to check out Kelly and any of his clients who might have wanted you eliminated."

"A terrible thing," Alexander said without emotion. "Unthinkable, that someone would attempt to assassinate a Van Dorn agent."

Bell gave Alexander a long hard look. "I can only wonder how Kelly knew where I was staying."

"Kelly was a well-known crime boss on the Barbary Coast in San Francisco," said Irvine. "Could any of your former friends who you put in jail or friends and families of those who were executed because you arrested them be from San Francisco?"

"None that I can name," answered Bell. "If I had to make a guess, I'd have to say the Butcher Bandit was behind it."

"Knowing you were on the case," said Irvine, "he'd certainly have a motive."

Alexander said, "We won't rest until we get to the bottom of this." To Bell, his words rang hollow. "I can't tell you how glad I am that you are alive and well." Then he turned and walked back to his office.

As soon as he was out of earshot, Bell said, "Another nail in the coffin, gentlemen. The key to the bandit's whereabouts *is* San Francisco."

18

When Bell, Irvine, and Curtis stepped off the ferry from Oakland and entered the huge Ferry Building, they found themselves in a three-story-tall hall with repeating arches and skylights overhead. They exited onto the Embarcadero, at the foot of Market Street. While Irvine and Curtis went to hail a motor cab, Bell turned and looked up at the two-hundred-forty-foot clock tower, modeled after the twelfth-century Giralda bell tower in Seville, Spain. The long hands on the expansive dial read eleven minutes past four.

Bell checked the time on his watch and duly noted that the ferry building clock was one minute fast.

Because of the huge crowds in the terminal after pouring off four ferryboats at the same time, the agents were unable to find a free motor cab. Bell stopped a horse-drawn carriage, haggled a price with the driver, and commandeered it to carry them to the Palace Hotel on Montgomery Street. As they settled in the carriage, Curtis spoke to Bell.

"How do you plan to handle the Van Dorn San Francisco office?"

"We're having dinner with the district director. His name is Horace Bronson. I once worked with him in New Orleans. He's a fine fellow and very efficient.

When I sent him a telegram, he wired back and offered every cooperation in his power. He promised to send his agents out to obtain the names of people from gun dealers who might have purchased a thirty-eight-caliber Colt automatic."

Irivne rolled an unlit cigar around in his fingers. "On my end, I'll start with the Cromwell and Crocker banks and see if they can help trace any of the stolen currency serial numbers."

Bell said to Irvine, "You might check out the other major banks, too, such as Wells Fargo and the Bank of Italy, in case any stolen bills might be in their possession. If the bandit is from San Francisco, it stands to reason he'd have passed them around town."

"We have our work cut out for us," said Curtis. "I'll see if I can't track down the O'Brian Furniture car."

Bell stretched out his feet in the carriage and said, "After we meet with Bronson, I'll write out news releases about the fake currency shipment to the San Miguel Valley Bank in Telluride and prevail upon the editors of the city's major newspapers to run the story."

The carriage reached the magnificent Palace Hotel and turned into the Garden Court, the hotel's elegant carriage entrance that was commanded by seven stories of gleaming white marble balconies with over a hundred ornamented columns. Light from above filtered through a huge stained-glass-domed skylight.

Bell paid off the coachman as porters took the luggage inside. The three Van Dorn detectives walked into a vast, majestic lobby. After registering, they went up to their rooms in a redwood-paneled hydraulic elevator. Bell arranged for the rooms to be joined together to create a large suite.

"Tell you what," said Bell to Irvine and Curtis. "It's almost five o'clock, so nothing can be accomplished today. Let's get cleaned up. Then we'll go out, have a good meal, get a good night's sleep, and start beating the bushes first thing in the morning."

"Sounds good to me," Irvine said, his stomach growling, since they had eaten nothing in the last eight hours.

"What have you got in mind for a restaurant?" asked Curtis.

"Bronson is a member of the Bohemian Club. He's arranged for us to eat with him in their dining room."

"Sounds exclusive."

Bell smiled. "You don't know *how* exclusive."

At eight o'clock, the men exited a motor cab at the Taylor Street entrance of the powerful and elite Bohemian Club. Founded in 1872 as a gathering place for newspaper journalists and men of the arts and literature, its members included Mark Twain, Bret Harte, Ambrose Bierce, and Jack London. Over the years, powerful and influential men who made up the business elite of the city joined and soon became the dominant group. No women were allowed, and wives and unmarried guests of the members had to enter through a back door.

This evening, women were permitted into the dining room because Enrico Caruso was being honored and he insisted upon his wife being present. The club directors considered it a special occasion and so had made it one of the few exceptions.

Irvine and Curtis followed Bell into the main reception room and stood for a moment until a tall man with a youthful face in a well-conditioned, muscular body that gave the impression of towering height came forward and shook Bell's hand vigorously. "Isaac, how good to see you."

"The pleasure is mine," returned Bell, pleased to see an old friend and prepared for a bone-crushing handshake. "You're looking fit."

"I still work at it." He nodded at Irvine and Curtis and smiled. "Hello, I'm Horace Bronson."

His voice was husky and went with the broad shoulders that looked as though they were about to burst the seams of his neatly tailored gray suit. His facial features made him look like a schoolboy under a thick forest of sun-bleached hair.

Bell made the introductions and was amused to see the tight expressions on his agents' faces and their eyes blink as Bronson compressed their hands in his big paw. Though he headed up an office with ten agents in a major city, Bronson deferred to Bell, who outranked him in the agency. He also greatly admired

Bell for his wide experience and enviable reputation in apprehending lawbreakers. And he was also indebted to the master detective who had recommended him to Van Dorn for the post in San Francisco.

"Come this way into the dining room," he said warmly. "The club is noted for its gourmet fare and fine wine."

Bronson led the way from the imposing grand lobby into the large and impressive dining room finished majestically with mahogany on the floors, walls, and ceiling. He had a few words with the maitre d'.

Bronson put his hand on Bell's shoulder. "I asked him for a table I usually reserve for talking business. It's in a corner of the dining room where we can't be overheard."

The maitre d' showed them to a table off by itself but with an unimpaired view of the other diners throughout the room. A waiter was standing by, who laid napkins in their laps and waited until Bronson perused the wine list and made his selection. As soon as the waiter was out of earshot, Bronson relaxed and looked at Bell.

"I checked out the number of businesses that have sold thirty-eight-caliber Colt automatics since they were introduced on the market. The total comes to sixty-seven. I've put four agents on the investigation. They should have an answer in two or three days – earlier, if they get lucky."

"Thank you, Horace," said Bell. "That will save us much-needed time to look into our other leads."

"It's the least I can do," Bronson said with a broad smile. "Besides, Mr. Van Dorn ordered me to give you my fullest cooperation."

"We'll need all the help we can get."

"Do you have any other leads on the Butcher Bandit?"

"I'll have to swear you to secrecy. I've found that the bandit has spies inside our agency."

"You're safe confiding with me," Bronson said with growing concern. "It's hard to believe such an intrusion can happen. Does Van Dorn know about it?"

Bell nodded. "He knows."

Then Bell gave Bronson a rundown on the evidence, slim as it was, that led them to San Francisco. He explained Irvine's tracking of the serial numbers on the money, Curtis's discovery of the getaway freight car, and his own revelation about the bandit's hair and missing finger. He told it carefully, with the details but without embellishment. Irvine and Curtis also added comments on what they had uncovered during their investigations. When Bell finished his report, Bronson sat silent for several moments.

At last, he said, "Your investigation has shown great progress, Isaac. You have something tangible when there was nothing a few weeks ago. But, unfortunately, it's hardly enough to identify the bandit."

"No, it's not," Bell agreed, "but it's a thread that can lead to a string that can lead to a rope."

The wine that Bronson selected, a California chardonnay reserve from Charles Krug, the oldest winery in the Napa Valley, arrived and, after the proper tasting ceremony, was poured. As they studied the menu, all talk of the bandit was put on hold while they enjoyed the wine and made their selections.

"What intrigues you?" Bronson asked Bell.

"The kitchen has sweetbreads in béchamel sauce. I'll give them the taste test since I am a lover of sweetbreads."

"Aren't they bull's testicles?" said Curtis.

"You're thinking of Rocky Mountain oysters," said Bronson, laughing.

"Prized by gourmets throughout the world," explained Bell, "they are the thymus glands of veal. There are two glands, one in the throat and the other near the heart. The heart sweetbread is considered the most delicious by chefs—"

Suddenly, Bell stopped in midsentence and stared intently across the dining room. His violet eyes narrowed, as if focusing in the distance. His relaxed position stiffened and he sat up, as if lost in preoccupation.

"What is it, Isaac?" asked Irvine. "You look like you've seen the Resurrection."

"I have," Bell murmured, his eyes staring at a couple who had walked in the door and were talking to the maitre d'. They were a striking pair that turned every head in the dining room. Both had the same flame red hair. The woman was as tall as the man, who was slight in stature.

She wore a yellow two-piece dress suit of the

Empire style, with a gored skirt that created an elongated trumpet-bell shape with a short trail on the floor. The blouse was embroidered with lace trim and worn under a short jacket that had an extremely low neckline which allowed her to show off a magnificent diamond necklace. In an era dominated by formality, her fashionable *Merry Widow*–wide hat with lavish feather trim was perfect for a dressy function. A fox boa was draped around her shoulders.

The man wore an expensive black suit with vest. A large gold chain hung from one pocket and threaded through a buttonhole to another pocket that held a watch. A large diamond-encrusted fob hung from it. There was a confident look in his eyes that missed nothing. He surveyed the room as if he owned it. Seeing several people he knew, he smiled slightly and graciously bowed his head. The couple was shown to a table in the center of the dining room in a position highly visible to the other diners. It was a rehearsed entrance that was carried off with sophisticated elegance.

"Who is that couple who made the grand entrance?" Bell asked Bronson.

"That's Jacob Cromwell, who owns the Cromwell National Bank. He's a member of the Bohemian Club. The handsome woman at his side is his sister."

"Sister?"

"Yes, her name is Margaret, a member of the social elite. Keeps busy with charity work. She and her brother are very wealthy and influential. They live on Nob Hill."

"So her name is Margaret Cromwell," Bell said quietly. "I knew her in Denver as Rose Manteca."

Irvine looked at Bell. "Is she the woman you told us about who was a spy for the Butcher Bandit?"

"Unless she has a twin sister," Bell answered, "that's her."

"Impossible," said Bronson in a tone heavy with derision. "The assumption is utterly ridiculous. She and her brother do more for San Francisco than half the wealthy of the city put together. They support orphan homes, the humane society for the lost and wandering animals of the city, and city beautification. They give large donations to worthy causes. They are highly respected and admired."

"He makes a strong case," said Curtis. "If the Cromwells own a large San Francisco bank and are already wealthy, what's their percentage in robbing and killing?"

"Is Miss Cromwell married?" Bell asked Bronson.

"No, she's single, and has the reputation of being on the wild side."

"Could you have been wrong about her being a spy for the bandit?" Irvine suggested.

Bell gazed intently at Margaret Cromwell, taking in every detail of her face. She seemed deep in conversation with her brother and did not turn in his direction. "I could be mistaken," he murmured without conviction. "The resemblance between her and the woman I met in Denver is uncanny."

"I know Cromwell personally," said Bronson. "He

cooperated with Van Dorn on a bank swindle that a gang of con men were using to bilk local businesses. I'll introduce you."

Bell shook his head and came to his feet. "Not to bother. I'll introduce myself."

He stood, dodged the chairs of the diners, and made his way to the Cromwells' table. He purposely came up behind and slightly off to the side of Margaret so she wouldn't notice his approach. He ignored Cromwell and looked down at her with a condescending smile and wondered how she would react. "I beg your pardon, Miss Cromwell, but I believe we met in Denver. My name is Isaac Bell."

She went rigid, and did not turn and look up at him. She stared across the table into her brother's eyes with an unfathomable expression – surprise, maybe, or consternation, or something else – something bordering on shock or distress. For an instant, it was as though she did not know how to react. And then she recovered in the blink of an eye.

"I'm sorry, but I don't know a Mr. Isaac Bell." Her voice was steady without the least indication of a tremor. She spoke without looking at him. She knew that if she did it would come like a physical blow to her stomach. She was grateful she wasn't standing or her legs would have turned to rubber and she'd have fallen to the carpet.

"Forgive me," said Bell, certain now from her reaction that she was the woman he knew as Rose Manteca. "It must be a case of mistaken identity."

Cromwell had come to his feet out of courtesy and was holding his napkin. He gazed at Bell like a prize-fighter sizing up his opponent before the bell of the first round. He showed not the least bit of surprise or incomprehension. He held out his hand. "Jacob Cromwell, Mr. Bell. Are you a member of the club?"

"No, a guest of Horace Bronson, of the Van Dorn Detective Agency."

Bell shook Cromwell's hand, thinking it strange the banker would keep his gloves on while he ate. Out of years of investigative habit, he glanced at the little finger of the glove on the left hand. The material over the finger was filled out and solid. Not that he thought there was the remotest chance Cromwell was the bandit. That was a crazy idea.

Cromwell nodded. "I know Horace. A fine man. A credit to your company."

Bell noticed close up how Cromwell's red hair was closely trimmed and was beginning to thin at the rear of the head. The banker was short and thin and carried himself with more feminine grace than masculine roughness. Bell saw the same expression in the eyes as he'd once seen in a mountain lion he had shot in Colorado. There was a cold, almost dead, look from deep inside.

"Yes, that he is."

"Bell? I do not think I've heard the name before," Cromwell said as if trying to place it. He dismissed the thought as if it were of no great importance. "Do you live in San Francisco?"

"No, Chicago."

Margaret still could not bring herself to look at Bell. She felt an uncontrollable fire down deep in her body. Her discomfort flared and she blushed red as a cherry. Then she turned angry, not so much at Bell but at herself for showing emotion. "My brother and I would like to enjoy our dinner in private, Mr. Bell. If you will excuse us."

He saw her long neck turn red and felt pleased. "I'm very sorry for the intrusion." He nodded at Cromwell. "Mr. Cromwell." Then Bell turned and walked back to his table.

As soon as he was certain Bell had moved out of earshot, Cromwell snorted. "What in hell is *he* doing in San Francisco? I thought Red Kelly took care of him."

"Apparently, Kelly failed," Margaret said with a small feeling of satisfaction in her stomach.

"How did he know *you* were here?"

"Don't look at me," said Margaret angrily. "I took the train from Denver to Los Angeles as Rose Manteca and bought a horse there under another name. Then I rode it to Santa Barbara, where I took a train to San Francisco under yet another name. There is no way he could have traced me."

"Are we to consider it coincidence?"

She looked like a lost dog. "I don't know. I just don't know."

"Regardless of why he's in San Francisco, his presence spells trouble," said Cromwell, staring openly with a constrained smile at the four agents seated around their table. "I don't think he's put two and two together, but after seeing you, suspecting you might have a connection with the bandit, and learning you're my sister, he'll be nosing around."

"Maybe it's time for me to take a vacation."

"Not a bad idea."

"I'll book passage to Juneau, Alaska, first thing in the morning."

"Why Juneau?" asked Cromwell. "It's colder than a witch's nipple up there."

"Because it's the last place he'd look." She paused, and her eyes took on a shrewd look. "And there is the fact that Eugene's father, Sam Butler, oversees his mining operations outside of Juneau." Margaret laughed, loosening the bond on her emotions. "It gives me a chance to look over my future financial interests."

"Dear sister," Cromwell said genially, "you are a never-ending, constant source of amazement." Then he brazenly looked across the dining room at Bell. "I wonder," he muttered, "what happened to Red Kelly."

"Maybe Bell killed him."

"Maybe," said Cromwell. "If that's the case, Bell is far more dangerous than I gave him credit for. Next time, I'll handle the matter myself."

When Bell returned to the table, his dish of sweetbreads had arrived. He picked up a fork, looking forward to tasting the delicacy, but he was stopped by questions from everyone at the table.

"Was she the woman you think you met in Denver?" demanded Bronson.

Bell dodged the question, not wanting to dwell on what he knew was a touchy subject with Bronson. "I am probably wrong. I admit it. But the resemblance is quite extraordinary."

"You have an eye for beauty," Bronson said with a mild chuckle.

"How did you find Cromwell?" asked Irvine. "Do you think he will be helpful when I make an appointment with him to discuss the stolen currency that passed through his bank?"

"You'll have to ask Horace. I didn't mention our investigation. He seemed nice enough, if a little lordly."

"He has a reputation of being lofty," said Bronson. "But, one on one, he's quite solicitous, and I'm sure he will be very cooperative in your investigation."

"We shall see," Bell said, finally savoring the sweetbreads. After swallowing, he nodded at Irvine. "I think I'll accompany you to the Cromwell National Bank."

"You want to meet him again?" asked Bronson.

Bell shook his head. "Not a priority, but I would like to probe around his bank."

"What do you expect to find?" wondered Curtis.

Bell shrugged, but there was a faint gleam in his eyes. "You know, I haven't the faintest idea."

19

Marion sat at her desk, typing a letter, when two men entered the office. She turned from her Underwood Model 5 typewriter and looked up. One man, with a thicket of unbrushed brown hair, smiled a friendly smile. He was thin, and would have appeared sickly if not for his tanned face. The other was tall, with blond hair. She could not see his face because he had turned away and seemed to be studying the luxurious décor of the office.

"Miss Morgan?"

"Yes, may I help you?"

"My name is Irvine." He handed her his agency card. "My fellow agent, Isaac Bell, and I are from the Van Dorn Detective Agency. We have an appointment with Mr. Cromwell."

She came to her feet but did not smile. "Of course. Your appointment was for nine-thirty. You're five minutes early."

Irvine made an open gesture with his hands. "You know the saying . . ."

"About the early bird getting the worm?" she said as if amused.

The tall blond-haired man faced her. "But the second mouse gets the cheese."

"Very astute, Mr. Bell . . ." said Marion, her voice trailing off.

Their eyes met, and Marion suddenly felt something she had never felt before as she gazed into the blue-violet eyes. She realized now that he was well over six feet tall, with a wiry body clothed by a nicely tailored white linen suit. A large mustache was the exact shade of his flaxen, well-groomed hair. He was not handsome in the pretty-boy sense, but his features were craggy and masculine. There was a look of ruggedness about him, a man who was at home in the wild country of the West as well as the comforts of city life. She openly gazed at him, her usually well-restrained emotions in upheaval. No man had ever moved her this way before, certainly not on the first meeting.

Bell was also moved by the beauty of Marion and her aura of loveliness. The floor trembled beneath his feet as he stared back at her. She looked dainty but strong as a willow. There was a serene confidence about her that suggested she could surmount any complicated problem. She was poised and graceful, and, from the narrow waist to the flared bottom of her lengthy skirt, he could tell that she had long legs. The thick, lustrous hair was piled atop her head, with one long, narrow strand falling nearly to her waist. He guessed that she was the same age as he, give or take a year.

"Is Mr. Cromwell busy?" he asked, tearing himself back to the purpose of the visit.

"Yes . . ." she said with a trace of a stammer. "But he is expecting you."

She knocked on Cromwell's door, entered, and announced Bell and Irvine's arrival. Then she stood aside and motioned them in as Cromwell came from behind his desk to greet them. As they passed through the door, Bell purposely brushed his hand against Marion's. She felt as if an electric shock had passed through her, before closing the door.

"Sit down, gentlemen," said Cromwell. "Horace Bronson tells me you've come about the stolen currency that passed through my bank."

Irvine seemed not to notice it, but Bell again found it intriguing that Cromwell wore gloves.

"That is correct," Irvine said as Bell let him handle the conversation. "One of the bills, serial number 214799, was reported as being deposited in your bank."

"That is entirely possible," said Cromwell, toying with an unlit cigar. "I assume it was a fifty- or hundred-dollar bill, because we never record any currency less than that amount."

Irvine checked his notations in a notebook. "Actually, it came from a merchant on Geary Street, a florist's shop. The manager, whose name is Rinsler, contacted the Van Dorn Detective Agency because he thought the bill might be counterfeit. It proved to be genuine. He stated that he'd obtained it from the Cromwell National Bank when he was transferring cash to a private safe."

"Rinsler's reasons sound a bit shady," added Bell. "But if he's violated the law, that's a problem for the local police department."

"Millions of dollars pass through this bank during the course of a year," said Cromwell. "I don't see why one bill is so important."

"Because a check of the serial number revealed that it came from a bank robbery in Elkhorn, Montana, where the bandit murdered four bank employees and customers," Bell explained.

Cromwell waited for more, but Bell and Irvine went silent. Irvine was examining his notes, but Bell was watching Cromwell intently. The banker met the unrelenting gaze without shifting his eyes. It stimulated his ego knowing that he was in a game of wits with the best agent Van Dorn had.

"I'm sorry, gentlemen," said Cromwell, moving his gaze from Bell to his unlit cigar. "I fail to see how I can help you. If other bills from the robbery passed through the Cromwell Bank, they have long gone into general circulation and there is no way to trace them, no way of knowing who deposited them."

"That is true," Bell replied. "But we have to check out every lead, no matter how remote."

"The bills were new and had consecutive serial numbers," explained Irvine. "Is it possible you recorded them before they were put into circulation?"

"Quite possible, since, as I've said, we record fifty- and hundred-dollar bills."

"Could you have your bookkeeper check your records?" Bell asked.

"Happy to oblige." Cromwell paused to press a buzzer under his desk. Within seconds, Marion Morgan was standing in the doorway. "Miss Morgan, would you please have Mr. Hopkins come up to my office?"

She nodded. "Of course."

When Hopkins showed up, he was not what Bell expected. Instead of a colorless, lackluster little man with glasses and a pencil behind one ear who spent his working life poring through numbers in ledgers, Hopkins looked like a star athlete, big robust, and quick of movement. He nodded as Bell and Irvine were introduced.

"Mr. Bell and Mr. Irvine are from the Van Dorn Detective Agency. They are here to check out serial numbers on currency that was stolen during a bank robbery in Elkhorn, Montana. A fifty-dollar bill was deposited in our bank before it was given to a customer cashing a check. These gentlemen think that other stolen bills might have passed through the bank. They would like you to check the list of serial numbers that we recorded."

Hopkins looked positively congenial as he smiled. "I'll need the serial numbers."

"Check for consecutive bills above and below 214799," answered Cromwell, relying on his memory.

"Right away, sir," acknowledged Hopkins. He made a slight bow to Bell and Irvine. "I should have the numbers, if they exist, within a few hours."

"I'd be grateful," said Bell.

"Anything else, gentlemen?" said Cromwell, ending the interview.

"No, you've been most helpful. Thank you."

Bell let Irvine move out ahead of him to the elevator, lagging behind. He stopped at Marion's desk and gazed at her. "Miss Morgan?"

She swirled her chair from her typewriter in his direction but shied from looking into his eyes.

"I know this is terribly presumptous of me, but you look like an adventurous lady, and I was wondering if you might throw caution to the winds and have dinner with me this evening?"

Her first impulse was to reject him, but some forbidden door had opened and she fought a battle of principle against desire. "I'm not allowed to date bank customers. Besides, how do I know I can trust a complete stranger?"

He laughed and leaned toward her. "Number one, I am not a bank customer. And, number two, if you can't trust a bonded detective, who can you trust?" He reached out and took her hand in his.

A terrifying wave of anxiety swept over her as she fought a losing battle. Her last barrier crumpled and, along with it, her final grip on control. All self-restraint had evaporated.

"All right," she heard herself say, as if she was listening to a total stranger. "I get off work at five o'clock."

"Good," he said, a little too enthusiastically, he thought. "I'll meet you at the front entrance."

She watched him walk toward the elevator. "Good Lord," she murmured to herself. "I must be made to have agreed to have dinner with a perfect stranger."

Yet, as she berated herself, there was a twinkle in her eye.

Irvine waited for Bell in the elevator. "What was all that about?"

"I have a dinner date with Cromwell's personal secretary."

"You work fast." Irvine said admiringly.

Bell grinned. "Things just sort of fell into place."

"Knowing you like I do, I'll bet you have an ulterior motive."

"You might say that I'm mixing business with pleasure."

"You may be playing with fire," said Irvine seriously. "If she catches wise that you're using her to probe into Cromwell's affairs, there could be trouble."

"I'll worry about that when the time comes," Bell said comfortably.

On the ride back to the hotel, Bell's thoughts were not on the business part of the coming evening but rather the pleasure.

20

Marion could not explain it. The sensation was one she had not experienced since a boy she dreamed about in school had smiled at her. That was all. He never approached or talked to her. Now, as she sat across an intimate table for two, she felt as giddy as a schoolgirl.

Bell had picked her up outside the Cromwell Bank at exactly five o'clock in a motor cab. The driver drove directly from the street into the seven-story building that contained the city's most famous French restaurant, Delmonico's. They entered an elevator that took them to the top floor, where the maitre d' showed them into an enclosed private dining room with a large picture window that overlooked the city and the bay.

People who could afford it thought nothing of consuming ten-course meals, each accompanied by a different wine. Bell ordered oysters Rockefeller with a tangy curry sauce, followed by a flavorful broth, poached Great Lakes sturgeon, frog's legs à la poulette, pork chops, chicken Kiev, assorted roasted game birds, boiled potatoes, and creamed peas.

Marion had never dined this sumptuously in her life. True, she had been wined and dined by the city's eligible and moneyed bachelors, but none had treated her this lavishly. She was more than thankful the portions were small but regretted not loosening her corset in advance.

For dessert, Bell ordered crêpes suzette, the flaming orange-flavored delicacy. When the waiter stood at their table expertly spooning the flaming mixture over the crêpes, Marion forced herself to look directly into Bell's eyes.

"May I ask you a question, Mr. Bell?"

His smile was engaging. "I believe we know each other well enough for you to call me Isaac."

"I'd prefer Mr. Bell, if you don't mind," she said in what she thought was a proper manner.

The smile remained. "Suit yourself."

"How can you afford all this on the pay of a detective?"

He laughed. "Would you believe I saved up all month just to impress you?"

"Not for an instant," she said haughtily.

"Is Cromwell the biggest bank in San Francisco?"

She was taken back by his question to her answer. "No, there are two others that are larger, including Wells Fargo. Why do you ask?"

"My family owns the largest bank in New England."

She tried to digest it but could not. "Would you be upset if I said I didn't believe you?"

"Ask your boss. He'll verify my claim."

She frowned, confused. "Why are you a hired detective when you could be president of a bank?"

"I happen to like criminal investigation more than banking. I felt trapped at a desk. There is also the challenge of matching wits with the criminal mind."

"Are you successful?" she asked, teasing.

"I win more times than I lose," he answered honestly.

"Why me?" she asked him. "Why wine and dine a mere secretary instead of a socialite more your equal?"

Bell did not mince words. "Because you're attractive, intelligent, and I'm captivated."

"But you don't know me."

"I hope to change that," he said, devastating her with his eyes again. "Now, enough talk. Let's enjoy the crêpes."

When they finished the savory dessert, Bell asked the waiter for two glasses of fifty-year-old port. Then he leaned back, fully sated. "Tell me about Jacob Cromwell."

The food and wine had done its work. Marion was too mellow to see the trap she was stepping into. "What would you like to know?"

"Where he came from, how he launched his bank, is he married. After meeting him, I found him most interesting. I heard he and his sister Margaret are the city's leading philanthropists."

"I've worked for Mr. Cromwell for nine years and I can safely say he is a very smart and perceptive man who is a confirmed bachelor. He started the bank in 1892 with very little in assets and weathered the depression of the nineties. He made money through the worst of it. Most all the banks in the city came close to closing their doors during hard economic times. Not Cromwell National Bank. Through shrewd management and sound banking principles, he built a financial empire with assets running in the many millions of dollars."

"A resourceful man," said Bell admiringly. "Obviously, a self-made man."

She nodded. "The growth of Cromwell National Bank is nothing short of a financial miracle."

"Where did he find the money to open a bank?"

"That's a bit of a mystery. He's very close-lipped about his business affairs prior to launching a small bank on Market Street. Rumor has it, he started with no more than fifty thousand dollars. When I came to work, the bank's assets were well over a million."

"What sort of investments does he make with his fortune?"

She held up her hands in a helpless gesture. "I honestly don't know. He's never mentioned his personal finances to me, and I've seen no paperwork or correspondence. I assume he plunges his profits back into the bank."

"What of his family? Where did he and his sister come from?"

Again, Marion looked lost. "He's never spoken of his past. One time, he mentioned that he and

Margaret's father had a farm in North Dakota, in a little town called Buffalo. Other than that, his family ties are buried in the past."

"I'm sure he has his reasons," said Bell. He did not want to push Marion too far, so he turned the conversation to his own childhood growing up in the elitist society of Boston. Going to Yale University, and his father's extreme displeasure when he went to work at the Van Dorn Detective Agency and not the family bank. He took a circuitous route back to Cromwell. "Cromwell stuck me as an educated man. I wonder where he went to school."

"Margaret once said they attended college in Minnesota," said Marion, dabbing a napkin to her lips after finishing her crêpes.

"Margaret is a beautiful woman," he said, watching for a reaction.

Marion barely veiled her dislike of Cromwell's sister. "I know she's involved with a number of charities, but she is not someone I'd have as a close friend."

"She can't be trusted?" Bell guessed.

"She doesn't always tell the truth. And there are always rumors of scandal, which Mr. Cromwell manages to cover up. Strangely, he doesn't seem disturbed by her antics. It's almost as if he enjoys them."

"Does he travel much?"

"Oh, yes, he's often away fishing in Oregon, enjoying the Bohemian Club's retreat in the redwoods, or hunting in Alaska. He also attends at least three banking conferences a year in various parts of the country. Once a year, he and Margaret tour Europe together."

"So he doesn't manage the day-to-day business of the bank."

She shook her head. "No, no, Mr. Cromwell is always in weekly contact with the bank when he's away. He also has a board of directors that has the best brains in the business."

The waiter brought their glasses of port on a silver tray. They sipped in silence for a few moments before Marion spoke.

"Why are you asking me all these questions about Mr. Cromwell?"

"I'm an investigator. I'm just naturally curious."

She pushed a curl from her forehead and patted her hair. "I feel rejected."

He gazed at her carefully. "Rejected?" he echoed.

"Yes, you ask all these questions about my boss, but you haven't asked about me. Most men I've known always asked about my past on the first date."

"Dare I go there?" he asked, teasing her.

"Nothing risqué," she said, laughing. "My life's been pretty dull, actually. I am a California native, born across the bay in Sausalito. My mother died when I was quite young, and my father, who was an engineer for the Western Pacific Railroad, hired tutors for me until I was old enough to go to the city's first secretarial school. When I graduated, Jacob

Cromwell hired me, and I've worked in his bank ever since, working up from an office typist to his personal secretary."

"Ever been married?"

She smiled coyly. "I've had a proposal or two but never walked down the aisle to the altar."

He reached across the table and took her hand. "Hopefully, Prince Charming will come along one day and sweep you off your feet."

She pulled her hand back, more from exerting her authority than rejecting him. "Prince Charmings are few and far between. I've yet to see one in San Francisco."

Bell decided not to go there. He was determined to ask her out again and see where their wave of mutual attraction might take them. "I've enjoyed the evening. It's not often I can value the company of such a lovely woman who can hold her own in conversation."

"You're very good at flattery."

He dropped his eyes from hers. Bell did not want to push his luck, but there was one more enigma he had to have answered. "There's another thing about Cromwell that intrigues me."

He could see from her expression that she was disappointed and had expected him to say something about them getting together again, and he sensed that she was beginning to doubt her feelings toward him.

"What is it?" Her tone suddenly went icy.

"When I first saw him in the dining room of the

Bohemian Club, and today in his office, he was wearing gloves. Does he always wear them when dining or working at his desk?"

She folded her napkin and laid it on the table as a sign that for her the evening was over. "When he was a boy, he was in a fire. Both his hands were badly burned, so he wears gloves to cover the scars."

Bell felt guilty for using Marion. She was a vital, beautiful, and intelligent woman. He stood, came around the table, and pulled her chair out for her. "I'm truly sorry for letting my detective's undue inquisitive nature get the best of me. I hope you'll forgive me. Will you give me a chance to make it up to you?"

She could tell that he was sincere and felt a tickle of excitement, her hope rising again that he was truly interested in her. He was far more enticing than she could have imagined. "All right, Isaac, I'll go out with you again. But no questions."

"No questions," he said with a tingle of pleasure at hearing her use his first name. "That's a promise."

21

Two days later, the four detectives met in the Van Dorn Detective Agency offices on the fifth floor of the Call Building on Market Street. They sat in a semicircle at a round table and compared notes. They were all in shirtsleeves, their coats hanging on the back of their chairs. Most wore straight, conservative neckties under their stiff collars. Only one wore a bow tie. Three sipped coffee from cups with the Van Dorn logo baked on the porcelain surface, the fourth drank tea. Loose papers and bound reports covered the top of the table.

"I've written up a story telling how one of the largest shipments ever of newly printed currency from the San Francisco Mint will be shipped under heavy guard to the mining town of Telluride, Colorado, to make the payroll and a bonus to ten thousand miners," Bell told them. "I merely alluded to the exact amount but suggested that it was in the neighborhood of five hundred thousand dollars."

"I used my contacts with the newspaper editor to run the article," said Bronson. "It will be printed in tomorrow's papers."

Irvine spun his cup slowly around on its saucer. "If the bandit lives in San Francisco, it should tantalize him into making a try for it."

"*If* he lives in San Francisco," repeated Curtis. "We're going out on a limb on this one. We may have run up a dead-end alley."

"We know the boxcar and several of the stolen bills ended up here," said Bell. "I think the odds are good he lives somewhere in the Bay Area."

"It would help if we knew for certain," Bronson said wearily. He looked at Irvine. "You say your search to backtrack the stolen currency went nowhere."

"A bust," Irvine acknowledged. "The trail was too cold and there was no way to trace the bills before they were recirculated."

"The banks had no record of who turned them in?" asked Bronson.

Irvine shook his head. "The tellers have no way of knowing because they don't list the serial numbers. That's done later by the bank's bookkeepers. By the time we made a connection, it was too late. Whoever traded in the bills was long gone and forgotten."

Bronson turned to Curtis. "And your search for the boxcar?"

Curtis looked as if he had just lost the family dog. "It disappeared," he replied helplessly. "A search of the railyard turned up no sign of it."

"Maybe it was sent out on a freight train that left the city," Bell offered.

"Southern Pacific freight trains that left on scheduled runs in the last week show no manifest that includes a freight car owned by the O'Brian Furniture Company."

"You're saying it never left the railyard?"

"Exactly."

"Then why can't it be found?" inquired Bronson. "It couldn't have vanished into thin air."

Curtis threw up his hands. "What can I say? Two of your agents and I searched the railyard from top to bottom. The car is not there."

"Did the Southern Pacific's dispatchers know where the car was switched after it arrived?" asked Bell.

"It was switched to a siding next to the loading dock of a deserted warehouse. We checked it out. It wasn't there."

Irvine lit a cigar and puffed out a cloud of smoke. "Could it have been coupled to a train without the dispatcher knowing about it?"

"Can't happen," Curtis came back. "They would know if a car was covertly added to their train. The brakemen use a form to list the serial numbers on a train in the sequence the cars are coupled together. When the boxcars arrive at their designated destination, they can easily be switched from the rear of the train before it continues on its run."

"Perhaps the bandit figured the car had outlived its usefulness and he had it scrapped and destroyed," said Bronson.

"I don't think so," Bell said thoughtfully. "My guess is that he simply had it repainted with a new serial number and changed the name to another fictitious company."

"Won't make any difference," said Curtis. "He couldn't use it anyway."

"What do you mean?" Bell asked.

"Only the Rio Grande Southern Railroad runs into Telluride."

"So what's stopping him from repainting that railroad's insignia over one advertising the Southern Pacific?"

"Nothing. Except it would be a waste of time. The Rio Grande Southern runs on a narrow-gauge track. The Southern Pacific trains run on standard gauge, nearly a foot wider. There's no way the track can accommodate the bandit's boxcar."

"How stupid of me," muttered Bell. "I forgot that only narrow-gauge railroads run through the Rocky Mountains."

"Don't feel bad," said Bronson. "I never thought of it either."

Irvine struck the table with his fist in frustration. "He'll never bite the hook, knowing that he can't escape in his private freight car."

Bell smiled tightly. "He has his strengths, but he also has his weaknesses. I'm counting on his greed and his ego, his sense of invincibility. I'm certain he will take the bait and attempt to rob the bank in Telluride. The challenge is too mighty for him to ignore."

"I wish you the best of luck," said Bronson. "If anybody can catch the Butcher, you can."

"What about you, Horace? Any luck on tracing the bandit's gun?"

"Nothing encouraging," Bronson said soberly. "New firearm purchases don't have to be registered. All any buyer has to do is lay down the money and walk out with the gun. We've drawn a blank with dealers. Even if they remember who they sold a Colt thirty-eight automatic to, they won't give out any names."

Irvine stared at a wall without seeing it. "It would seem, gentlemen, that all our hard-earned leads have turned into blind alleys."

"Setbacks, yes," Bell muttered softly. "But the game isn't over – not yet. We still have a chance to make the final score."

22

Cromwell sat at the table, eating his breakfast and reading the morning paper. He folded the first section on a front-page article and passed it across the table to Margaret without comment.

She read it, her eyes squinting as the story hit home, then she looked up quizzically. "Do you intend on going for it?"

"I find it very tempting," he replied. "It's as though a gauntlet was thrown at my feet."

"What do you know about Telluride?"

"Only what I've read. It lies in a box canyon. Has an extensive redlight district, and Butch Cassidy robbed the San Miguel Valley Bank there in 1889."

"Was he successful?"

Cromwell nodded. "He and his gang got away with over twenty thousand dollars."

"I suppose you're thinking if he could do it, you could do it."

"Cassidy conducted an amateur holdup and rode away on horses," Cromwell said pompously. "My methods are more scientific."

"If Telluride is in a box canyon, there is only one way in and one way out. A posse would have time to stop a train and search the cars."

"I can't use my boxcar anyway. It will have to be left behind."

"I don't understand."

"The railroad running in and from Telluride is the Rio Grande Southern. The tracks are narrow gauge, the rails too closely spiked for my Southern Pacific car. I'll just have to find another means of leaving town without the threat of capture."

Margaret scrutinized the story again. "I don't have a good feeling about this."

"I don't consider feelings. I work with hard facts, and I play it safe by taking into account every contingency, no matter how small."

She watched him across the table as he poured another cup of coffee. "You'll need help with this job."

He looked over his cup. "What have you got in mind?"

"I'll come with you."

"What about your little journey to Juneau, Alaska?"

"I'll simply postpone it."

Cromwell considered that for a few moments. "I can't put you at risk."

"You haven't failed yet," Margaret admonished him. "But, this time, you may need me."

He was quiet for a while. Then he smiled. "I do believe you'd come along if I ordered you not to."

She laughed. "Have I ever bowed to your demands yet?"

"Not even when we were children," he said, remembering. "Though you were two years younger, I could never get the upper hand."

She patted a napkin against her red lips. "It's settled, then. We're in this job together."

He sighed. "You win. But I hope I won't be sorry I didn't put you on the boat to Alaska."

"What do you want me to do?"

He stared down at the table, as if seeing an abstract image, while he circled his fork on the tablecloth. "Take a train to Colorado tomorrow and then make a connection to Telluride."

She stared at him. "You want me to leave before you?"

He nodded. "I'll deviate from my usual routine. Instead of my spending time mingling with the locals and studying the bank operation, you can do it. As a woman, you can conduct a close scrutiny without arousing suspicion."

"A *woman* in Telluride?" she mused. "I'll have to pass myself off as a prostitute."

"Better yet, claim that you're an abandoned wife whose husband left her to strike it rich in the mines and disappeared. That way no one will be suspicious of you asking questions and snooping around."

"But in order to live and eat, I have to find work in a bordello."

"Have it your own way," he said, resigning himself as always to his sister's whimsical ways.

"And you?"

"I'll come a few days later, after I've checked out the shipment and firmed up my plans for the robbery and our getaway." He paused and gazed at her with a look of brotherly love. "I must be mad for involving you in such a risky venture."

"I'm mad, too." She laughed a lilting laugh. "Insane with excitement and a growing rage for adventure." She threw him the feminine expression of a cat about to leap on a mouse. "Of course, the thought of acting like a prostitute is an attraction I find delicious."

"Spare me the details."

Then she suddenly became serious. "What about Isaac Bell?"

He shrugged. "What about him?"

"He seems to show up everywhere, maybe even Telluride."

"The thought crossed my mind, but, once I verify the currency shipment, I believe that pretty much eliminates him. He's too busy chasing ghosts all over San Francisco to show up out of the blue in Telluride."

"I don't trust him any more than I can throw this house."

He laughed. "Cheer up, sister dear. This will be a walk in the park just like the other robberies. You'll see."

23

The spring day was cool and brisk as Bell departed the train at the town depot and walked to the corner of Aspen Street and Colorado Avenue, where he found a three-story wooden building with a sign out front that read MAMIE TUBBS BOARDINGHOUSE. He carried a battered valise and wore a worn wool coat with a vest and flannel shirt underneath. His pants were heavy cotton with almost the consistency of canvas. Boots that looked as if they had walked five thousand miles protected his feet while a rumpled old Stetson sat solidly on his head. The fabricated image was embellished with a Dublin-style bent pipe wedged between his teeth. Bell also walked with a pronounced limp as if his left leg was stiff.

He stepped into the parlor of the boardinghouse and was greeted by Mamie Tubbs, a jolly woman as round as a huge pear. Her gray hair hung down her back in two braids, and she had a face that looked like a large saucer with a nose.

"Greetings, stranger," she said in a voice as deep as a man's. "Looking for a place to stay?"

"Yes, ma'am," said Bell politely. "I'm new in town."

"Seven dollars a week including meals, providing you're at the table when I dish up."

He reached into a pocket, brought out a few folded bills, and counted out seven dollars. "Here's your money, in advance. "I don't have much, but enough to tide me over for a while."

She had noticed his limp when he came into the parlor. "You lookin' to work in the mines?"

Bell tapped a hand against his leg. "My mining days ended when I was injured by a badly laid stick of dynamite."

She eyed him suspiciously, beginning to wonder where any future rent was going to come from. "Where do you expect to find a job?"

"A friend found me work as a cleanup man at the New Sheridan Hotel."

She smiled. "They couldn't find you a room in the basement?"

"All beds in the basement were taken by miners," Bell lied. He had no idea if miners slept in the basement.

The impression of a crippled miner, he knew, would satisfy Mamie Tubbs enough so she wouldn't gossip around town about her new boarder. She showed him to his room, where he unpacked his valise. He removed a towel wrapped around a Colt Browning model 1905 .45 caliber automatic pistol with a custom twenty-shot magazine and shoulder stock that fit in a slot behind the grip. He slipped the weapon under the bed but kept his trusty Remington derringer inside his Stetson. He retightened the wrapping around his knee so it hindered normal movement.

After a beef stew dinner in Mamie's dining room, he met the other people who were staying at the boardinghouse. Most were miners, but there were a few store clerks, and a husband and wife who were opening a restaurant. After dinner, Bell strolled up Pacific Avenue and studied the layout of the town.

Telluride – the name supposedly came from the saying "to hell you ride" – was launched after gold was discovered in the San Miguel River. The gold, along with silver-bearing ore, found high in the San Juan Mountains, quickly attracted an army of prospectors and miners over the next fifty years. By 1906, more millionaires per capita lived in Telluride than in New York City.

The miners eventually dug three hundred fifty miles of tunnels that honeycombed the surrounding mountains, some as high as twelve thousand feet above sea level. The population soared to over five thousand, and the rip-roaring town soon overflowed with wild and crazy living mixed with a healthy dose of corruption. There were three dozen saloons and one hundred eighty prostitutes to keep the army of miners in a good mood after long twelve-hour shifts in the Silver Bell, Smuggler-Union, and Liberty Bell mines at three dollars a day.

When the sun dropped behind the mountains and darkness came, a blaze of lights flashed on up and down the streets. In 1892, mine owner L. L. Nunn had hired the electrical wizard Nikola Tesla to build the world's first alternating-current power plant to move ore on cables down the mountain and miners up from town. After running lines from the power plant into town. Telluride became the first town in history to have electric streetlamps.

Bell walked past the notorious cribs where the scarlet women plied their trade. The upper-class houses were called the Senate and the Silver Belle. Music could be heard through the windows out on the street as a piano player pounded out the "Dill Pickles Rag" and other ragtime tunes. The street was called Popcorn Alley, its name coming from the constant opening and closing of doors all night.

He moved up to the main section of town on Colorado Avenue and looked through the windows of the Telluride First National Bank. Tomorrow, he would meet with the town sheriff and the bank manager to plan a reception for the Butcher Bandit, should he swallow the bait and make an attempt to rob the bank. He passed the old San Miguel Valley Bank that Butch Cassidy had robbed seventeen years previously.

The evening air had turned cold, once the sun took its heat beyond the mountain peaks. Bell noticed that the nine-thousand-foot altitude caused him to take deeper breaths. He ignored the main street saloons and headed for the New Sheridan Hotel.

Bell stepped inside the lobby and asked the desk clerk to see the manager. In a minute, a short man with a florid face and bald head came out of the office with quick, hurried steps, like a mouse running from a hole in the wall. He smiled an official smile, but not too warmly, as he sized up Bell's rather dowdy appearance.

"I'm sorry, all our rooms are taken. The Sheridan is full up."

"I don't want a room," said Bell. "Are you Mr. Marshall Buckman?"

The smile straightened and the eyes narrowed. "Yes, I'm Buckman."

"I'm Isaac Bell with the Van Dorn Detective Agency."

Buckman eye's widened again and he bowed. "Mr. Bell. I received your telegram. Permit me to say the Sheridan will cooperate in every way."

"The most important thing," explained Bell, "is to confirm to anyone who asks that I work here as a janitor."

"Yes, of course," Buckman said in a patronizing manner. "You can count on me."

"Thank you, Mr. Buckman. Now, if you don't mind, I think I will enjoy the best whiskey in your bar."

"We serve only superior whiskey from the finest distillers. No local rotgut is tolerated at the Sheridan."

Bell nodded and then turned his back on Buckman and stepped toward the bar. He paused and read a plaque listing rules for the hotel patrons.

Don't shoot the pianist, he's doing his damndest.
No horses above the first floor.
No more than 5 in a bed.
Funerals on the house.
Beds 50 cents, with sheets 75 cents.

At the doorway, he stood aside as a blond lady whose face was hidden under a wide-brimmed hat stepped past him. All he saw was that she had a fine figure.

Conversely, she paid no attention to the limping man who walked by her as she headed for the carpeted stairway leading to her room.

Much later, Bell cursed himself for not recognizing the blonde just as Margaret blamed herself for not identifying the limping man until it was too late.

24

Bell explained the situation to Sheriff Henry Pardee and the bank manager, Murray Oxnard. The three men sat around a table eating a breakfast served by the sheriff's wife. Pardee's house sat directly behind his office and the jail. He walked to the door, made sure it was locked, and drew the curtains so nobody could see inside.

Bell was impressed with the sheriff. One wall of the parlor had bookshelves from floor to ceiling stacked with works by Shakespeare. Plato, Voltaire, Bacon, and Emerson, along with several volumes in Latin. Bell had never met a peace officer in a small town who was so well read.

Pardee ran a hand through a thick mane of graying hair and tugged at a shaggy mustache. "What you're saying. Mr. Bell, is that you think the Butcher Bandit is going to hit our town bank."

"I can't say for certain," Bell replied. "But if he's true to form, he'll be lured by the large payroll that is being shipped to the bank from the First National Bank of Denver."

"I know of no such payroll shipment," said Murray Oxnard. He was a tall, quiet man with broad shoulders and narrow hips. He seldom smiled, and his face was always fixed with a dour expression.

"There is no shipment," explained Bell. "It is a ruse to smoke out the bandit."

Pardee rapped the fingers of one hand on the table. "If he is as smart as I've read, he'll dig into the true facts and find it's all a sham."

Bell shook his head. "No, sir, the directors of the bank in Denver are primed to go along with the story."

"If I may ask," said Pardee, "why did you choose Telluride?"

"Because you sit in a box canyon with its only entrance and exit to the west. The situation that makes it ideal to block off his escape route if we don't apprehend him during the attempted robbery."

"I don't like it," said Oxnard. "The bandit is known to murder without batting an eye. I cannot put my employees at risk, nor will I have their blood on my hands."

"I do not intend to have you or your people in the bank when and if the robbery occurs. Myself and one other Van Dorn agent will man the bank. Another agent will watch the trains coming in and out, since the bandit is known to escape his crimes by using a railroad freight car."

"What about my customers?" Oxnard pressed on. "Who will tend to their transactions?"

"My agent and I are fully experienced in running

the daily affairs of a bank. If the bandit steps up to a teller's cage, we'll be ready for him."

"Do you know what he looks like?" asked Pardee.

"Except for the fact we know he's missing the little finger on his left hand and he has red hair, we have no description."

"That's because he murders everyone who can identify him. You don't have much to go on."

"I still cannot bring myself to go along with this," said Oxnard. "One of my customers could be in the wrong place at the wrong time and get shot."

"We'll take every precaution," said Bell soberly. "There may be some risk, but this bandit must be stopped. He's already killed over thirty people. There's no telling how many more will die before we can apprehend him and stop the murders."

"What can I do to help?" Pardee said, giving Oxnard a cold stare.

"Don't patrol the bank with your deputies and scare off the bandit," answered Bell. "Stand by – out of sight, if possible – but be ready to act in case he shows up. We'll arrange a signal when he makes his play."

Though Oxnard had his demons about the trap, Pardee was already imagining the notoriety he would receive if the bandit were caught in the act under his jurisdiction. As far as he was concerned, the debate was decisive and now it was over. He had only one more question.

"When is the supposed money shipment due?"
"Tomorrow," Bell told him.
Oxnard looked at him inquiringly. "What about the shipment that's already sitting in the safe for the real payroll?"
"Leave it in the safe. I guarantee, the bandit won't get it."
Pardee twisted the ends of his mustache. "Ever been in a mining town on payday, Mr. Bell?"
"I haven't had the luxury, but I hear it can get pretty wild."
"That's true," said Oxnard with a faint grin. "Every payday, all hell breaks loose from one end of town to the other."
Pardee matched his grin. "Yes, the cribs will be busy until the miners have wasted their hard-earned money on whiskey and gambling." He paused a moment and looked at Bell. "Where are you staying, in case I have to get in touch with you?"
"I'm staying at Mamie Tubbs Boardinghouse."
"A good place to keep a low profile," said Oxnard. "Mamie's a fine old gal, and a good cook."
"I can vouch for her stew," Bell said with humor.
After breakfast, the meeting broke up. Bell and Oxnard thanked Mrs. Pardee for a fine breakfast. Then the three men stepped outside and walked toward town, Pardee leaving them when he got to his office and jail. Bell went with Oxnard to the bank to study its interior layout.

The floor plan was the same as a thousand other banks'. The bank manager's office sat behind the teller's cage, which was enclosed in glass except for the area in front of the cash drawers. This section of the counter was open through narrow bars. The vault was more like a large safe and stood in an alcove off to the side of the lobby. Bell learned that it was closed during business hours and opened only to withdraw currency or when all cash and coins were returned after closing.

"You don't have a vault?" Bell said to Oxnard.

"Don't need one. Payroll money usually goes up to the mines under heavy guard the second day after the shipment comes in."

"Why the second day?"

"We need the time to make a count to verify the amount shipped from the bank in Denver."

"So the bandit has a limited window of opportunity."

Oxnard nodded. "If he's going to make his play, it will have to be tomorrow."

"Have you seen or had contact with any new depositors or people who simply walked into the bank and then walked out again?"

"A new superintendent for the Liberty Bell mine opened a checking account." He paused to gaze up at the ceiling in thought. "Then there was a very attractive woman who opened an account. A very small account. Very sad."

"Sad?"

"Her husband left her back in Iowa to strike it rich in Colorado. She never heard from him again, and the last thing she learned was from a friend, a conductor on the railroad. He told her that her husband left word he was going to Telluride to work in the mines. She came here in an attempt to find him. Poor soul. Chances are, he was one of the many men who died in the mines."

"I'd like the name of the mine superintendent," said Bell, "so I can check him out."

"I'll get it for you." Oxnard went into his office and returned in less than a minute. "His name is Oscar Reynolds."

"Thank you."

Oxnard stared at Bell. "Aren't you going to check out the woman?"

"The bandit has never worked with a woman – or any man, for that matter. He always commits his crimes alone."

"Just as well," Oxnard sighed. "Poor thing. She only opened an account for two dollars. In order to eat, she'll probably have to work in a bordello, since jobs for women are scarce in Telluride. And those jobs that do exist are filled by the wives of the miners."

"Just to play safe, I'd like her name, too."

"Rachel Jordan."

Bell laughed softly. "Her, you remembered."

Oxnard smiled. "It's easy to remember a name with a pretty face."

"Did she say where she was staying?"

"No, but I can only assume it's in a crib." He gave Bell a sly look. "You going to look her up?"

"No," said Bell thoughtfully. "I hardly think a woman is the Butcher Bandit."

25

Margaret was not enduring the life of a prostitute in a crib on Pacific Avenue. She was living in style in the New Sheridan Hotel. After opening a small account at the town bank to examine the floor plan, number of employees and where they were located, and the type of safe, she made the rounds of the mining companies to make inquiries about a long-lost husband who never existed. The effort gave her story substance, and soon she became the source of gossip around town.

She went so far as to call on Sheriff Pardee with her bogus story, to see what kind of man he was face-to-face. Mrs. Alice Pardee came into the office when Margaret was asking the sheriff for his cooperation in finding her husband. Alice immediately felt sorry for the woman in the cheap, well-faded cotton dress who poured out her sad tale of the abandoned wife desperately seeking the man who had deserted her. Alice assumed that this Rachel Jordan was half starved and invited her up to their house for dinner. Margaret accepted and arrived in the same cheap dress, which she had bought in San Francisco at a used-clothing store for the poor.

That evening, Margaret made a display of helping

Alice Pardee in the kitchen, but it was obvious to the sheriff's wife that their guest was not at home over a hot stove. Alice served a homemade meal of mutton chops, boiled potatoes, and steamed vegetables, topped off by an apple pie for dessert. After dinner, tea was served and everyone settled in the parlor, where Alice played tunes on an old upright piano.

"Tell me, Mrs. Jordan," Alice asked, pausing to change the sheet music, "where are you staying?"

"A nice lady, Miss Billy Maguire, hired me as a waitress at her ladies' boardinghouse."

Pardee and his wife exchanged pained glances. Alice sucked in her breath. "Big Billy is the madam of the Silver Belle bordello," she said. "Didn't you know that?"

Margaret made a display of looking sheepish. "I had no idea."

Alice bought Margaret's lie, Pardee did not. He knew there was no way any woman could fail to recognize the difference between a boardinghouse and a bordello. The germ of suspicion began to grow in his mind, but his wife was swept by compassion.

"You poor thing," she said, putting her arm around Margaret. "You'll not stay at the Silver Belle another minute. You'll stay here with Henry and me until you find your husband."

"But he may not be in Telluride," Margaret said as if about to weep. "Then I would have to move on, and I don't want to inconvenience you."

"Nonsense," said Alice. "You march right back to Big Billy's and bring back your things. I'll make up the spare bed for you."

Margaret went into her act and shed a few tears. "How can I ever thank you? How can I ever repay you?"

"Don't give it a thought. Henry and I are only too glad to help a poor soul in distress. It's the Christian thing to do."

As she sipped her coffee, Margaret moved the conversation to Pardee's job as sheriff. "You have to live an exciting life," she said. "Telluride seems like an uninhibited town. You must be kept quite busy."

"The miners can get pretty rowdy at times," Pardee agreed, "but serious crimes like murder don't happen but once every six months or so. It's been peaceful since the union strikes by the miners two years ago, when the governor sent in the army to squelch the rioting."

Margaret was slow and deliberate in her answers to Pardee's questions about her missing husband. She in turn made general inquiries about the town and the mines. "A lot of money must pass through the bank to the mining companies," she said casually.

Pardee nodded. "The payrolls can add up to a considerable amount."

"And you never have a fear of robbers and thieves?" she asked innocently.

"The miners are a solid lot and rarely indulge in crime. Except for occasional fights in the saloons, or a killing when a confrontation gets out of hand, the town is pretty quiet."

"When I was in the bank, I saw that the safe looked very strong and secure."

"It's strong, all right," said Pardee, lighting his pipe. "Five sticks of dynamite couldn't blow it open."

"And the bank manager is the only one who knows the combination?"

Pardee thought it strange a question like that came from a woman, but he answered without hesitation. "Actually, the locking bolts are set to spring open at ten o'clock every morning. At three o'clock in the afternoon, the manager closes the door and sets the clock."

"Someone at the Silver Belle told me Butch Cassidy robbed the local bank."

Pardee laughed. "That was a long time ago. We've never had a bank robbery since."

Margaret was leery of pushing too hard, but there was information she had to know if her brother was to carry out a successful robbery. "The miners' payroll. Is it taken directly to the mining companies when it arrives?"

Pardee shook his head and went along with Bell's story. "It came in today and went directly to the bank. Tomorrow, it will be counted and sent to the mines the next day."

"Are there extra guards in the bank to protect the money?"

"No need," said Pardee. "Anyone who tried to rob

the bank wouldn't get far. With the telegraph lines running alongside the railroad tracks, peace officers around the county would be alerted and posses formed to wait for the robbers when they tried to escape."

"Then such a crime would be impossible to commit successfully."

"I guess you could say that," Pardee replied confidently. "There's no way it could succeed."

Margaret left the Pardee house and walked toward the Silver Belle. As soon as she was out of sight, she ran down an alley to the New Sheridan Hotel to pack her meager clothes. She felt pleased with herself and could not believe her luck. Staying with the sheriff and his wife would give her access to most of the town. When her brother arrived, she would have enough information for him to plan a fool-proof crime.

Her only problem was the whereabouts of her brother. To her knowledge, he had not arrived in town, and tomorrow was the only day the payrolls could be robbed before they went to the mines for distribution to the miners. She began to feel extremely uneasy.

26

The following morning, a black-haired woman drove a smart-looking buggy pulled by a dappled gray horse on the road into Telluride. The road led from the ranching community of Montrose, a rail terminus for the Rio Grande Southern Railroad. She had arrived from Denver and rented the rig and horse at the local stable. She was dressed in a long buckskin skirt over a pair of pointed-toe leather boots. Her upper torso was covered by a nicely knit green sweater under a wolfskin fur coat. A lady's-style flat-topped cowboy hat was set squarely on her head. She was fashionably attired for the West, but not ostentatious.

She came onto Colorado Avenue, passed the San Miguel County Courthouse, and pulled the horse to a stop in front of the town stable. She climbed down from the buggy and tied the horse to a hitching post. The stable owner came out and lifted his hat.

"Good afternoon, ma'am. Can I help you?"

"Yes, I wonder if you would please feed and water my horse. I have to be on the road back to Montrose this afternoon."

"Yes, ma'am," said the stable owner politely, slightly

taken aback by a voice that had a gentle harshness about it. "I'll take care of it. While I'm at it, I'll tighten your front wheels. They look a mite loose."

"You're very kind, thank you. Oh, and by the way, my sister will come for the buggy and pay you."

"Yes, ma'am."

The woman left the stable and walked a block to the New Sheridan Hotel. She approached the desk clerk and asked, "Do you have a Miss Rachel Jordan registered here?"

The clerk shook his head, stared at what he saw as an attractive woman, and said, "No, ma'am, she checked out last night." He paused, turned, and pulled an envelope out of a mail-and-key slot. "But she said if someone asked for her to give them this."

The woman thanked the clerk, walked out onto the sidewalk, opened the envelope, and read the note. She stuffed it in her purse and began walking through town. After a short hike, she came to the Lone Tree Cemetery, on a hill north of the San Miguel River. She passed through the gate and walked among the tombstones, noting that most of the deceased had died from mine accidents, snow slides, and miner's consumption.

A pretty blond woman was sitting on a bench beside a grave site, leaning back and sunning herself. Out of the corner of one eye, she caught the approach of another woman. She sat up and stared at the intruder, who stopped and looked down at her. Margaret began to laugh.

"My God, Jacob," she finally gasped. "That's the most ingenious disguise you've ever created."

Cromwell smiled. "I thought you'd approve."

"A good thing you're short, thin, and wiry."

"I don't know why I never thought of it before." He awkwardly bunched up his buckskin skirt and sat down on the bench next to Margaret. "Tell me, sister dear, what have you learned since you've been here?"

Margaret told him how she became friendly with the sheriff and his wife. She handed him a sketch she'd made of the Telluride First National Bank's interior and a description of the employees. Her report included the arrival of the payroll shipment from the bank in Denver and the counting today before it was sent to the mines tomorrow.

Cromwell looked at his watch. "We have one more hour before the bank closes. The best time to remove the currency and leave town."

"I spotted a man hanging around the railroad depot. I couldn't tell for sure, but I suspect he might have been a Van Dorn agent who was on the lookout for you."

Cromwell looked thoughtful. "Even if Van Dorn sends agents to watch train arrivals and departures during payroll shipments, they're only chasing a phantom. No way they could know where I'll strike next."

"If they're wise to your boxcar, it's a good thing you had it repainted." She looked at him quizzically.

"Just how do you expect us to make a clean escape after you rob the bank?"

Cromwell grinned wolfishly. "Who would suspect a pair of clean-cut, attractive ladies riding slowly out of town in a horse and buggy?"

She placed her arm around his shoulders. "The simplest plan is the best plan. You are brilliant, brother. You never cease to amaze me."

"I appreciate the compliment," he said, rising to his feet. "We don't have much time. The payroll awaits."

"What would you like me to do?"

"Go to the stable and pick up my horse and buggy. I told the stable owner my sister would come by to get the rig. Then wait at the back door of the bank."

While Irvine watched the train station and town railyard, Bell and Curtis manned the Telluride Bank. Sitting in Murray Oxnard's office, Bell began to think he had bet on the wrong horse. There were only ten minutes left before closing time and no sign of the bandit. Playing the role of a teller, Irvine was getting ready to close out his cash-box in anticipation of waiting on the last customer.

Bell glanced down at the .45 Colt automatic he'd kept in an open desk drawer and regretted that he would not get to use it on the Butcher Bandit. Blowing the scum's head off was too good for him, Bell mused. Not after he had murdered so many unsuspecting people. His death would save the taxpayers the expense of a trial. Now Bell was faced with admitting defeat and starting over again with the meager clues he and his agents had ferreted out.

Irvine walked over to the office door and leaned his shoulder against the frame. "I can't deny it was a good try," he said with a tightness in his voice.

"It looks as if the bandit failed to take the bait," Bell said slowly.

"Perhaps he didn't read the article in the paper because he doesn't live in San Francisco."

"It's beginning to look that way."

Just then the door opened and a woman wearing a buckskin skirt walked into the bank, her hat pulled low so it covered her eyes. Bell gazed past Irvine but relaxed at seeing what appeared to be a well-dressed woman. He nodded to Irvine, who walked back to his teller's cage and said, "How may I help you, ma'am?"

Cromwell lifted his head slightly so he could look into Irvine's face. Then with a pang of alarm he stiffened as he instantly remembered the Van Dorn agent as one of the men who were sitting with Bell and Bronson in the Bohemian Club dining room only days earlier. He did not answer Irvine for fear his voice would give him away to the agent. Cromwell became charged with tension as he realized this was a trap. There came a pause as he lowered his head, his mind racing with alternatives. His advantage was that the agent did not recognize him, not dressed as a woman, and was not alert to the fact that the bandit was less than four feet away on the other side of the counter.

He could shoot the agent and take what money was in the safe or he could simply turn around and walk out of the bank. He chose the latter option and was about to beat a hasty retreat when Bell stepped from the office. Cromwell immediately recognized Bell. For the first time in his criminal career, he felt the spur of panic.

"How may I help you, ma'am?" Irvine repeated, vaguely wondering why the woman did not answer him the first time.

Already, Bell was looking at him with a questioning expression on his face, as if the female customer looked familiar. Bell was a master of identification and had a photographic memory when it came to faces. His eyes betrayed the fact that he was trying to recall where he'd seen her. Then his eyes dropped to Cromwell's hands, which were covered by leather gloves. Abruptly, as if he had seen an apparition, he realized that he was staring at the bandit. It struck him like a hammer blow to the head. Bell's eyes flared open and he gasped: *"You!"*

Cromwell did not waste another second. He reached into his large cloth purse and jerked out his .38 Colt, which had a heavy cloth taped around the muzzle. Without the slightest hesitation, he pointed the Colt at Irvine's chest and pulled the trigger. A loud thump reverberated in the bank's lobby. Then he swung the muzzle around and shot at Bell even before Irvine hit the floor like a rag doll.

If Bell hadn't instinctively whirled around and thrown his body over the top of the desk, crashing to the floor behind it, the bullet would have caught him square in the stomach. The violent thrust saved him, but the bullet still plowed through the fleshy part of his thigh. He hardly felt the piercing blow. In a single movement, he reached up and snatched his Colt from the desk drawer. Without the luxury of time, he snapped off a shot at Cromwell that missed the neck of the bandit by less than half an inch.

Then, faster than lightning could strike, both men fired again, the shots coming so closely together they sounded as one.

Cromwell's second bullet gouged a small trench across the side of Bell's head, barely piercing the skin but creasing the skull. Bell's vision became a blurred mist and he fell into the black pit of unconsciousness. Blood quickly seeped from the wound and covered the side of his head. It had not been a decisive wound, but to Cromwell, who was still standing, it looked as if he had shot off half of Bell's head.

The bandit did not come out of the gun battle unscathed. Bell's bullet had caught Cromwell in the waist but had passed through without striking any internal organs. He swayed, and only by reaching out and grasping the edge of the teller's cage did he prevent himself from falling to the floor. He stood there for a few moments, fighting the pain. Then he turned and unlocked the rear door, standing aside as Margaret burst in.

"I heard shots outside," she shouted shock. "What went wrong?"

"It was a trap," he murmured as anger replaced fear. Holding a hand over his wound, he motioned the muzzle of his Colt toward the office floor. "I killed Isaac Bell."

Margaret stepped into the office and looked down at the bloodied Van Dorn agent and a look of horror came into her eyes as she recognized Bell despite the blood covering much of his face. "Oh, my God!" She felt as if she was going to be sick, but the nausea quickly passed when she turned and saw that her brother was also bleeding. "You're hurt!" she gasped.

"Not as bad as it looks," he said through clenched teeth.

"We've got to get out of here. The shots will bring the sheriff and rouse half the town."

Margaret half carried, half dragged her wounded brother through the rear door of the bank. Outside, the horse and buggy were waiting. She used all her strength to push him onto the seat of the rig, untied the horse from the fence post, and climbed aboard.

She raised the whip to urge the horse to a gallop, but he grabbed her wrist. "No, go slowly, as if we're two women out for a buggy ride. It will look suspicious if we charge out of town."

"The sheriff is a smart man. I know him. He won't fool easily."

"Even a smart man won't suspect a woman of robbing a bank and killing two men," muttered Cromwell.

At the end of the alley, Margaret turned the buggy up a side street and then headed west toward the town limits. Cromwell took off the wolfskin coat and draped it over his lap to cover the blood that soaked his sweater. He slipped the Colt into one of his cowboy boots and sat back, trying to keep his mind clear by ignoring the throbbing pain in his side.

Bell had instructed Sheriff Pardee that he would fire a shot as a signal if the bandit made his appearance. But Pardee knew there was trouble when he heard five shots, some of them muffled like the distant dynamite charge in a nearby mine. He rushed into the street from a hardware store where he had been hiding, fearful that the woman he'd seen walk into the bank might have been shot by the bandit.

Seeing him running toward the bank, four of his deputies leaped from their hiding places and rushed after him, while a fifth deputy ran to the railroad depot to alert Curtis. With his single-action Smith & Wesson drawn and the hammer pulled back, Pardee burst through the door of the bank. At first, he didn't see anyone. Irvine was lying out of sight, behind the teller's cage, and Bell was down on the other side of the desk. Then he came around the cage, saw the Van

Dorn agent sprawled on the floor in a pool of blood. He checked to make sure Irvine was dead before he entered the office and found Bell.

"Is he a goner?" asked one of his deputies, a great bear of a man with a huge stomach bulging over pants with suspenders stretched to their limits, who stood poised with a sawed-off shotgun at the ready.

"The bullet only creased his skull," answered Pardee. "He's still alive."

"What about the woman?"

Pardee's mind did not register for a moment. Then it hit him. "The woman who came into the bank before the gunshots?"

"That one."

"She must have been abducted by the bandit."

"But we saw no one else enter the bank before or after her."

Pardee stood up in confusion and disbelief. It took all his imagination to believe a woman was the Butcher Bandit.

"The bandit must have entered through the back door."

"I don't know, Sheriff," said the deputy, scratching his chin. "The door should have been locked from the inside, like it always is."

Pardee rushed over to the rear door and found it unlocked. He jerked it open and peered up and down the alley but saw no one. "Hell's fire," he muttered. "She got away."

"She can't get far," said the deputy.

"Round up the men!" snapped Pardee. He motioned to another deputy, who was standing at the entrance of the bank. "Get Doc Madison. Tell him the Van Dorn agent is down with a head wound and to get over to the bank double-quick." Pardee knelt down and quickly examined Bell again. "Also tell him there looks like there's a bullet in the agent's leg."

The deputy was no sooner out the door than Pardee was on his heels, running toward his horse tied to the hitching post in front of his office. It didn't seem possible, he thought, that everything had gone so terribly wrong. Only then did it begin to strike him that the bandit was a man disguised as a woman and that the poor widow he and his wife had taken in was an accomplice.

As soon as they left the city limits of Telluride and passed the road leading to the mines of Ophir to the south, Margaret gave the horse the whip and urged it to run through the canyon and down the road heading west toward Montrose. During the ten minutes since they left the bank, Cromwell had time to think. He pointed to a break in the trees that led to a bridge over the San Miguel River. It was an overgrown access road used by the railroad for maintenance crews repairing the track.

"Get off the road," Jacob said to Margaret. "Go over the bridge and head down the track bed."

She turned and looked at him. "I thought you

said they'd never be suspicious of two women in a buggy?"

"That was before it occurred to me that the sheriff and his deputies were watching the bank."

"That goes without saying, but what does it have to do with our escape?"

"Don't you see, dear sister? I was the last one to enter the bank and never came out. If what you say is true, Pardee is no fool. He must have put two and two together by now and is looking for both of us. But he'll never think to search for us riding over the track bed. He'll be certain we took the road."

"And if he doesn't find us, what do you think he'll do then?"

"He'll backtrack, thinking that we hid out in the trees while he and his posse rode past. By then, we'll be on a train out of Montrose, dressed as two men."

As usual, Cromwell was miles ahead of his pursuers when it came to matching wits. Though he was disheartened that Bell had outsmarted him in laying a well-conceived trap, he gained a certain amount of satisfaction believing he had killed the famous Van Dorn agent.

Just as he had predicted, the sheriff and his posse charged down the road that was out of sight of the railroad tracks in the trees and, not finding any sign of their quarry, had doubled back toward Telluride. It was a bumpy ride over the railroad ties, but it was compensated for by knowing that Pardee had been hoodwinked and would end up empty-handed.

27

Bell was carried to the Telluride Hospital, where he was treated by the town doctor. The first bullet out of Cromwell's Colt had entered and exited his thigh, causing only minor damage to the tissue. The doctor said it would heal within a month. The doctor then stitched the scalp wound, sewing up the crease as neatly as a tailor mending a torn suit pocket.

After ignoring the doctor's demands that he remain in the hospital for a few days, Bell limped to the depot to take the next train to Denver. Wearing a hat to cover the bandage around his head, he, along with Curtis, watched with anger and sadness as the coffin containing Irvine was lifted into the baggage car by Sheriff Pardee's deputies. Then he turned and held out his hand to Pardee. "Sheriff, I can't thank you enough for your cooperation. I'm grateful."

Pardee shook Bell's hand. "I'm sorry about your friend," he said sincerely. "Did he have a family?"

"Fortunately, no wife or children, but he lived with an aging mother."

"Pour soul. I suppose it's the county poorhouse for her."

"She'll be taken care of in a good nursing home."

"A good nursing home doesn't come cheap. Did Irvine have money?"

"No," replied Bell, "but I do."

Pardee refrained from any more questions. "If only things had fallen our way."

"Our well-laid plans certainly turned into a fiasco," said Bell, seeing the baggage car door close behind the coffin. "The bandit made me out the fool."

"Not your fault," said Pardee. "He fooled us all, and I was the biggest fool. I'm certain now the destitute widow who my wife and I took in was in cahoots with him. I should have been suspicious when she finagled information out of me about the bank's operations."

"But you didn't tell her there was a trap being set. Cromwell would have never walked into the bank if he suspected a trap."

Pardee shook his head. "They bought your story – hook, line, and sinker. If only we had known he was going to wear women's clothing, we might not have thought twice before we shot him down like the dog he is."

"According to reports of his other robberies, he never dressed as a woman."

"Even if the trap turned sour, my posse and I should have apprehended them. Stupidly, I thought they'd stay on the road. It never crossed my mind they would use the railroad track bed as an escape route until it was too late. By the time I figured out how they had outfoxed me, they were long gone."

"Were the train passenger lists checked in Montrose?"

"I wired the stationmaster, but they had already left on the train to Grand Junction," answered Curtis. "He didn't remember two women boarding, but he noticed two men. He said that one looked as if he were sick."

"There was blood on the back step of the bank," said Pardee with a tight smile. "You must have plugged him."

"Not seriously enough to stop him," Bell muttered quietly.

"I telegraphed the marshal of the territory. He had deputies in Grand Junction search all the trains going east and west but found no trace of two women traveling together."

Bell leaned on a cane given to him by Pardee. "I'm beginning to know how the bandit's mind works. He went back to wearing men's clothes and dressed his sister as a man, too. The marshal, looking for two females, never suspected them."

"A clever man, Cromwell."

"Yes," admitted Bell, "he is that."

"Where do you go from here?" asked Pardee.

"Back to Denver and start all over again."

"But now you know the bandit's name and habits."

"Yes, but making a case is impossible. No federal prosecutor would waste time on an indictment with such flimsy evidence."

"You'll nail him," Pardee said confidently.

"We'll work even harder now that we've got a personal reason to see him hung," said Bell.

When Bell and Curtis reached Denver late in the evening, a hearse was waiting to take Irvine to the local mortuary.

"He was my closest friend," said Curtis. "I'll console his mother and take care of the funeral arrangements."

"Thank you," Bell said. "I'll take care of the costs."

Bell took a taxi to the Brown Palace Hotel. Entering his suite, he removed his clothes and relaxed in a tub of hot water, propping his wounded leg on the edge to keep the bandage from getting wet. He closed his eyes and let his mind wander over the events of the past few days. Bell now knew the woman he'd passed in the New Sheridan Hotel was Margaret Cromwell. When her brother entered the bank from the front door, she was waiting in the rear with a horse and buggy. The picture of Cromwell made up as a woman disgusted him, yet he could not help but respect the shrewd, calculating mind of the Butcher Bandit. Avoiding Sheriff Pardee's posse by driving the rig down the railroad track bed was a stroke of genius.

At first, Bell thought Cromwell would not tempt fate with another robbery. The possibility seemed extremely remote, but, as he had with all the criminals he'd apprehended, Bell began to make inroads inside Cromwell's mind. He trained himself to think like the bandit. The more Bell thought about it, the more he became convinced that Cromwell believed he was invincible and immune to every investigation by law enforcement officers, especially the agents of the Van Dorn Detective Agency.

The next step would have to be carefully thought out. His mind was considering alternatives to accumulate enough evidence to arrest Cromwell when he heard a knock on his door. Favoring his good leg and suffering a brief bout of dizziness caused by his head wound as he stood, Bell climbed awkwardly out of the tub, put on a robe, and limped to the door. After pulling it open, he was surprised to see Joseph Van Dorn standing in the hallway.

Van Dorn looked up at the bandage around Bell's head, which had seeped a spot of red, and he grinned tightly. "You're a sorry sight."

"Come in, sir, and make yourself at home."

Van Dorn studied his wounded agent. He was concerned, but he made an effort to look nonchalant. "Is there much pain?"

"Nothing aspirin won't cure."

Van Dorn stepped into the suite and looked around. "I like an agent who travels in style when it's not my money."

"Can I call room service and get you something to eat or drink?"

Van Dorn waved a hand. "No, thanks, I ate on the train from Chicago just before it arrived in Denver. A glass of port would hit the spot."

Bell phoned Van Dorn's request to room service and hung up the phone. "I did not expect the head man to travel over a thousand miles just to see me."

"A meeting between us is not only appropriate but vital to the investigation." Van Dorn sank into an overstuffed chair. "I prefer a detailed report to a few words on a telegram. Now, tell me what happened in Telluride, and leave out nothing."

"Most of what I can tell you went wrong," Bell said sourly.

"Don't blame yourself," Van Dorn consoled him. "I wish I had a dollar for every plan I conceived that turned bad."

A waiter brought a glass of port, and then Bell spent the next forty minutes filling Van Dorn in on the scheme to catch the Butcher Bandit and how Cromwell turned the tables on him and Sheriff Pardee. He told of the murder of Irvine and his own wounding, ending up with him waking up in the Telluride Hospital.

When Bell finished, Van Dorn asked, "You're certain Jacob Cromwell is the Butcher Bandit?"

"His disguise was the work of genius, and Irvine and I were caught off guard. But there is no doubt in my mind Cromwell was the person I recognized wearing women's clothing at the bank. Both Pardee and I also identified his sister, Margaret, who was staying in town to help him rob the bank."

Van Dorn pulled a cigar case from his vest pocket,

retrieved a long, thin corona, and lit it with a wooden match he flamed with his thumbnail. "It makes no sense. If Cromwell is wealthy, owns a bank with assets in the millions, and lives on Nob Hill in San Francisco, what does he gain by risking it all to pull off a string of robberies and murders?"

"From what I've been able to put together, the money he stole was used to build his bank's assets."

"But why now, when he is financially secure and his bank well established? Why continue the crime spree?"

Bell gazed through a window at the blue sky above the city. "The simple answer is, the man is insane. I've put together a profile of him in my mind. I'm certain he robs and kills because he enjoys it. The money is no longer his intent. It has lost its importance. Like a man addicted to whiskey or opium, he is driven to commit mayhem and murder. He believes himself too untouchable by law enforcement. In his mind, he is invincible and considers every criminal act as a challenge to outwit the law."

"You have to admit," said Van Dorn, blowing a large blue smoke ring across the room, "so far, he's done a pretty good job of making us and every peace officer west of the Mississippi look like a bunch of amateurs."

"Cromwell is not flawless. He's human and humans make mistakes. When the time comes, I intend to be there."

"Where do you go from here?"

Bell grimaced. "I wish everybody would stop asking me that."

"Well?"

Bell's gaze was focused and calm as he stared at Van Dorn. "It's back to San Francisco to build a case against Cromwell."

"From what you've told me, that won't be easy. You have little evidence to make a case. A defense attorney would crucify you on the witness stand. He'd laugh at your identification of a man dressed like a woman, claiming it was impossible to tell the difference. And, without another witness or any fingerprints, I'd have to say you're fighting a lost cause."

Bell fixed Van Dorn with an icy stare. "Are you suggesting I resign from the investigation?"

Van Dorn scowled. "I'm not suggesting anything of the sort. I'm only pointing out the facts. You know perfectly well this is the number one priority case within the agency. We won't rest until Cromwell is behind bars."

Bell tenderly touched the side of his head, as if to feel if the wound were still there. "As soon as I sew up a few loose ends here in Denver, I'm returning to San Francisco."

"I can arrange a team of agents to assist you. You have but to ask."

Bell shook his head. "No. With Carter as my right-hand man, and backed by Bronson and the agents in his office, I'll have all the manpower I'll need. Better we continue to work undercover without an army of agents to cause complications."

"What about Colonel Danzler and the Criminal Investigation Department in Washington? Can the government be of help in this matter?"

"Yes, but only at the opportune moment. Cromwell has an incredible amount of influence with the political and wealthy elite in San Francisco. He is the city's leading philanthropist. If we obtain enough evidence to indict him, his friends will circle the wagons and fight us every step of the way. At that time, we'll need all the help from the federal government we can get."

"What is your plan?"

"At the moment, I have no set plan. Cromwell is fat, dumb, and happy, not knowing we're getting closer to him with each passing day."

"But you're no closer now to seizing him than you were three weeks ago."

"Yes, but now I have the advantage."

Van Dorn's eyebrows raised in curiosity and he muttered skeptically, "What advantage is that?"

"Cromwell doesn't know I'm still alive."

"It will come as a blow to his ego when he sees you've been resurrected."

Bell smiled faintly. "I'm counting on it."

28

Cromwell's wound from Bell's bullet was not serious. He held off having it tended by a physician until he returned with Margaret to San Francisco, where the entry-and-exit wound in his side was cleaned with antiseptic, stitched, and bandaged. The doctor, an old friend, asked no questions, but Cromwell told him a lie anyway about accidentally shooting himself when cleaning a gun. Because his wife received a generous donation from Cromwell for her pet project, the ballet company of San Francisco, the doctor filed no police report and vowed the incident would never be mentioned.

Cromwell returned to his office at the bank and quickly settled into the old routine of managing his financial empire. His first project for the day was to write a speech to give at the opening of a sanitarium for the elderly, funded and built through his generosity. Modesty was not one of his virtues and he named the hospital the Jacob Cromwell Sanitarium. He called in Marion Morgan to transcribe his notes on the speech.

She sat in a chair beside his desk and gazed at him. "If you forgive me for asking, Mr. Cromwell, but are you feeling all right? You look a bit pale."

He forced a smile as he instinctively, lightly, touched his side. "I caught a cold from fishing at night. It's almost gone away."

He handed her his notes, swung around in his leather chair, and stared out the window at the surrounding city. "Edit my sanitarium speech, and please feel free to make any suggestions you feel are pertinent."

"Yes, sir."

Marion rose to leave Cromwell's office but hesitated at the door. "Excuse me, but I was wondering if you ever heard from the detective from the Van Dorn Agency again?"

Cromwell swung back around from the window and stared at her curiously. "Isaac Bell?"

"I believe that was his name."

He could not help a mild grin as he said, "He's dead. I heard he was killed during a bank robbery in Colorado."

Marion's heart felt as if it was squeezed between two blocks of ice. She could not believe Cromwell's words. Her lips quivered, and she turned away from him so he couldn't see the shock written on her lovely face. Barely maintaining her composure, she said nothing and stepped from the office and closed the door.

Marion sat at her desk as if in a trance. She could not understand the sense of grief over a man she hardly knew, a man with whom she had shared only one dinner. Yet she could see his face in her mind as if he was standing in front of her. The short-lived bond between them had been cruelly cut. She could not explain her feeling of sorrow and she didn't try. She felt as if she had lost a dear friend.

With trembling hands, she inserted a sheet of paper in her typewriter and began transcribing Cromwell's notes for his speech.

At five o'clock, late in the afternoon, Cromwell stood on the steps of a new three-story redbrick building on Geary and Fillmore Streets, listening to a long and flowery introduction by city mayor Eugene Schmitz, a close friend of Cromwell who had benefited from large contributions secretly transferred to his personal account at the Cromwell Bank. A crowd of five hundred people attended the inauguration, along with members of the city's fire and police departments, political bosses, and over fifty elderly patients sitting listlessly in their wheelchairs.

Cromwell's own remarks were short and to the point. He modestly referred to himself as a "humble messenger of the Lord" who had chosen to help those who could not help themselves. When he finished, the applause was polite and subdued, befitting the formal occasion. A ribbon was cut at the front entrance and Cromwell was heartily congratulated. He shook every hand that was thrust at him. He made a show of embracing all of the patients waiting to enter the building. Mayor Schmitz gave him a bronze plaque for his philanthropic efforts and announced that, henceforth, April 12th would be known as Jacob Cromwell Day.

Making his way through a throng of well-wishers and admirers, Cromwell reached the parking space that held the Mercedes Simplex. Margaret was already seated behind the wheel, looking lovely in a green wool dress with cape.

"Well done, brother. Another good deed under the Cromwell banner."

"It never hurts to have friends in high places, as well as the adoration of the foul-smelling rabble."

"Aren't *we* the humanitarian?" she said sarcastically.

"What about *your* benevolent pet projects that somehow get publicized in the society pages of the newspapers?" he retorted.

"Touché."

Cromwell moved to the front of the car and cranked the engine. Margaret retarded the spark and set the hand throttle. The engine caught and coughed into a throaty roar. Cromwell climbed into the seat as Margaret advanced the spark, shifted gears, and advanced the throttle. The Mercedes Simplex bounded out into the street between a cable car and beer truck.

By now, Cromwell was used to his sister's mad driving antics and relaxed in the seat, but was prepared to jump should a disaster rear up its head. "Drive up to Pacific Heights and stop at Lafayette Park."

"Any particular reason?"

"We can walk the paths while we talk."

She didn't question him further. The Mercedes Simplex easily cruised up the hill to Pacific Heights. She turned off Fillmore Street and took Sacramento Street until she reached the park, then stopped at the foot of a path leading into the trees. A five-minute walk took them to the summit of the park, which presented them with a beautiful panoramic view of the city.

"What do you wish to talk about?" Margaret asked.

"I've decided to undertake another robbery."

She stopped in midstride and stared at him in distress. "You must be joking."

"I'm dead serious."

"But why?" she demanded. "What have you to gain? You almost got caught in Telluride. Why tempt fate again for no purpose?"

"Because I like a challenge. Besides, I rather enjoy being a legend in my own time."

She turned and looked away stunned. "That's stupid."

"You don't understand," he said, putting his arm around her waist.

"I understand that it's crazy, and that someday your luck will run out and they'll hang you."

"Not for a while, at any rate," he said. "Not while their best agent lies in his grave."

Margaret remembered the incredible blue-purple eyes and Bell's arm around her as they danced at the

Brown Palace. She seemed to hear her voice from far away. "Bell dead, it's hard to believe."

He looked at her curiously. "You sound like you had a crush on him."

She shrugged and tried to look uninterested. "Oh, he was nice-looking, in a strange sort of way. I imagine other women found him attractive."

"No matter. Isaac Bell is history." Cromwell stopped and began leading his sister back to the automobile. "I'm going to fool Van Dorn and all the other stupid peace officers who want me hung. They'll never suspect I'd commit another crime so quickly, at a bank in a town they'd never suspect. Once again, they'll be caught with their pants down."

A tear came to her eye and Margaret dabbed a handkerchief at it, not sure if her emotions were twisted by Bell's demise or her brother's madness. "Where this time?"

"Not a mining town payroll," he said, grinning. "I'll throw them a curve and hit a town that doesn't expect me, and leave them frustrated once again."

"What town?"

"San Diego, here in California."

"That's almost in our backyard."

"All the better," said Cromwell. "My escape will be that much easier."

"What makes San Diego so special?"

"Because the city's Wells Fargo is fat with deposits, from merchants and from ships importing goods into the port. And because I'd love to poke a hole in my biggest competitor."

"You're crazy."

"Do not call me crazy!" he said harshly.

"What do you call yourself? Everything we've worked for could come crashing down around us if you're ever caught."

"Not so long as they're dealing with a mastermind," Cromwell said brashly.

"When will you ever stop?" Margaret demanded.

"When the Cromwell Bank is as big as the Wells Fargo Bank and I am crowned king of San Francisco," he said with a nasty glint in his eyes.

She knew it was hopeless to argue with her brother. Without his knowledge, she had quietly moved assets, little by little over the years, into the Wells Fargo Bank, where he would never think to trace them. The expensive jewelry she had purchased was put away in a safe-deposit box. If the worst came to pass and her brother was caught and hung, she would leave San Francisco, go to Europe, and live a life of luxury before finding a rich and titled husband.

They reached the automobile and Jacob helped his sister into the driver's seat. As he cranked the engine to life, Cromwell's self-confidence was overwhelming. Like a ship sailing into a heavy sea with all sails set, danger became a challenge that bordered on addiction. At the thought of outwitting every law enforcement officer in the West once again, his face beamed like that of a religious fanatic who had just witnessed a miracle.

Neither of them paid any attention to a man sitting on a bench near the car dressed like a worker, with a toolbox perched in his lap, casually smoking a pipe.

29

Bell's train got him into San Francisco at eight o'clock in the morning. By nine, he was meeting with Carter, Bronson, and five of his agents. Everyone was seated around a large conference table that was twice as large as the one in the office in Denver. Bell was dead tired, and his wounds still gave him trouble, but he ignored the pain, as he had with earlier injuries, and soldiered on.

"Gentlemen," he began, "now that our number one suspect for the Butcher Bandit is Jacob Cromwell, we are going to put him and his sister, Margaret, under twenty-four-hour surveillance."

"That means their every movement outside their palace on Nob Hill," added Bronson.

One agent held up a hand. "Sir, we'll need photos for identification, since most of us have no idea of what they look like."

Bronson picked up a bulky file on the table. "Photographs of them were taken while they were out and about town."

"Who took them?" asked Bell.

Bronson smiled and nodded at one of his agents across the table. "Dick Crawford here is an ace photographer."

"Didn't the Cromwells get suspicious about a photographer following them around, shooting their picture?" asked Carter.

Bronson nodded at Crawford. "Dick, tell everyone how you pulled it off without them getting wise."

Crawford had a narrow saturnine face with a small jaw and bushy eyebrows beneath a bald head. A serious man, he did not show any humorous disposition. "I wore coveralls and carried a toolbox with a small hole cut out in one end for the camera lens. All I had to do was reach into the box to adjust the focus and shoot their picture. They didn't have a clue and never so much as gave me a glance." He then set a small camera on the table and explained its application. "What you see is a Kodak Quick Focus box camera that takes postcard-sized images."

As Crawford talked, Bronson passed out photos of Jacob and Margaret Cromwell.

"You will note that the photos are remarkably sharp and distinct," Crawford continued. "The unique feature of the camera is that, unlike other cameras with a set focus, I could set the distance using the small wheel you see on the side. Then all I had to do was press a button and the front of the lens would pop out to the correct distance for exposure."

Everyone studied the photos. They showed the Cromwells, individually or together, walking down the street, coming out of stores and restaurants. Several photos were of Jacob Cromwell entering and exiting his bank. Two showed him speaking at the opening of his sanitarium for the elderly. Crawford even followed them to Lafayette Park and shot them walking along a path. Bell was particularly interested in the pictures showing Margaret behind the wheel of an exotic-looking car.

"A Mercedes Simplex," he said admiringly. "The Cromwells have good taste in automobiles."

Bronson examined the photos showing the car. "It looks expensive. How fast will it go?"

"At least seventy, maybe eighty, miles an hour," replied Bell.

"I doubt if there is a car in San Francisco that could catch it in a chase," said a bushy-haired agent at the end of the table.

"There is *now*," Bell said, his lips spread in a grin. "It was unloaded from a freight car this morning." He looked at Curtis. "Am I correct, Arthur?"

Curtis nodded. "Your automobile is sitting in the Southern Pacific freight warehouse. I hired a boy who works in the railyard to clean it up."

"You sent a car here from . . ."

"Chicago," Bell finished.

"I'm curious," said Bronson. "What automobile is so special that you'd have it shipped all the way from Chicago?"

"A fast motorcar can come in handy. Besides, as it turns out, it's more than a match for Cromwell's Mercedes Simplex, should it come to a pursuit."

"What make is it?" asked Crawford.

"A Locomobile," answered Bell. "It was driven

by Joe Tracy, who drove it to third place in the 1905 Vanderbilt Cup road race on Long Island."

"How fast is it?" inquired Bronson.

"She'll get up to a hundred and five miles an hour on a straight stretch."

There came a hushed silence. Everyone around the table was astounded and disbelieving.

They had never seen or heard of anything that could go so fast. Professional auto races with competing factory cars had not come to the West Coast yet.

"Incredible," said Bronson in awe. "I can't imagine anything traveling a hundred miles an hour."

"Can you drive it on the street?" asked Curtis.

Bell nodded. "I had fenders and headlamps installed and the transmission modified for street traffic."

"You've got to give me a ride in it," said Bronson.

Bell laughed. "I think it can be arranged."

Bronson turned his interest back to the photos of the Cromwells. "Any thoughts on what the bandit will do next?"

"After Telluride," said Curtis, "I would bet his days of robbery and murder have ended."

"Sounds logical if he knows we're onto him," agreed Bronson.

"We can't be sure of that if he thinks all witnesses to the fiasco in Telluride are dead, including me," said Bell. "He is a crazy man, driven to rob and kill. I don't believe he can ever stop cold. Cromwell believes his criminal acts can never be traced. He simply does not fit the mold of Black Bart, the James Gang, the Daltons, or Butch Cassidy. Compared to Cromwell, they were crude, backwoods amateurs."

One of the agents stared with growing admiration at Bell. "So you think he will strike again."

"I do."

"You may have suckered him with your story about Telluride," said Bronson. "But if he is as smart as you say he is, Cromwell won't make the same mistake twice and step into another trap."

Bell shook his head. "There is little hope of that, I'm afraid. For the moment, all we can do is try to outguess him, and, failing that, we keep gathering evidence until we can convict him."

"At least we know he isn't infallible."

Bronson grunted. "He's about as close as you can come."

Bell poured himself a cup of coffee from a pot sitting on the conference table. "Our edge is that he doesn't know his every move is being watched. You will have to be very careful and not make him or his sister wary. If we can stay on his tail the next time he leaves town for a robbery, we have a chance of bringing his crime wave to a halt."

Bronson looked around the table at his agents. "It looks like we have our job cut out for us, gentlemen. I'll let you work out your surveillance shifts among yourselves. I received a telegram from Mr. Van Dorn. He said to pull out all the stops. He wants the

Butcher Bandit caught, whatever the cost, whatever the effort."

Bell said to Bronson, "I wonder if you could do me a favor."

"You have but to name it."

"Call Cromwell's office and ask for Marion Morgan. Tell her you're calling in the strictest confidence and she is to say nothing to no one, including her boss. Tell her to meet you at the northeast corner of Montgomery and Sutter Streets, a block from the Cromwell Bank, during her lunch hour."

"And if she asks me the purpose?"

Bell made a crooked smile. "Just be vague and tell her it's urgent."

Bronson laughed. "I'll do my best to sound official."

After the conference, Bell and Carter took a cab to the Southern Pacific freight warehouse. They checked in with the superintendent, looked over the car for damage, and, finding none, signed off the necessary transport paperwork.

"She's a beauty," Curtis said admiringly, gazing at the bright red-painted automobile with its gleaming brass radiator topped by a custom-sculpted bronze eagle with wings outspread and a temperature gauge in its chest. Behind the radiator was a barn-roof-cut hood. A big cylindrical gas tank sat mounted behind the two seats. The narrow tires were moored to huge wooden spoked wheels that had sped over the twisting roads of Long Island during the Vanderbilt Cup race.

Bell climbed into the seat behind the big steering wheel, mounted on its long shaft, turned the ignition switch on the wooden dashboard, set the throttle lever on the steering wheel, and moved the spark lever to retard. Next, he took a hand pump and pressurized the fuel tank, forcing gas to the carburetor. Only then did he walk to the front of the car, grip the big crank with his right hand, and heave vigorously. The engine coughed and kicked over on the second try, with a thunderous roar from the exhaust pipe.

Then Bell, joined by Carter, sat in the red leather driver's seat and advanced the spark as he eased the throttle to an idle position. After releasing the brass hand brake, he pushed in the clutch and pulled the shift lever into first gear. Next, he moved the throttle lever and released the clutch, having attracted a crowd of warehouse workers who cheered as the rakish car rolled forward.

As soon as the Locomobile was speeding down a road alongside the railroad tracks, Carter asked loudly, "Are we headed back to the office?"

Bell shook his head. "Show me the way to the warehouse where the O'Brian Furniture boxcar was parked."

"Then turn left at the next crossing over the tracks," directed Carter.

A few minutes later, Bell parked the Locomobile behind the empty warehouse and turned off the big engine. With Carter leading the way, they walked up a ramp to the loading dock. A single freight car sat on the siding.

"Is this where you found Cromwell's phony furniture freight car?" asked Bell.

"According to the Southern Pacific's freight-movement schedule," said Curtis. "I ran a check of company freight car movements. Car 16173 is no longer listed on Southern Pacific freight records. No one knows what happened to it. It's as if it vanished overnight."

Bell studied the sides of the car parked alongside the loading dock. "It could have been repainted and given a new serial number."

"It's entirely possible." Curtis stared at the number and then nodded. "Car 16455. I'll check it out."

"This car has had a new paint job recently," said Bell slowly. "There isn't a scratch on it."

"You're right," Curtis murmured thoughtfully. "It's as clean as the day it came out of the factory."

Bell walked up to the boxcar's loading door and placed his fingers around a bronze lock that sealed the interior from entry. "Why would an empty car on a siding be locked up?"

"Maybe it's been loaded with cargo and is waiting to be coupled to a train."

"I wish I knew what was inside," Bell mused.

"Shall we break it open?" Curtis inquired with a growing sense of anticipation.

Bell made a slight shake of his head. "Better we

leave well enough alone for the time being. Until we check out the serial number, we won't know the history of this car. And should it belong to Cromwell, he'll know if we tampered with the lock."

"If we proved this is the freight car he used to escape his criminal acts, we can arrest him."

"Nothing is that simple. It might simply be an empty car that was shunted to this siding temporarily. Cromwell's no fool. He wouldn't leave evidence lying around just waiting to be found. Chances are, there is nothing incriminating inside, certainly not enough to stand him under the hangman's noose."

Curtis shrugged in understanding. "We'll keep a sharp eye on it, but I doubt if he'll be using it anytime soon, if ever again, considering how he came within a hair of being caught in Telluride."

"And, sooner or later, he'll learn I'm still alive and know I identified him," Bell said with a wide grin. "Then he'll really make things interesting."

Marion put down the phone and looked toward the doorway leading to Cromwell's office. As usual, it was closed. He almost always worked in private, handling his day-to-day business over the telephone or a speaker system he had installed around the bank.

She glanced up at a big Seth Thomas Regulator wall clock, with its enclosed pendulum swinging back and forth. The hands were pointing at Arabic numerals that read three minutes to twelve. When she put down the phone after listening to Bronson's instructions, she was torn between her loyalty to Cromwell – and whether she should tell him about the call – and the building sense of excitement that coursed through her body at the thought of performing an act of secrecy. Because a distinct rift had built between her and Cromwell over the past year, especially since that night in the Barbary Coast when he and Margaret had acted so strangely, she felt less loyalty and respect toward him. He was not the same man she had come to trust for so many years. He had become distant and aloof, cold and rude toward her much of the time.

The minute hand clicked over the hour hand, both pointing to twelve, when she took her purse, put on her hat, and stepped out of the office, all the while keeping an eye on the closed doorway to Cromwell's office. She bypassed the elevator and flew down the stairway to the lobby. Passing through the big entrance doors, she turned and hurried down Sutter Street to Montgomery. The streets and sidewalks were busy during the lunch hour and it took her a good ten minutes to skirt the crowds. Reaching the corner, she stood there, looking around, but found no one looking in her direction or coming toward her. She had never met Bronson and had no idea what he looked like.

After a minute, her attention, and that of many people passing along the street, was drawn to a big red car that moved effortlessly through traffic. There was a brute strength about its appearance that made it look as if it were hurtling over the pavement, even though it was moving no more than twenty miles an hour. Its bright red paint had been hand rubbed to a glistening finish. Everything about it portrayed a powerful elegance.

With her attention focused on the car, she did not notice the man behind the wheel until it came to a stop in front of her and he said, "Please climb in, Marion."

She paled, one hand flying up and holding her throat, startled to find herself gazing into the violet eyes of Isaac Bell that seemed to draw her into his soul. "Isaac," she murmured in shock. "Jacob told me you were dead."

He held out his hand, grasped hers, and pulled her up onto the leather passenger seat with an case and strength that stunned her. "It just goes to show, you can't believe all you hear."

Oblivious to the crowd that had gathered around the car, Bell circled his arm around Marion's waist. Then he took her in his arms and kissed her.

"Isaac!" she gasped when he released her. Her protest was one more of enjoyment than embarrassment. "Not in front of all these people."

By now, the crowd that had assembled to stare at the car found themselves being entertained by the man and woman in the front seats. They began to applaud and cheer them on.

Bell pulled back and smiled wickedly. "I was never able to resist a beautiful lady."

Marion was almost swept away by the moment

– almost but not quite. "Can we please move away?" she insisted.

Bell laughed, tipped his hat to the people cheering him on, and shifted the Locomobile into first gear. He stepped lightly on the gas pedal and moved into the street amid the flow of traffic. He drove north on Montgomery before turning left into Chinatown. He swung into an alley and came to a stop behind a large Mandarin-style restaurant, painted red and gold and with a pagoda roof. An attendant waiting there bowed.

"I will watch your car, sir."

Bell gave him a tip that made the attendant's eyes pop. "I'm counting on you." Then he helped Marion from her seat to the ground.

"The Empress of Shanghai," she said, staring at the ornate entrance. "I've always wanted to eat here."

"It came highly recommended."

"I wondered how you knew about the rear parking."

After they entered a long hallway, they were greeted by a beautiful woman with long shiny black hair wearing a Chinese sheath silk dress slit high on the sides. She led them upstairs to a small private dining room and seated them. While they were studying the menu, a pot of tea arrived and was poured.

"You were limping," she said.

"A little memento of Telluride, Colorado."

For the first time, she noticed the bandage on his head as he removed his hat. She frowned and raised her eyebrows. "Another memento?"

He nodded and smiled gamely.

Marion looked into Bell's eyes and her own eyes became misty. "You don't know how happy I am that you weren't killed."

"Your boss certainly tried."

"Mr. Cromwell!" she exclaimed as her mood altered from compassion to alarm. "I don't understand."

"He's the man who shot me and killed a Van Dorn agent who was my friend."

"You can't be serious."

"Like it or not, Jacob Cromwell is the Butcher Bandit who has held up over twenty banks in the past twelve years and killed nearly forty innocent people."

"That's crazy!" Marion bit her lower lip. She looked as if she was lost and had nowhere to turn. "He couldn't have done what you say."

"What I said is true," Bell said with a sudden gentleness. "We have evidence. Maybe not enough to convict, but it falls at Cromwell's doorstep."

"But he's helped so many people in need," she protested.

"A front," said Bell icily. "He's built a wall around his empire, guarded by an army of good citizens who believe he and Margaret are generous people who want to help the poor out of the goodness of their hearts. It's an act. Cromwell couldn't care less about those who are destitute. He uses them to promote his own purposes. In the eyes of the city's crooked politicians, he can do no wrong so long as he supports them with secret donations."

Confused, Marion sipped at her tea, her hand noticeably trembling. "I simply refuse to believe it," she murmured.

Bell reached across the table and took both her hands in his. "Believe me, Marion, it's true. I looked into his eyes and recognized him the instant he shot me at the bank in Telluride."

She pulled her hands back and clasped them together tightly. "Oh, Isaac, it's all too fantastic. Why would Jacob rob banks when he already owns the second-largest bank in San Francisco? The thought is too absurd to be real."

"I can't give you an answer, Marion. In the beginning, he took the money to build his own bank. But when he became rich, the robbery and killings became an obsession. I've seen many cases like Cromwell's. The robberies and the murders are like a narcotic for him. He can't help himself, and will go on killing until I stop him."

She looked up into his sensitive violet eyes across the table. They had turned dark and cold. "You, Isaac? Does it have to be you?"

"I can't let him go on murdering people." Bell spoke the words in a monotone, as if he were reading an accusation in a courtroom. "I am not going to let him thumb his nose at the law and continue to run around free, living the life of a wealthy Santa Claus." Then he added, "And that goes for his sister,

Margaret. She's buried in his evil operations up to her pretty neck."

Marion dipped her head in utter confusion as her hat covered her eyes. "I've known Jacob and Margaret for years and yet I didn't know them."

"It's hard," Bell said softly, "but you'll have to accept it."

She tilted her head back and the forward brim of her wide flowered hat rose until he could look directly into her coral–sea green eyes. "What can I do?" she asked softly.

"For one thing, you must go on as if you know nothing. Continue your duties as his loyal secretary. Our agents will have both brother and sister under constant surveillance. All you have to do is report anything suspicious or unusual regarding Jacob's actions."

"You mean, of course, report to *you*."

He nodded. "Yes."

She suddenly had the feeling she was being used, that Bell's interest in her was purely as an informer. She turned away so he couldn't see the tears welling up in her eyes.

Bell immediately sensed what was whirling in her mind. He moved his chair around the table until he was sitting close enough to put his arm around her shoulders. "I know what you're thinking, Marion, and it's not true. I know I am asking you to commit a devious act, but lives hang in the balance. Yet there is much more. It goes far beyond a request for your help." He paused to build up his courage. "I'm in love with you, Marion. I can't explain why it happened so suddenly, but it did. You must believe me."

Marion looked into his face and saw only affection and fondness. Her fears vanished in an instant as she leaned forward and kissed him solidly on the lips. When she pulled back, she smiled wickedly. "You must think I'm a brazen hussy."

He laughed at seeing her blush. "Not at all. I enjoyed it."

Then her eyes turned soft. "I have to admit I felt something when I looked up and saw you standing there in the office."

This time, *he* kissed her.

After a long moment, he pulled back and grinned. "Perhaps we should order before they ask us to leave for disorderly conduct."

30

As soon as Marion returned from her lunch with Bell and was in the midst of typing a letter, Cromwell called her into his office. She concealed her nervousness by not looking him in the face as he spoke.

"Marion, I'm going to attend the National Conference for Community Banks. It is being held in Los Angeles this year on March twenty-eighth to March thirtieth. Could you please make the necessary travel arrangements, and book me a room at the Fremont Hotel downtown?"

"To be in Los Angeles by the twenty-eighth, you'd have to leave tomorrow," said Marion. "That's awfully short notice."

"I know," Cromwell said with an offhand shrug. "I wasn't going to attend, but I changed my mind."

"Will you wish to charter a private car?"

"No. I'll leave private cars to the presidents of the Crocker and Wells Fargo banks. When I go on bank business, I'll travel as a simple passenger so my depositors will know I have their best interest at heart and am not squandering their money."

Marion rose to her feet with a rustle of her skirts. "I'll see to it."

As soon as she returned to her desk, she picked

up her telephone and in a low voice, nearly that of a whisper, asked the operator for the Van Dorn Detective Agency. When Marion gave the receptionist her name, she was immediately put through to Bell.

"Isaac?"

"Marion? I was just going to call and ask you out for dinner and a play."

She felt pleased that he was happy to hear her voice. "I have some information for you," she said seriously. "Jacob is going out of town."

"Do you know where?"

"Los Angeles," she answered. "He's going to attend the National Conference for Community Banks. It's a forum for bankers, to exchange the latest in banking operations."

"When does it take place?"

"The twenty-eighth to the thirtieth of this month."

Bell thought a moment. "He'd have to be on a train tomorrow if he was going to make Los Angeles by the twenty-eighth."

"Yes, that's right," said Marion. "As soon as I ring off, I have to make his reservations. He's traveling in a coach, as an ordinary passenger."

"Not like your boss to save a buck."

"He claimed it would impress Cromwell depositors by not squandering the bank's assets."

"What do you think, Marion? Is this trip legitimate?"

She did not hesitate in answering. "I do know there

really is a National Conference for Community Banks on those dates in the City of Angels."

"I'll see that one of our agents is with him all the way."

"I feel soiled going behind his back," she said remorsefully.

"Do not regret it, sweetheart," Bell replied tenderly. "Jacob Cromwell is an evil man."

"What time should I expect you?" Marion asked, happy to get off the subject of Cromwell.

"I'll pick you up at six so we can have an early dinner before making the play."

"Are we going in your red racer?"

"Do you mind?"

"No, I enjoy the exhilaration of speed."

He laughed. "I knew there was something about you that attracted me."

Marion hung up the phone, surprised to find her heart beating at a rapid rate.

On gut instinct, and the knowledge that Bell and his agent Irvine had been nosing around before he killed them, Cromwell made elaborate plans to cover his tracks even more thoroughly. He was certain that with the loss of two of his agents, Van Dorn would add fuel to the investigation by probing ever deeper into every lead. He could expect more agents to come around asking more questions about the stolen money that had been dispersed through merchants and other banks around the city.

Just to be on the safe side, Cromwell called the chief dispatcher of the Southern Pacific and informed him that he was sending in a written request to move his disguised freight car, now serial number 16455, sitting at the abandoned warehouse, to a new location across the bay in Oakland. Within minutes, the order was received by the yardmaster, who sent a switch engine that was coupled to the car and pulled it onto a boxcar ferry.

Cromwell also ordered a special train, a private Pullman car pulled by an engine and tender; destination: San Diego. The order went through the O'Brian Furniture Company of Denver, which had a long-standing account and was a respected customer of the Southern Pacific Railroad Company.

Only then did he sit back in his chair, light an expensive cigar, and relax, totally self-assured that he was once again ten steps ahead of any remote suspicion that might be held by Van Dorn or any other law enforcement agency.

He would have been even more smug if he had known that before Bronson could send an agent to keep an eye out for anyone approaching the freight car, it had been switched onto the ferry and transported to a siding in the Southern Pacific railyard in Oakland.

31

Early the next morning, Cromwell bid Margaret good-bye and stepped into his Rolls-Royce limousine. Abner smoothly steered the car through the city traffic to the Southern Pacific passenger station for trains running directly north or south that did not have to cross the bay. Stopping at the station entrance, he opened the car door and handed Cromwell a valise.

As the Rolls pulled away from the curb, Cromwell casually walked into the station, showed his ticket to the gatekeeper, and joined the other passengers moving along the platform. He climbed the steps to the third coach and boarded the train.

A Van Dorn agent watched him board and then loitered until the train began to move, making sure that Cromwell did not step back on the platform, in case he had missed the train. Only then did the agent swing aboard the last car and begin walking through the passenger cars until he reached the one Cromwell had entered. To his amazement, Cromwell was nowhere to be seen. Alarmed, the agent rushed through the remaining cars, searching until he reached the locked door to the baggage car. Still no Cromwell. Then he hurried to the back of the train, entertaining the possibility that he had missed the banker, but Cromwell was still nowhere to be found.

Unseen, Cromwell had departed the passenger car by the opposite door and stepped down and crossed the tracks to another platform, where the special train he had chartered was waiting. He climbed aboard his private car, where he relaxed in the luxury and glamour of what was a veritable yacht on wheels. He removed his coat, sat back casually in an overstuffed velvet chair, and opened the morning paper. A steward served him breakfast that had been specially prepared by the car's private chef. He was leisurely reading the *San Francisco Chronicle* when the train pulled away from the station and onto the main track for the run to Los Angeles, just fifteen minutes behind the regularly scheduled passenger train on which Marion had booked him a seat.

"No word from my agent, so I can safely assume Cromwell is on his way to Los Angeles," said Bronson.

Bell looked up from a map depicting San Francisco and its neighboring big city to the south. "His train is scheduled to arrive in Los Angeles at four-thirty this evening. I'm told he's staying at the Fremont Hotel."

"I was lucky. I managed to wire Bob Harrington, who heads up the Southern California Van Dorn office, before the flash flood somewhere to the south took out the line. He's going to have a man disguised as a cabbie pick up Cromwell and take him to his hotel. My agent on the train will point him out. From there, Harrington's agents can keep a tight rein on him."

"His trip sounds innocent enough," Bell said slowly. "But I don't trust him. He's up to something. I feel it in my bones."

"He won't get far if he tries anything." Bronson said confidently. "Should he make even a tiny false move, a dozen agents will land on him like a ton of bricks."

Bell walked back to an empty office and rang up Marion over at the bank. "Did you survive last night?" he asked lovingly.

"I had a wonderful time, thank you. The meal was scrumptious and the play was delightful."

"Now that the cat is away, how about the mouse coming out and play – say, for lunch?"

"I'm game."

"I'll pick you up in front of the bank."

"I'll meet you where we met before," she said without hesitation. "I don't want our relationship to be obvious. If any of the employees see me getting in your flashy red car, they're liable to talk, and it will get back to Jacob."

"Same time, same place," he said before he hung up.

Later that morning, a Western Union messenger came running into the office. "I have an urgent message for a Mr. Horace Bronson," he said to the receptionist, gasping because of his dash from the Western Union office.

Bronson, who was coming back from the bathroom down the hall, said, "I'm Bronson. I'll take it." He flipped the messenger a coin and tore open the envelope. As he read the message, his lips tightened and his forehead turned into a hard frown. He rushed through the office until he came to Bell.

"We're in trouble," he announced.

Bell looked at him questioningly. "Trouble?"

"My man lost Cromwell."

Bell faltered, taken completely off balance. "How could he lose him on a train?"

"Cromwell must have gotten on the train and immediately jumped off the opposite side without being seen."

"Your agent should have alerted us sooner," Bell snapped, anger flaring.

"The train had departed the station and he couldn't get off until it stopped in San Jose," Bronson explained. "He sent a telegram from there."

"He could have saved thirty minutes by using the telephone."

Bronson shrugged helplessly. "The phone lines are unreliable and in constant repair."

Bell sank into a chair, stunned and furious at having the rug pulled out from under him. "He's going to rob and kill again," he said, his face flushed with frustration. "The bastard is rubbing it in our faces."

"If we only knew where," said Bronson, overcome with defeat.

Bell walked over to the window and looked across the roofs of the city buildings. He stared without seeing, lost in thought. Finally, he turned. "Cromwell is taunting us," he said slowly. "He expects us to run around like chickens with our heads cut off, wondering where he went."

"He's obviously heading in the opposite direction he told his secretary." Bronson gave Bell a hard stare. "Unless she's lying."

Bell didn't meet his stare. The possibility crossed his mind, too. He merely shook his head. "No, I'm certain Marion told the truth."

Bronson walked over to a map of the United States hanging on one wall. He stared at it, perplexed. "I doubt if he'll head north into Oregon or Washington. He probably doubled back to the Ferry Building, crossed the bay, and took a train heading east."

A smile slowly began to curve and spread across Bell's face. "I'll bet my Locomobile Cromwell is still heading south."

Bronson looked at him. "Why would he continue south if he literally threw us off the track?"

"I know how the man thinks," said Bell in a voice that defied argument. "Though he doesn't know his every movement is being watched, he never takes chances, every possibility is carefully thought out."

Bronson looked at his pocket watch. "The next train isn't until noon."

"Too late," Bell disagreed. "He has too much of a head start."

"But how do we know that, since he jumped the train?"

"He gave Marion a cock-and-bull story about riding in coach so his depositors would think he's a down-to-earth kind of guy. Ten will get you twenty he chartered a private train."

Bronson's apprehension appeared to loosen. "Harrington can still have his agents follow him when he arrives in Los Angeles."

Bell shook his head. "His agents won't be able to identify him. Your agent got off the train in San Jose to notify you Cromwell wasn't on board. He's probably waiting for the next train back to San Francisco."

"That is a problem," Bronson agreed. "But they can still grab him when he checks into the Fremont Hotel."

"*If* Cromwell checks into the Fremont," Bell said shrewdly. "Since he slipped off the passenger train, it's unlikely the rest of his story to Miss Morgan was true."

"If not Los Angeles, then where is he going?"

"Cromwell could stop his train anywhere between here and there, but my guess is that he's going on through Los Angeles."

"*Through?*" wondered Bronson. "Through to where?"

"The last place we would expect him to go for a robbery, the least likely destination."

"Which is?"

"San Diego."

Bronson thought quietly for several moments. Finally, he said, "That's a long shot."

"Maybe. But that's all we have going," said Bell. "He's demonstrated that he doesn't always rob mining towns. Why not a city with a bank bulging with profits from goods imported by rich merchants and the owners of large ranches around Southern California?"

"A long shot or not, we can't overlook it. If only I could alert Harrington to send his agents to the San Diego railroad terminal and be on the lookout for a private train. But the telephone and telegraph lines from San Jose to Los Angeles are still down due to flooding."

Bell shook his head. "Cromwell's too smart to run his train directly into the city. He'll park in on some remote siding and use another mode of transportation to get to the city, probably the motorcycle he used on other robberies."

"If only Harrington's had a description," said Bronson.

"They couldn't identify him anyway; he'll probably be wearing a disguise."

Bronson's optimism suddenly vanished out the window. "Then where does that leave us?"

Bell smiled. "I'll have to go to San Diego and confront him myself."

"Not possible," Bronson said. "By the time we can

hire a special express train, have it on the tracks, and leave town, he will have conducted his dirty business and be halfway back to San Francisco."

"Very true," acknowledged Bell. "But, with a little luck, I can make it to Los Angeles before his train arrives and be waiting for him."

"So how are you going to beat him to Los Angeles, fly on a big bird?" Bronson said sarcastically.

"I don't need a big bird." Bell gave Bronson a canny look. "I have something just as fast." Then he smiled bleakly. "But, first, I have to break a date."

32

The big red Locomobile swept through San Francisco like a bull running through the streets of Pamplona, Spain, during the Fiesta of San Fermin. Bell sat back in the red leather seat, his two hands tightly gripping the bottom of the big spoked steering wheel, turning the car with his palms facing up, using his biceps to twist the stiff mechanism around curves and street corners.

The time was fifteen minutes before ten o'clock.

Next to him, in the shotgun seat, sat Bronson, whose job was to keep the fuel pressure pumped up. Every few minutes, he pulled out the pump handle that was mounted on the upper wooden panel just above the slanting floorboard and shoved it forward, sending gas to the carburetor. Besides keeping the big hungry engine fed, he took on the job of navigator, since Bell had no knowledge of the California countryside. As Bell drove, Bronson braced his feet on the floorboard and pressed his back into the leather seat to keep from being thrown to the pavement, feeling as if he was being shot through the muzzle of a cannon.

Not wanting to take either hand from the steering wheel, Bell also gave Bronson the job of sounding the big horn bulb. The agent seemed to enjoy squeezing out squawking honks at the people and traffic, especially at intersections. It was not long before his hand ached.

Bronson was wearing a long leather coat, his feet and lower legs encased in boots. His head was covered by a leather helmet with huge goggles that made him look like an owl on a quest for a rodent. The goggles were a necessity since the Locomobile did not have a windshield.

The car hadn't traveled a hundred yards when Bronson had dire misgivings about what he had gotten himself into by insisting that he accompany Bell on this mad dash to San Diego in an open car over roads that weren't much better than cow paths.

"How are the brakes on this mechanical marvel of engineering?" Bronson asked caustically.

"Not great," Bell answered. "The only brakes are on the shaft driving the chains to the rear wheels."

"Do you have to go so fast through town?" Bronson protested.

"Cromwell's private train has over an hour's head start," yelled Bell through the exhaust. "We need every minute we can gain."

Pedestrians, who heard the throaty exhaust roar coming up the street followed by a strange blaring sound from the bulb horn, were stunned when they saw the red Locomobile bearing down on them. Staring incredulously, they quickly stepped out of the street until the machine sped past. The twin exhaust pipes, barely protruding from the left side of the hood, throbbed like cannon.

Two workmen, who were carrying a large windowpane alongside the street, froze in total shock as the car thundered past, the explosive roar of the Locomobile's exhaust shattering the glass in their hands. Neither Bell nor Bronson ever looked back, their complete focus being on the traffic that ran thick or thin in front of them, forcing Bell to swing the wheel violently back and forth as though he was driving through an obstacle course. His great satisfaction came in pointing the car in the direction he wanted to go and having it respond as if anticipating his thoughts.

Bell jockeyed his foot from the accelerator to the brake and back again, as he tore down the streets, hammering turns at the intersections onto the main street leading from the city, wishing he was a sorcerer who could magically make the traffic disappear. Bell narrowly missed a laundry truck, throwing the Locomobile into a four-wheel drift to avoid it. He spun the thick wooden rim of the steering wheel fiercely as he dove between vehicles littering the streets. Drivers of other motorized vehicles stared in awe at the speed of the car as it flashed up from behind and quickly disappeared up ahead. Horses harnessed to buggies and wagons reared at the noise of what their drivers thought was the devil's chorus.

As they neared the outer edge of the city's southern

limits, the traffic began to thin. Bell slowed the Locomobile around a sweeping turn onto the main road south that paralleled the railroad tracks. He breathed a sigh of relief at seeing automobiles and wagons becoming sparse. He was also thankful that he now had ample room to swerve around any vehicle that blocked his path. The huge automobile was incredibly responsive. Bell pressed the accelerator within an inch of the floor, as the car began to rocket along a road that ran straight with few curves. The faster the Locomobile traveled, the more solid her feel of stability, as the drive chains on her axles whirred at a high, metallic pitch.

Soon the road became straight and rural. Picturesque farming communities came up on the horizon and quickly slipped behind the automobile's dust trail. San Carlos, Menlo Park, and then San Jose, towns that were linked together by the El Camino Real, the old road used in the late 1700s by the Franciscan friars who built twenty-one missions, each a day's journey apart.

Enjoying a straight, open road with little traffic, Bell pressed the accelerator to the floor and pushed the automobile as hard as it could go. The Locomobile was in its element now, running as strongly as when it had in the Vanderbilt Cup race, the first American car to place in an international speed event. Like a racehorse that had been retired and then brought back to run again, the Locomobile roared down the road like a maddened elephant, the cavernous cylinders of its mighty engine turning the huge crankshaft effortlessly.

Bell loved the big machine. He had an exceptional sense of its temperament and idiosyncrasies. He gloried in its strength and simplicity, felt intoxicated by the speed produced by the big pounding engine, and drove like a demon possessed, reveling at the vast, swirling cloud of dust the Locomobile hurled in its wake.

Bronson looked over at Bell, who wore a short leather jacket and jodhpur riding pants with boots. He wore goggles but no helmet, preferring to hear the beat of the engine. There was a look of unfathomable concentration about him. He looked relentlessly determined to beat Cromwell at his own game. Bronson had never seen anyone with such fierce, decisive resolve. He turned away and studied his map. Then he tapped Bell on the shoulder.

"There is a fork in the road coming up. Veer left. The road is better inland than along the coast. At this rate, Salinas will come up in another hour. After that, Soledad."

"How's our time?" Bell asked without taking his hands from the wheel and digging out his pocket watch.

"Ten past eleven," Bronson answered over the exhaust. "Without knowing how fast we're going, I have no way of knowing how much time, if any, we've gained on Cromwell's train."

Bell nodded in understanding. "The auto does not

have a speedometer or a tachometer, but I'd guess our speed to be over ninety miles an hour."

Bronson had been slowly becoming attuned to the wind rushing against his face, the telegraph poles streaking past at lightning speed. But then a stretch of road became violently rough and rutted, and Bronson soon realized what it would be like inside the rattle of a maddened sidewinder. He clutched the arm of his seat in a death grip with one hand and gamely worked the fuel pump with the other.

They hurtled over the narrow, rolling farm road and crossed into Monterey County before coming to the agricultural community of Salinas. The farmland along the sides of the road was strikingly beautiful, turning green under the spring sun. Fortunately, the main road through town was quiet, with only one or two automobiles and a few horse-drawn wagons parked along the sidewalks. People heard the booming bellow of the Locomobile's exhaust as it crossed the city limits. They turned and looked speechlessly as the big fire red machine shot through the business section of town. They had no time to indulge their curiosity before the hard-charging machine was heading into the open country to the south.

"What's the next town?" asked Bell.

Bronson consulted his map. "Soledad."

"How far?

"About twenty-five miles. We'd better fill the tank there, because it's a good two hundred miles to the next major town." He turned and looked at the huge cylindrical brass tank mounted behind the seats. "How much does it hold?"

"Forty-five gallons."

"They should have a garage in Soledad that services automobiles and farm machinery."

The words were no sooner out of Bronson's mouth than the left rear tire went flat after striking a sharp rock in the road. The Locomobile fishtailed for a hundred yards before Bell brought it under control and braked it to a stop.

"Only a matter of time," said Bell resignedly. "One of the predicaments of road racing."

He was out of the automobile and shoving a jack under the rear axle within three minutes while Bronson removed one of the two spare tires on the rear of the automobile. Bell removed the wheel and replaced it inside of ten minutes. He had changed tires that gave out at breakneck speeds many times since he owned the Locomobile. Then he separated the tire from the wheel and tossed the tire to Bronson. "There's a patching kit under your seat. Patch the hole while we drive. I'll remount it on the wheel after we reach Salinas."

No sooner were they on their way again over a reasonably smooth road than a hay wagon hitched to a team of horses loomed up. The farmer, believing he was the only one for a mile around, was driving right down the center of the road, with only a few feet to spare before the weeds and brush along the edge of the dirt thoroughfare met fences surrounding fields of artichokes, chilies, mushrooms, and lettuce.

Bell began to slow but had no choice but to pull the Locomobile half off the road and pass the hay wagon with only inches to spare, but he hadn't been left enough room for a free-and-clear passage. He took out a good thirty feet of a frail wooden fence, luckily without causing severe damage to the car. Only the front right fender was bent and twisted, scraping the tire when it hit a bump in the road. Bell did not look back to see the farmer shaking his fist and cursing him as his horses reared and nearly turned the wagon over on its side. Nor was he happy at being inundated by the dust storm that spewed from the Locomobile's drive wheels.

"That's one mad sodbuster," said Bronson, turning in his seat and looking behind him.

"He probably built and owns the fence we destroyed," Bell said with a sly grin.

Within ten miles, Soledad came into view. Named after the Mission Nuestra Señora de la Soledad that had been founded over a hundred years before, the town was a major railroad stop in the valley for transporting to market as quickly as possible the produce grown there. Bell quickly slowed as he entered town and soon found a garage where he could purchase gasoline for the Locomobile. While Bronson and the garage owner poured cans of fuel into the big tank, Bell wrestled with the crumpled right front fender, bending it back away from the tire. Then he took the tube Bronson had patched, inserted it back inside the tire, and remounted it on the wheel before bolting it on the rear of the Locomobile.

"You fellas the first car in a race passing through?" the garage owner asked, clad in a pair of greasy coveralls.

Bell laughed. "No, we're alone."

The garage owner looked at the dusty and damaged automobile and shook his head. "You fellas must be in a mighty big hurry."

"That we are," said Bell, pressing bills that more than covered the price of the gasoline into the garage owner's hand.

He stood there, scratching his head, as the Locomobile roared away and quickly became a red speck down the main street of town before traveling out into the farm country. "Them fellas must be crazy," he mumbled. "I hope they know the bridge over Solvang Creek is out."

Fifteen minutes later and twenty miles down the road from Soledad, a sharp left-angled curve with a down slope came rushing toward them. A sign that stood beside the road flashed past.

"What did it say?" asked Bell.

"Something about a bridge, was all I caught," replied Bronson.

A barricade of railroad ties blocked the center of the road, and Bell could see the upper part of a bridge that looked as if it had broken apart in the middle. A crew of men were working to repair the center span while another crew were installing poles and restringing the telegraph and phone lines that had been torn away by a flash flood.

Bell jerked his foot off the accelerator, made a hard twist of the wheel. He jammed both feet on the brake, locking the rear wheels, fishtailing the rear end across the road, and causing the Locomobile to slow into a four-wheel drift. He straightened the front of the automobile with one second to spare and they flew through the air over the edge of the slope and dove down the steep bank of a broad ravine that had once been a dry wash. They landed in an explosion of dust less than twenty feet from a wide stream two feet deep that flowed toward the sea.

The heavy steel chassis and massive engine, driven by momentum, smacked into the water with an enormous eruption of silty brown water that burst over the Locomobile in a giant wave. The violent thump jarred Bell and Bronson in their every joint. Water gushed over the radiator and onto the hood before flooding over the men, drenching them in a deluge of liquid mud. Taking the full brunt of the surge, they felt as if they were driving through a tidal wave.

Then the big automobile burst into clean air on the opposite shore, as it shuddered and shed itself free of the stream. Bell instantly jammed the accelerator to the floor, hoping against hope that the powerful engine would not drown and die. Miraculously, the spark plugs, magneto, and carburetor survived to do their job and kept the big four-cylinder combustion chambers hitting without a single miss. Like a faithful steed, the Locomobile charged up the opposite slope until it shot onto level ground again and Bell regained the road.

With great relief after their narrow brush with disaster, Bell and Bronson pulled off their goggles and wiped them clean of the mud and silt that splattered the lenses.

"It would have been nice if that garage guy had warned us," said Bronson, soaked by their ordeal.

"Maybe they're close-lipped in these parts," Bell joked.

"That was where the flash flood took out the phone and telegraph lines."

"We'll contact your counterpart in the Los Angeles office when we stop for gas again."

The road flattened out and appeared well maintained for the next ninety miles. Bell, with his ear tuned to any miss of the brawny engine's cylinders, let the Locomobile run as fast as he dared over the dirt-and-gravel road, thankful there were no sharp turns, and especially happy the tires held without going flat.

Finally, his luck ran out when he hit a stretch of the road that was rock infested but worn smooth by eons of rain. He slowed to save the tires, but one became embedded with a sharp stone and hissed flat within a hundred yards. One of the spares was quickly thrown on the axle and, with Bronson patching the tube once again, Bell continued his mad dash toward Los Angeles.

San Luis Obispo and Santa Maria came and went. Then they dropped down in altitude as the road ran along the Pacific Coast. The ocean glittered blue under the sky, turning white as the breakers rolled onto the white sandy beach that was flecked with black rocks.

Outside of Santa Barbara, they became airborne over a large hump in the road, crashing down on the other side with an impact that knocked the wind out of Bronson, who was amazed that the sturdy car held together without flying to pieces.

They entered Santa Barbara, where they refueled, filled the radiator with water, and installed the spare tire. A quick stop was made at the railroad depot, where Bronson sent a wire to his fellow agent Bob Harrington asking him to meet them at the Los Angeles railroad terminal.

Instead of taking the treacherous winding road called the Grapevine over Tejon Pass before plunging down into Los Angeles, Bronson directed Bell to run the Locomobile along the railroad tracks that were laid with far more gradual turns. The rough ride strained the automobile's chassis as it rolled through the narrow pass below the 4,183-foot summit, but it held together until they reached the long slope leading down into the San Fernando Valley.

At last, the worst was behind them. Now they were in the homestretch, and the Locomobile was pressing hard and gaining on Cromwell's private train with every mile. According to Bronson's time estimate, they were only fifteen minutes behind. With luck, they just might reach the Los Angeles railroad terminal ahead of the Butcher Bandit.

Most cheering was the sight of tall buildings in the far distance. As they neared the outskirts of the city, the traffic began to build. Bronson marveled at Bell's physical endurance. His blue eyes, hard and unblinking, never left the road. The man was born to sit behind the wheel of a fast car, Bronson thought. He looked at his watch. The hands on the dial read four-twelve. They had averaged over sixty miles an hour for the four-hundred-mile run.

Traffic thickened the closer they came to the main part of the city and Bell began his now accustomed routine of swerving around horse-drawn wagons and buggies and automobiles. He was vastly relieved when the dirt road finally became paved with bricks. He raced in and around big red trolley cars that rode tracks down the center of the street. He was surprised by the number of automobiles he rushed past, unaware that there were over two thousand of them traveling the streets of the mushrooming city of one hundred twenty thousand.

Bell found the thoroughfares of the City of Angels were considerably wider than those of San Francisco, and he made good time with more room to negotiate around the traffic. They passed through downtown, heads turning in awe at the speed of the red Locomobile. A police officer blew his whistle and became angered when Bell ignored it and sped on. The policeman jumped on his bicycle and took up the chase but was soon left far behind, until the automobile was completely out of sight.

The big train depot came into view as Bell rounded a corner on two wheels. A man in a brown suit and wide-brimmed hat was standing on the curb at the entrance frantically waving his arms. Bell braked to a stop in front of Bob Harrington, the Van Dorn agent in charge of Southern California operations. At first, Harrington didn't recognize Bronson. The man in the mud-encrusted leather coat and helmet looked like an apparition until the goggles were raised.

"My God, Horace, I didn't recognize you," said the intense man with a tanned face and sharp features. At six foot five inches, Harrington towered over Bell and Bronson.

Bronson stiffly stepped to the pavement and stretched his aching muscles. "I doubt if my own mother would know me." He turned and pointed at Bell, still sitting exhausted behind the wheel. "Bob, this is Isaac Bell. Isaac, Bob Harrington."

Bell pulled off his driving glove and shook Harrington's hand. "Good to meet you, Bob."

"I heard a lot about your exploits, Isaac. It's an honor to meet *you*."

Bell wasted no more time in pleasantries "What's the status of Cromwell's private train? Are we in time to stop it?"

Harrington slowly shook his head. "Sorry to have

to tell you, but the regularly scheduled passenger train pulled off on a siding in Ventura and let it go through. When it came to Los Angeles, it bypassed the depot and took the express track south to San Diego. By doing that, it cut off nearly half an hour."

"How long ago?" asked Bell, his hopes dashed.

"About twenty minutes."

"We would have beat it by ten minutes," Bronson observed morosely.

Bell looked at the tired Locomobile, wondering if there was enough left in her for the final dash. He knew, without looking in a mirror, that he was more exhausted than the automobile.

Harrington studied the worn-out men. "I can have my agents in San Diego apprehend Cromwell when his special train stops at the San Diego depot."

"He's too smart to get off at the depot," said Bell. "He'll stop the train outside of town and enter in one of his many disguises."

"Where do you think he's headed?"

"One of the local banks."

"Which one?" queried Harrington. "There are at least ten."

"The one with the most assets."

"You honestly believe a lone bandit will attempt robbing the San Diego Wells Fargo Bank?" Harrington asked skeptically. "It's the most secure bank in Southern California."

"All the more reason he'd attempt it," answered Bell. "Cromwell loves a challenge."

"I'll telephone ahead and have my agents standing by the entrance."

Bell shook his head doubtfully. "He'll spot them and call it off. Unless we can catch him in the act, we still haven't enough evidence to convict. And your agents have no idea what he looks like, and, if they did, they'd never see through his disguise. He's *that* good."

"We can't stand around and let him waltz into the bank unhindered," protested Bronson. "He'll murder everyone inside."

Bell turned to Harrington. "Tell your agents to close the bank until Horace and I get there."

"You're not continuing on to San Diego?" Harrington asked incredulously.

"Yes," Bell said simply as he wearily climbed behind the wheel of the Locomobile. "What's the fastest way out of town to the south?"

"Just stay on the road that runs alongside the railroad tracks. It will take you straight south to San Diego."

"What's the condition?"

"Well maintained all the way," said Harrington. He stared doubtfully at the tired machine. "You should make good time if your automobile holds up."

"She got us this far," said Bell with a tight smile. "She'll see us through."

"Tell your agents we're on our way," Bronson said tiredly. He looked like a man stepping up to the gallows.

Harrington stood for a few moments watching the Locomobile roar down the road. Then he slowly shook his head and walked to the nearest telephone.

Ten minutes later, Bell reached the outer limits of the city and aimed the eagle ornament on the big brass radiator down the open road toward San Diego. Even after the wild ride from San Francisco, Bronson still marveled at Bell's expertise and mastery at timing the engine rpms and judging the precise moment to engage the clutch and grip the tall brass lever that meshed the unsynchronized gears.

Bell's weary mind was divided between his driving over the road ahead and the image of Jacob Cromwell robbing another bank and killing everyone in it. As they closed in on their destination, his nerves tightened and his blood churned with adrenaline while the faithful engine beat with the steadiness of a healthy pulse.

33

The time sped away swiftly as the Locomobile ate up the one hundred twenty miles between the two cities in nine minutes under two hours. The last light was glimmering over the ocean to the west when they dropped down from Mount Soledad toward the heart of the city that opened up before them like a carpet of buildings tinted gold by the final rays of the setting sun. Though the Locomobile sported huge acetylene headlamps, Bell did not wish to take the time to stop the car and light them.

"How's our gas?" Bell asked in a rasping voice, his mouth coated with dust.

Bronson turned in his seat, unscrewed the big gas tank cap, and dipped a stick down to the bottom. He withdrew the stick and stared at the moisture at its very tip.

"Let's just say we'll have to finish the race on fumes."

Bell nodded without answering.

The grinding strain had taken its toll on him. After hours of twisting the big steering wheel in a thousand gyrations to turn the stiff linkage to the front wheels, his arms felt numb, as if they were no longer a part of his body. His ankles and

The Race to San Diego

knees also ached from constant clutch, accelerator, and brake pedal action. And both his hands were blistered inside his leather driving gloves. Yet Bell drove at full throttle the last few miles, forcing the Locomobile to leap toward the final destination like a bear sprinting after an elk.

The Locomobile was badly worn down, too. The knobby tread on the Michelin tires was nearly shredded, the wheels were wobbling from the beating they had endured, the faithful engine was beginning to emit strange noises, and steam was billowing from the radiator cap. Still, the magnificent machine pushed on.

"I wonder what's in Cromwell's mind," said Bell. "He's too late to commit robbery today. The bank is closed until tomorrow morning."

"This is Friday," answered Bronson. "The banks in San Diego stay open until nine o'clock in the evening."

They were sprinting down India Street, parallel to the railroad tracks, with the depot no more than a mile away, when Bell flicked his eyes from the road for an instant and glanced in the direction of a train with only one car that was slowing to a halt.

The locomotive pulling the private Pullman car came to a stop on a siding four tracks over from the street. Smoke lazily rose from its stack as the engineer vented steam from exhaust tubes. The fireman had climbed on top of the tender, preparing to take on water from a large wooden tank. With the growing darkness, lights blinked on in the Pullman car, which was now parked a mile away from the depot and the city's downtown.

Bell knew immediately that this had to be Cromwell's private train.

He did not hesitate. He spun the wheel hard left and sent the Locomobile bouncing wildly across the railroad tracks. By the time he had bounded over three tracks, he had blown all four of the badly worn tires and rolled the rest of the way up to the train on the rims of the wheels, showering sparks like meteors as they smashed against the steel rails.

Bronson said nothing. He had been frozen in confused shock, until he saw the train and realized what Bell had up his sleeve. Excitement grew to elation at knowing that, after their five-hundred-mile daredevil drive, they had finally come within spitting distance of their goal.

Bell slammed the Locomobile to a stop across the tracks in front of the locomotive. Its momentum finally spent, the battered automobile sat forlornly with its overheated engine crackling, its radiator hissing steam, and the smell of shredded tires. Its mad and wild chase had come to a fitting climax in front of the quarry it had pursued through the backwoods of hell.

"We may be jumping the gun," said Bronson. "He hasn't attempted to rob the bank yet. We can't arrest him without a crime."

"Maybe. But on the drive down here from San

Francisco, I had much to think about. Better we take Cromwell now, before he has time to act. If he sees through our trap again, we're lost. I'll worry about gathering enough evidence to convict him later. Besides, he's not on home ground. He can't call in expensive attorneys to get him out on bond."

Bell was well aware that no one had had the time to exit the train during the few minutes since it had come to a standstill. He climbed from the automobile and walked unsteadily toward the Pullman car, the aches and pain and weariness slowly falling away. He halted abruptly, and slipped between the Pullman and the coal tender, as two stewards wrestled a motorcycle from the car to the ground beside the track.

He waited patiently for a few minutes until a man dressed in the uniform of a railroad conductor stepped from the Pullman car and threw one leg over the seat of the motorcycle that Bell recognized as a Harley-Davidson. The man's back was to Bell as Bell stepped silently alongside the Pullman car and stopped only when he was no more than five feet behind the man, who was leaning down to open the fuel valve to the carburetor in preparation for starting the engine.

"The Harley is a good machine," Bell said calmly, "but I prefer the Indian."

The man on the motorcycle froze at the sound of the familiar voice. He slowly turned and saw an apparition standing behind him. Eerie illumination fell from overhead electric lights along the railroad siding. The figure wore a short leather coat over jodhpurs and boots that looked like they had been dragged through a swamp. A pair of goggles was pushed back on his head, revealing strands of blond hair coated in dried mud. But there was no mistaking the face, the piercing eyes, and the begrimed mustache that covered the upper lip.

"You!"

"Not very original," Bell said cynically. "But since I used the same expression at the bank in Telluride, I won't criticize."

A silence came over the two men that seemed to last a lifetime, but it was only the few seconds that it took Cromwell to see that the apparition really was Isaac Bell. Cromwell just stood there in growing disbelief, his face suddenly turning pale.

"You were dead!" he gasped. "I shot you!"

"Twice, as a matter of fact," said Bell with a hard edge to his voice. His right hand gripped the 1905 Colt. 45 automatic, its muzzle aimed squarely between Cromwell's eyes and held as steady as an iron bar in concrete.

For the first time in his life, Jacob Cromwell was taken completely off guard. His agile mind, filled with overconfidence, had never considered how he would act should the time ever come when he was apprehended. The unthinkable was never dwelled upon. He had always thought of himself as untouchable. Now he stood face-to-face with his archenemy, who should have been dead. He felt like a captain whose unsinkable ship had run up on the rocks.

Cromwell's Colt .38 was in his coat pocket, but he knew Bell would blow his brains out before he could reach for it. Slowly, he lifted his hands into the air in abject defeat.

"What happens now?" he asked.

"I'm going to borrow your special train to take you back to San Francisco. There, I'll turn you over to the police, until such time as you're tried for murder and hung."

"You have it all mapped out."

"The day had to come, Cromwell. You should have quit when you were ahead."

"You can't arrest me. I have committed no crime."

"Then why are you disguised as a railroad conductor?"

"Why don't you shoot me now and get it over with?" Cromwell asked, his composed arrogance coming back on keel.

"A mere slap on the hand for your crimes," Bell said caustically. "Better you have plenty of time to think about the hangman's noose tightening around your murdering neck."

Bronson came from around the rear of the Pullman car, his Smith & Wesson double-action .44 revolver drawn and pointed at Cromwell's chest. "Nice going, Isaac. You nabbed our friend here before he could commit another crime."

Bell handed Bronson a pair of Tower nickel-plated, double-lock handcuffs. The agent wasted no time in snapping them on Cromwell's wrists. Then he gave the bandit a thorough search and found the .38 Colt automatic.

"The weapon you used to commit three dozen murders," Bronson said with a cold voice.

"Where did you come from?" Cromwell demanded at seeing Bronson and knowing with certainty that these men would not hesitate to shoot him if he gave the slightest indication of trying to escape.

"Isaac drove us from San Francisco in his automobile," he answered as if it were an everyday event.

"Impossible!" snorted Cromwell.

"I thought so, too," said Bronson, leading Cromwell up the steps into the Pullman car, where he took his own handcuffs, placed them around Cromwell's ankles, and roughly shoved him onto a couch.

Bell walked back up the track and stared sadly at the mauled Locomobile. A barrel-chested man carrying an oil can in the coveralls and denim striped hat of a locomotive engineer came up behind him and stared dumbly at the automobile.

"How in God's name did that derelict come to be on the tracks in front of my engine?"

"It's a long story," said Bell wearily.

"What's going to happen to it?"

Bell spoke quietly, almost reverently: "It's going

to be shipped back to the factory in Bridgeport, Connecticut, where it will be rebuilt until it is as good as new."

"Fix this wreck?" said the engineer, shaking his head. "Why bother?"

Bell looked at the Locomobile with a loving expression in his eyes and said, "Because she deserves it."

34

"You're a fool, if you think you can get away with kidnapping me," Cromwell stated contemptuously. "You have no authority to arrest me without a warrant. As soon as we get back to San Francisco, my attorneys will demand my release. After making fools of the Van Dorn Detective Agency, I shall walk free as a bird. Then I'll launch a series of lawsuits that will break your agency and drown it in a sea of scandal."

Cromwell sat manacled to a large couch in the center of the parlor car. His wrists, legs, and even his neck were encased in steel bands that were chained to tie-down rings on the floor of the forward baggage section of the car. No chances were taken. Four heavily armed Van Dorn agents from the Los Angeles office sat in the car less than ten feet from the bandit, sawed-off shotguns, loaded and cocked, laid across their knees.

"You may have a chance to demonstrate your arrogant ego with your pals in city hall, my friend," said Bell. "But you'll walk free only as far as a pig to a butcher shop."

"I am an innocent man," said Cromwell matter-of-factly. "I can prove I was nowhere near the bank robberies you accuse me of. Where is your evidence? Where are your witnesses?"

"I'm a witness," Bell answered. "I saw through your disguise as a woman in Telluride before you shot me."

"*You*, Mr. Bell? What jury in San Francisco would buy your testimony? The trial will be a farce. You have nothing to bring an indictment, much less conviction."

Bell gave Cromwell a foxlike smile. "I am not the only witness. There are other people in the towns where you committed your murders who can identify you."

"Really." Cromwell leaned back in the couch as if he hadn't a care in the world. "From what I read of the Butcher Bandit, he always used disguises during his crimes. How can he be identified?"

"You'll have to wait and see."

"I have great influence in San Francisco," Cromwell said with total conviction. "I have contributed heavily to the election of every superior and federal court judge on the bench. They owe me. Same with the good citizens of San Francisco. Even if you could bring me to trial, no jury of my peers will convict me, not when they take into account the many thousands of dollars I've spent on their behalf."

"You're betting your hand before you see it," said Bell. "A federal judge will be sent out from Washington to hear your case and the venue will be moved elsewhere, where you're not the city's darling."

"I can afford the finest attorneys in the country," Cromwell continued haughtily. "No jury, regardless of what judge sits on the bench, will ever sentence me for crimes with so little evidence, certainly not with my reputation as a man who is beloved by the poor and homeless of San Francisco."

Bronson's face was clouded with disgust. It took all his willpower not to plant his fist in Cromwell's face. "Tell that to the families of the victims you shot down in cold blood. Tell them how the money you stole went to give you a lavish lifestyle as a banker in a mansion on Nob Hill."

Cromwell smiled brazenly and said nothing.

The train began to slow. Bronson stepped over to a window and peered out. "We're coming into Santa Barbara. The engineer will probably stop to take on water."

"I'd like to get off at the depot," said Bell. "There's a little matter I'd like to take care of."

As soon as the train came to a stop, Bell jumped down the stairs to the platform and quickly disappeared into the depot. Ten minutes later, as the engineer tooted the whistle warning that he was going to engage the drive wheels, Bell trotted out and climbed back aboard the Pullman car.

"What was that all about?" asked Bronson.

Cromwell immediately suspected something that was not to his liking. He shifted in his chair and leaned forward to listen.

"The phone lines have been repaired over the ravine

where the flash flood went though," Bell answered Bronson. Then he looked down at Cromwell with a sardonic grin. "I put a call through to the Van Dorn office and instructed our agents to take your sister into custody as an accomplice."

"You're insane," Cromwell cried out.

"I think we can prove she is implicated in the murders carried out by the Butcher Bandit."

Cromwell surged up from the couch, his face a mask of loathing and hate, but was stopped dead by his chains. "You dirty swine," he hissed. "Margaret had nothing to do with any of this. She knew nothing about my . . ." He hesitated, before he incriminated himself. He slowly lowered himself back onto the couch, his composure and presumptuous behavior regaining control. "You'll pay dearly for involving an innocent woman in your ridiculous accusations. Margaret will be back in her parlor within an hour after she's falsely accused of crimes she knows nothing about."

Bell stared into Cromwell's eyes with the self-assurance of a panther about to take a bite out of an antelope. "Margaret will talk," Bell said firmly. "She will tell what she knows in an effort to save her brother. She'll lie, of course, but she'll be tripped up on a thousand details she can't answer. Margaret will be the witness who will unwittingly lead you to the gallows."

"Even if I was guilty, Margaret would never utter a single word against me," Cromwell said with conviction.

"She will if she knows she's going to jail for the rest of her natural life. That, and the loss of a luxurious lifestyle. Turning state's evidence will be quite simple if there is a heavy price to pay for not doing so."

"You've badly underestimated Margaret."

"I don't think so," said Bell quietly.

Cromwell smiled tightly. "You'll never connect Margaret with the crimes any more than you can convince a jury that I am guilty."

Bell stared at the banker. "Are you guilty?"

Cromwell laughed and nodded around the parlor car. "Admit to being your Butcher Bandit in front of witnesses? Come now, Bell." There was no "Mr." this time. "You're skating on thin ice and you know it."

Then Bell pulled off the glove on Cromwell's left hand and revealed a metal tube where his finger once extended.

"We'll see," Bell mused aloud. "We shall see."

Bell was taking no chances. When they reached San Francisco, he ordered the engineer to bypass the main depot and head onto the siding of the railyard. Bronson had a small army of agents on hand to escort Jacob Cromwell to an ambulance, where he was tied down to a stretcher, for the ride through the city.

"We can't run the risk of putting Cromwell in the country jail," said Bell. "He's right about his friends springing him within an hour. Take him across the bay to the state prison at San Quentin. We'll keep him on ice until we're ready to bring formal charges."

"Every reporter with every newspaper in town will be on hand to report that event," said Bronson.

"They'll send the story across the country by telegraph to every newspaper from here to Bangor, Maine," Bell said with a grin. "Now all we have to do is keep him from slipping through our fingers. Cromwell will attempt to bribe any guard that comes near him."

"I know the warden at San Quentin," said Bronson. "He's as straight as an arrow. Cromwell will be wasting his breath if he thinks he can bribe him into escaping."

"Don't think he won't try." Bell looked at Cromwell as he was toughly lifted into the ambulance. "Put a hood over his head so no one will recognize him. Swear the warden to secrecy, and have him lock Cromwell in solitary confinement, away from the other prisoners. We'll give the warden the necessary paperwork in the morning."

"What about Margaret? I doubt a judge with his hand in Cromwell's pockets would fill out arrest papers for her."

"Go through the motions," Bell instructed. "Put pressure on her. Once she knows her brother is in custody and that she may go down with him, I'm betting Margaret will gather up all the cash she can and make a run for it. Then she'll sail right into our hands."

Before heading for Bronson's office, Bell stopped off at a telegraph office and sent a lengthy wire to Van

Dorn reporting the capture of the notorious Butcher Bandit. He also asked for whatever help Colonel Danzler could offer from the federal government.

Cromwell was right about one thing. Margaret walked out of the police department less than thirty minutes after she was escorted there by two Van Dorn agents. Cromwell's attorneys were already there arranging bond when she arrived. Even her chauffeur was on hand to drive her home, waiting in the Rolls-Royce out front, parked in a zone where no vehicle was allowed. A court magistrate miraculously appeared to sign the necessary release papers. It seemed to a reporter, who happened to be present covering a burglary case, that Margaret's arrest and almost-instant release were a staged formality.

Meanwhile, Bronson and his agents had driven the ambulance carrying Cromwell onto the ferry that took them across the bay to Marin County. After moving off the dock, they drove to the state prison at San Quentin. As Bronson had claimed, the warden was very cooperative and even proud to have the famous Butcher Bandit in his prison until Bell and Bronson could orchestrate an arraignment.

After Bell left the telegraph office, he walked to Cromwell's bank. He took the elevator up to the main office and approached Marion's desk. "Get your hat," he said without preamble in a no-nonsense tone. "You're taking the rest of the day off."

She faltered, taken completely off balance by his

sudden appearance after three days. Her sensual feelings toward him came flooding back. She could see that there was no arguing with him, yet she said, "I just can't leave when I feel like it. I could lose my job."

"Your job is already lost. Your boss is behind bars." He walked around her desk and pulled her chair out so she could stand.

She rose slowly and stared at him, dazed. "What are you saying?"

"The show is over. I'm holding Cromwell until we obtain the necessary warrant for his arrest and documents for an indictment."

Almost as if she were moving in a fog, she retrieved her hat and purse from a cabinet behind her desk and then stood there unsure of what else to do. Her eyes slipped away and she stared hesitantly at the floor, disbelieving. She had never thought it possible that Jacob Cromwell, regardless of his crimes, was vulnerable.

Bell had seen Marion's cheeks blush before and he was always taken by the demure reaction. He took her hat from her fingers and placed it on her head at a jaunty angle. "I like that," he said, laughing.

"Well, I don't," she said with womanly irritation in her voice as she straightened the hat to its proper position on her lovely head of hair. "Where are you taking me?"

"Down to the beach, where we can walk in the sand and have a long talk about recent events."

"Are we taking your fancy automobile?"

She was surprised at the pained look that crossed his face. "I'm afraid we won't be taking it anywhere anytime soon."

35

Construction on San Quentin Prison began auspiciously on Bastille Day, July 14, 1852. Why it was later named after a notorious inmate serving time for murder whose name was Miguel Quentin is anybody's guess. The term *San* is Spanish for male saint. Quentin was no saint, but his name stuck, and the prison became known as San Quentin.

The oldest state prison in California, it held its first execution in 1893 by hanging José Gabriel for murdering an aged couple he worked for. Women were also confined there, in a separate building. By 1906, over a hundred prisoners had died behind the prison walls, from inmate murders to suicides to death from natural causes. They were buried in the cemetery outside the prison walls.

Richard Weber, the warden, was a big man, agile as a gymnast and energetic, a workaholic who was dedicated to his job. Heavyset but solid as a rock, he wore a perpetual grin that ever so slightly curled the corners of his lips. A strict disciplinarian with a strong approach to reform, he put the prisoners to work making products, working the gardens, and joining a number of educational studies. His program of compensating the inmates in a small way, along with rewarding them with reductions in their sentences, enhanced his reputation as the "Tough But Fair Warden."

Bronson was close to the mark in claiming Weber could not be bribed. He was known as a man far above the taint of corruption or graft. A devout Catholic, Weber and his wife had raised a family of eight children. His salary as chief of the state's largest prison facility was ample but left little for extra niceties. His dream of retiring someday to a ranch in the San Joaquin Valley was only that, a dream.

Though it was often said that every man has his price, all who knew Warden Weber thought of him as untouchable. But, as it turned out, beneath that hard veneer of integrity he was only human.

Soon after Cromwell was locked up in solitary confinement, Weber visited the bandit/banker in his small cell two levels below the main prison building. After ordering the guard to unlock the steel door, Weber entered the cell and sat down on a small folding chair he had brought with him.

"Mr. Cromwell," he said politely, "welcome to San Quentin."

Cromwell rose from his bunk and nodded. "Perhaps I should say I'm grateful for your hospitality, but that would be a lie."

"It's my understanding that you'll only be with us for a short time."

"Until I'm arraigned in federal court," said

Cromwell. "Is that what Bronson of the Van Dorn Detective Agency told you?"

Weber nodded. "He said he was waiting for instructions from the Criminal Investigation Department in Washington."

"You know why I was arrested?"

"I was told you were the notorious Butcher Bandit."

"Are you familiar with my status in the community?" asked Cromwell.

"I am," replied Weber. "You own the Cromwell Bank and are an admired philanthropist."

"Do you think such a man could rob banks and kill dozens of people?"

Weber shifted on his seat. "I must admit I find the idea a bit far-fetched."

Cromwell circled for the kill. "If I gave you my word that I did not commit any crimes and these are false charges by the United States government to take over my bank, would you release me?"

Weber thought a moment, then shook his head. "I'm sorry, Mr. Cromwell, I am not authorized to release you."

"Even though formal charges have not been filed?"

"I have been assured that charges are being filed as we speak."

"If I guarantee that I do not intend to escape but need go directly to my attorneys in the city and obtain the necessary release papers from a court magistrate, then would you allow me to leave the prison?"

"I might if I could," said Weber. "But, as warden, I cannot permit you leaving the prison grounds before the release papers are in my hands. Besides, there are Van Dorn agents patrolling outside the prison walls to prevent you from escaping."

Cromwell looked around the concrete, windowless cell with its steel door. "Has any inmate ever escaped from solitary?"

"Not in the history of San Quentin."

Cromwell paused to lay his trap. "Suppose – just suppose, Warden – that you personally took me into San Francisco?"

Weber looked at him with interest. "What do you have in mind?"

"Deliver me to County Prosecutor Horvath's office and fifty thousand dollars in cash will be delivered to your house on the prison grounds by private messenger precisely one hour later."

Warden pondered Cromwell's offer for several moments. He knew it was not an idle offer. The banker was worth many millions of dollars and the offer was in cash, which would leave no trail should law enforcement investigators come sniffing around. Fifty thousand dollars was an enormous sum. He could keep the money hidden until his retirement. Weber also did his arithmetic and knew that it was more than enough to buy him a ranch second to none in the state. It was an offer even an honest man of integrity could not refuse.

Finally, Weber rose from his chair, stepped to the steel door, and rapped three times. The door opened and the uniformed guard entered. "Put a hood over the prisoner's face and take him to the office behind my house. I'll be waiting there." Then he turned and left the cell.

Ten minutes later, the guard pushed Cromwell into Weber's office. "Remove his hood and manacles," Weber instructed. As soon as the hood was off and the manacles around Cromwell's feet and hands removed, the guard was dismissed.

"I trust I can rely on your word as a gentlemen that my compensation will arrive an hour after I safely deposit you on the steps of the city hall?"

Cromwell nodded solemnly. "You can rest assured, the money will be in your hands this afternoon."

"Good enough." Weber rose and walked to a closet. He returned with a woman's dress, hat, purse, and shawl. "Put these on. You are a small man and about the same size as my wife. You will be disguised as her when we drive through the inner gates and the main gate. Keep your head down and the guards will take no notice. She and I often take drives around the countryside or into town."

"What about Van Dorn's agents who are patrolling the outer walls?"

Weber smiled thinly. "I am the last man they would suspect of foul play."

Cromwell looked at the clothes and laughed.

"Something funny?" asked Weber.

"No," replied Cromwell. "It's just that I've been here before."

When Cromwell had slipped on the warden's wife's clothes, he wrapped the shawl around his neck and pulled the hat down so it would cover the beard that was beginning to stubble his chin. "Ready as I'll ever be," he announced.

Weber led him out of the office across a yard to the garage that housed the warden's Ford Model Tautomobile. Cromwell effortlessly cranked over the engine and climbed behind the wheel. The car began rolling over the gravel road toward the inner gates and was passed through with a wave from the warden. The main gate was another story. Here, two guards approached the warden for his personal authority to open the gate. "Shari and I are running into the city to buy a gift for her sister's birthday," he said placidly.

The guard on the left side of the car dutifully gave the warden a salute and waved him on. The guard on the right gazed at Cromwell, who made a show of looking for something in the purse. The guard dipped his legs to look under her hat, but Weber caught the movement and snapped, "Stop gawking and open the gate."

The guard straightened up and waved to the engineer in the tower who controlled the mechanism that opened the massive steel doors. As soon as they spread wide enough to permit the Ford through, Weber pulled down the throttle lever and raised his foot off the high-gear pedal. The automobile jumped forward and was soon chugging down the road toward the landing to board the ferry for San Francisco.

36

"He what?" Bell roared over the telephone.

"What is it?" asked Bronson, coming into the office as Bell hung up the phone.

Bell looked up at him, his face twisted in rage. "Your friend, the righteous and incorruptible warden of San Quentin, released Cromwell."

"I don't believe it," Bronson blurted in utter disbelief.

"You can believe it, all right!" snapped Bell. "That was Marion Morgan, Cromwell's personal secretary. She said he walked into his office five minutes ago."

"She must be mistaken."

"She's right on the money," said Curtis from the doorway. He looked at Bronson. "One of your agents who was following his sister, Margaret, saw him come down the steps of the city hall and get in her automobile."

"Warden Weber taking a bribe," Bronson muttered. "I would have never thought it."

"Cromwell probably offered him a king's ransom," said Bell.

"My agents at the prison reported that Weber left in his automobile with his wife for a shopping trip to the city."

"Not the first time Cromwell disguised himself as a woman," Bell murmured angrily. "He no doubt shed the dress once they were out of sight of San Quentin and before they reached the ferryboat."

"Where does that leave us?" inquired Curtis.

"I telegraphed Colonel Danzler, chief of the United States Criminal Investigation Department. He's arranging for a federal judge to swear out a warrant for Cromwell's arrest that cannot be overridden by city or state judicial system. As soon as it is in our hands, we can take Cromwell out of circulation for good."

"That will take at least four days by rail," said Bronson. "What if he attempts to flee the country? We have no legal means to stop him."

"We had no legal means to grab him in San Diego," retorted Bell. "We'll snatch him again and keep him on ice in a secret location until the paperwork arrives."

Bronson looked doubtful. "Before we can put our hands on Cromwell again, his pals the mayor, police chief, and county sheriff will protect him with an army of policemen and deputies armed to the teeth. My seven agents will be outnumbered twenty to one if they attempt to seize him."

"Cromwell has that kind of influence?" asked Curtis.

"The degree of corruption in San Francisco makes the Tammany Hall political machine of New York City look like a convent," said Bronson. "Cromwell has done more than his share to keep city officials fat and rich."

Bell smiled a hard, canny smile. "We'll have our own army," he said quietly. "Colonel Danzler will call out the army regiment that's stationed at the Presidio, if I request it."

"We may need them sooner than you think," said Bronson. "If Cromwell cleans out the cash in his bank and charters another train, he'll be over the border into Mexico free as a bird before we can lift a finger."

"He's right," agreed Curtis. "As it stands, we're helpless. We can't touch him. By the time Danzler can contact the Presidio's commander and order troops called out and marched into the city, it will be too late. Cromwell's graft will have greased his way out of town."

Bell leaned back in his chair and stared at the ceiling. "Not necessarily," he said slowly.

"What's going through that devious mind?" asked Curtis.

"Suppose the president of the United States requests the president of the Southern Pacific Railroad not to charter a train to Cromwell?"

Bronson looked at him. "Is that possible?"

Bell nodded. "Colonel Danzler has great influence in Washington. I was told by Van Dorn that he and President Roosevelt are very close. They fought side by side at San Juan Hill in the war. I think it's safe to say he could persuade the president to go along."

"And if Cromwell charters a ship?" probed Bronson.

"Then a United States warship will be sent to stop the ship at sea, take Cromwell off, and return him to San Francisco. By that time, we'll have the necessary warrants for his arrest and trial."

"It sounds like you have all the bases convered," Bronson said admiringly.

"Cromwell is a slippery customer," said Bell. "If there is a way to slip through our net, he'll think of it." He paused to look up at a clock on the wall. "Four thirty-five. I have a dinner date at six o'clock."

"Marion Morgan?" Curtis asked with a sly smile. "It strikes me that besides her keeping tabs on Cromwell, you two have a thing going."

Bell nodded. "She's an exquisite lady." He rose to his feet and slipped on his coat. "She's fixing dinner at her place."

Bronson winked at Curtis. "Our friend is a lucky man."

"I've lost track of time," said Bell. "What day is it?"

"Tuesday, April seventeenth," answered Curtis. Then he added humorously, "The year is 1906."

"I'm aware of the year," Bell said as he stepped through the door. "See you all in the morning."

Sadly, one of the three men in the room would never see tomorrow.

Margaret stopped the Mercedes under the porte cochere that sheltered vehicles at the front door of the mansion before they passed into the courtyard beyond. Since picking her brother up in front of city hall, she had driven him to the bank, where he had spent two hours locked in his office. When he emerged, they rode to Nob Hill in silence. Their chauffeur came from the carriage house and drove the car inside. The instant they stepped into the foyer, Margaret pulled off her hat and spun it across the floor, glaring at her brother with fire in her eye.

"I hope you're satisfied now that you've sent our fortunes crashing down around us."

Cromwell walked like an old man into the sitting room and slumped wearily in a chair. "I made the mistake of underestimating Bell," he said. "He caught up to me before I could hit the bank in San Diego."

The floor tilted beneath Margaret's feet as her entire mood changed. "Isaac alive? You saw him?"

He looked at her intently. "You appear to take an uncommon interest in him," he said with dry amusement. "Are you glad our nemesis still walks the earth?"

"You said you killed him in Telluride."

Cromwell spoke as if he were describing a truckload of coal. "I thought I did, but he apparently survived. The only mistake I've made in twenty years."

"Then it was he who brought you back from San Diego and put you into San Quentin."

Cromwell nodded. "He had no right. He stepped

outside the law. Now Bell is going to move heaven and earth to proclaim me the Butcher Bandit and send me to the gallows."

"It won't be an easy matter of escaping the city. Van Dorn agents are watching our every move."

"I have no intention of fleeing like a thief in the night. It's time those who have curried our favor and funds repay their obligations by keeping us out of Van Dorn's hands until we're ready to quietly depart for greener pastures."

She looked at him resolutely, her mind on an unwavering course of action. "We'll hire the finest lawyers in New York. It will be impossible to convict you. We'll make Isaac Bell and the Van Dorn Detective Agency the laughingstock of the nation."

"I don't doubt we'll win in court," he said quietly, staring at his sister with a serious expression. "But we'll be finished as an admired institution in San Francisco. The bank will suffer a financial disaster as our depositors, fearful of scandal, run to competing banks. The Cromwell National Bank will close its doors." He paused for effect. "Unless . . ."

"Unless what?" she asked, meeting his unrelenting gaze.

"We quietly and secretly move our assets to another city in another country where we can launch a new financial empire under another name."

Margaret visibly relaxed now that she began to realize that all was not lost, her lifestyle might not fall off the edge of the cliff after all. "What city and what country did you have in mind? Mexico? Brazil, perhaps?"

Cromwell grinned wickedly. "My dear sister, I can only hope Mr. Bell thinks as you do."

He felt smug with self-satisfaction, believing that all he needed was no more than three hours in the morning to arrange for the shipment of the cash reserves from his bank. His paper assets had already been sent out of the country by telegraph when he went to the bank. Now all he and Margaret had to do was pack a few things and lock up the house, leaving it with a realtor to sell. Then it would be clear sailing, once they crossed the border and left the United States behind.

Bell sat staring thoughtfully at a small fire in the fireplace of Marion's apartment while she was busy in the kitchen. He had brought a bottle of California Beringer 1900 Cabernet Sauvignon and was halfway through a glass when Marion entered the dining room and began setting the table. He looked up and had a strong desire to walk over and press his lips to hers.

She looked stunning, with her fashionable hourglass silhouette of ample curves and full breasts. She wore a pink satin bodice of cascading lace that reached up under her chin and elongated her tall, graceful neck. The skirt was also pink and long and flowing like an inverted flowering lily. Even with her torso half covered by a large apron, she looked elegant.

Her straw blond hair shined under the light from the candles on the table. It was pulled back in a silky bun like a whorl behind her delicate ears. Bell suppressed his desire to kiss her and simply reveled at the sight of her.

"Nothing fancy," she said, coming over and sitting on the arm of his chair. "I hope you like pot roast."

"I have a passion for pot roast," he said, losing all control and pulling her down onto his lap, where he kissed her long and ardently. She tensed, then trembled, and her eyes became huge and flashed a deep sea of green. As they drew apart, her poise altered. The eyes turned brazen and her expression spicy. Her breathing became quick, and she enjoyed the sensation of deep sensuality, a sensation that she had never experienced with another man. With slow deliberation, she eased out of his lap and stood shakily, brushing back a wisp of hair that had fallen along her temple.

"Enough of this, unless you want a burned pot roast."

"How long do I have to suffer on an empty stomach?"

She laughed. "Ten more minutes. I'm waiting for the potatoes to soften."

He watched as she returned to the kitchen, her walk as fluid as a gazelle's.

As she set the bowls on the table, he refilled their glasses, and they sat down. They ate in silence for a few moments. Then Bell said, "Everything is delicious. You'll make some lucky man a wonderful wife one day."

The words came like a warm breeze across the nape of her neck and a flush of blood flowed across her breasts, hardening the nipples. Deep down, she hoped his feelings were moving in that direction, but she was also afraid that his affection might cool and he would walk off into the dark some evening, never to return.

Bell read Marion's confusion and became afraid to go there. He changed the course of the conversation. "How long did Cromwell remain in the bank today?"

Her emotion quickly turned to anger. She was mad at herself for responding with the proper words instead of calmly expressing her feelings towards him. "Most of the time he spent in the office, he seemed very secretive. He also made three trips downstairs to the vault."

"Do you have any idea of what he was about?"

She shook her head. "It seemed very mysterious." Then she lifted her head and a small smile parted her lips. "But when he was in the vault, I sneaked into his office and glanced at the paperwork he had spread across his desk."

He waited expectantly as she took a few moments to let him twist in the wind, as if getting even with him for ignoring her feelings for him. "He was filling out bank drafts and money transfers."

"It figures. Our guess is that he and Margaret are going to skip out of the country and move the bank's funds to their destination. There's no way Cromwell will stay in town and fight us in federal court."

"It would look that way," said Marion quietly, wishing they could keep their time together more close and personal.

"Could you tell where he was sending the bank's funds?"

She shook her head. "Only the amounts were filled in, not the banks that were to receive them."

"What do you think he was doing in the vault?"

"My best guess is he was packing the bank's cash reserves in crates in preparation to ship them to a bank in whatever city they're going to."

"You're a very asture lady," he said, smiling. "And if you were Jacob and Margaret, where would you go?"

"They wouldn't be safe anywhere in Europe," Marion answered without hesitation. "The banks on the Continent work with the U.S. government in freezing illegal funds. There are too many other countries where they could hide their money and begin building their empire again."

"How about Mexico?" Bell asked, impressed with Marion's intuition.

She shook her head. "Margaret could never live in Mexico. The land is too primitive for her tastes. Buenos Aires in Argentina is a possibility. The city is very cosmopolitan, but neither of them speaks a word of Spanish."

"Singapore, Hong Kong, Shanghai," suggested Bell. "Any of those cities hold any interest?"

"Australia or New Zealand, perhaps," she said thoughtfully. "But I've learned over the years in his employ that Jacob doesn't think like most men."

"My experience with the man has led me to the same conclusion," Bell said.

Marion went quiet as she passed him more helpings of the pot roast, potatoes, and vegetables. "Why don't you give your brain a rest and enjoy the fruits of *my* labors?" she said, smiling.

"Forgive me," he said honestly. "I've been a bore as a dinner companion."

"I hope you like lemon meringue pie for dessert."

He laughed. "I adore lemon meringue pie."

"You'd better. I baked enough for a small army."

They finished the main course and Isaac stood up to help clear the table. She pushed him back down in his chair.

"Where do you think you're going?" she demanded.

He looked like a young boy startled by his mother. "I wanted to help."

"Sit down and finish your wine," Marion said smartly. "Guests don't work in my house, especially male guests."

He looked at her slyly. "And if I wasn't a guest?"

She turned away from him for fear her inner emotions might show. "Then I'd make you fix a plumbing leak, a squeaky door hinge, and a broken table leg."

"I could do that," he said staunchly. "I happen to be very handy."

She looked at him disbelieving. "A banker's son who is handy?"

He feigned a hurt look. "I didn't always work in my father's bank. I ran away from home when I was fourteen and joined the Barnum and Bailey Circus. I helped put up and take down the tents, fed the elephants, and made repairs on the circus train." He paused and a sad expression came across his face. "After eight months, my father found me, hauled me home, and sent me back to school."

"So you're a college man."

"Harvard. Phi Beta Kappa, in economics."

"And smart," she added, properly impressed.

"And you?" he probed. "Where did you go to school?"

"I was in the first graduating class of Stanford University. My degree was in law, but I soon found that law firms were not in the habit of hiring women lawyers, so I went into banking."

"Now it's my turn to be impressed," said Bell honestly. "It seems I've met my match."

Suddenly, Marion went silent and a strange look came over her face. Bell thought something was wrong. He rushed to her side and slid his arm around her.

"Are you ill?"

She looked up at him from her coral green eyes. They seemed dark in thought. Then she gasped. "Montreal!"

He leaned toward her. "What did you say?"

"Montreal . . . Jacob and Margaret are going to make a run across the Canadian border to Montreal, where he can open another bank."

"How do you know that?" asked Bell, bewildered at Marion's strange attitude.

"I just remembered seeing the city Montreal scrawled on a notepad beside his telephone," she explained. "I didn't think it meant anything of importance and dismissed it from my mind. Now it all makes sense. The last place authorities would look for the Cromwells is in Canada. They can easily take on new identities and buy off the right people to become upstanding citizens who start up a solvent financial institution."

The look of confusion faded from Bell's face. "The piece fits," he said slowly. "Canada is probably the last place we'd think to look. The obvious escape route used by felons over the years is over the southern border into Mexico, using that as a springboard to travel farther south."

Then, slowly, his thoughts of the Cromwells evaporated and he became quiet, gentle, and loving as he picked her up in his arms. "I knew there was a reason I fell in love with you," he said, his voice becoming low and husky. "You're smarter than I am."

Her whole body trembled as she entwined her arms

around his neck. "Oh, God, Isaac. I love you, too."

He gently touched his lips to hers as he carried her from the living room into the bedroom. She pulled away and looked up, her eyes now mischievous. "What about the lemon meringue pie?"

He gazed down at her lovely features and laughed. "We can always eat it for breakfast."

Bell could not have predicted nor much less have known that within a few hours the pie would become but a dim memory.

37

Called the hallmark of the West, the San Francisco of 1906 was a maze of contradictions. One writer described the city as the Babylon of grandiloquence, the Paris of romance, and the Hong Kong of adventure. Another went so far as to portray it as the gateway to paradise.

It may have been dynamic and exciting, but, in truth, San Francisco was a sprawling, filthy, soot-ridden, foul-smelling, brawling, corrupt, vulgar city with less charm than London in the seventeen hundreds. It intermingled incredible wealth with sordid poverty. Coal smoke from steamboats, locomotives, foundries, house furnaces and stoves enveloped streets already blanketed by the dung of thousands of horses. There were no sewage-treatment plants to be found and the blackened skies reeked of foul odors.

Most all the houses were built of wood. From the nice homes on Telegraph Hill to the stylish mansions of Nob Hill to the shacks and hovels in the outlying districts, it was described by the city's fire chief as a sea of tinderboxes waiting to be lit.

The image and the myth were to change dramatically within two and a half minutes.

At 5:12 A.M., on the morning of April 18th, the

sun was beginning to lighten the eastern sky. The gas streetlights had been shut off and the cable cars began to clatter from their barns for their runs up and down the many hills of the city. Early workers began walking to their job as those who worked during the late-night hours headed home. Bakers were already at their ovens. Police on the early-morning shift still patrolled their beats, expecting another quiet day, as a light wind without the prevailing fog blew in from the west.

But at 5:12, the peaceful world of San Francisco and its surrounding towns was shattered by an ominous, rumbling roar that came from the depths of the earth a few miles under the sea beyond the Golden Gate.

Hell had come to San Francisco.

The foreshock shook the surrounding countryside and was felt throughout the Bay Area. Twenty-five seconds later, terrifying, undulating shock waves from the massive earthquake surged across the city like a monstrous hand sweeping stacks of books off a table.

The rock of the San Andreas Fault, whose walls had been grinding against each other for millions of years, abruptly split apart as the North American Plate under the land and the Pacific Plate beneath the sea unleashed their grip on each other and shifted in opposite directions, one to the north, the other to the south.

The unimaginable force raged toward the helpless city at seven thousand miles an hour in a disastrous spree that would leave monumental death and destruction in its wake.

The shock wave struck with savage swiftness. The pavement of the streets running east and west began to rise and crest before falling into troughs, as the quake rolled relentlessly forward and sent block upon block of tall buildings rocking and swaying like willow trees in a hurricane. Wood, mortar, and brick were never meant to withstand such an onslaught. One by one, the buildings began to crumble, their walls falling and avalanching into the streets under a cloud of dust and debris. Every window in the stores along the avenues burst and shattered onto the sidewalks in a shower of jagged shards.

Huge five- and ten-story buildings in the downtown business section toppled in a horrendous crash that sounded like a cannon barrage. Chasms opened and closed on the streets, some filling with groundwater and spilling into the gutters. The rails of streetcars and cable cars were twisted and bent like strands of spaghetti. The most violent shocks lasted for slightly more than a minute before diminishing, although smaller aftershocks continued off and on for several days.

When the full light of day showed through the chaos, all that was left of a major city of tall buildings, comprising a vast number of stores, offices, banks, theaters, hotels, restaurants, saloons and brothels, houses and apartments, was now a hundred square miles of jagged mounds of shattered masonry, splintered wood, and twisted iron. Though they'd looked substantial, most of the buildings were not reinforced and fell to pieces before the earthquake was thirty seconds old.

The city hall, the most impressive edifice west of Chicago, sat smashed and destroyed, its cast-iron columns lying shattered in the street. The Hall of Justice was a skeleton of mangled steel girders. The Academy of Sciences gone as though it had never stood. The post office was still standing but effectively demolished. The Majestic Theater would never stage a show again. Only the redoubtable six-story Wells Fargo Building had refused to tumble down despite a ravaged interior.

Thousands of chimneys had been first to fall. None was built with an earthquake in mind. Reaching through and high above the roofs, unable to bend and sway and with no support, they shuddered, then fractured and fell through houses and onto streets that were already clogged with debris. Later, it was determined that over a hundred people died from being crushed in their beds by falling chimneys.

Wooden two- and three-story homes leaned drunkenly in all directions, twisted on their foundations and tilted crazily in grotesque angles. Oddly, they stood intact but had shifted as much as twenty feet off their foundations, many across sidewalks and into the streets. Though their exterior walls were intact, their interiors were devastated, floors having collapsed, beams ruptured, the furniture and the inhabitants ending up crushed and buried in the basement. The cheaper houses in the poor part of town had collapsed in a pile of splintered beams and siding.

Those who had survived the earthquake were frozen in stunned shock, unable to speak or conversing in whispers. As the great clouds of dust began to settle, the cries of those who were injured or trapped under the fallen structures came as muffled wails. Even after the main force of the quake had passed, the earth still shuddered with aftershocks that continued to shake walls of brick onto the streets, causing their own tremors and strange rumbling sounds.

Few cities in the history of human civilizations had suffered as much devastating destruction as San Francisco. And yet it was only the opening act of an even-worse scene of disintegration that was yet to come.

The shock hurled the bed Isaac and Marion were occupying across her bedroom. The apartment house around them rumbled and shook in a series of convulsions. The noise was deafening as dishes crashed to the floor, bookcases collapsed and the books scattered, pictures were slung off the walls, and the upright piano rolled like a boulder down a mountain across the slanting floor only to fall into the street because the entire front wall of the apartment house had detached itself from the rest of the building and cascaded in a flood of rubble onto the street below.

Bell grabbed Marion by the arm and half carried, half dragged her through a hail of falling plaster to the doorway, where they stood for the next thirty seconds while the horrendous noise became even more deafening. The floor moved like a stormy sea beneath their feet. They had barely reached the temporary shelter of the doorway when the great chimney at the top of the roof toppled and fell crashing through the two apartments above and smashed through the floor not ten feet away from them.

Bell recognized the bedlam as an earthquake. He had endured one almost as had as the one that destroyed San Francisco while traveling with his parents in China when he was a young boy. He looked down into the pale face of Marion, who looked up at him, dazed and paralyzed by shock. He smiled grimly, trying to give her courage, as the shock waves tore the floor in the parlor from its beams and sent it collapsing into the lower apartment. He could only wonder if the occupants had been killed or were somehow managing to survive.

For nearly a full minute, they kept on their feet, clutching the doorframe, as their world turned into a nightmarish hell that went far beyond imagination.

Then slowly the tremors died away and an eerie silence settled over the ruin of the apartment. The cloud of dust from the fallen plaster ceiling filled their nostrils and made it difficult to breathe. Only then did Bell realize that they were still on their feet, clutching the doorframe, with Marion wearing a flimsy nightgown and him in a nightshirt. He saw that her radiant long hair had turned white from the plaster's fine powder that still floated in the air like a mist.

Bell gazed across the bedroom. It looked like the contents of a wastebasket that had been dumped on the floor. He put his arm around Marion's waist and pulled her toward the closet, where their clothes still hung on hangers, free of the dust.

"Dress and be quick about it," he said firmly. "The building isn't stable and might collapse at any minute."

"What happened?" she asked in utter confusion. "Was it an explosion?"

"No, I believe it was an earthquake."

She stared through the wreck of her parlor and saw the ruined buildings on the other side of the street. "Good Lord!" she gasped. "The wall is gone." Then she discovered that her piano was missing. "Oh, no, my grandmother's piano. Where did it go?"

"I think what's left of it is down on the street," replied Bell sympathetically. "No more talk. Hurry and throw on some clothes. We've got to get out of here."

She ran to the closet, her composure back on keel, and Bell could see that she was as tough as the bricks that had fallen around them. While he put on the suit he'd worn the night before, she slipped into a cotton blouse under a coarse woolen jacket and skirt for warmth against the cool breeze blowing in from the sea. She was not only beautiful, Bell thought, she was also a practical, thinking woman.

"What about my jewelry, my family photos, my valuables?" she asked. "Shouldn't I take them with me?"

"We'll come back for them later, when we see if the building is still standing."

They dressed in less than two minutes, and he led her around the gaping hole in the floor made by the fallen chimney and past the overturned furniture to the front door of the apartment. Marion felt as if she were in another world, as she stared out into open air where the wall once stood and saw her neighbors beginning to wander bewildered out into the middle of the street.

The door was wedged tight. The earthquake had shifted the building and jammed the door against its frame. Bell knew better than to attack the door by charging against it with his shoulder. That was a fool's play. He balanced on one leg and lashed out with the other. The door failed to show the least sign of give. He looked around the room and surprised Marion with his strength when he picked up the heavy sofa and shoved it against the door like a battering ram. On the third thrust, the door splintered and swung crazily open on one hinge.

Thankfully, the stairway was still standing, winding its way to the floor below. Bell and Marion made it past the main entrance and found a high mountain of debris piled outside the apartment house, thrown there when the front wall crashed and buried the street. The front section of the structure looked as if it had been sliced clean by a giant cleaver.

Marion stopped, her eyes welling with tears at the sight of her mother's piano sitting smashed on the crest of the rubble. Bell spotted two men making their way down the street through the wreckage on a wagon drawn by two horses. He left Marion for a few moments, walked over and conversed with the two men as if striking a deal. They nodded and he came back.

"What was that about?" asked Marion.

"I offered to pay them five hundred dollars to take your mother's piano to Cromwell's warehouse by the railyard. When things get back to normal, I'll see that it's rebuilt."

"Thank you, Isaac." Marion stood on her toes as she kissed Bell on the cheek, stunned that a man could be so thoughtful about such a little thing in the midst of such disaster.

The army of people crowding the middle of the street was strangely subdued. There were no wails or cries, no hysteria. Everyone talked in whispers, glad they were alive, but not knowing what to do next or where to go or whether the earthquake would strike again. Many were still in their nightclothes. Mothers cuddled young children or clutched babies while men talked among themselves studying the damage to their homes.

A lull settled over the ruined city. The worst, everyone thought, had to be over. And yet the greatest tragedy was yet to come.

Bell and Marion walked to the intersection of Hyde and Lombard, seeing the cable car rails that now snaked like a meandering silver stream to the streets below Russian Hill. The cloud of dust hung tenaciously over the devastation, slowly dissipating as it was carried toward the east by the offshore breeze. From the docks protruding into the water around the Ferry Building west to Fillmore Street, and from the north bay far to the south, the once-great city was a vast sea of ruin and devastation.

Scores of hotels and lodging houses had collapsed, killing hundreds who had been sleeping soundly when the quake struck. The screams and cries of those trapped under the rubble and the badly injured carried up to the hill.

Hundreds of electrical poles had toppled, their high-tension wires snapping apart, whipping back and forth like desert sidewinders, sparks shooting from the tattered ends. At the same time, pipes carrying the city's gas had split apart and now unleashed their deadly fumes. Tanks in the basements of manufacturing plants holding kerosene and fuel oil ran toward the fiery arcs thrown from the electrical wires where they met and burst in an explosion of orange flame. In destroyed houses, coals from the fallen chimneys ignited furniture and wooden frameworks.

Soon the wind helped merge the big and small fires into one massive holocaust. Within minutes, the city was blanketed by smoke from fires erupting across San Francisco that would take three days and hundreds of lives before they were contained. Many of the injured and trapped who could not be rescued in time would go unidentified, their bodies incinerated and turned to ashes by the intense heat.

"It's going to get worse, much worse," said Bell slowly. He turned to Marion. "I want you to go to Golden Gate Park; you'll be safe there. I'll come and find you later."

"Where are you going?" she whispered, shuddering at the thought that she would be alone.

"To the Van Dorn office. The city is going to need every law enforcement agent available to help control the chaos."

"Why can't I stay here, near my apartment?"

He took another look at the growing conflagration. "It's only a matter of a few hours before the fire reaches Russian Hill. You can't stay here. Do you think you can make it on foot to the park?"

"I'll make it," she said, nodding gamely. Then she reached up and circled her arms around his neck. "I love you, Isaac Bell. I love you so much I hurt."

He slipped his arms around her slim waist and kissed her. "I love you, too, Marion Morgan." He hesitated before pushing her back. "Now, be a good girl and get a move on."

"I'll wait for you at the bridge over the pond."

He held her hand a moment before turning away and moving through the mass of people who were crowded in the center of the street as far away as they could get from the buildings as a series of light aftershocks rippled through the city.

Bell took one of the long stairways leading from Russian Hill. It was split apart in several places but did not block his way down to Union Street. Then he cut over to Stockton and then to Market Street. The scene of destruction went far beyond anything his mind could have created.

There were no streetcars running, and all automobiles, many of them new models commandeered from dealer showrooms, as well as horse-drawn vehicles, were being pressed into service as ambulances to carry the injured to makeshift hospitals that were springing up in the city squares. The bodies of the dead, those who could be retrieved, were carried to warehouses that had been turned into temporary morgues.

The falling walls had not only crushed unlucky humans walking the sidewalks but also horses pulling the city's huge fleet of freight wagons. They were felled by the dozens under tons of bricks. Bell saw a driver and horse that had been smashed to pulp by an electrical pole that had fallen on their milk wagon.

Reaching Market Street, Bell ducked into the remains of a still-standing doorway that was once the entrance into the Hearst Examiner Newspaper Building. He sought refuge as a herd of cattle appeared that had escaped their pen at the docks. Maddened by fright, they charged down the street and almost immediately vanished, swallowed up by one of the great chasms where the violent thrust of the earthquake had split the streets.

Bell could not believe how the great thoroughfare of the city, with its magnificent buildings, had changed from the evening before. Gone were the fleets of vehicles, the throngs of happy, contented people working or shopping in the heart of the city's business district. Now the boulevard was scarcely recognizable. The tall buildings had crumbled to pieces, huge pillars with their decorative cornices and ornamentations had been wrenched from the façades of the structures and hurled to the sidewalk and street in jumbled fragments. The enormous office and store windows were shattered. Signs that once advertised the businesses occupying them lay scattered amid the wreckage.

As Bell made his way down through the destruction, he could see that the blocks to the south were becoming an ocean of flame. He knew it was only a matter of time before the big hotels, government buildings, tall office skyscrapers, the great department stores, and the theaters would be burned-out skeletons. There were far too few firemen and almost all of the underground water mains had been ruptured by the earthquake. Hundreds of the city's fire hydrants and water taps trickled and then ran dry. The firemen, helpless in fighting the mushrooming fires, began a heroic struggle to repair the water lines.

After dodging the automobiles transporting the

injured and making his way over the landslides of brick, Bell came within sight of the Call Building. At first, the twelve-story skyscraper looked in good shape, but as he walked closer he saw that the base of one side of the building had moved two feet over the sidewalk toward the street. Inside, he found that none of the elevators were working because the interior was twisted out of alignment. He made his way up the five flights of stairs to the Van Dorn office and stepped over the mounds of plaster that had fallen from the ceiling. Footprints in the plaster told him others had preceded him.

The furniture scattered about the office by the quake had been set upright where originally positioned.

Bell walked into the conference room and found four Van Dorn agents including Bronson, who rushed over and pumped his hand. "Am I ever glad to see you alive. I was afraid you might be lying under a ton of rubble."

Bell managed a smile. "Marion's house lost the front wall, but her apartment is a mess." He paused and looked around room. Not seeing Curtis, he asked, "Have you heard from Art?"

The look on everyone's face told Bell what he needed to know. "Art is missing, assumed to have been crushed under tons of brick as he made his way from the Palace Hotel to our office," Bronson answered solemnly. "From what reports we've managed to gather, two of my agents are either injured or dead.

We don't know yet. Those you see here are the only ones who survived without injury."

Bell's chest felt as if a belt had been cinched around it and pulled tight. He had seen and known death, but to lose someone close was an enduring hurt. "Curtis dead," Bell muttered. "He was a fine man, a good friend, and one of the best detectives I ever worked with."

"I lost good men, too," Bronson said slowly. "But now we must do what we can to ease the suffering."

Bell looked at him. "What is your plan?"

"I met with the chief of police and offered Van Dorn's services. Despite our differences in the past, he was only too glad to have our help. We're going to do what we can to combat looting, apprehend looters stealing from the dead and their demolished homes and take them to the city jail. Thankfully, because it's built like a fortress, it still stands."

"I wish I could join you and the others, Horace, but I have another job."

"Yes, I understand," Bronson said quietly. "Jacob Cromwell."

Bell nodded. "The earthquake and the bedlam left in its wake have given him the ideal opportunity to escape the country. I intend to stop him."

Bronson held out his hand. "Good luck to you, Isaac." He gestured around the room with one hand. "This building isn't safe. And if it doesn't fall down on its own, it will probably be consumed by the approaching fire. We'll have to take our records and abandon it."

"Where can I reach you?"

"We're setting up a command center in the Customs House; it was only slightly damaged. The army units that are arriving to maintain order and help battle the fires are also setting up their headquarters there."

"One of us has to report what has happened to Mr. Van Dorn."

Bronson shook his head. "Not possible. All telegraph lines are down."

Bell shook Bronson's hand. "Good luck to you, too, Horace. I'll be in contact as soon as I learn Cromwell's whereabouts."

Bronson smiled. "I bet nothing like this happens where you live in Chicago."

Bell laughed. "Aren't you forgetting the great Chicago fire of 1871? At least your calamity came from an act of God. Chicago's came from a cow who kicked over a lantern."

After saying his good-bye, Bell retraced his route down the twisted stairs to the devastation on Market Street. He quickly made his way over the rubble and past the crowds of people who had assembled to watch the fire that was now burning throughout Chinatown and relentlessly moving toward the city's primary business district.

He reached the Palace Hotel, which had fared better than the Call Building. Standing just outside the entrance was a man Bell instantly recognized:

Enrico Caruso, who had sung the role of Don José in *Carmen* the night before at the Grand Opera House, was waiting as his valet pulled his trunks out onto the sidewalk. He was dressed in a long, bulky fur coat over his pajamas and smoking a cigar. As Bell passed, he heard the great tenor muttering, "'Ell of a place, 'ell of a place. I never come back."

The elevators were not running due to the lack of electricity, but the stairways were relatively clear of debris. After entering his room, Bell did not bother to pack his clothes. He saw no reason to burden himself with luggage. He threw only a few personal items in a small valise. Not planning on life-threatening danger in San Francisco, he had left his Colt .45 and the derringer in the room. The Colt went in the valise and the derringer back into its small holster inside his hat.

As he walked up Powell Street toward Cromwell's mansion on Nob Hill, he saw a small group of men frantically struggling to lift a huge beam from a pile of rubble that had once been a hotel. One of them motioned to him and shouted, "Come give us a hand!"

The men were frantically working to free a woman pinned in the debris and the wreckage around it was burning fiercely. She was still dressed in her nightgown, and he saw that she had long auburn hair.

He gripped her hand for a moment and said softly, "Be brave. We'll get you free."

"My husband and my little girl – are they safe?"

Bell looked up into the somber faces of the rescuers. One of them slowly shook his head. "You'll see them soon," he said, feeling the intense heat of the fire closing in.

Bell lent his strength to the others and vainly tried to lift the beam that covered the woman's legs. It was an exercise in futility. The beam weighed tons and could not be moved by six men. The woman was very courageous and watched the efforts in silence until the flames began scorching her nightgown.

"Please!" she begged. "Don't let me burn!"

One of the men, a fireman, asked for her name and wrote it on a small piece of paper he had in his pocket. The rest of the men retreated from the intense heat and menacing flames, horrified at losing their battle to save the woman.

Her nightgown ignited and she began to scream. Without hesitation, Bell held up his derringer and shot her in the forehead between the eyes. Then, without a backward glance, he and the fireman ran for the street.

"You had to do it," said the fireman, his hand on Bell's shoulder. "Dying by fire is the worst death. You couldn't let her suffer."

"No, I couldn't do that," Bell said, his eyes rimmed with tears. "But it's a terrible memory I'll take to my grave."

38

Cromwell awoke in his bed to see the chandelier in the middle of the room swinging like a wild pendulum, its crystal pendants tinkling madly. The furniture danced about as if possessed by crazed demons. A large painting of a fox hunt dropped from the wall with a loud crash as it struck the polished teak floor. The entire house creaked as the stone blocks of the walls ground against each other.

Margaret came staggering into his room, struggling to remain upright as the quake continued. She was wearing nothing but her nightgown, too shocked to throw on a robe. Her face was as white as the breast of a seagull, her golden brown eyes wide with fright, and her lips trembling.

"What's happening?" she gasped.

He reached out and pulled her against him. "An earthquake, dear sister. Nothing to fret about. It will pass. The worst is over."

His words were quiet and calm, but she could see the nervous tension in his eyes. "Will the house fall on us?" she asked fearfully.

"Not this house," he said resolutely. "It's built like the Rock of Gibraltar."

The words were no sooner said than the great chimneys above began to topple and crash down. Fortunately, they were constructed on the outside of the house walls and collapsed outward without smashing through the roof. Most of the damage came from sections of the outer wall surrounding the house that cracked and crashed to the ground like rumbling thunder. Finally, the tremors began to taper away.

The house had stood through the worst of the earthquake and retained its structural integrity, looking as it had before except for the collapsed outer wall and three fallen chimneys. And because the inner walls were board over stone, decorated with paint or wallpaper, and the ceilings were mahogany, there were no clouds of dust from fallen plaster.

"Oh, Lord," murmured Margaret. "What are we going to do?"

"You see to the house. Assemble the servants and see if any are injured. Then put them to work cleaning up the mess. Outwardly, act as if restoring the house was your first priority. But begin packing only those valuables and clothes that you consider essential for our flight out of the country."

"You're forgetting Van Dorn's agents," she said, looking up quickly.

"The quake will prove to be a blessing. The city is in chaos. Bell and his fellow Van Dorn detectives have more-pressing problems on their hands than keeping an eye on us."

"What about you?" asked Margaret, pulling her nightgown tightly around her body.

"I'm going to the bank to finish cleaning out the vault of all cash. I put most of the currency in trunks yesterday. When it is all packed, Abner and I will transport the trunks in the Rolls to the warehouse and load them on my railcar for our trip across the Canadian border."

"You make it sound easy," she said drily.

"The simpler, the better." He climbed from bed and headed for the bathroom. "By this time tomorrow, our curtain will ring down on San Francisco and, within a few short months, we'll launch a new banking empire in Montreal."

"How much do you figure we'll have?"

"I've already transferred fifteen million by telegraph wire to four different Canadian banks in four different provinces," he pointed out. "We'll carry another four million with us in currency."

Now she smiled broadly, the fear of the earthquake suddenly pushed aside. "That's more than we had when we came to San Francisco twelve years ago."

"A lot more," Cromwell said comfortably. "Nineteen million more, to be exact."

Bell missed Cromwell by twenty minutes when he reached the mansion on Cushman Street. He studied the house and was surprised at the superficial damage after witnessing the unbelievable destruction of the buildings in the main part of the city. He climbed over the mound of fallen bricks that had been an eight-foot wall and walked up the driveway to the front door.

He pulled the doorbell knob, stood back, and waited. After a long minute, the door cracked open and the housekeeper peered out at Bell. "What do you want?" she demanded, all formal courtesy lost from the lingering fright of the earthquake.

"I'm from the Van Dorn Detective Agency, here to see Mr. Cromwell."

"Mr. Cromwell is not at home. He left soon after the awful earth shuddering."

He could see a figure approach through the curtains covering the glass of the door. "Do you know if he went to his bank?"

The housekeeper moved back as Margaret stepped onto the threshold. She stared at the man standing on the step in a suit covered with dust, grime, and soot. The face was blackened with ash, the eyes tired of seeing too much misery. She barely recognized him.

"Isaac, is that you?"

"A little worse for wear, I'm afraid. But, yes, it's me." He removed his hat. "Good to see you, Margaret. I'm happy you survived the quake without injury."

Her dark eyes were wide and soft, as if she were seeing him for the first time. She stood back from the door. "Please come in."

He entered and saw that she had been working at cleaning up the mess littering the floors of the mansion, mostly broken china, porcelain figurines, and Tiffany lampshades. She wore a comfortable red cotton skirt and a woolen sweater under a long apron.

Her hair was wrapped in a tight curl atop her head, with loose strands falling beside her cheeks. Despite her plain appearance, she filled the air around her with a sweet fragrance. Whether she wore an expensive silk gown or an ordinary work dress, Margaret was still a stunning woman.

She led him into the parlor and offered him a chair by the fireplace, whose ashes had fanned out over the carpet when the chimney collapsed. "Would you like a cup of tea?"

"I'd sell my soul for a cup of coffee."

She turned to her housekeeper, who had overheard and simply nodded, then scurried off to the kitchen. Margaret found it difficult to gaze directly into Bell's hypnotic eyes. She found herself with a growing lust that she had experienced earlier in his presence.

"What do you want with Jacob?" she demanded without preamble.

"I think you know the answer to that question," he replied in a flat tone.

"You cannot abduct him again. Not in San Francisco. You must know that by now."

"You and he have bribed too many corrupt politicians in this town to ever be held for your crimes," Bell said bitterly. He paused and looked around at the servants cleaning up the house and putting the furniture and décor back in its proper place. "Looks like you intend on remaining in the city."

"Why not?" she said, faking indignation. "This is our city. We have a thriving business and close friends.

Our hearts are open to the poor who live here. Why on earth should we leave?"

Bell was almost tempted to believe Margaret. She was good, he thought, remembering the night they danced in the Brown Palace Hotel. Very good.

"Is Jacob at the bank?"

"He left to survey the damage."

"I saw what's left of Market Street. Most all the buildings are ruined, few still stand, and the Cromwell Bank is right in the path of the growing inferno."

Margaret seemed unconcerned. "Jacob built the bank to stand for a thousand years, as he did this house, which, you can see, survived the earthquake while the more-pretentious Nob Hill mansions were heavily damaged if not destroyed. The House of Cromwell was built to endure."

"Be that as it may, Margaret," said Bell with deadly seriousness. "But I warn you and Jacob not to consider leaving town."

Her anger flared and she came to her feet. "Do not threaten me, and do not think for a moment you can bully my brother. You're all bluff, Isaac. You have no authority, no influence, in this city. My brother and I will be here long after you're gone."

He came to his feet. "I admit defeat on that score. I have no influence in this city or with its political machine. But once you cross the city limits, the two of you belong to me. You can count on it."

"Get out!" she hissed fiercely. "Get out now!"

For a long moment, they glared at each other

through wild eyes, infuriated with sudden hostility. Then Bell rose slowly and put on his hat as he walked to the front door.

Margaret jumped to her feet and shouted, "You'll never lay your hands on my brother again. Never in a thousand years! Over my dead body!"

He paused to give her one final look. "I wish you hadn't said that." And then he was gone out the door.

Abner expertly zigzagged the Rolls-Royce to the Cromwell National Bank on Sutter and Hyde Streets, evading the heaps of bricks and swarms of people littering the streets. At one corner, a policeman stopped the car and ordered Abner to go to the Mechanics' Pavilion, the immense building and arena that housed a huge archive and was the scene for many fairs, sports events, and concerts. In desperate need of an emergency facility, the city had converted the pavilion into a hospital and morgue. The policeman insisted Cromwell put the Rolls into service as an ambulance for the injured.

"I have other uses for my car," Cromwell said loftily. He spoke through the speaking tube: "Continue on to the bank, Abner."

The policeman pulled out his revolver and pointed the muzzle at Abner. "I'm personally commandeering this car and seeing that you go directly to the pavilion or I'll blow your driver's head off and turn the car over to someone with decency."

Cromwell was not impressed. "A pretty speech, Officer, but the car stays with me."

The policeman's face flushed with anger. He waved his revolver. "I'm not going to warn you again—"

The policeman reeled back in shock, his eyes wide, as a bullet from Cromwell's Colt .38 ripped into his chest. He stood for a moment, bewildered, until his heart stopped and he crumpled to the pavement.

There was no hesitation, no concern, no remorse. Abner quickly slid from behind the wheel, snatched up the body as if it were a dummy, and set it on the front seat. Then he resumed his position behind the wheel, shifted into first gear, and drove away.

There was so much pandemonium on the streets – people shouting, the occasional thunder of another building collapsing, and the shriek of the fire equipment – that no one noticed the murder of the policeman. The few people who saw him fall to the ground thought he was injured and being picked up by a driver using his automobile as an ambulance.

"You'll dispose of him?" Cromwell asked, as if suggesting that a servant throw a dead cockroach in the trash.

Abner spoke into his speaking tube: "I'll take care of the matter."

"When you're finished, drive into the freight-and-service entrance at the rear of the bank. Let yourself in the back door – you have the key. I'll need you to help carry several trunks to the automobile."

"Yes, sir."

As the Rolls-Royce reached the corner of Sutter and Market Streets and Cromwell saw the approaching inferno and the magnitude of the destruction, he began to feel apprehensive about what he would find when they drove up to his bank. His growing fear quickly turned to elation when the building came into view.

The Cromwell National Bank had withstood the earthquake nearly unscathed. The unyielding stone structure had lived up to Cromwell's boast that it would last a thousand years. None of the walls or the great fluted columns had fallen. The only apparent damage was the shattered stained-glass windows, whose shards turned the sidewalk around the bank into a kaleidoscope of colors.

Abner pulled the Rolls to a stop and opened the rear door. Several bank employees were milling around the front entrance, having come to work out of habit, not knowing how else to deal with the tragic interruption of their lives. Cromwell got out and was only halfway up the steps when they surrounded him, all talking at once, bombarding him with questions. He held up his hands for silence and reassured them: "Please, please, go home and stay with your families. You can do nothing here. I promise your salaries will continue to be paid until this terrible calamity has ended and normal business can resume."

It was an empty promise. Not only did Cromwell have no intention of continuing their salaries while the bank was shut down; he could see that the flames sweeping through the business district of the city were only a few hours away from consuming the bank building. Though the walls were stone and unyielding, the wooden roof beams were highly susceptible to fire, which would quickly gut the building to an empty shell.

As soon as his employees were walking away from the bank, Cromwell took a set of large brass keys from his coat pocket and unlocked the massive bronze front door. He didn't bother to lock it after him, knowing the fire soon would consume any records inside. He headed straight for the vault. The time lock was set to engage the combination at eight o'clock. It was now seven forty-five. Cromwell calmly walked over to a leather chair at the loan officer's desk, brushed off the dust, sat down, and produced a cigar from a case in his breast pocket.

Feeling as if he were in full command of the situation, he leaned back, lit the cigar, and blew a cloud of blue smoke toward the ornate ceiling of the lobby. The earthquake, he thought, could not have come at a more-opportune time. He might lose a few million, but the insurance would cover any damage to the bank building itself. His competitors tied up their assets in loans, but Cromwell always kept his assets in cash and invested on paper. Once it became known he had fled town, bank examiners would land on the Cromwell National Bank like vultures. With luck, his depositors might get ten cents on their invested dollar.

At precisely eight, the vault mechanism made a

chiming sound as the locks clicked off one by one. Cromwell walked over to the vault and turned the huge wheel, which had spokes like a ship's helm, turned it, and released the bars from their shafts. Then he pulled the giant door open on its gigantic well-oiled hinges as easily as if it were attached to a kitchen cupboard and entered.

It took him two hours to finish loading four million dollars in large-denomination gold certificate bills into five large leather trunks. Abner arrived, after hiding the body of the policeman under the collapsed floor of a hardware store, and carried the trunks out to the Rolls. Cromwell was always impressed with the Irishman's brute strength. He himself could barely lift one end of a filled trunk off the floor, but Abner hoisted it onto one shoulder with barely a grunt.

The Rolls was parked in the underground freight entrance used by armored trucks and wagons that delivered currency or coins from the nearby San Francisco Mint. Cromwell helped Abner load the trunks in the spacious rear compartment before covering them with blankets he'd brought from his mansion. Under the blankets, he placed cushions from the chairs in the lobby of the bank, positioning them so that it looked as if they were dead bodies.

Cromwell went back inside and left the vault door open so the contents would be destroyed. Then he walked out and climbed in the open driver's section of the Rolls and sat beside Abner. "Drive to our warehouse at the railyard," he instructed.

"We'll have to detour to the north docks and come around behind the fires if we want to reach the railyard," said Abner, shifting the car into first gear. As he skirted the huge fire consuming Chinatown, he headed toward Black Point, to the north. Already, wooden buildings were disintegrating into beds of smoldering ashes as broken chimneys stood like blackened tombstones.

Some streets were clear enough to drive through, Abner avoiding those that were impassable because they were buried under collapsed walls. The Rolls was stopped twice by police, demanding the car be used as an ambulance, but Cromwell merely pointed to the makeshift bodies under the blankets and said they were on their way to the morgue. The police duly stepped back and waved them on.

Abner had to weave his way around crowds of refugees from the burned-out areas, carrying their meager belongings. There was no panic; people moved slowly, as if they were out for a Sunday stroll. There was little conversation, and few looked back at what had been their homes before the calamity.

Cromwell was stunned at the intensity and swiftness of the fire as it consumed a nearby building. The towering blaze sent a shower of flaming sparks and debris onto the roof, which became a flaming torch within two or three minutes. Then a firestorm enveloped the entire building and consumed it in less time than it takes to boil water.

Regular army troops from the surrounding military

installations began arriving to maintain order and help the city firemen fight the flames. Ten companies of artillery, infantry, cavalry, and the Hospital Corps – seventeen hundred men in all – marched into the city with guns and cartridge belts, prepared to guard the ruins, the bank and store vaults and safes, the post office, and the Mint from looters. Their orders were to shoot any man caught stealing.

They passed a caravan of soldiers in four automobiles whose backseats were stacked with boxes of dynamite from the California Powder Works. Within minutes, explosions rocked the already-devastated city, as homes and stores were detonated and leveled to slow the rage of the fire. Losing the battle, the army quickly began to dynamite entire blocks in a last-ditch attempt to stop the onslaught of the conflagration.

A sickly pale yellow light crept through the growing pall of smoke. There was no sun falling on the ruins except around the outskirts of the city. The dull ball of the sun appeared red and seemed smaller than its usual size. The army troops, firemen, and police retreated from the flames, herding the homeless to the west away from the approaching holocaust.

Abner twisted the wheel of the Rolls as he evaded the rubble in the streets and the crowd of people struggling to reach the ferry terminal in the hope of crossing the bay to Oakland. At last, he came across a railroad track and followed it into the main Southern Pacific railyard until he reached Cromwell's warehouse. He drove up a ramp and parked next to the boxcar sitting at the loading dock. He noted the serial number painted on the side: 16455.

Cromwell did not know that Bell was aware the boxcar was not what it appeared to be. But the agent who was assigned to observe it had been called away by Bronson for other duties after the quake. All looked secure. Cromwell studied the padlock on the big sliding door of the boxcar to make sure it had not been tampered with. Satisfied, he inserted a key and removed the lock, which was more for show than for protection. Then he crouched under the car and came up through the trapdoor into the interior of the car. Once inside, he turned the heavy latches that sealed the door from within and slid it open.

Without instructions, Abner began carrying the heavy trunks filled with currency from the Rolls, hoisting them up to the floor of the boxcar, where Cromwell dragged them inside. When the last of the four million dollars was removed from the limousine, Cromwell looked down at Abner and said, "Return to the house, gather up my sister and her luggage, then return here."

"You're staying, Mr. Cromwell?" asked Abner.

Cromwell nodded. "I have business to conduct across the yard at the dispatcher's office."

Abner knew that making a round-trip from the warehouse to the mansion on Nob Hill was a near-impossible task, but he gave Cromwell a casual salute and said, "I'll do my best to bring your sister here safe and sound."

"If anyone can do it, you can, Abner," said Cromwell. "I have complete faith in you."

Then Cromwell closed the sliding door of the boxcar and dropped down through the trapdoor. As Abner drove the Rolls down the ramp, he saw Cromwell making his way across the tracks toward the dispatcher's shack.

39

Bell hiked down Nob Hill and stopped to help a crew of men removing the debris of a small hotel that was little more than a mound of splintered wooden beams and crushed bricks. Underneath the wreckage, a little boy's voice could be heard sobbing. Bell and the men worked feverishly, throwing rubble off to the side and digging a hole toward the pitiful cries.

After nearly an hour, they finally reached a small air pocket that had protected the boy from being crushed. In another twenty minutes, they had him free and carried him to a waiting car that would rush him to a first-aid facility. Except for his ankles, which appeared to be fractured, he had suffered no other injuries but bruises.

The little boy looked to be no more than five years old to Bell. As the boy cried for his mother and father, the men who had saved him looked at each other with great sorrow, knowing his parents, and possibly brothers and sisters, were lying crushed deep within the collapsed hotel. Without a word, they went their separate ways, saddened, but glad they were at least able to save him.

Two blocks farther on, Bell passed by a soldier supervising a group of men who were pressed into service removing bricks from the street and stacking them on the sidewalk. Bell thought one of the men with a handsome profile looked familiar. Out of curiosity, he stopped and asked an older man, who was observing the operation, if he could identify this man who had "volunteered" to clean up the street.

"He's my nephew," the older man said, laughing. "His name is John Barrymore. He's an actor, performing in a play called *The Dictator*." He paused. "Or should I say *was* performing. The theater was destroyed."

"I thought I recognized him," said Bell. "I saw him play Macbeth in Chicago."

The stranger shook his head and grinned. "It took an act of God to get Jack out of bed and the United States Army to get him to work."

The soldier also tried to put Bell to work picking up bricks from the street, but again Bell showed his Van Dorn identification and moved on. By now, the crowds had scattered and the streets were nearly empty, except for soldiers on horseback, and a few sightseers, who lingered to watch the fires.

In the time it took Bell to walk another eight blocks to Cromwell's bank, the heart of the city on both sides of Market Street was burning fiercely. The wall of fire was only half a dozen blocks away from the bank when he reached the steps leading up to the huge bronze doors. A young soldier, no more than eighteen years of age, stopped Bell and menaced him with the bayonet on the end of his rifle.

"If you were going to loot the bank, you're a dead man," he said in a voice that meant business.

Bell identified himself as a Van Dorn agent and lied, "I'm here to check on the bank, to see if there are any records or currency that can be saved."

The soldier lowered his rifle. "All right, sir, you may pass."

"Why don't you accompany me? I might need some extra muscle to remove anything of value."

"Sorry, sir," said the soldier, "my orders are to patrol the street ahead of the flames to prevent looting. I don't suggest you spend much time inside. It's only a question of about an hour before the fire reaches this area."

"I'll be careful," Bell assured him. Then he walked up the steps and pushed open one of the doors, which Cromwell fortunately had left unlocked. Inside, it appeared as though the bank were closed for Sunday. The tellers' windows, desks, and other furniture made it look as if they were just waiting for business to resume on Monday morning. The only apparent damage was to the stained-glass windows.

Bell was surprised to find the vault door open. He entered and quickly saw that most of the currency was missing. Only silver and gold coins, along with some bills, their denominations no higher than five dollars, were still in the tellers' drawers and in their separate bins and containers. Jacob Cromwell had come and gone. The time Bell had spent helping to save the little boy had kept him from catching

Cromwell in the act of removing his bank's liquid assets.

There was no doubt in Bell's mind now that Cromwell meant to use the disaster to escape the city and flee over the border. Bell cursed that his Locomobile was not drivable. Making his way on foot through the ruins was costing him time and was draining his strength. He left the bank and set out for the Customs House, which was also in the path of the fire.

Marion did not fully accept Bell's instructions. Against his advice, she climbed back up the shaky stairs and into her apartment. She packed a large suitcase with her family photographs, personal records, and jewelry, topping it off with some of her more-expensive clothes. She smiled as she folded two gowns and a silk cape. Only a woman would save her nice things, she thought. A man would care less about saving his good suits.

Marion lugged the suitcase down the stairs and joined the other now-homeless people in the streets who were carrying or dragging trunks filled with their meager possessions, bedding, and household treasures. As they trudged up the hills of the city, none looked back at their homes and apartments, not wanting to dwell on the shattered and smashed remains where they had lived in peace and comfort until this day.

Through the night, tens of thousands fled the relentless fires. Strangely, there was no panic, no disorder. None of the women wept, none of the men showed anger at their misfortune. Behind them, picket lines of soldiers retreated before the flames, urging the horde to keep moving, occasionally prodding those who had become exhausted and stopped to rest.

Dragging heavy trunks up and down steep hills, block after block, mile after mile, eventually became too heavy a burden. Trunks by the thousands and their contents were abandoned, their owners completely played out. Some people found shovels and buried their trunks in vacant lots, hoping to retrieve them after the fires had died out.

Marion's spirit and fortitude rose within her to a level she had not known existed before. She carried or dragged her suitcase as if she was lost in a stupor. She toiled hour after hour alone, no man offering his assistance. Men, and their families, were all occupied in the heroic attempt to save their own belongings. Finally, when Marion could carry her suitcase no farther, a teenage boy asked if he could help her. Marion cried as she thanked him for coming to her aid.

It was not until five o'clock in the morning that she and the boy reached Golden Gate Park and met a soldier, who directed them to tents that were being set up for the refugees. She entered one, thanking the boy, who refused her offer of money, and sagged onto a cot and fell deeply asleep in less than ten seconds.

* * *

When Bell reached the Customs House, it was like walking through a wall of fire. Though late at night, the city was lit by an eerie, oscillating orange light. Crowds were fleeing the flames, but not before hurriedly loading goods from houses and stores onto wagons and rushing to safety at the last minute. The fire was approaching the Customs House on three sides and threatening the entire block. Soldiers on the roofs of neighboring buildings fought a nonstop battle to extinguish the flames and save the Customs House, whose upper level had been badly damaged in the earthquake. The lower floors, however, were undamaged and being used as an operations center by the army and by a detachment of marines and navy personnel who'd been given the job of providing and maintaining fire hoses.

Bell passed through the army guards posted around the building and stepped inside. In a room off the main lobby, he found Bronson consulting with two policemen and an army officer over a large-scale map laid out on a conference table.

Bronson saw an ash-covered man, his face blackened by soot, standing in the door and did not recognize him for a few seconds. Then a smile spread across his face and he came over and embraced Bell.

"Isaac, am I ever glad to see you."

"Do you mind if I sit down, Horace?" said an exhausted Bell. "I've walked a very long way."

"Of course." Bronson led him to a chair in front of a rolltop desk. "Let me get you a cup of coffee.

Despite the inferno around us, we have no way of heating it – but nobody cares."

"I'd love some, thank you."

Bronson poured a cup from an enamel pot and set it on the desk in front of Bell. A tall man with topaz brown eyes, shaggy dark brown hair, and wearing an unblemished white shirt with tie, came over and stood beside Bronson.

"Looks like you've seen better days," he said.

"Many of them," replied Bell.

Bronson turned to the stranger. "Isaac, this is the writer Jack London. He's writing an essay on the earthquake."

Bell nodded and shook hands without standing. "Seems to me you'll have enough material for ten books."

"Maybe one," said London, smiling. "Can you tell me what you've seen?"

Bell gave London a brief report of what he had seen around town, leaving out the horror of shooting the woman in the burning wreckage. When Bell was finished, London thanked him and walked over to a table, where he sat down and began organizing his notes.

"How did you make out with Cromwell? Did he and his sister survive?"

"Alive and well and headed over the border out of the country."

"Are you sure?" asked Bronson.

"I got to Cromwell's bank too late. The vault was

cleaned out of all denominations over five dollars. He must have made off with three, maybe four, million."

"He won't be able to leave the city. Not with the mess it's in. The wharfs are jammed with thousands of refugees trying to get over to Oakland. No way he could smuggle *that* much money in just a couple of suitcases."

"He'd find a way," said Bell, enjoying the cold coffee and feeling almost human again.

"What about Margaret? Did she go with him?"

Bell shook his head. "I don't know. I went by the house before noon and Margaret acted as if she and Jacob were staying in the city and going to fight us in court. After I found out he had fled with his bank's currency, I could not return to Nob Hill because of the advancing wall of fire. I barely made it here as is."

"And Marion?" Bronson asked cautiously.

"I sent her to Golden Gate Park. She should be safe there."

Bronson started to reply, but a boy no older than twelve ran into the room. He wore a broad cap, heavy sweater, and knickers – short pants gathered at the knee. It was obvious that he had been running a long distance because he was so out of breath he could barely speak.

"I'm . . . I'm looking for . . . for Mr. Bronson," he gasped haltingly.

Bronson looked up, interested. "I'm Bronson," he answered. "What do you want with me?"

"Mr. Lasch . . ."

Bronson looked at Bell. "Lasch is one of my agents. He was at our meeting shortly after the quake. He's guarding a government warehouse at the railyard. Go on, son."

"Mr. Lasch said you would pay me five dollars for coming here and telling you what he said."

"Five dollars?" Bronson stared at the boy suspiciously. "That's a lot of money for somebody your age."

Bell smiled, retrieved a ten-dollar bill from his wallet, and passed it to the boy. "What's you name, son?"

"Stuart Leuthner."

"You've come a long way from the railyard through the fire and devastation," said Bell. "Take the ten dollars and tell us what Lasch told you."

"Mr. Lasch said to tell Mr. Bronson that the boxcar parked in front of Mr. Cromwell's warehouse is gone."

Bell leaned toward the boy, his face suddenly clouded. "Say again," he instructed.

The boy looked at Bell, apprehension in his eyes. "He said Mr. Cromwell's boxcar was gone."

Bell stared at Bronson. "Damn!" he muttered. "He *has* fled the city." Then he gave the boy another ten-dollar bill. "Where are your parents?"

"They're helping pass out food in Jefferson Square."

"You'd better find them. They must be worried

about you. And, mind you, stay away from the fire."

Warren's eyes widened as he stared at the two ten-dollar bills. "Gosh almighty, twenty dollars. Gee, thanks, mister." Then he turned and ran from the building.

Bell sank back into the chair at the rolltop desk. "A train?" he murmured. "Where did he come by a locomotive?"

"All I know is, every ferry is jammed with refugees fleeing across the bay to Oakland. From there, the Southern Pacific is gathering every passenger train within a hundred miles to transport them away from the area. No way he could have hired a locomotive, crew, and tender."

"His freight car didn't roll away by itself."

"Trust me," said Bronson, "no freight cars are being ferried to Oakland. Only people. The only moving trains are those coming in with relief supplies from the east."

Bell came to his feet again, his eyes cold and fixed on Bronson. "Horace, I need an automobile. I can't waste hours hiking the part of the city that's not in flames."

"Where are you going?"

"First, I have to find Marion and make certain she's safe," Bell answered. "Then I'm heading for the railyard and the dispatcher. If Cromwell hired, or stole, a train to take him out of the city, there has to be a record at the dispatcher's office."

Bronson grinned like a fox. "Will a Ford Model K do?"

Bell looked at him in surprise. "The new Model K has a six-cylinder engine and can churn out forty horsepower. Do you have one?"

"I borrowed it from a rich grocery store owner. It's yours, if you promise to have it back by noon tomorrow."

"I owe you, Horace."

Bronson placed his hands on Bell's shoulders. "You can pay me back by seizing Cromwell and his evil sister."

40

Marion slept for six hours. When she awoke, she found the tent inhabited by five other single women. One was sitting on her cot, weeping. Two looked dazed and lost, while the others showed their strength by volunteering to help feed the suffering at the kitchen facilities that were being set up in the park. Marion rose from her cot, straightened her clothes, and marched with her new friends to several large tents that had been erected by the army as emergency hospitals.

She was immediately instructed by a doctor to treat and bandage wounds that did not require the services of doctors, who were busy in surgery helping to save the lives of the badly injured. Marion lost track of time. She shrugged off sleep and exhaustion by working in a shelter for children. Many were so brave it tore her heart. After tending the cuts and bruises of a little three-year-old girl who had lost her family, she turned away in tears when the girl thanked her in a tiny voice.

She moved to the next cot and knelt beside a boy brought in from surgery after having his broken leg set. As she tucked him in a blanket, she felt a presence behind her. Then came a familiar voice.

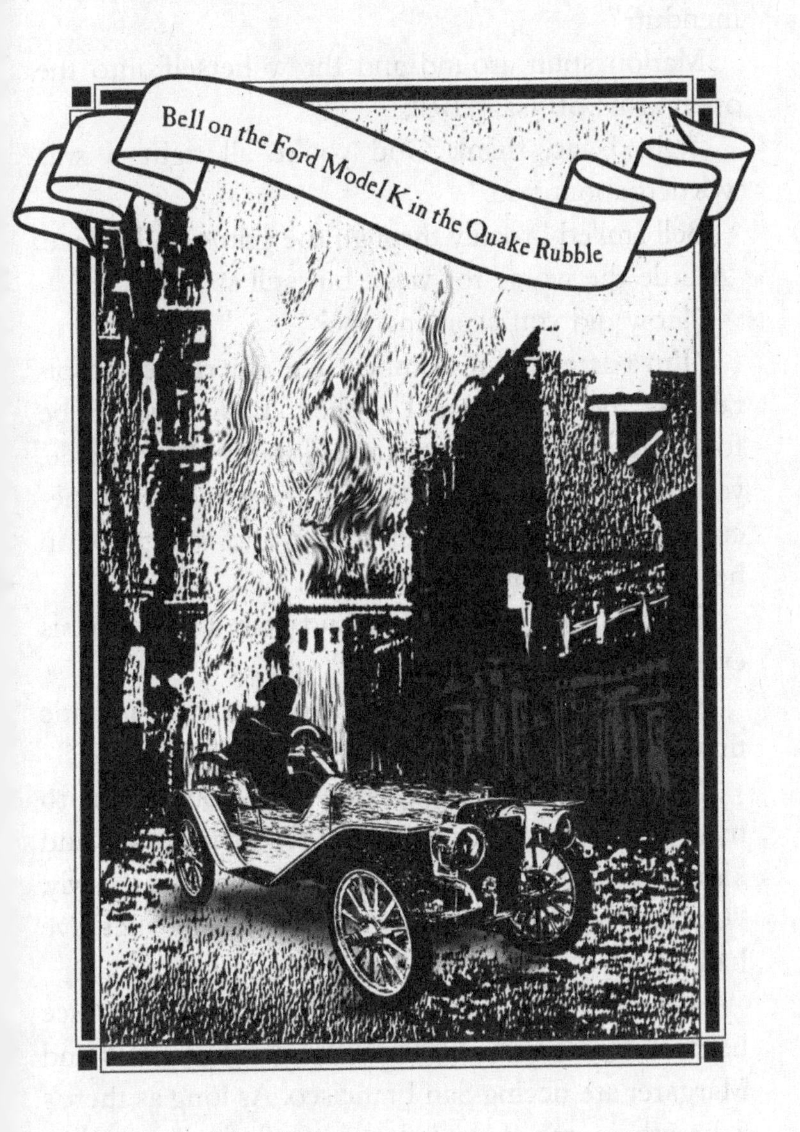
Bell on the Ford Model K in the Quake Rubble

"Pardon me, nurse, but my arm fell off. Can you mend it?"

Marion spun around and threw herself into the open arms of Isaac Bell.

"Oh, Isaac, thank God you're all right. I was worried about you."

Bell smiled broadly through the grime on his face. "A little the worse for wear, but still standing."

"How did you ever find me?"

"I'm a detective, remember? The emergency hospital was the first place I looked. I knew you'd be following in the footsteps of Florence Nightingale, your heart is too big not to help those in need, especially children." He squeezed her and whispered in her ear. "I'm proud of you, Mrs. Bell."

She pushed herself back and stared up into his eyes in confusion. "Mrs. Bell?"

Bell's smile remained fixed. "Not exactly a romantic time or place to propose, but will you marry me?"

"Isaac Bell," she cried, "how dare you do this to me." Then she softened, pulled his head down, and kissed him. When she released him, she said slyly, "Of course I will marry you. It's the best offer I've had all day."

His smile faded, his lips tightened, and his voice harshened. "I can't stay but a minute. Cromwell and Margaret are fleeing San Francisco. As long as there's a breath in me, I can't let a murdering scum like Cromwell go free."

His fervor frightened her, but she embraced him

fiercely. "It isn't every day a girl is proposed to by her lover who then runs away." She kissed him again. "You come back, you hear?"

"As soon as I can."

"I'll be waiting here. I don't expect any of us will be leaving our shantytown soon."

Bell held up her hands and kissed them both. Then he turned and disappeared from the hospital tent.

Bell did not consider returning to the Cromwell mansion on Nob Hill to see if Margaret had flown. He was certain she had fled with her brother.

The palace houses of the rich and powerful were great blazing bonfires. From every part of town came the roaring of the flames, the rumble of crashing walls, and the explosions of dynamite.

The Model K Ford was light and fast. And it was durable. It climbed over the rubble in the streets like a mountain goat. Unknowingly, Bell took nearly the same route as Cromwell and Abner, skirting along the northern waterfront away from the fire. Barely half an hour had passed since he had left Marion when he stopped the car on the ramp at Cromwell's warehouse, satisfying himself that the boxcar was indeed missing.

Switch engines were coupling cars to passenger trains in order to evacuate refugees to the southern part of the state, which still had open tracks, while freight cars were being dispatched to transport food supplies and medicine from Los Angeles. He drove the Ford into the railyard along the tracks until he reached a wooden building with a sign above the roof advertising it as the DISPATCH OFFICE. Bell stopped the car, leaped to the ground, and stepped inside.

Several clerks were busily working on the paperwork to dispatch trains and none looked up as Bell entered. "Where can I find the chief dispatcher?" he asked a harried clerk.

The clerk nodded toward a door. "In there."

Bell found the dispatcher writing numbers on a huge blackboard that displayed the tracks leading to and from the railyard. The sign on the desk read MORTON GOULD. He was a short man with a recessed chin and hawklike beak for a nose. The board showed over thirty different trains dispatched over track that spread from the railyard like a spiderweb. Bell could not help but wonder which one included Cromwell's boxcar.

"Mr. Gould?"

Gould turned and saw a man who looked as though he'd walked from one side of hell to the other. "Can't you see I'm busy? If you want to catch a train out of the city, you'll have to go to the Southern Pacific depot – or what's left of it."

"My name is Bell. I'm with the Van Dorn Detective Agency. I'm looking for a boxcar with the serial number 16455."

Gould motioned toward the board. "Southern Pacific is moving heaven and earth transporting thousands of homeless out of the city on our fleet of ferryboats and tugs over to Oakland, where we've assembled passenger trains waiting to evacuate them from the area. Over fourteen hundred relief cars are coming in from all over the country. Cars – passenger and freight – on this side of the bay, all three hundred of them, are being routed around the lower part of the state. How do you expect me to keep track of just one car?"

Bell studied Gould's eyes. "This particular car belonged to Jacob Cromwell."

It was there, a barely perceivable indication of recognition. "I don't know any Jacob Cromwell." Gould paused to stare apprehensively at Bell. "What's this all about?"

"You dispatched a locomotive to pull his private freight car."

"You're crazy. I wouldn't dispatch private trains during an emergency such as this."

"How much did he pay you?"

The dispatcher lifted his hands. "I couldn't be paid by a man I don't know. It's ridiculous."

Bell ignored Gould's lie. "Where was the destination of Cromwell's train?"

"Now, look here," Gould said, fear growing in his eyes. "I want you out of here, Van Dorn cop or no Van Dorn cop."

Bell removed his hat and made a motion as if cleaning the inside band. The next thing the dispatcher knew, he was staring into the business end of a derringer. Bell pressed the twin barrels against the side of

Gould's left eye socket. "Unless you tell the truth in the next sixty seconds, I will shoot and the bullet will horribly disfigure your face besides blasting away both of your eyes. Do you wish to spend the rest your life as a mutilated blind man?"

The hypnotic grip of terror crossed Gould's face. "You're mad."

"You have fifty seconds left before you see nothing."

"You can't!"

"I can and I will, unless you tell me what I want to know."

The cold expression, along with the icy voice, was enough for Gould to believe the Van Dorn detective was not bluffing. He looked around wildly, as if there was a way to escape, but Bell continued remorselessly.

"Thirty seconds," he said, pulling back the hammer of the derringer.

Gould's shoulders collapsed, his eyes filled with terror. "No, please," he murmured.

"Tell me!"

"All right," Gould said in a low tone. "Cromwell was here. He paid me ten thousand dollars in cash to hook his car up to a fast locomotive and direct the train onto a track heading south."

Bell's eyes partially closed in incomprehension. "South?"

"It's the only way out of the city," replied Gould. "All the train ferries are being used to transport people over to Oakland and the relief trains back. There was no other way he could go."

"How was he routed?"

"Down to San Jose, then around the bay to the north until his train turned east on the main line over the mountains and across Nevada to Salt Lake City."

"How long ago did he leave the railyard?" Bell demanded.

"About four hours."

Bell continued the pressure. "When is he scheduled to reach Salt Lake City?"

Gould shook his head in quick spasms. "Can't say. His engineer will have to spend a lot of time on sidetracks so the relief trains can fireball through. If he's lucky, his train will reach Salt Lake by late tomorrow afternoon."

"What type of engine did you assign to pull Cromwell's private freight car?"

Gould leaned over a desk and examined the notations in large ledger. "I gave him number 3025, a 4-6-2 Pacific, built by Baldwin."

"A fast engine?"

Gould nodded. "We have a few that are faster."

"When will one be available?"

"Why do you ask?"

"I want the fastest engine you've got," answered Bell, menacing Gould with the derringer. "This is a vital emergency. I have to catch Cromwell's train."

Gould consulted his big board. "I have number

3455, a 4-4-2 Baldwin Atlantic. She's faster than a Pacific. But she's in the Oakland yard for repairs."

"How long before she's ready to run?"

"The repair shop should have her ready to go in another three hours."

"I'll take her," Bell said without hesitation. "See that Van Dorn is charged for the time it's in use."

Gould looked as if he was going to protest and argue with Bell, but, staring at the derringer, he thought better of it. "If you report me, I could lose my job and go to jail."

"Just give me that engine and route me around San Jose toward Salt Lake City and I'll say nothing."

Gould sighed thankfully and began making out the paperwork to charter and dispatch a route for the locomotive under the Van Dorn Detective Agency. When he was finished, Bell took the papers and studied them for a moment. Satisfied, he left the office without another word, climbed in the Ford, and drove toward the Ferry Building.

41

Nearing the Ferry Building, Bell threw a blanket over his head as he drove through a shower of cinders. He could see that Chinatown was gone, leaving little more than hundreds of piles of charred, smoldering ruins. The Ferry Building had survived with only minor damage to its clock tower. Bell noted that the clock had stopped at 5:12, the time the earthquake struck.

The streets and sidewalks around the Ferry Building looked like a vast mob scene. Thousands were fleeing, believing the entire city would be destroyed. There was pandemonium and bedlam in the jumbled mass of people, some wrapped in blankets and loaded down with what possessions they were able to carry onto the ferryboat. Some pushed baby buggies or toy wagons, and yet, amid the nightmare, everyone was gracious, courteous, and considerate toward others.

Bell stopped beside a young man who seemed to be merely standing around and watching the fire across the street from the wharfs. He held up a twenty-dollar gold piece. "If you know how to drive a car, take this one to the Customs House and turn it over to Horace Bronson of the Van Dorn Detective Agency and this is yours."

The young man's eyes widened in anticipation, not so much from the money but the chance to drive an automobile. "Yes, sir," he said brightly. "I know how to drive my uncle's Maxwell."

Bell watched with amusement as the boy clashed the gears and drove off down the crowded street. Then he turned and joined the mass of humanity that was escaping the destruction of the city.

Within three days, over two hundred twenty-five thousand people left the peninsula where San Francisco stood, all carried free of charge by the Southern Pacific Railroad to wherever they wished to travel. Within twenty-four hours of the quake, overloaded ferryboats were departing San Francisco for Oakland every hour.

Bell showed his Van Dorn credentials and boarded a ferry called the *Buena Vista*. He found an open place to sit above the paddle wheels and turned back to watch the flames shooting hundreds of feet into the air, with the smoke rising over a thousand feet. It looked as if the whole city was one vast bonfire.

Once he stepped off the Mole in Oakland, a railroad official directed him to the repair shop where his locomotive was sitting. The mammoth steel monster was a grand sight up close. It was painted black from the cowcatcher to the rear of its coal tender. Bell guessed the cab's roof was at least fifteen feet above the rails. The big drive wheels were eighty-one inches in diameter. In its time, the Atlantic-type locomotive was a masterwork of mechanical power.

To Bell, it looked mean and ugly. The number 3455 was painted in small white letters on the side of the cab; SOUTHERN PACIFIC, in larger type, ran across the side of the tender, which fueled the boiler with coal and water. Bell walked up to a man wearing the traditional striped engineer's coveralls and striped cap with brim. The man held a big oil can with a long spout and looked to be oiling the bearings on the connecting rods running from the piston cylinder to the drive wheels.

"A mighty fine locomotive," said Bell admiringly.

The engineer looked up. He was shorter than Bell, with strands of salt-and-pepper hair straying from under his cap. The face was craggy from years of leaning out a cab window into the full wind stream from a speeding engine. The eyebrows over a pair of sky blue eyes were curved and bushy. Bell judged he was younger than he looked.

"None better than *Adeline*," the engineer answered.

"*Adeline?*"

"Easier to remember than her four-figured number. Most locomotives are given a woman's name."

"*Adeline* looks very powerful," said Bell admiringly.

"She's built for heavy passenger service. Came out of the Baldwin Works no more than five months ago."

"How fast will she go?" asked Bell.

"Depends on how many cars she's hauling."

"Let's say none."

The engineer thought a moment. "On a long, straight stretch of open, empty track, she'd top a hundred miles an hour."

"My name is Bell." He handed the engineer the paperwork. "I've chartered your engine for a special job."

The engineer studied the papers. "Van Dorn detective outfit, huh. What's so special?"

"Ever hear of the Butcher Bandit?"

"Who hasn't? I've read in the newspapers he's about as deadly as they come."

Bell wasted no detailed explanation. "We're going after him. He chartered a Pacific-type locomotive to haul his special private car. He's steaming to Salt Lake City before heading north for the Canadian border. I reckon he has a five-hour head start."

"More like six, by the time we take on coal and get a load of steam up."

"I was told there were repairs. Are they completed?"

The engineer nodded. "The shop replaced a faulty bearing in one of the truck wheels."

"The sooner we get going, the better." Bell paused to extend his hand. "By the way, my name is Isaac Bell."

The engineer's shake was vigorous. "Nils Lofgren. My fireman is Marvin Long."

Bell pulled his watch from its pocket and checked the time. "I'll see you in forty-five minutes."

"We'll be at the coal-loading dock just up the track."

Bell hurried toward the Oakland terminal until he came to a wooden building that housed the Western Union office. The wire chief told him that only one wire was open to Salt Lake City and it was hours behind getting messages through. Bell explained his mission and the chief was most cooperative.

"What's your message?" he asked. "I'll see that it's sent straightaway to our office in Salt Lake."

Bell's wire read:

To the Van Dorn office director, Salt Lake City. Imperative you stop locomotive hauling freight car number 16455. It is carrying the Butcher Bandit. Use every precaution. He is extremely dangerous. Seize and hold until I arrive.

Isaac Bell, special agent

He waited until the telegrapher tapped out the message before leaving the office and walking to where Lofgren and Long were taking on coal and water. He climbed up into the cab and was introduced to Long, a heavy, broad-shouldered man with large muscles stretching the sleeves of his denim shirt. He wore no hat and his red hair almost matched the flames inside the door to the firebox. He pulled off a leather glove and shook Bell's hand with a hand that was hard and callused from long hours wielding a coal shovel.

"Ready whenever you are," announced Lofgren.

"Let's do it," answered Bell.

As Long stoked the fire, Lofgren took his seat on the right side of the cab, locked the reverser Johnson bar into place, opened the cylinder cocks, and pulled the rope above his head down twice, causing the steam whistle to scream an about-to-move-forward warning. Then he gripped the long throttle lever and pulled it back. *Adeline* began to move and slowly gather speed.

Ten minutes later, Lofgren was signaled to switch onto the main track east. He eased the throttle back and the big Atlantic began to move forward. Slowly, the train wound through the yard. Long began maintaining his fire, light, level, and bright. In the five years he'd stoked locomotive fires, he'd developed a technique that kept the fire from burning too thin or too thick. Lofgren yanked on the throttle, the drive wheels churned amid a loud blast of steam, and black smoke spewed out the top of the stack.

Bell took the seat on the left side of the cab, feeling vastly relieved that he was at last on what he felt certain was the final chase to catch Cromwell and hand him over to the authorities in Chicago, dead or alive.

He found the vibration of the locomotive over the rails as soothing as floating in a rubber raft on a mountain lake, the chug of the steam propelling the drive wheels and the warm heat from the firebox positively restful for a man on a mission. Before they reached Sacramento and swung east across the Sierra Nevada Mountains, Bell slid down in his seat, yawned, and closed his eyes. Within a minute, he was in a sound sleep, amid the clangor of the speeding locomotive, as *Adeline* aimed her big cowcatcher toward the Sierra Nevada and Donner Pass.

42

Abner Weed's barrel chest and beefy shoulders were sweating as he shoveled coal into the firebox. There was an art to creating an efficient fire, but he had no idea how. He simply heaved coal through the open door into the fire, ignoring the complaints from the engineer who shouted that too much coal would drop the fire temperature.

Abner took on the job only to spell the fireman, Ralph Wilbanks, a big, burly man who soon became exhausted after a few hours of sustaining the necessary steam temperature that kept the big Pacific locomotive running up the steep grades of the Sierra Nevada Mountains. They traded one hour shoveling, one hour of rest.

Abner stayed alert during the effort, his Smith & Wesson revolver stuffed in his belt. He kept an eye on the engineer, who was constantly busy maintaining a fast but safe speed around the many mountain curves while watching the track ahead for any unforeseen obstacle, such as an unscheduled train coming in the opposite direction. At last, they crested the summit and it was all downhill until they met the flatlands of the desert.

"We're coming into Reno," yelled Wes Hall, the engineer, above the roar of the flames in the firebox. An intense man with the features of a weathered cowboy, he would have stopped the train in protest when he found his passengers demanded he set speed records across the mountains but relented after Abner put the Smith & Wesson to his head and threatened to kill him, and his fireman, if they didn't do as they were told. A thousand dollars in cash from Cromwell added to the persuasion, and Hall and Wilbanks now pushed the Pacific locomotive through the mountains as fast as they dared.

"The signal ahead reads red," said Wilbanks.

Hall waved that he saw it, too. "We'll have to stop and lay over on a siding."

Abner pointed the gun at the engineer's head. "Lay on the whistle. We're going through."

"We can't," said Hall, staring Abner in the eye. "There must be an express carrying relief supplies to San Francisco coming toward us on the same track. I'd rather you shoot me than cause a collision with another train that would kill all of us and stop traffic in both directions for maybe a week."

Abner slowly slid the revolver back under his belt. "All right. But get us back on the main track as soon as the relief express passes."

Hall began closing the throttle arm. "We can use the delay to take on coal and water."

"All right. But mind your manners or I'll blow holes in the both of you."

"Ralph and I can't go on much longer. We're done in."

"You'll earn your money – and stay alive – by pushing on," Abner said threateningly.

Leaning out the left side of the cab, Abner could see the train depot and the small town of Reno, Nevada, looming in the distance. As they came nearer, Abner spotted a figure waving a small red flag standing by a switch stand. Hall blew the whistle to announce their arrival and to let the flagman know that he understood the signal to slow down and was prepared to be switched off the main track.

Hall precisely stopped the Pacific's tender directly under an elevated wooden water tank on one side of the track and a coal bin on the other. Wilbanks jumped up on the tender, grabbed a rope, and pulled down the spout hinged to the tank until water flowed on board due to gravity. Climbing down from the cab with an oil can, Hall began checking all the bearings and fittings of the locomotive, and, since Cromwell had refused to wait for the arrival of a brakeman, he had to examine the bearings on the wheels of the tender and freight car as well.

Keeping a sharp eye on Hall and Wilbanks, Abner moved past the tender to the door of the freight car. He rapped twice with the butt of his Smith & Wesson, waited a moment, then knocked again. The door was unlatched from the inside and slid open. Jacob and Margaret Cromwell stood there, looking down at Abner.

"What's the delay?" asked Cromwell.

Abner tilted his head toward the locomotive. "We switched to a siding to let an express relief train through. While we're waiting, the crew is taking on coal and water."

"Where are we?" asked Margaret. She was dressed uncharacteristically in men's pants, with the legs tucked into a pair of boots. A blue sweater covered the upper half of her body, and she wore a bandanna on her hair.

"The town of Reno," answered Abner. "We're out of the Sierras. From now on, the landscape flattens out into desert."

"How about the track ahead?" inquired Cromwell. "Any more relief trains to delay our passage?"

"I'll check with the switchman for scheduled westbound trains. But we'll have to stand aside as they come."

Cromwell jumped to the ground and spread out a map on the ground. The lines drawn across it displayed the railroads in the United States west of the Mississippi. He pointed to the spot signifying Reno. "Okay, we're here. The next junction with tracks going north is Ogden, Utah."

"Not Salt Lake City?" asked Margaret.

Cromwell shook his head. "The Southern Pacific main line joins the Union Pacific tracks north of Salt Lake. We swing north at the Ogden junction and head toward Missoula, Montana. From there, we take the Northern Pacific rails into Canada."

Abner kept his eyes trained on the crew. He saw the fireman struggle with the coal flowing from the chute into the tender and the engineer moving about as if he were in a trance. "The crew is dead on their feet. We'll be lucky if they can run the locomotive another four hours."

Cromwell consulted the map. "There's a railyard in Winnemucca, Nevada, about a hundred seventy miles up the track. We'll pick up another crew there."

"What about these two?" inquired Abner. "We can't let them run to the nearest telegraph office and alert law enforcement up the line that we're coming."

Cromwell thought for a moment. "We'll keep them with us, then make them jump the train in a desolate part of the desert. We'll take no chances of Van Dorn agents getting wise to our leaving San Francisco and wiring officials down the line to stop our train, so we'll cut the telegraph lines as we go."

Margaret took a long look toward the Sierras and the track they had traveled. "Do you think Isaac is onto us?"

"Only a question of how long, dear sister," he said with his usual high degree of self-assurance. "But by the time he realizes we've flown San Francisco and finds a locomotive to give chase, we'll be halfway to Canada and he'll have no chance to stop us."

43

Adeline was Lofgren's pride and sweetheart, and he spoke to her as if the locomotive were a beautiful woman instead of a steel, fire-breathing monster that charged up the curving grades of the Sierras and through Donner Pass. Without having to pull two hundred tons of cars weighed down with passengers and luggage, she performed effortlessly.

The spring air was cool and crisp, and snow still covered the ground. Donner Pass was the notorious section of the mountains where the most poignant event in western history had taken place. A wagon train made up of a dozen families that would pass into legend as the Donner party became trapped in the winter blizzards of 1846 and suffered terribly until rescued. Many survived by eating the dead. Out of the original eighty-seven men, women, and children, only forty-five lived to reach California.

Bell had been fully awake since passing through Sacramento and was finding the scenery spectacular – the towering, rocky peaks; the forest of fir trees, some with branches still laden with snow; the summit tunnels, which were blasted out of granite by Chinese laborers in 1867. *Adeline* plunged into the black mouth of a long tunnel, the roar of the train's exhaust reverberating like a hundred bass drums. Soon, a tiny circle of light materialized ahead in the darkness and quickly grew wider. Then *Adeline* burst into the bright sunlight with a noise like thunder. A few miles later came the panoramic view of Donner Lake, as the train began its long, curving descent to the desert.

Bell stared with some uneasiness down the sheer thousand-foot drop that was within a step or two of the edge, as the locomotive swung around a sharp bend. He did not need to urge Lofgren to go faster. The engineer was pushing the big locomotive at nearly thirty-five miles an hour around the mountain curves, a good ten miles faster than was considered safe.

"We're across the summit," announced Lofgren, "and have a downgrade for the next seventy-five miles."

Bell stood and gave Long his fireman's seat on the left side of the cab. Long thankfully sat down and took a break, as Lofgren closed off steam and allowed *Adeline* to coast down through the pass in the mountains. Long had been shoveling coal almost nonstop since they had swung onto the main line at Sacramento and up the steep grade into the Sierras.

"Can I give you a hand?" asked Bell.

"Be my guest," said Long, lighting up a pipe. "I'll tell you how to shovel the coal into the firebox. Even though we're loafing along for the next hour, we can't let the fire die down."

"You don't just throw it in with a shovel?"

Long grinned. "There's more to it than that. And it's not called a *shovel*; it's a *fireman's scoop*, size number four."

For the next two hours, Bell labored in front of the maze of pipes and valves as he learned the intricacies of firing a locomotive. The tender was rocking from side to side around the turns, making it difficult to shovel coal into the firebox. It was easy work, however, with *Adeline* running downhill. He shoveled just enough coal to keep the steam up. He quickly learned to open the firebox door wide, after hitting the scoop against it and spilling coal over the floor. And instead of stacking the coal in a fiery pile, he developed the knack for making a level fire that burned bright and orange.

The sharp curves were left behind as their arc increased as they dropped down to the foothills. An hour after Bell turned the scoop over to Long, the fireman shouted to Lofgren: "We've only got enough water and coal for another fifty miles."

Lofgren nodded without taking his eyes from the track ahead. "Just enough to make Reno. We can put in for coal and water there and take on a relay crew."

Bell realized that the race over the mountains had taken its toll on Lofgren and Long. He could see that the strain on body and mind had drained the staunch engineer, and the physical effort of maintaining steam on the steep grades had sapped the strength of the indefatigable fireman. It seemed evident to Bell that

Cromwell's train crew must be worn out as well. He checked his watch and could only wonder if they had narrowed the gap.

"How long will it take to assemble another crew?" Bell asked.

"As long as it takes to coal and water the tender," replied Lofgren. Then he smiled wearily, revealing a set of crooked teeth, and added, "Providing we're lucky and one happens to be standing by."

"I'm grateful to you both," Bell said sincerely. "You did a heroic job getting over the Sierras. You must have set a record."

Lofgren pulled out his big Waltham railroad watch with its locomotive engraved on the back of the case. "Indeed," he laughed. "We shaved eight minutes off the old record set by Marvin, me, and *Adeline* six months ago."

"You love this engine, don't you?" said Bell.

Lofgren laughed. "Take all the Atlantic locomotives ever put on rails: they're the finest in the world, all built exactly the same, with identical dimensions and construction. Yet, every one is different – like people, they all have diverse personalities. Some can run faster than the others, with the same steam pressure. Some are finicky while others are jinxed, always having bad luck with repair problems. But *Adeline*, she's a sweetheart. No whims; never cranky, eccentric, or ill-tempered. Treat her like a lady and she's like a thoroughbred mare that wins races."

"You make her sound almost human."

"*Adeline* may be a hundred seven tons of iron and steel, but she's got a heart."

They were nearing Reno, and Lofgren pulled the whistle cord to announce his intention of switching to the siding for coal and water. He eased back on the throttle to slow the locomotive. The switchman threw the switch lever to link the tapering rails, as he had done for Cromwell's train earlier. Then he waved a green flag to alert Lofgren that the siding was open.

Even before *Adeline* rolled to a stop, Bell had jumped from the cab and took off running across the railyard to the depot, which looked like a thousand other small-town depots across the nation. It was characterized by wooden slat walls, arched windows, and a peaked roof. The loading platform was empty, giving Bell the impression that no passenger trains were due to stop there anytime soon.

He stepped inside, past the freight-and-ticket office, and stopped at the telegrapher's small room. Two men were in the middle of a deep conversation when he walked in. It struck him that their faces looked serious and grim.

"I beg your pardon," said Bell, "I'm looking for the stationmaster."

The taller of the two men stared at Bell for a moment before nodding. "I'm the stationmaster, Burke Pulver. What can I do for you?"

"Has a train come through with only one freight car in the last ten hours heading east?"

Pulver nodded. "They were stopped on the siding for two hours while two express trains carrying relief supplies for the San Francisco earthquake victims rolled through."

"They were delayed two hours?" said Bell, suddenly feeling optimistic. "How long ago did they leave?"

Pulver glanced up at the Seth Thomas clock on the wall. "About four and a half hours ago. Why do you ask?"

Bell identified himself and briefly explained his chase of Cromwell.

Pulver stared Bell in the eye. "You say that freight car was carrying the notorious Butcher Bandit?"

"He was on it, yes."

"If only I had known, I'd have told the sheriff."

The time gap was less than Bell had dared hope. "Do you have a relay crew available? Mine is worn out, after their record run over the Sierras."

"Who's your crew?"

"Lofgren and Long."

Pulver laughed. "I might have known those two would try to beat their own record." He studied a blackboard on one wall. "I have a crew on hand." He paused. "I thought there was something funny about that train. Reno is a relay stop for just about every train going either east or west. Highly unusual, not taking on a relay crew. Your bandit won't get far with an engineer and fireman who are used up."

Bell looked down at the telegrapher, a bald-headed man with a green visor perched on his forehead and garters on his shirtsleeves. "I'd like to alert lawmen in the towns ahead to stop the train and seize the bandit, whose name is Jacob Cromwell."

The telegrapher shook his head. "No can do. The lines are down. I can't get a message through to the east."

Bell said, "I'll lay money Cromwell is cutting the lines."

Pulver studied a large blackboard on another wall that showed the trains scheduled to pass through Reno. "I'll have a crew for you in twenty minutes. You should have a clear run until you reach Elko. After that, I hope you'll find the telegraph in operation or you'll run the risk of colliding with a train traveling west."

"In that case," Bell said cynically, "I'll have the satisfaction of knowing Cromwell collided with it first."

44

Adeline was hitting her stride on the flat, open stretch of track. She was touching ninety miles an hour, roaring across trestles over dry gulches, flying through small towns, and hurtling past signals indicating open track ahead. The telegraph poles running alongside the track swept by in a confused blur. Gray smoke tinged with sparks and cinders spewed from the stack, streaming back in a horizontal cloud over the cab and flattened by the head-on rush of wind.

A doleful, flaxen-haired descendant of the Vikings, Russ Jongewaard, sat in the engineer's seat, one hand on the throttle, while Bill Shea, a tall, humorous Irishman, shoveled coal into the firebox. After hearing from Bell that he was in a do-or-die attempt to capture the famed Butcher Bandit, they gladly came aboard to join the chase.

Lofgren and Long stayed aboard, too. "We're volunteering for the duration," said Lofgren. "With the four of us spelling each other, we won't have to stop for another relay crew."

Bell pitched in with the coal-shoveling duties. His thigh wound from Cromwell's bullet in Telluride had not completely healed, but as long as he didn't put too much weight on it there was little pain. His scoop held half as much coal as those that Long or Shea pitched in the firebox, but he made up for it with two shovels to their one.

The two Southern Pacific firemen took turns keeping an eye on the water gauge and watching the steam gauge, making sure it showed their fire was burning well and the engine was operating at just under two hundred pounds of steam pressure, within a hair of the redline mark. They studied the smoke coming from the stack. When it started to go from gray to clear, they added more coal. When it turned black, it meant the fire was too thick and they had to ease off.

A competition, unchallenged and unspoken, developed between Lofgren and Jongewaard, but it did not go unnoticed. *Adeline* may have shown the immense power of her machinery and the lightning speed of her churning drive wheels, but it was the strength and endurance of the men who drove her to her limits that set records across Nevada that day. The engineers had the bit in their teeth and worked hard to catch the train of the killer of so many innocent people.

Seeing the semaphore that signaled the track was clear beyond Elko, Lofgren kept the throttle against its stop as he swept past the depot at ninety-five miles an hour. People waiting on the platform for a passenger train stared aghast as *Adeline* shot by like an immense cannonball.

Fortunately, junctions were few and far between – a few spur lines running off the main track – so they kept up their rapid speed without slowing. Then agonizing slowdowns began to occur at the town of Wells, and again farther up the track at Promontory, to allow westbound relief trains through. The delays were utilized by taking on coal and water, but a total of eighty minutes was lost.

At each stop, Bell questioned the stationmasters about Cromwell's train. At Wells, the stationmaster told him that the engineer and fireman who had driven Cromwell's train from Oakland had been found by a section hand checking the ties and rails. He'd had them brought into town, barely able to stand because they were so fatigued and dehydrated. They had confirmed what Bell had feared: Cromwell had frequently ordered the train to stop so his hired gun could climb the poles and cut the wires.

"How are we doing?" asked Lofgren when Bell climbed back in the cab.

"The stationmaster said they passed through three hours ago."

"Then we've picked up an hour and a half since Reno," Long said with a wide grin, knowing their untiring efforts were paying off.

"From here to Ogden, you'll have to keep out a sharp eye. Cromwell is cutting the telegraph wires, We'll be running blind, should we come upon a west-bound train."

"Not a great threat," said Jongewaard. "The company won't risk sending trains down the main line if they can't contact stationmasters to set schedules.

Still, we'll have to be on the alert, especially around turns where we can't see more than a mile ahead."

"How far to Ogden?" asked Bell.

"About fifty miles," replied Jongewaard. "We should make the station in about an hour."

With Lofgren at the throttle, *Adeline* pulled into Ogden's Union Station forty-two minutes later. He was switched to the coal- and water-loading siding and brought the locomotive to a halt. Their routine was now well established. While Long and Shea loaded the coal and water, Lofgren and Jongewaard checked the engine and oiled the drive connectors and wheel bearings. Bell hurried into the big station and found the dispatcher's office.

A pudgy man sat at a desk, staring out the window at an arriving passenger train. His interest was particularly taken by the young pretty women who showed ankles when stepping down the Pullman car steps. Bell read the name on a small sign sitting on the front of the desk.

"Mr. Johnston?"

Johnston looked Bell's way and smiled a friendly smile. "Yes, I'm Johnston. What can I do for you?"

Bell ran through his story of chasing Cromwell for perhaps the sixth time since leaving San Francisco. "Can you tell me when the train came through?"

"Never came through," answered Johnston.

"Never came through your station?" Bell's thick eyebrows lifted toward his mane of blond hair.

"Yep," Johnston said, leaning back in his swivel chair and setting a booted foot on a pulled-out drawer. "They were switched onto the line heading north."

"How?" snapped Bell. "It was not a scheduled train."

"Some rich woman showed papers to the dispatcher at the junction up the track that said she had chartered a train with right-of-way clearance to Missoula, Montana."

"The bandit's sister," said Bell. "They're trying to reach the border and cross into Canada."

Johnston nodded in understanding. "The dispatcher checked with me on southbound trains. None was scheduled until tomorrow morning, so I told him to go ahead and allow the lady's train to travel north."

"When did this take place"

"A little less than two hours ago."

"I've got to catch that train," Bell said firmly. "I'd appreciate clearance to Missoula."

"Why not telegraph the sheriff in Butte to stop the train and take the bandit and his sister into custody?"

"I've tried to do that since leaving Reno, but Cromwell has cut every telegraph line between here and there. No reason for him to stop now."

Johnston looked stunned. "My God, he could have caused a head-on collision."

"Until he and his sister reach the Canadian border, they have nothing to lose, even if it means killing anyone who gets in their way."

Shocked understanding had come to Johnston. "Get that dirty coward," he said, desperation creeping into his voice. "I'll gladly give you clearance through to Missoula."

"I'm grateful for any help you can give," said Bell sincerely.

"What's your train number?"

"No train, only a tender and engine number 3455."

"What kind of engine?"

"A Baldwin Atlantic 4-4-2," answered Bell.

"She's a fast one. What about relay crews?"

"I have two crews who insist on sticking to the chase until we grab the bandit."

"In that case, all I can do is wish you luck." Johnston rose and shook Bell's hand.

"Thank you."

"Two hours is a hell of a lead," said Johnston quietly.

"We gained two and a half since leaving Oakland."

Johnston thought a moment. "You've got a real chase on your hands. It will be close."

"I'll stop him," Bell said gamely. "I've got to stop him or he'll kill again."

45

There was hope in the hearts of the men who sweated and toiled to drive *Adeline* over the rails. They had all risen up and reached beyond themselves to do the impossible. Men and women who worked the farms and ranches alongside the track stopped their labor and stared in surprise at the speeding lone locomotive that shrieked its whistle in the distance and thundered past beyond their sight in less than a full minute except for the lingering trail of smoke.

With Lofgren in the driver's seat, he pressed *Adeline* harder and harder until they swept over the border from Utah to Idaho at a speed of nearly one hundred miles an hour. Pocatello, Blackfoot, and Idaho Falls came and went. Stationmasters could only stand in shock and confusion, not able to comprehend a locomotive and tender that came out of nowhere with no advance warning and plunged past their depots at unheard-of speed.

Before they raced out of Ogden, Bell had procured a pile of blankets so the crews could catnap between shifts of driving the locomotive and feeding its boiler. At first, they found it impossible to sleep for short periods because of the clamor of the drive train, the hiss of steam, and the clatter of the steel wheels over the rails. But as exhaustion set in, they found it easier and easier to drift off until their turn came at the scoop and throttle again.

Except for quick stops for coal and water, *Adeline* never slowed down. At one stop, in Spencer, Idaho, Bell learned that they were only fifty minutes behind Cromwell's train. Knowing they were rapidly closing the distance inspired them to renew their efforts and work even harder.

The mystery in Bell's mind was the report given him by the Spencer stationmaster. It seemed that the Southern Pacific main track stopped at Missoula, with only a spur that went another eighty miles to the small port of Woods Bay, Montana, on Flathead Lake.

"How do you read it?" Lofgren asked Bell after his place at the throttle was taken by Jongewaard.

"Cromwell must have found another crew after driving the engineer and fireman from Winnemucca half to death," said Bell.

Lofgren nodded. "Without telegraph messages coming through and informing us otherwise, I have to believe he dumped them in the middle of nowhere, too, and forced a relay crew to come aboard for the final dash across the border."

"Then he'll have to do it by driving over a road in an automobile."

Lofgren looked at him. "Why do you say that?"

Bell shrugged. "The stationmaster at Spencer told me Southern Pacific's tracks end at Woods Bay on the east shore of Flathead Lake. I assume the only way Cromwell can continue north into Canada is by road."

"I disagree. My guess is, he's going to take his train onto the car ferry that runs across the lake."

Bell stared at Lofgren questioningly. "Car ferry?"

Lofgren nodded. "Logs from timber operations in Canada are hauled on flatcars across the border to a small port on the west side of the lake called Rollins. From there, they are rolled onto a ferry that carries them across the lake. When they reach Woods Bay, they are coupled to trains that transport them to lumberyards around the Southwest."

"Why doesn't Southern Pacific simply run their tracks north to Canada?"

"The Great Northern Railroad received land rights from the government to cross the upper United States. They laid tracks that run from a landing on the west shore of Flathead Lake north to the border, where their locomotives are coupled to flatcars carrying logs hauled by the Canadian Pacific Railroad from the logging camps. Officials from both Great Northern and Southern Pacific refused to work together and never laid tracks that merged around the ends of the lake."

"How do you know all this?"

"My uncle lives in Kalispell, above the lake. He's retired now, but he was an engineer for the Great Northern Railroad. He drove an engine between Spokane and Helena."

The interest in Bell's voice gave way to trepidation.

"So what you're telling me is that Cromwell can ferry his train across the lake to the Northern Pacific tracks and go north into Canada without stepping off his freight car."

"That's about the size of it."

"If he gets across on the car ferry before we can stop him . . ." His voice trailed off.

Lofgren saw the apprehension in Bell's eyes. "Don't worry, Isaac," he said confidently. "Cromwell can't be more than ten miles up the track ahead of us. We'll catch him."

For a long moment, Bell said nothing. Then he slowly reached in a breast pocket and pulled out a piece of paper. Slowly, he unfolded it and handed it to Lofgren.

The engineer studied and then spoke without looking up. "It looks like a list of names."

"It is."

"Names of who?"

Bell dropped his voice until it was barely audible above the clangor of the charging locomotive. "The men, women, and children Cromwell murdered. I've been carrying it since I was put in charge of chasing him down."

Lofgren's eyes lifted and gazed through the front window of the track ahead. "The others should see this."

Bell nodded. "I think now is an appropriate time."

* * *

Three hours later, with Lofgren back on the throttle, *Adeline* began to slow as she came into Missoula. He brought the locomotive to a halt fifty feet before a switch stand. Shea jumped from the cab, ran up the track, and switched the rails to those of the spur leading to Flathead Lake. He ignored the switchman, who came running out of a shack.

"Here, what are you doing?" demanded the switchman, who was bundled up against a cold wind.

"No time to explain," said Shea as he waved to Lofgren, signaling that it was safe to roll onto the spur from the main track. He looked at the switchman as *Adeline* slowly rolled past and said, "Did another train pass onto the spur in the last hour?"

The switchman nodded. "They switched onto the spur without permission either."

"How long ago?" Shea demanded.

"About twenty minutes."

Without replying, Shea ran after *Adeline* and pulled himself up into the cabin. "According to the switchman," he reported, "Cromwell's train passed onto the spur twenty minutes ago."

"Eighty miles to make up twenty minutes," Jongewaard said thoughtfully. "It will be a near thing." He pulled open the throttle to the last notch and, five minutes after leaving the junction, he had *Adeline* pounding over the rails at eighty-five miles an hour.

Flathead Lake came into view as they ran up the eastern shore. The largest freshwater lake in the western United States, it was twenty-eight miles long, sixteen miles wide, and covered one hundred eighty-eight square miles, with an average depth of one hundred sixty-four feet.

They were in the homestretch now of a long and grueling chase. Lofgren sat in the fireman's seat and helped Jongewaard survey the track ahead. Bell, Shea, and Long formed a scoop brigade to feed the firebox. Not having leather gloves like the firemen, Bell wrapped his hands with rags the engineers used to wipe oil. The protection helped, but blisters were beginning to rise on his palms from the long hours of shoveling coal.

They soon reached a speed higher than the spur tracks were ever built to endure from a speeding train. There was no slowdown over bridges and trestles. Curves were taken on the outer edge. One double-reverse turn they whipped around in a violent arc rattled the bolts in the tender. Luckily, the tracks then became as straight as the crow flew. Jongewaard held the eighty-five-mile-an-hour pace for the next forty miles.

"Eureka!" Lofgren suddenly yelled, vigorously pointing ahead.

Everyone leaned from the cab, the icy wind bringing tears to their eyes. But there it was, four, maybe five, miles directly ahead, a faint puff of smoke.

46

Margaret lounged on a settee, wearing an embroidered silk robe, and stared at the champagne bubbles rising in her saucer-shaped coupe glass. "I wonder if it's true," she said softly.

Cromwell looked at her. "What's true?"

"That this glass was modeled from the breast of Marie Antoinette."

Cromwell laughed. "There is an element of truth in the legend, yes."

Then Margaret gazed out the window Cromwell had raised in the back of the car – it was recessed into the rear wall and was inconspicuous when closed. The tracks that flashed under the wheels seemed to be stretching to infinity. She could see that they were traveling through a valley surrounded by forested mountains.

"Where are we?"

"The Flathead Valley in the heart of the Rocky Mountains."

"How much farther to the border?"

"Another thirty minutes to the ferry landing at Flathead Lake," said Cromwell, opening their second bottle of champagne for the day. "Half an hour to cross over onto the Great Northern tracks and we'll be in Canada by sunset."

She held up her glass. "To you, brother, and a brilliant flight from San Francisco. May our new endeavor be as successful as the last."

Cromwell smiled smugly. "I'll drink to that."

Ahead, in the cab of the locomotive, Abner was pressing the crew he had abducted at gunpoint from a small café beside the railyard in Brigham City, Utah: Leigh Hunt, a curly-red-haired engineer, and his fireman, Bob Carr, a husky individual who had worked as a brakeman before becoming a fireman, a step he hoped would eventually lead to his becoming an engineer. They had just come off a run and were having a cup of coffee before heading home when Abner held his gun to their heads and forced them into the cab of the engine pulling Cromwell's fancy freight car.

As was the earlier crew, Wilbanks and Hall were thrown from the engine in the middle of nowhere at the same time Abner cut the telegraph wires.

Abner sat on the roof of the tender above the cab so he could prod Hunt and Carr to keep the Pacific locomotive hurtling over the rails to Flathead Lake. The black swirling clouds over the Rocky Mountains to the east caught his attention.

"Looks like a storm brewing," he shouted to Carr.

"A chinook, by the look of it," Carr yelled back over his shoulder as he scooped coal into the firebox.

"What's a chinook?" asked Abner.

"It's a windstorm that roars down out of the Rockies. Temperatures can drop as much as forty degrees in an hour and winds can blow over a hundred miles an hour, enough to blow railcars off the tracks."

"How long before it strikes here?"

"Maybe an hour," replied Carr. "About the time we'll reach the train ferry dock at Woods Bay. Once we arrive, you'll have to sit out the storm. The ferry won't sail during a chinook."

"Why not?" Abner demanded.

"With hundred-mile-an-hour winds, the lake turns into a frenzy. The wind whips the water into waves as high as twenty feet. The train ferry wasn't built for rough water. No way the crew will take it out on the lake during a chinook."

"We telegraphed ahead to have the ferry waiting for our arrival," said Abner. "We're going across, wind or no wind."

Back in Cromwell's rolling palace, Margaret had drifted into a light sleep from the champagne while her brother sat and relaxed with a newspaper he'd picked up when Abner abducted the train crew at Brigham City. Most of the news was about the San Francisco earthquake. He read that the fires had finally been put out and wondered if his mansion on Nob Hill and the bank building had survived.

He looked up, hearing a strange sound different from the clack of the steel wheels on steel rails. It came faint and far off. He stiffened as he recognized it as a train whistle. Cromwell was stunned, knowing now for certain that he was being pursued.

"Bell!" he exploded in anger.

Startled at his loud voice, Margaret sat up awake. "What are you shouting about?"

"Bell!" snapped Cromwell. "He's chased us from San Francisco."

"What are you saying?"

"Listen," he ordered her. "Listen."

Then she heard it, the unmistakable sound of a train's steam whistle, barely perceptible, but it was there.

Margaret rushed to the rear window and peered down the track. It was as if a fist had struck her in the stomach. She could see a stream of black smoke rising beyond a curve above a windbreak of small trees.

"You must tell Abner!" she screamed.

Cromwell had anticipated her and climbed a ladder to the vent opening in the roof of the boxcar. He pushed aside the lid to the vent, stood above the roof, and shot off his revolver to get Abner's attention over the clamor of the locomotive. Abner heard and hurried over the top of the tender, until he was only a dozen feet away from Cromwell.

"There is a train coming up behind us," Cromwell shouted.

Abner braced his feet apart against the pitch and roll of the tender and gazed over the roof of the boxcar. The onrushing train had come around the curve now and was visible in the distance. It looked to be a locomotive and its tender, pulling no cars. It was coming, and coming on fast, as evident from the smoke exploding from its stack and laid flat by the headwind.

Now the two trains were in sight and sound of each other, with the ferry dock at Woods Bay on Flathead Lake only twenty miles away.

47

It was as if *Adeline* was a come-from-behind thoroughbred pounding around the far turn into the back stretch, flying through the herd and vying for the lead. Her connecting rods were a blur as they whipped the massive drive wheels over the rails. No locomotive ever worked harder. From the Oakland railyard to the wilds of Montana, she had covered more distance faster than any locomotive in history. No one timed her speeds, but none on board her cab or those who had seen her hurtle past ever doubted that she had surpassed ninety miles an hour on straight and level stretches of track.

Jongewaard had the throttle against its stop, throwing *Adeline* over tracks that were never meant for such speeds. Both engineers sat in the cab seats, their eyes fixed on the track ahead. Bell and Long shoveled while Shea systematically banked the fire to keep it burning evenly for the maximum amount of heat for proper combustion.

The chugging sound of the steam exhaust became one continuous hiss and the smoke poured from the stack in an ever-growing cloud. Bell stopped shoveling every so often to stare at the train ahead, growing larger by the minute. There was no effort to sneak up on Cromwell now; he pulled the cord and gave the whistle a long shriek that cut through the breeze beginning to blow in over the lake. Bell's lips were spread in a tight smile. He hoped Cromwell sensed that it was he who was charging down his throat.

Bell turned, looked up to the sky, and saw it had changed from a blue sea to a gray shroud from the chinook wind that howled out of the Rocky Mountains to the east. Great swirls of dust, leaves, and small debris were thrown like wheat chaff through a threshing machine. The water of Flathead Lake had gone from a dead calm to a turbulent mass in less than twenty minutes.

Then, suddenly, both Jongewaard and Lofgren shouted at once: "Wagon on the track!"

Every eye swung and stared at the track ahead.

A farmer with a hay wagon pulled by a team of horses was on a road crossing the tracks. He must have heard the engine's whistle, Bell thought, but the farmer had badly misjudged the speed of the train, believing he could cross the tracks in plenty of time. Jongewaard heaved back the reverser Johnson bar, slowing the drive wheels until they stopped and spun backward in reverse, braking the speeding locomotive.

When the farmer realized the iron monster was only a hundred yards away, he whipped his horses in a frenzied attempt to drive them out of the path of onrushing death. By then, it was too late.

Adeline plowed into the wagon in an explosion of hay, wooden planks, splinters, and shattered wheels.

The men in the cab instinctively ducked behind the protection of the boiler as debris clattered along the sides of the engine and flew over the roof onto the tender.

Miraculously, the horses had jumped forward and escaped without harm. Bell and the others did not witness the farmer's fate. As soon as Jongewaard brought *Adeline* to a halt a hundred yards down the track, Bell and crew leaped from the cab and ran back to the crossing.

They were all vastly relieved to find the farmer lying no more than five feet from the rails with all his hands and feet intact. He had pushed himself to a sitting position and was looking around, befuddled at the demolished wreckage of his wagon.

"Are you injured?" asked Bell anxiously.

The farmer surveyed his arms and legs while feeling a rising bump on the head. "A rash of bumps and bruises," he muttered. "But, wonder of wonders, I'm still in one piece, praise the Lord."

"Your horses also survived without injury."

Shea and Long helped the farmer to his feet. And led him to the horses that had seemingly forgotten their narrow brush with death and were eating the grass beside the road. He was glad to see his horses in sound shape but angered that his wagon was scattered over the landscape in a hundred pieces.

Bell read his mind and gave him a Van Dorn card. "Contact my detective agency," he instructed. "They will compensate you for the loss of your wagon."

"Not the railroad?" the farmer asked, confused.

"It wasn't the railroad's fault. A long story you'll read about in the newspapers." Bell turned and gazed in frustration down the tracks at the fading smoke from Cromwell's locomotive. He refused to believe he had failed so close to his goal. But all was not lost. Already, Jongewaard had backed up *Adeline* to pick up Bell and the crew.

Seeing the farmer able to fend for himself, Jongewaard yelled to Bell. "Hop aboard. We've got time to make up."

Bell, Lofgren, and the fireman had barely climbed back into the cabin when Jongewaard had *Adeline* barreling down the rails once again in hot pursuit of the bandit's train. The chinook was upon them now. The wind blew the dust and loose foliage like foam flying from surf plunging onto a beach. Visibility had been cut to no more than two hundred yards.

Jongewaard could no longer peer out the side of the cab or his squinting eyes would have filled with the dust. Instead, he stared though the cab's forward window, having no choice but to cut *Adeline*'s speed from seventy-five miles an hour down to forty-five.

He saw a semaphore beside the track with its flag in the horizontal position, signaling the locomotive to stop, but he ignored it. Next came a sign proclaiming the outer town limits of Woods Bay. Not knowing the exact distance to the ferry landing, he slowed down even more until *Adeline* was creeping along at twenty-five miles an hour.

Jongewaard turned to Bell. "Sorry about the slowdown, but I can't see if the town docks are five hundred yards or five miles away. I've got to lower the speed in case we come upon the bandit's freight car, or flatcars with logs, sitting on the main track."

"How much time do you figure we lost?" asked Bell.

"Twelve minutes, by my watch."

"We'll catch them," said Bell with measured confidence. "Not likely the ferry crew will risk crossing the lake in this weather."

Bell was right about the ferry not normally running across the lake in rough water, but he missed the boat by underestimating Cromwell. The Butcher Bandit and his sister had not come this far to surrender meekly.

Cromwell and Margaret were not to be stopped. Already, their train was rolling across the dock onto the ferry.

48

The railcar ferry was waiting at the dock when Cromwell's train arrived. The locomotive was switched onto the track that led across the wooden dock onto the ferry. But that was as far as it would go. The three-man crew had decided it wasn't safe to attempt a crossing until the chinook passed and the lake's surface settled down. They were sitting in the small galley drinking coffee and reading newspapers and did not bother to get up when Cromwell's train rolled on board.

Cromwell stepped down from his freight car and walked to the locomotive, bending into the stiff wind. He paused and studied the waves that were building and chopping on the lake. It reminded him of a furious sea. Then he studied the side-paddle, steam-powered ferryboat.

A faded wooden sign attached to the wheelhouse read KALISPELL. The boat was old. The paint was chipped and peeling, the wooden deck worn and rotted. It had seen many years of service – too many. But to Cromwell it looked sturdy enough to endure the severe wind and the valleys forming between the growing waves. He felt secure that it could steam to the west side of the lake. He was irritated at seeing no sign of the crew.

He looked up the track and felt gratified that the pursuing train was not in sight. He could only wonder why it became delayed. Whatever the reason, there was no time to dally. He waved to Abner in the cab of the locomotive. "See that the fireman feeds the firebox so we have steam when we reach the Great Northern tracks."

"Consider it done," replied Abner, pointing the muzzle of his gun at fireman Carr, who had overheard the conversation. "You heard the man. Keep shoveling."

"Have you seen the boat crew?"

Abner shrugged. "I've seen no one."

"Better roust them. We've got to get under way. That locomotive behind us may arrive any minute."

"What about the train crew?" said Abner. "If I leave them alone, they might make a run for it."

"You cast off the lines," Cromwell ordered. "They can't go anywhere if we drift away from the dock. I'll look for the boat crew myself."

Abner jumped to the deck, ran onto the dock. He found the bow and stern lines securing the ferry. The waves surged in from the middle of the lake and rocked the boat back and forth against the bumpers hanging along the starboard paddle box. Abner waited while the boat drifted away from the dock and the lines became taut. When the water surged back, the lines became slack, and Abner pulled them off their bollards and threw them over the railings of the *Kalispell*. Agile as a cat, he leaped back on the deck and returned to the cab of the locomotive.

Cromwell climbed a ladder to the wheelhouse and was thankful to get inside out of the howling wind. He found it empty and went down a stairwell that led to the galley, where he found the crew sitting around reading impassively. They looked up as he came down the stairs but showed little sign of response or interest.

"You Mr. Cromwell?" said a big, red-faced, heavily bearded man in a red plaid lumberman's coat.

"Yes, I'm Cromwell."

"We heard your train come onboard. I'm Captain Jack Boss, at your service."

The laid-back attitude of Boss, who remained sitting, and his two-man crew, who showed utmost indifference, angered Cromwell. "It is of the greatest importance that we get under way immediately."

Boss shook his head. "No can do. The lake is kicking up. It's best if we wait until the storm blows over."

As calmly as if he were lighting a cigar, Cromwell pulled his .38 Colt from a coat pocket and shot one of the crewmen in the forehead. The surprise was so complete the crewman slumped over and stared blankly, as if he were still reading newsprint.

"Good God!" was all Boss uttered, his face frozen in shock.

Cromwell pointed his gun at the face of the other crewman, who began to shake uncontrollably. "You will get this boat under way immediately or he goes, too."

"You're crazy," gasped Boss.

"My attendant has already cast off the lines. I suggest you waste no more time protesting."

Boss looked at his dead crewman and slowly, dazedly, came to his feet. He glared at Cromwell with a combined expression of disgust and fury. "You might as well shoot the rest of us," he said slowly. "We'll all die before we get to the other shore."

"A chance we have to take," Cromwell said, his voice hard and venomous.

Boss turned to his crewman, Mark Ragan. "You'll have to operate the engine alone."

Ragan, a young man yet to see seventeen, nodded with a pale face. "I can do it."

"Then stoke the boiler and get up enough steam to make good headway."

The crewman left the galley quickly and dropped down a ladder to the engine room. Boss, closely followed by Cromwell, climbed to the wheelhouse.

Cromwell stared at Boss. "Do not even think about going against my instructions, Captain, or your crewman in the engine room will die. Nor will I have any reservation of killing you, should you not take me to the rail landing on the far shore."

"You're diabolical scum," Boss said, his face twisted with rage.

Cromwell laughed and gave Boss a look as cold as death. Then he turned and left the wheelhouse.

As he walked back to his palace boxcar, he heard the shrill blare of a steam whistle. It sounded as if it came from no more than a few hundred yards away. And then his ears caught the hiss of steam and the clatter of locomotive drive wheels. Through the debris hurled by the gusts from the chinook, he saw a large engine materialize from the gloom.

Too late, he thought complacently. The *Kalispell* had already drifted five feet from the end of the dock. No one or nothing could stop him now. Smiling to himself, he made his way back the boxcar and climbed inside.

Jongewaard brought *Adeline* to a grinding halt only thirty feet from the end of the dock's tracks. Even before the big drive wheels stopped turning, Bell hopped from the cab and ran toward the end of the dock. The railcar ferry was drifting past the pilings out into the lake and the paddle wheels began to turn. The gap had broadened to eight feet when Bell reached the dock's edge.

He did not hesitate, did not think about or analyze his actions, did not step back for a running start. It seemed too far, but without an instant's interruption, he leaped from the dock. Knowing the distance was too great for him to land on his feet, he reached out and grabbed the railing with his hands, his body falling and swinging like a pendulum against the hull of the ferry. He came within a hair of losing his grip and falling in the water, as the impact knocked the wind from his body. He held the railing in a death grip until his breath returned, but the growing ache in his chest did not fade. Slowly, almost agonizingly, he pulled himself over the railing onto the deck of the ferry alongside Cromwell's boxcar.

Bell lightly ran his fingers over his chest and realized he had cracked one, maybe two ribs. Clenching his teeth against the pain, he struggled to his feet and grabbed one of the ladder rungs leading to the roof of the boxcar to support himself from the pitching and heaving of the ship, plowing into the teeth of the chinook. As the *Kalispell* moved farther into the middle of the lake, the windswept waves surged over the bow and onto the low track deck, swirling around the wheels of the locomotive. The terrible winds brought a stunning rise in temperature of over twenty degrees.

Bell cast off any thought of caution. He threw open the loading door of the boxcar and rolled onto the floor, gasping from the agony in his chest, the .45 Colt steady in his hand. Surprise was in his favor. Cromwell was not alarmed, believing that it was Abner who was entering the car. Too late, he saw that it was his worst enemy.

"Hello, Jacob," Bell said with a cordial grin. "Did you miss me?"

There came a few moments of stunned stillness.

Bell came to his knees and then his feet, keeping the Colt aimed at Cromwell's heart, and closed the door to the boxcar to seal it off from the gusts of wind that were battering the old ferry. He made a quick scan of the interior of the car. "Well, well, well," he said with interest. "My compliments." He swung his free hand around the exotically furnished car. "So this is how you escaped your crimes in style."

"I'm glad you approve," Cromwell said conversationally.

Bell smiled in narrow-eyed guardedness without lowering his Colt. He glanced at the leather trunks lined against one wall. "The cash from your bank. Must be an impressive amount."

"Enough to initiate a new enterprise," Cromwell answered cordially.

"You followed us?" Margaret said, baffled and incredulous. It was more a question than a statement.

"Not exactly *followed*," Bell said curtly. "More like *chased*."

Predictably, Cromwell recovered his composure. "How did you arrive so quickly?"

"Fortunately, I had a faster engine and dedicated crewmen."

"You knew Margaret and I left San Francisco?"

"I tracked down this freight car and figured you had it repainted with a new serial number. My agents had it under surveillance, waiting for the moment when you would use it again. Unfortunately, the earthquake came and my agents had more-pressing duties elsewhere."

"And you discovered that it had left the railyard," Cromwell assumed.

Bell nodded. "Only after I went to your bank and saw that you had cleaned out the vault of all large-currency bills."

"But how could you have known we were heading for Canada?"

"The dispatcher at the Southern Pacific office," Bell said, lying so as not to involve Marion. "I put a gun to his head and persuaded him to tell me what tracks your chartered train was traveling. Then it was only a matter of filling in the cracks."

"Very ingenious, Mr. Bell." Cromwell, champagne glass in hand, stared at Bell appraisingly. "It seems I have a penchant for underestimating you."

"I've misjudged you a time or two."

Margaret spoke in a tone barely above a whisper. "What do you intend to do?" Her shock had turned to desperation.

"Hold your brother for the local sheriff after we reach shore. Then assemble the necessary papers to escort the two of you to Chicago, where he'll have a speedy trial without a fixed jury of your old pals and hang for his crimes." Bell's smile turned cold and his voice ominous. "And you, dear Margaret, will probably spend the best years of your life in a federal jail."

Bell caught the exchange of knowing looks between Cromwell and Margaret. He could only wonder what they were thinking, but he was pretty sure it didn't bode well. He watched as Cromwell sank into one end of an ornate couch.

"Our voyage may take a while in this weather." As if to accent his statement, the bottle of champagne slid off its table and onto the floor. "A pity. I was going to offer you a drink."

Bell could only guess where Cromwell kept his Colt .38. "I never drink while on duty," Bell said facetiously.

The car took another sudden lurch as the ferry tipped over to one side, the entire hull vibrating as one of the paddle wheels thrashed out of the water. Margaret gasped in fear and stared at the water that was seeping in widening puddles along the bottom of the freight door.

Outside, the wind shrieked, and the *Kalispell* creaked and groaned against the onslaught of the mounting waves that rolled down the length of Flathead Lake. The tired old vessel burrowed her bow into the gale-driven crests before dropping sickeningly into the troughs. A towering wave broke out the forward windows, sending sheets of water into the wheelhouse.

Captain Boss pulled up his coat collar and grasped the helm desperately as the gale lashed him with spray that stung the skin of his face and hands.

A whistle shrilled through the speaking tube from the engine room. Boss picked it up, said, "Wheelhouse."

Ragan's voice came with a hollow tone through the tube. "I'm taking water down here, Captain."

"Can the pumps handle it?"

"So far. But the hull is creaking something awful. I fear the bulkheads might give way."

"Get ready to clear out if it gets bad. Make your way to the roof over the galley and unlash the raft."

"Yes, sir," replied Ragan. "What about you, Captain?"

"Call me when you leave the engine room. I'll follow if I can."

"What about the people on the train? We can't just abandon them."

Boss was a man with moral depth, a God-fearing man of great inner strength from the old school whose word was his bond. He was well respected by all who lived around the lake. He gazed through the broken wheelhouse window at the far shore and the mad water thrashing over the bow and felt certain the *Kalispell* was not going to make it.

"They're my responsibility," he said slowly. "You save yourself."

"God bless you, Captain."

Then the tube went silent.

49

The tornado winds of the chinook were the most destructive in memory. Barns were flattened, roofs carried away, trees ripped by their roots, and telegraph and telephone lines downed. The full force of the warm winds roared over Flathead Lake and flogged the water into a swirling turbulence that battered the weary old *Kalispell* unmercifully as she wallowed in the valleys between the waves. Already, the lifeboat that Captain Boss had hoped would save lives had been torn from its lashed mounting and shattered, its wreckage swept into the restless water.

Boss struggled with the helm in a desperate attempt to keep the *Kalispell* on a straight course toward the west shoreline, now only two miles away. He nurtured a slim hope that they might reach the safety of the little harbor of Rollins, but, deep inside, he knew the odds were stacked against him and his boat. There was a constant danger the ferry might swing. The engine, tender, and freight car were the straws that would break the camel's back.

Without their weight, the *Kalispell* might have ridden higher in the water and not have suffered as badly from the huge waves that swept across her lowered track deck. Boss looked down at the bow and saw that it was badly damaged. Timbers on the exposed part of the bow were being smashed and torn from their beams.

His clothes and lumberman's coat soaked through to his skin. Boss grimly took one hand off the wheel, held the speaking tube to his mouth, and whistled. There was a lag of nearly thirty seconds before Ragan answered.

"Yes, Captain?"

"How does it look down there?"

"I've got good steam, but the water is still rising," Ragan's voice was tinged with fear. "It's over my ankles."

"When it gets to your knees, get out of there," Boss ordered him.

"Do you still want me to unlash the boat?" Ragan asked anxiously.

"You don't have to bother," Boss said bitterly. "It's been swept away."

The fear was noticeably heavier in Ragan's voice now. "What will we do if we have to abandon the boat?"

Boss said flatly, "Pray there's enough loose wreckage that will float that we can hang on to until this storm blows over."

Boss hung up the speaking tube and gave a mighty heave of the wheel to keep the boat moving against the swell, as a huge wave fell against the left bow of the *Kalispell* and shoved her broadside to the surge. This was what Boss was afraid of. Caught by a huge wave on the side of the hull and unable to recover, the ferry would capsize and then sink like a stone under the weight of the train.

Fighting the ferry around to head into the teeth of the gusts, he stole a glance down at the train and was stunned to see it violently rocking back and forth, as the boat fell into the troughs before being struck by the crests that now swirled around the engine's drive wheels.

Bell took little satisfaction in knowing that if the *Kalispell* sank into the depths of the lake the criminals on the train would die with him.

In the locomotive, Hunt and Carr were hanging on to any valve, gauge, or lever within reach to keep from being flung against the boiler and sides of the cab. Abner sat in the fireman's seat, his feet braced against the front panel below the window. He felt no need to keep his gun aimed at the engineer and fireman. Not with everyone fighting to keep from being hurled about and becoming injured. He was no longer their threat. It was the storm around them that was menacing.

The last thing that occurred to Abner was that Hunt and Carr might conspire against him. He had not heard their exchanged muffled words nor seen their discreet hand signs to each other. There was nothing for him to do but stare with great trepidation at the vicious water battering the ferry. The engineer fell from his seat and reeled across the cab, colliding against Abner. The impact momentarily stunned Abner, but he roughly pushed Hunt back to his side of the cab.

Abner did not pay any attention to Carr, as the fireman struggled to shovel coal into the firebox while fighting to keep his balance against the lurching and rolling of the *Kalispell.* Hunt staggered against him again. Irritated, Abner tried to heave the engineer back to his side of the cab. But, this time, Hunt had flung himself on Abner, pinning the big man's arms to his side. Then Hunt fell backward, pulling the startled and angered Abner down to the floor of the cab on top of him.

Galvanized into action, Carr swung his coal scoop over his head and brought it down heavily between Abner's shoulder blades. The ferry plunged into a trough just as Carr swung with whiplash speed, but the scoop missed Abner's head and surely would have cracked his skull if it had connected. To Carr, it felt as though he had struck a fallen log.

It was a vicious blow, a bone-crushing blow, and it would have paralyzed most men and left them unconscious. Not Abner. He gasped, his face twisted in pain, and rolled off Hunt and came to his knees. He reached for his Smith & Wesson and leveled it at Carr. His face was expressionless and his eyes stared unblinkingly as he pulled the trigger. Cart's scoop was poised for another strike, but the fireman froze as the bullet drilled into the center of his chest. The shock threw him against the maze of valves before he slowly sank to his knees and keeled over onto the floor of the cab.

Without the slightest hesitation, Abner swung the muzzle of the revolver toward Hunt and shot the engineer in the stomach. Hunt doubled over, his eyes locked on Abner with cold hatred mixed with pain and shock. He staggered backward, one hand clutching his stomach, the other outstretched. Too late, Abner realized what Hunt had in mind. Before he could react, Hunt had reached out and struck the engine's brass horizontal brake lever, moving it from right to left. In his last act, the dying man swung his arm around the throttle lever, pulling it toward him as he fell dead.

The drive wheels spun and the locomotive lurched forward. Abner, weakened by the crushing blow to his back, was too slow to respond. There was a mist surrounding his vision, and it took a long three seconds to realize the locomotive was forging across the deck of the ferry. Any attempt to stop the inevitable came too late. By the time Abner could push back the throttle, the hundred-thirty-four-ton locomotive began its plunge off the *Kalispell*'s bow into the cold depths of Flathead Lake.

50

At first, no one in Cromwell's boxcar realized the train was rolling off the ferry because of the violent motion caused by the waves and wind. Bell quickly distinguished a different movement and sensed the wheels beneath the car were beginning to turn. He threw open the freight door and was met by a blast of wind that staggered him for an instant. But then he lowered his head and leaned out. He took in two macabre sights at once. One, the deck appeared to be moving toward the stern because of the train's forward motion. And, two, the locomotive's front four-wheel truck was rolling off the bow and diving into the surging turbulence below.

Bell spun around. "The train is falling off the boat!" he shouted over the gale. "Quick, jump while you still can!"

Cromwell thought he saw an opportunity and did not immediately consider the disaster-in-the-making. Without a word, he launched himself off the couch and drew his automatic as he leaped. A foolish mistake. Instead of instantly squeezing the trigger and killing Bell, he hesitated to say, "Farewell, Isaac."

Suddenly, the hand clutching the gun was knocked

off to the side and the bullet smashed into the doorframe beside Bell's head.

Margaret stood in front of Cromwell, her dark eyes on fire and her lips pressed tightly together until she spoke. There was no fear, no fright; she stood with her legs firmly planted on the freight car's floor. "Enough, Jacob," she said.

She had no time to say more. Bell grabbed her by the arm. "Jump!" he urged her. "Quickly!"

Only Bell grasped the inevitable. He glanced out the door again and saw the engine had almost disappeared beneath the waves and the tender and the freight car were moving faster as they were rapidly dragged by the immense weight into the water. The deck was tilted at a sharp angle, and the *Kalispell* was in dire danger of going down with the train. There were only seconds left before the freight car was pulled over the bow.

His face contorted with hate, Cromwell swung the Colt's muzzle toward Bell again, but Margaret stepped between the two men. Cromwell was finally aware of the danger now, his eyes sick in the realization that defeat and death were only moments away. He tried to push Margaret aside so he could leap out the door, but she wrapped her arms around her brother's waist, pulling him back inside the car. He swung the barrel of the gun and struck her across the cheek. Blood seeped, but she clutched him in a death grip he could not shake off.

The freight car's front wheels were irresistibly

following the tender off the front of the ferry. Bell tried to yank Margaret out the door, but she was clutching her brother too tightly. The sleeve on her blue sweater tore away and he lost his grip on her arm.

She looked at Bell and her eyes turned soft. "I'm sorry, Isaac."

He reached out for her but it was too late. Bell was falling through the door.

He twisted violently in midair and crashed to the wooden deck, striking the shoulder opposite his cracked ribs. The impact was still enough to make him gasp in agony. He lay there, watching in horror as Cromwell's freight car was drawn below the surface. A hope flashed through his mind that Margaret might still leap through the door and into the water and be saved. But it was not to be. A seething white wall of water washed over the boxcar and penetrated the interior through the open freight door with a surge that made it impossible for anyone inside to escape. Still hoping against hope, Bell lay on the deck, water swirling around him, staring at the bubbles rising from the depths as the ferry steamed over them. He was still staring at the place where the train sank when it fell far astern, but neither Margaret nor her brother came to the surface.

The bow of the ferry swung up and the hull rose nearly a foot out of the water without the hundreds of tons of deadweight from the train. Almost immediately, to the immense relief of Captain Boss in the wheelhouse, the *Kalispell*'s stability increased dramatically and she began to burrow through the waves, her paddle wheels driving her toward the western shore of the lake.

It took Bell nearly ten minutes to struggle across the deck to the door leading to the stairs up to the wheelhouse. When he got to the wheelhouse, looking like the proverbial drowned rat. Boss stared at him in astonishment.

"Well, now, where did you come from?"

"I jumped on deck as you pulled away from the deck in Woods Bay. My name is Bell. I'm an agent with Van Dorn."

"You were lucky you didn't go down with the others."

"Yes," he said softly. "I was lucky."

"Who were those people?"

"Two were innocent members of the train crew who were held hostage. The other three were wanted for murder and robbery. I was going to arrest them when we reached port."

"Poor devils. Drownin' isn't a good way to go."

Bell was deeply marked by guilt and grief. His face was expressionless as he turned his gaze to the waters of the lake. The waves no longer looked deadly and were settling down to a mild chop. The chinook was moving east and the terrible winds had subsided to a stiff breeze.

"No," he murmured. "Not a good way to go at all."

UP FROM THE DEPTHS

Kalispell Riding Through the Storm

April 16, 1950
Flathead Lake, Montana

After the coal tender was brought up and set on the barge behind the big Pacific locomotive, the divers concentrated on running the steel lift cables under the bottom of the freight car and attaching them to a cradle so it could also be raised. Despite the muck and slime, the name SOUTHERN PACIFIC was still readable across the sides of the tender.

Late in the afternoon, the director of the salvage operation, Bob Kaufman, paced the deck impatiently, as the divers were lifted from the bottom on a platform that was swung onto the barge. He looked up at the clouds, which were dark but not threatening, and lit a cigar while he waited for the brass helmet to be lifted off the dive master's head.

As soon as it was lifted from the diver's head, Kaufman asked, "How's it look?"

The diver, a balding man in his early forties, nodded. "The cables are secured. You can tell the crane operator he can begin the lift."

Kaufman waved to the man who operated the big crane that rose skyward from the deck of the salvage barge. "All cables secure!" he shouted. "Lift away!" Then Kaufman turned and spoke to the tall, older, silver-haired man standing next to him on the deck of the barge. "We're ready to raise the freight car, Mr. Bell."

Isaac Bell nodded. His face was calm, but there was an expression of expectancy. "All right, Mr. Kaufman. Let's see what it looks like after all these years on the bottom of the lake."

The crane operator engaged the lift levers, tightening the cables as the diesel engine on the crane rose from an idle to a high rpm before flattening out as it strained to hoist the freight car. The operation was not nearly as complex as bringing up the hundred-thirty-four-ton locomotive. Once the car was pulled free from the bottom, the lifting operation went smoothly.

Bell watched with an almost-morbid fascination as the freight car broke the surface of the water and was raised up high before the crane slowly swung it over the barge. Deftly coordinating the controls, the crane operator cautiously lowered the car until it settled onto the deck behind the locomotive and tender.

Gazing at the train, Bell found it hard to visualize in his mind how it looked so many years ago. He walked up to the car and wiped the lake growth away from the serial number that was barely visible through the oozing slime. The number 16455 now became distinct.

Bell looked up at the freight door. It was still as

open as when he fell through it so long ago. The interior was dark because the sunlight was diminished by the clouds. Memories flooded back as he recalled that fateful day when the train rolled across the ferry and plummeted to the bottom of the lake. He dreaded what he would find inside.

Kaufman came with the ladder they had used to enter the locomotive's cab and propped it against the open floor of the freight car. "After you, Mr. Bell."

Bell nodded silently and slowly mounted the ladder until he was standing on the threshold of the boxcar. He stared into the darkness and listened to the water dripping throughout the freight car. He suppressed a shudder. The dampness and the smell of muck and slime seemed to reek of death, hoary and evil and infinitely ghastly.

The once-ornate furnishings and décor of the palatial car now looked like something out of a nightmare. The plush-carpeted floor was covered with sediment decorated with long slender weeds. The intricately carved bar, the leather chairs and couch, the Tiffany lamps overhead, even the paintings on the walls, looked grotesque under their coating of ooze and growth. Small fish that had not escaped as the car came out of the water were flopping on the floor.

As if delaying the inevitable, Bell sloshed through the mud and found the five leather trunks along one wall where he remembered seeing them back in 1906. He pulled a folding knife from his pocket and pried open the rusting and nearly frozen latches on the first trunk. Lifting the lid, he saw that the interior was relatively free of silt. He carefully picked up one of the bundles. The paper currency was soggy but had held its shape and consistency. The printing on the gold certificate bills still appeared distinct and well defined.

Kaufman had joined Bell and stared fascinated at the stacks of bills stuffed in the trunk. "How much do you reckon there is?"

Bell closed the lid and motioned at the other four trunks. "A wild guess? Maybe four or five million."

"What happens to it?" asked Kaufman with a glint in his eyes.

"Goes back to the bank whose depositors were robbed of their savings."

"Better not let my crew know about this," said Kaufman seriously. "They may get it in their heads it's open salvage."

Bell smiled. "I'm certain the banking commissioners in San Francisco will be most generous in granting a reward to you and your crew."

Kaufman was satisfied, his gaze sweeping through the car. "This must have been one luxurious palace on wheels before it sank. I've never seen a boxcar fixed up like a private Pullman parlor car."

"No expense was spared," said Bell, eyeing several bottles of vintage champagne and expensive brandy that were scattered in the sediment on the floor.

Kaufman's expression turned grim as he nodded

at two misshapen mounds protruding from the floor. "These the two you were looking for?"

Bell nodded solemnly. "Jacob Cromwell, the infamous Butcher Bandit, and his sister, Margaret."

"The Butcher Bandit," Kaufman said softly in awe. "I always thought he'd disappeared."

"A legend handed down through the years because the money was never recovered."

The adipose tissue that once stored Cromwell's fat had broken down and his body, like the corpses in the cab of the locomotive, had turned waxlike in saponification. The notorious killer looked less than something that had once been a living human being. It was as though he had melted into an indiscernible lump of brown gelatin. His body was twisted, as if he'd died writhing in terror when tons of water gushed into the freight car as it followed the locomotive down to the bottom of the lake. Bell knew better. Cromwell might have struggled to survive, but he would never have been gripped with terror. No longer was he a menacing figure. His reign of robbery and murder had ended forty-four years ago under the cold waters of Flathead Lake.

He waded through the muck to where Margaret's body lay. Her lustrous hair was fanned out in the silt and tangled with strands from a reedlike weed. The once-lovely face looked like a sculpture an artist had left unfinished. Bell could not help but remember her beauty and vivaciousness the night they met in the elevator of the Brown Palace Hotel.

Kaufman interrupted Bell's thoughts. "His sister?"

Bell nodded. He felt an overwhelming sense of sorrow and remorse. Her final words before he fell from the car came back to haunt him. He could never explain his feelings toward her. There was no endearing love on his part, more a fondness coated with hatred. There was no forgiving her criminal actions in league with her brother. She deserved to die as surely as he did.

"Can't tell from the look of her now," said Kaufman. "She might have been a beautiful woman."

"Yes, she was that," said Bell softly. "A beautiful woman full of life but veiled in evil." He turned away saddened but his eyes dry of tears.

Shortly before midnight, the salvage barge tied up at the old railroad dock in Rollins. Bell made arrangements with Kaufman to see that the bodies were taken care of by the nearest mortuary and the next of kin of Hunt and Carr notified. He recognized Joseph Van Dorn standing on the dock surrounded by four of his agents and was not surprised to see him.

Van Dorn was in his eighties but stood straight, with a full head of gray hair and eyes that never lost their gleam. Although his two sons now ran the detective agency from offices in Washington, D.C., he still worked out of his old office in Chicago and consulted on the cases that had never been solved.

Bell walked up and shook Van Dorn's hand. "Good to see you, Joseph. It's been a long time."

Van Dorn smiled broadly. "My work isn't as interesting since you retired."

"Nothing could stop me from coming back on this case."

Van Dorn stared at the freight car. Under the dim lights on the dock, it looked like some odious monster from the depths. "Was it there?" he asked.

"The money?"

Bell merely nodded.

"And Cromwell?"

"Both he and his sister, Margaret."

Van Dorn sighed heavily. "Then at long last it's over. We can write finish to the legend of the Butcher Bandit."

"Not many of the Cromwell Bank's depositors," Bell said slowly, "will still be alive to receive their money."

"No, but their descendants will be notified of their windfall."

"I promised Kaufman and his crew a fat finder's fee."

"I'll see that they get it," Van Dorn promised. He placed a hand on Bell's shoulder. "Nice work, Isaac. A pity we couldn't have found the train fifty years ago."

"The lake is two hundred seventy feet where the train sank," explained Bell. "The salvage company that was hired by the San Francisco banking commissioners dragged the lake but couldn't find it back in 1907."

"How could they have missed it?"

"It had fallen in a depression in the lake bed and the drag lines passed over it."

Van Dorn turned and nodded toward a car parked by the dock. "I guess you'll be heading home."

Bell nodded. "My wife is waiting. We'll be driving back to California."

"San Francisco?"

"I fell in love with the town during the investigation and decided to remain after the earthquake and make my home there. We live in Cromwell's old mansion on Nob Hill."

Bell left Van Dorn and walked across the dock to the parked car. The blue metallic paint of the 1950 Custom Super 8 convertible Packard gleamed under the dock lights. Although the night air was chilly, the top was down.

A woman was sitting in the driver's seat wearing a stylish hat over hair that was tinted to its original blond. She gazed at him approaching with eyes that were as coral–sea green as when Bell met her. The mirth lines around her eyes were the lines of someone who laughed easily, and the features of her face showed the signs of an enduring beauty.

Bell opened the door and slipped into the seat beside her. She leaned over and kissed him firmly on the lips, pulled back, and gave him a sly smile. "About time you came back."

"It was a hard day," he said with a long sigh.

Marion turned the ignition and started the car. "You found what you were looking for?"

"Jacob and Margaret and the money, all there."

Marion looked out across the black water of the lake. "I wish I could say I'm sorry, but I can't bring myself to feel grief, not knowing about their hideous crimes."

Bell did not wish to dwell on the Cromwells any longer and changed the subject. "You talk to the kids?"

Marion stepped on the accelerator pedal and steered the car away from the dock toward the main road. "All four this afternoon. Soon as we get home, they're throwing us an anniversary party."

He patted her on the knee. "You in the mood for driving all night?"

She smiled and kissed his hand. "The sooner we get home, the better."

They went silent for a time, lost in their thoughts of events long gone. The curtain to the past had come down. Neither of them turned and looked back at the train.